Wine for Tomorrow

A Novel

By

Rupert Pratt

Wine for Tomorrow: A Novel

I dedicate this book to the memory
of my wife, Millie Pratt,
and to the other members of my family,
Greg, Jon, Bobbi, Purvesh,
Lizzie, Nathan, and Andy.

I love you all.

Contents

Part One

1931–1943

Dreams

Part Two

1943–1945

Nightmares

Part Three

1945–1948

Wine

Part One

1931–1943

Dreams

CHAPTER ONE

May 15, 1931

Obie Gainsworthy, five years old to the day, sprinted in long looping circles around the spacious Hunt family lawn. He could fly if he could just run fast enough—soar into the air like blue herons off the Morass. Instead, he tripped over the exposed roots of the giant elm at the edge of the lawn and sprawled face down in the grass. The Hunt's young dog, Slobber, licked his face. A rivulet of crimson trickled down his right forearm, and his left elbow stung like when he'd bumped against his mother's hot woodstove. He clenched his teeth. "Big boys don't cry," his father had said—and his father was smarter than most people.

He was playing with Laura and Cassie Hunt. It was Cassie's birthday, too. Yesterday, while with his mother and the sisters in Mercer's Grocery, Cassie had told Helen Mercer, "Obie and me were born on the same day." He hated that—saying private things where everyone could hear.

Laura pointed at his arm and scrunched her mouth. "Obie . . . I see blood."

Cassie skipped toward them, her yellow curls bouncing. "Are you hurt, Obie?" she asked.

"No."

"But it does hurt, doesn't it?"

It did, but he wasn't going to admit it. "No, let's race. I'll beat you both."

The challenge was a familiar one. "No, you won't," Cassie said as she turned and started running along the white picket fence that separated the lawn from the gravel driveway. Obie and Laura ran after her. Slobber stayed at their heels, yelping. Cassie was first to the corner post, the usual finish line. Slobber jumped on Obie, then on Laura, whose eyes flashed anger. She shoved the dog aside, none too gently.

"I won! I won!" Cassie's words rode on unrestrained screams of joy.

Laura crossed her arms and stood so straight she seemed to

3

bend backward. "No, you didn't. We weren't ready. You cheated."

Cassie grabbed Obie's hand. "I didn't cheat, did I, Obie?"

His mother had said to always be truthful, even when lying felt better. "You didn't cheat," he said. "You won."

Cassie still clutched his hand. "See, Laura! I won! Obie said so! I won!"

Laura smiled. "All right, you won the race. It doesn't matter. It was just a silly old race."

Calm ruled only briefly; as they walked back toward the house, Laura pushed Cassie, and Cassie shoved back. They did things like that to him—and worse things. Cassie yelled at Laura. "Just because you're older than me, you think you can push me around. I'm going to tell Mom on you."

"You'd better not if you know what's good for you."

Laura put her face close to Obie's. He liked it when she did that. "She's being a little brat, isn't she, Obie?" Her raven hair sparkled in the sunlight. Today she smelled like lemon drops. Sometimes it was flowers.

Obie had learned the best way to answer that kind of question. "I don't know," he said.

"Yes, you do, Obie. You know she's a brat. Say it."

Laura had once made him call Cassie a "stupid bitch." He hadn't even known what it meant. Mrs. Hunt found out and scolded him. Later, Cassie gave him a chocolate cupcake to tell Laura to "go to hell," and he was scolded again, more severely. Keeping quiet was best unless it really mattered; his mother and father agreed on that.

Sometimes, though, he couldn't keep from speaking out. It was hard to be quiet when the girls did bad things to him. But it was easy to forgive them because they were always sorry. Anyway, his mother said forgiveness was the best way to be happy, and he was "never to forget it."

Eventually, the sisters stopped quarreling and they all sat on a wooden bench Mr. Hunt had placed under the elm by the driveway gate. Obie sat between the girls. Cassie put an arm around his shoulder with her mouth close to his ear. "Obie loves me, don't you, Obie?"

She'd asked that question many times. "I love Cassie," he said, knowing what she expected.

"See, Laura, he loves me," Cassie said. Her round face barely contained her smile.

Laura frowned. "It's nothing to be so happy about. Obie loves me too."

Keeping the peace was important. "I love Laura too," he said. "I love you both."

Cassie looked annoyed, but then patted Obie's blood-streaked arm. "Vi will clean it up," she said.

Sitting between the sisters felt like times in winter when his mother brought hearth-warmed blankets to his bed. He glanced from one to the other. He liked Laura's lemon-drop scent, but it was Cassie who could make him smile.

* * *

Pinkerton Hunt sat on his open patio in a wooden chair of his own making. He lit his pipe, hoping the smoke might discourage a persistent yellow jacket buzzing about his head. He had for several minutes been watching the three children play on the lawn he had mowed that morning. The fresh-cut scent of spring grass lingered, but today that pleasure was blunted by anxiety about the future of his furniture manufacturing business. The Adirondack region of New York State and the rest of the world still reeled from the stock market collapse and bank failures.

Pinky had believed he would not be adversely affected by the economic turmoil, for he had put his money into his business, ignoring Abigail's advice to "buy stocks." Her way would have paved a sure road to financial ruin, but his way was also proving perilous. A sinking ship sucks down smaller vessels. Eight-year-old Stafford Rest Furniture was not escaping the undertow. Two of his ten employees were already laid off, a situation that had caused him much anguish, for making a living in the Adirondack Mountains, even in the best of times, was a struggle for most people. Other workers might have to go if the business were to survive—if survival was even possible.

It wasn't only about profit. Pinky loved Stafford Rest, and he respected its people. There was sincere pride in building his factory here. Lloyd Baumgartner, the part-time mayor, had stated in a recent village meeting that "Pinkerton Hunt has planted an oak in our town under whose branches our residents can take refuge." Lloyd's elegant speech, for which he was well-known, did little to dispel Pinky's fear that the oak was splintering. It could even fall.

The yellow jacket returned. Pinky stood, rolled up a New Yorker magazine, and batted the pest to the flagstone surface. He watched as it made an erratic path along the patio edge and into the grass. He sighed. The bee threat was gone, but worry remained.

The children, previously out of sight, roared around the lakeside corner of the house. Obie, with Slobber on his heels, was chasing the girls. Their housekeeper's son was a good child, big for his age, and bright as a new silver dollar. Pinky often wondered what obstacles might lie in store for the boy, considering Ken's fondness for drink. Vi was the anchor of the family.

"Laura Honey, is that blood on Obie's arm?"

"He fell over the roots."

"Obie, come here to me," Pinky called.

Obie hopped and skipped his way to the patio edge. "It don't hurt now, Mr. Hunt. Slobber licked it."

Pinky examined Obie's arm, saw that the injury was superficial, and sent him back to play with the admonition, "Maybe you'd better pay more attention to where you're going."

Pinky decided at that moment to give Slobber to Obie. The year-old mutt, a cross between a hound and retriever with some unknown pedigrees thrown in, loved the boy and followed him everywhere. Carl Burlingame, one of Pinky's employees, had insisted he take his pick from the litter. The little animal had licked Pinky's hand with such wet exuberance that he gave the pup its name on the spot. The girls might protest the gift to Obie, but Abigail wouldn't care. She often complained about Slobber's hair on her furniture.

A day away from the factory was rare. Abigail and Vi were in Tupper Lake buying last-minute birthday presents. Abigail had commandeered him to stay home with the children. "You're in that dirty old place too much anyway," she told him. He'd used the time to mow the lawn and catch up on other neglected chores, little jobs he could do and still watch the youngsters.

Desiring to submerge his ugly economic mindset, Pinky sucked spring air into his lungs and strolled out to the section of fence running parallel to the state highway. He tapped ashes from his pipe on top of a picket and refilled the bowl from his tobacco pouch. He never tired of eying the scene below which spread like a rumpled patchwork quilt over a disheveled plain, nor of viewing the green-topped mountains rolling off to all points of the compass. But the most awe-inspiring sight was north, where pinnacles of the High Peaks punched their way into the clouds. That ever-changing view was subject to season and weather, and today's rocky summits gleamed in the sunlight like beacons of hope for a troubled world.

Abigail may have been wrong about stocks, but had shown

excellent foresight when she insisted they build on Garnet Point where they could enjoy the whole panorama of lake, village, and mountains. From their "perfect house-site," they could see the two-mile-long natural ridge encircling the town and the largely uninhabited area beyond. Pinky imagined that, seen from the air, it would resemble a giant horseshoe with the town sitting in the open end by Diamond Lake. At the other end, east, and still within the horseshoe's curve, was a vast swampy area taking up most of the interior. Long ago, some poetic soul had named it the "Morass."

In many ways, the Morass appeared to be a sterile area with countless trunks of long-dead trees pointing skyward. It was, in fact, teeming with wildlife. Birdwatchers and other nature lovers often came to cautiously launch canoes into its enigmatic waters or walk an ever-shifting trail about its perimeter. On the north side of town, a stream from the Morass met and swelled little Cedar Creek on its way to the lake. The ridge itself stretched almost unbroken from Blackberry Hill north of town, around to Garnet Point. Along with the Morass, it was state land, as was a vast reach of the Adirondack Park beyond Pinky's sight.

Stafford Rest Furniture was well back from Diamond Lake, beyond the few dirt and gravel "streets" with their scattered homes, even beyond three small subsistence farms whose wandering boundaries and roads formed an interlocking jigsaw. His factory building sat at the edge of the Morass. Pinky had purchased the acreage at a bargain price soon after his arrival in town. The seller had been candid: "Too poor for farmland, and too close to the swamp for homes."

The building had been, at first, a two-room one-story structure barely large enough to accommodate himself and three employees. After a year, he expanded it, adding rooms vertically and horizontally. Additional local people were hired and trained, though he could have found more skilled workers elsewhere.

Stafford Rest Furniture gradually grew from serving a local clientele to a regional one. The Adirondack Chair had become popular, and Pinky produced his own version. Many people wanted quality rustic furniture, so he started advertising beyond the local markets. Eventually, he invested in a truck and driver to extend his market into Central New York and western New England. His hope of expanding into New York City and Boston had been dashed by the market collapse and widespread financial ruin.

A Model A Ford chugging down the road drew his attention away from his financial problems. Pinky waved to Jake Brown, then watched the car go on down the state highway, cross Garnet Creek concrete bridge, and continue into the village. The road flattened out between two rows of scattered buildings consisting of residences, small businesses, and vacant lots. The conglomeration was called "Main Street" by the locals.

He knew that Jake usually stopped at Mercer's Store or sometimes at the Gulf station for gasoline. Today, however, he went on through the village, crossed the new steel bridge over Cedar Creek, and climbed north up the steep pine-lined highway. That road divided Indian Knob on the left and Blackberry Hill on the right. The car finally disappeared against a horizon of evergreen and blue sky. Jake would be going to see his brother, Darius. Darius Brown was seriously ill. Prayers had been requested at the Sunday morning church service.

Pinky heard another automobile approaching. He could tell from the familiar sound of the Packard Eight engine that Abigail and Vi had returned from Tupper Lake. Abigail downshifted flawlessly before turning into their driveway. The children ran to the gate to greet the mothers. Pinky joined them there.

"What's in the packages?" Laura asked as she ran beside Abigail and tried to pull the bags down to her eye level.

Abigail shooed her away. "These are gifts for Cassie. It's her birthday. You'll have yours in October."

"I'll be seven, won't I, Mommy?"

"Yes, you'll be seven, but today we're celebrating Cassie's birthday. This is *her* day."

"And Obie's," Cassie said.

"Well . . . yes, there's something for Obie too."

"What? What do you have for Obie?"

Pinky saw that Abigail was ignoring Cassie's question. He wouldn't be surprised if she'd forgotten to get a gift for Obie. His wife had her flaws, despite her love for their daughters.

Cassie pulled at his pants leg. "Daddy, what do you think Mommy got for Obie?"

"I don't know, dear. We'll just have to wait and see."

* * *

Violetta Gainsworthy had trouble keeping ahead of Cassie as she tore wrapping papers from her packages and scattered them around her feet and about the Hunt family dining room. Vi had hoped to salvage the wrappings for her own use, but Cassie's exuberance had nearly ended that hope. Cassie had let Obie open a couple of her packages; one was a hobby horse. Vi hoped Obie understood it was Cassie's gift and not his.

The birthday celebration was a Hunt family affair. She and her son were there because she was "the help." She had no illusions and no regrets. In such troubled times she was lucky to be a servant in the household of a wealthy family.

The good fortune had come several years before, less than a month after her marriage. Stafford Rest was nothing like New York City or Albany. Life in the mountains was stark. It was not solitude that upset her, for she had quickly learned to love the scent of pine and cedar carried on evening air, and the mournful early morning cry of loons drifting up from the lake. The problem was separation from her family. Leaving her two sisters and brother had troubled her more than she expected. For several days after her marriage, she considered going home and bearing whatever consequences that action might bring. Sibino Petitucci would consider it a family disgrace.

Family honor was a serious matter to her father and Oria, her mother. During the voyage across the Atlantic when she was eight years old, their discomforts had not deterred Sibino from insisting they dress well and stay clean. After leaving Italy, he had been the leader of their group consisting of his own family, the family of his younger brother Enzo, and their mother and father. Sibino ran his household and small bakery in Albany in an orderly fashion and instilled in his children the same disciplines. The more relaxed lifestyle of the Gainsworthy family shocked Vi.

Beth Clarington, owner of Beth's Cafe on Main Street, set in motion events that diverted Vi from thoughts of returning to Albany. The restaurant catered to loggers, hunters, fishermen, and locals. Beth was an extraordinary cook. Gladys, Lloyd Baumgartner's wife, had eaten in the best restaurants in New York and Philadelphia and declared their fare was no better than Beth's. One of her occasional patrons was himself a restaurant owner in Plattsburgh.

The Plattsburgh restaurateur had booked a large wedding reception and was nervous about supplying what the couple, especially the woman, required. Beth and Vi had already formed a friendship. Beth, whose husband had died a year after their marriage, understood loneliness. Beth pecked on the front window one day as Vi passed the restaurant. "He wants me to come over there and cook," she explained. "I want to, but I'll need help. Can you go with me, Vi?"

Vi wangled with Ken. "I don't like it much," he said. ". . . maybe, this once."

The groom was Mr. Pinkerton Hunt, a Stafford Rest resident. Vi had seen him several times in the village, and Ken had spoken well of him. They hunted together in the fall, and Ken called him "Pinky." The bride-to-be, Abigail Beachton, was from Boston, from one of the "old families," Beth told her.

Vi worked hard to please Beth with the hope of future work. Abigail must have noticed her efforts. "My dear young lady," she said, as the newlyweds prepared to leave, "If you lived in Stafford Rest, I'd give you work."

Vi wanted to laugh at the "young lady" reference. She was eighteen and could see that Abigail was only a few years older. "I do live in Stafford Rest," Vi informed her.

"Really? That could be fortunate for us both. Would you like to try out for a job? What's your name?"

Vi had studied Abigail's face. She was pretty, not beautiful as she imagined rich girls had a right to be. Her black hair was too stark against the whiteness of her face, but without distracting from her pleasant features. She was already telling her new husband what he could and could not do. Would she want to work for such a person?

"My name is Violetta Gainsworthy." She wanted to suppress her doubts, but there was a nervous feeling in the pit of her stomach. "People call me 'Vi.' I will consider working for you, but my husband must approve."

Pinky, after listening quietly, said, "Dear, do we need someone? The house is small. I'm sure you can handle everything by yourself."

Abigail laughed. "You don't really think, do you Pinky darling, that I'll be spending all my time at home? And we'll not be in that little house for long." To Vi, the words seemed sarcastic, even though garnished with a smile.

Pinky looked from one woman to the other, clearly not knowing what to say. Vi could not understand why he allowed her to talk like that; not only was he the husband, he was also much older. She was cautious. "Maybe it is not a good idea."

"Oh, yes! It is. I need a housekeeper and someone to prepare at least one daily meal. You might work out. You have an accent. What nationality are you, Violetta . . . Vi?"

"I am Italian."

"I thought so. Were you born in Italy?"

"Yes, I came . . ."

Abigail waved a dismissive hand. "It's not a real concern." She was silent a moment before saying, "We'll be gone two weeks. I'll speak to you when we return."

"I will have to ask Ken, my husband."

Abigail smiled. "Vi, I see there are things I need to teach you, but we'll talk about that later."

Ken fumed for a while before agreeing. Two weeks later, Vi Gainsworthy became an employee in the Hunt household. Laura Abigail Hunt was born in October the following year, right after the Hunts moved into their new house on the hill. Vi had nursed Abigail through months of morning sickness and various health symptoms, imagined and real. Most of the care for the child fell on Vi.

On most days, she arrived at seven in the morning and did not go home until six. Sunday was the only day she had for catching up on neglected home chores. Ken complained because he wanted her home more but finally adjusted to her schedule. He managed the money, giving her funds for groceries and other necessities. Sometimes, it was not enough.

When Vi became pregnant, she told Abigail, to pave the way for stopping work. Abigail countered with, "I'm pregnant again too. We'll just have to get through this together."

"Together" meant Vi's workload multiplied. She worked until two days before giving birth. Even then, Abigail sent Pinky for her.

"Abigail's about to have her baby." There was fear in his eyes. "I went for Doctor Williamson, but his buggy's gone. He must be out on a call. Vi, can you come?"

Ken's brother's wife, Claire, was with Vi, and told Pinky, "It's Vi's time too, so you'll just have to get along and find someone else to take care of that wife of yours." Pinky had appealed to Beth Clarington, who went with him to assist Abigail.

Obadiah Kenneth Gainsworthy and Cassandra Beachton Hurt were born within fifteen minutes of each other. A week later, Vi was back at the Hunt house, her infant son with her. Altogether, she had the primary care for seven people, including herself.

As Vi watched Cassie open present after present, squealing with delight, there came a rare feeling of resentment against Abigail. She must know that Vi could not afford gifts for Obie except for some homemade items, yet she had just handed him a small book of religious verses the Methodist church was giving away. She had not

11

even addressed Obie by name.

Pinky, without seeming to realize it, soothed Vi's indignation. "Obie," he said, leading Slobber by his collar and taking hold of her son's hand, "I have the perfect present for you."

CHAPTER TWO

May 15, 1931

Ken Gainsworthy leaned his long-handled mattock against a section of chicken-wire fence that enclosed his hillside vegetable garden and took a bandanna handkerchief from his back pocket to wipe his face. Behind and above the house, the garden was host to lettuce, cabbage, and other hardy vegetables still in the beginning stages of growth.

A separate section, a quarter of the total garden space, held Vi's herbs. Perennials there were thriving. Ken had recently spaded the soil to ready it for her annuals. Today, he was preparing a plot outside the fenced-in area, nearly doubling the garden area. Once cleared, he would extend the enclosure with extra fencing scrounged from Abner, his brother. The fence was necessary to discourage rabbits and woodchucks. It would not deter deer, the menace of all Adirondack gardeners. Danger from frost would soon be past. This soil would be broken up and have organic material worked in by then. He would plant beans, corn, and melon seed. Tomato plants, growing inside by the window since February, would then go in with little fear of freezing.

Grubbing out roots of hardy bushes and shrubs, and removing stones on this section of Blackberry Hill, was strenuous work. Ken was used to manual labor and even took pleasure in the challenge to his forty-year-old body. Nevertheless, on days like this, he sometimes glanced out to a world beyond this patch of earth to the surrounding forests and mountains.

Before the war, Ken's work was in the Adirondack woods. At the age of eight, and over his mother's protests, he started tagging along with Jacob Gainsworthy. His father had been a wilderness guide, sought-after by clients who came back year after year from Eastern cities, and sometimes farther away. Eventually, he and Jacob worked as partners, a collaborative effort that continued until Ken, at nearly thirty years of age, answered the call to serve his country. He came home sick from the war. After months of recovery, and against the advice of his semi-retired father, he tried to take up wilderness guiding again.

13

"It's not the same," Jacob told him. Unless you can work for the state or hire on with a big private resort, you won't earn a living at it anymore."

Ken finally accepted the wisdom of his father's message, bought an old truck, took seasonal work at lumber camps, and promoted himself as a handyman. He saw himself as a "Jack of all trades" and ignored Jacob's advice to specialize in carpentry or the up-and-coming electrical field. Instead, he took pride in doing the "little jobs." People noticed his competence, and he was sought-after.

Nevertheless, a reluctant little devil often tapped him on the shoulder and whispered soothing words in his ear about not abandoning his dream. He solicited guiding opportunities as they came, often passing up better-paying jobs if they conflicted with a chance to lead a hunting or fishing party, or a college group studying flora on the high peaks. In the years right after the war, his mindset had made him content with limited earnings.

That attitude changed after he married Vi, leading him to seek the lucrative over the fanciful. Seasonal work in the lumber business was available and paid well. In addition, there were more calls for his handyman services than he could accommodate. Soon after Obie was born, Pinky Hunt made a trip up the hill to offer him a job at Stafford Rest Furniture. "I need good workers," Pinky told him.

That persistent little devil whispered again with the advice that accepting Pinky's offer would end any hope of ever following his dream. He put off committing himself, which was terrible timing. The stock market crashed and work opportunities dried up. Working a few hours a week at Abner's farm brought a pittance, and the occasional odd job paid little. Ken picked up the mattock and resumed his attack on the deep-rooted popple bush. This garden expansion was a necessity.

Vi's pay envelope came every week without fail, generous by standards of the day, but not overly so. She passed it to him without comment and he never failed to experience a feeling of humiliation that she was bringing home the more significant share of their sustenance. Once, he said, "Not being able to provide adequately for you and Obie makes me feel like I'm not much of a man."

She had laughed. "You are much the man, Ken. I do not worry. Times will get better. You will see."

But times hadn't gotten better. And there was no end in sight.

Vi was the best thing that had ever happened to him. A bachelor in his mid-thirties, he had fought the matrimony urge for a year before surrendering. They met while he was in Albany at the docks picking up supplies for a client. She was there with her father, trying to buy grain and other supplies for their struggling bakery. The older man knew little English, and Violetta translated. The man with whom she was attempting to strike a bargain was giving her a hard time. Ken came to her rescue, resulting in them going home with a bounty of goods. Ken went too, at the invitation of Sibino Petitucci.

Ken made frequent trips back to Albany for several months to see Vi. The Petitucci family was close-knit. Oria, the mother, obviously lacking English skills, seldom spoke and then only to Sibino or her children. Isabella, "Izzie," the middle sister, was married to John Brandon and lived in close-by Schenectady. Gerardo, the youngest in the family, kept to himself. Michelangela, who had Americanized her name to "Angie," was six years older than Vi.

Angie said to Ken one afternoon, "You are an old man and Violetta is not yet twenty years old. You are robbing the cradle. Why do you not come and court me, instead?"

Her hazel eyes held an expression hard to interpret. He was unsure how to respond to such a bold question, so he avoided an answer and avoided Angie whenever possible. She was more than pretty and had a lighthearted and disarming demeanor.

Angie would have interested him had it not been for Vi. Vi was the one he wanted, and it seemed marriage was the only way he could have her. Nevertheless, he worried he might be violating some old-world custom in passing up the older sister for the younger.

Vi set him straight when he hinted about it. "There is a man for Angie. His name is Andrew Temple. I think they may marry. He comes once a month from Poughkeepsie. He is serious. She just likes to tease you. She is like that."

One day the father, who appeared to have acquired a few English words, said, "Marry?"

"What?" Ken had responded, startled.

"Marry? Marry my daughter? You marry Violetta?"

Ken smiled at the memory of how quickly he had answered. "Yes, I will." He'd been vaguely aware of Vi waiting expectantly in the shadows with her mother and Angie.

Sibino had grabbed a wine bottle and uncorked it. "Good! We celebrate."

The entire Petitucci family, Sibino, Oria, Izzie, Angie, and Gerardo, came to Stafford Rest for a visit shortly after their marriage. The family stayed a week at Abner and Claire's farm across the lake because Ken and Vi didn't have room for them in the little house on Blackberry Hill.

Sibino, at first, believed Ken owned an interest in the farm. The misunderstanding was embarrassing to Ken, for although he'd never made more than a passing reference to the farm, he might have, in Sibino's eyes, misrepresented himself as a viable candidate for marriage. Vi quickly explained to her father that Ken merely helped his brother at odd times, adding, "The property where we live on Blackberry Hill belongs to Papa and Mama Gainsworthy. There are ten acres, and we have a deal. It will be ours someday." Sibino had seemed satisfied with the explanation. That conversation had taken place more than six years ago.

The "deal" with Jacob had become an uncertain one. Ken stopped chopping at the roots and looked around at the land he lived on but did not own. A sparrow landed on a bush above the garden. It stared at him, its red head bobbing from side to side in an obvious inspection. The bird stilled, cocked its red head to one side, and appeared to wait for a response to some unspoken question.

Ken had no answers. Jacob had promised to deed the property to them if improvements were made to meet his expectations. The house and barn were sturdy structures long-neglected, but the setting was splendid. His parents had bought the property when Jacob became too crippled to stay in the woods for long periods and had treated it more like a wilderness camp than a house in an established community. After his mother and father left, but before Ken and Vi married, he moved in and worked hard to prepare for the uncertain prospect of living with a wife.

They paid no rent. The problem was that, with Vi gone so much, and Ken working hard to keep his head above water, there had been little time to make more than a few minor improvements. Nor had there been enough money. He was lucky Jacob hadn't pressed the matter. Jacob had never been one to give things away without an accounting.

Another troubling thought came. It was galling that Pinky Hunt saw more of Vi and Obie than he did. Today, they were celebrating birthdays at the Hunt home, and not being invited felt like a slight, although he would have declined such an invitation.

He admired Pinky. They had hunted together every fall since Pinky's arrival in Stafford Rest, and the newcomer had proven himself a man's man. Notwithstanding the camaraderie, Ken hated the way Pinky looked at Vi. On the robust side, he was not a "handsome" man, but he had money and a sophistication Ken would never possess. He couldn't put too much blame on Pinky, however, for any man with a cold vixen of a wife like Pinky's might be attracted to a young and pretty woman like Vi.

He turned from the pile of brush he was building and walked down to the barn. At a corner, he reached inside a space left by a broken board and removed a bottle. He let his fingers roam the glass and felt the coolness. The old battle loomed, and he mulled pouring out the contents. That impulse swayed him only a moment before he lifted the bottle to his lips.

* * *

"Prissy, come with me. We've not been to the grove for a smart while." Jacob Gainsworthy took his wife's hand and tugged gently toward a circle of woods on the high section of open pasture, a site they frequently visited.

"All right . . . if you're up to it."

"Today's one of my good days."

"You're a wonder," she said as she moved closer. He felt a wave of affection, a familiar condition of the heart that still astonished him.

Jacob loved life and family. Above all, he loved Prissy. Had he not, he might, at eighty-nine years and burdened with "tolerable rheumatism," have given in and let nature lead him to the inevitable. Jacob was not one to give in. He still expected and welcomed magical days when body pains lessened and a hint of springiness returned to his legs.

He was experiencing such a day. He had been up since six o'clock, eaten a hearty breakfast, and pitched hay to the cows over Abner's protests. His son thought he should never again have to lift a finger. Jacob then walked the fence line until he found the gap where a cow had escaped the previous evening. Neal Eps, who owned the neighboring farm, had brought the roaming bovine home and suggested Abner might want to fix the break "afore it happens again." Jacob had found the problem without difficulty. A post had rotted, leaned, and allowed the barbed wire to sag enough for the enterprising cow to make her way across.

Jacob returned to the barn to find Abner but then decided to take on the repair job himself. He started back toward the pasture with pliers and hammer in his back pockets, a locust post on one shoulder, and a posthole digger on the other.

Prissy had caught him at a barn corner and declared that she was going along. She would never admit that she worried about him when he went off alone. Together, they checked the remaining fence line to ensure there were no other escape routes.

With the fence job complete, they approached the stand of trees in the middle of the broad pasture. The sun's rays on Jacob's back and bare head intensified his good feelings. Warm spring days in the Adirondacks were days to be outside, days for celebrating the passing of a cold and confining winter.

The island of woods was two hundred feet in diameter, with numerous varieties of shrubs growing within the circle, along with spruce, oak, elm, maple, hickory, and walnut trees. Highlighting the perimeter were grotesquely bent white birches whose horizontal strips of paper-thin bark ringed each trunk. Those misshapen trees were survivors of past winds whose fury had driven them to bend but not break. Like himself, Jacob reflected, buffeted and bent but unbroken.

They found their familiar sitting place. The smooth trunk of a large downed oak whose bark had been stripped by weather and time was just the right shape and height on which to rest. Black raspberry bushes with whitish stems spread out among the birches. June would bring succulent berries in the shaded places. He would come back then to pick fruit for jams and jellies to supplement a later harvest of blackberries from Blackberry Hill. Sparrows and finches flitted among the lower tree branches. On their approach, he had heard a catbird.

Claire had said that her parents, the Ashdowns, enjoyed this site during their many years on the one-hundred-acre farm. Jacob believed it to be the finest acreage in the area. It bordered Diamond Lake and produced enough grain and hay to feed the small herd of dairy cows, with some extra to generate additional income necessary in these troubled times.

He and Prissy had not actually "moved in" with Abner and Claire. There were two houses on the farm. Jacob and Prissy occupied the bungalow on a knoll a hundred yards from the main house and near Lake Road. Built soon after Abner and Claire were married, it had been the young couple's home for years until the death of Claire's parents when the much larger and older stone house became their residence. Abner had electricity installed in the big house as soon as it became available in the area, as well as indoor plumbing. The bungalow was also brought up to date.

Ken had lived in the bungalow for several years before trading places for the house on Blackberry Hill. Abner had, at first, insisted his mother and father move into the big house with them. Prissy, however, was adamant about having their private abode. Four small rooms were more than adequate, providing even more space than the house on the hill.

Jacob squinted against the sun's glare across the end of the lake to Stafford Rest and beyond. It was too far to see the house on Blackberry Hill, but he could make out the barn.

Prissy saw him looking and said, "You haven't forgotten that we're walking over there later today, have you?"

"Of course not. It's Obie's birthday."

Her smile widened. "Five years old. Can you imagine?"

"Violetta's a blessing for this family. I'd given up us ever having a grandchild."

Her happy eyes changed, revealing uneasiness. "She's settled Kenneth down some. I hope and pray . . ."

It was an old worry and one Jacob shared. "I know, Prissy. He's like a cracked pot that's been patched but is always about to fall apart. I believe it's still the war that bothers him."

"It's been over a dozen years. Seems like he'd of got over it by now, don't it?"

"Things have improved some, and that's Vi's doing. She's a rock. He's lucky she married him, her being so much younger."

Prissy laughed. "You forget, Jacob!" she said. He laughed too, for she was speaking of their own marriage. Jacob had been forty-three and Priscilla Carpenter nineteen.

"It worked out far better than folks thought it would."

It was on a night at a Long Lake Christmas square dance that he first caught sight of Prissy, a young woman from Rochester visiting relatives. Jacob enjoyed local respect as a decorated Civil War veteran and acclaimed Adirondack wilderness guide, so that may have been the reason other would-be suitors simply stepped aside. On that evening, he swept the young blonde belle into his arms and his life. They were married a month later, although some well-meaning friends suggested he might give the situation more consideration.

He still remembered what he said to her on the night he proposed. "Prissy, I'm more than twice your age. I live in the woods most of the time, and that's not too likely to change cause it's about all I know how to do. But you'll not find a man anywhere who'll love you more. I'm particular about things, which is evidenced by the time I took to choose me a wife. I may be older in years, but I'm young in all the ways that count."

"You'd better be," she had replied as she took his bearded chin in her hands and looked into his eyes.

They were married in January, and Abner was born before the end of the year. Kenneth was born two years later. They made their home in the Keene Valley, east of the high peaks, and raised their two boys there. Prissy was a worrier and was pleased when Abner married Claire Ashdown and moved to Stafford Rest to help run the Ashdown farm. But she was devastated when Kenneth went off to war a few years later. Those had been the darkest days of their marriage; she had kept to herself until Kenneth returned.

Jacob loved both his sons, although Kenneth remained a mystery. As a young man, all he'd wanted to do was ramble through the woods, which was all right with Jacob at the time; a son wanting to be like his father had been fine with him. Nevertheless, as the state of New York took a tighter grip on the Adirondack Park and Forest Preserve, and wealthy interests acquired more private land within the park, it became apparent that wilderness guiding was an endangered occupation.

Jacob's family had been in the Adirondacks for over a hundred years. His father entered the Champlain Valley from Boston early in the nineteenth century and resided in Elizabethtown before marrying Mary Ann Morehouse. The couple soon made their way west to Newcomb. Abraham Gainsworthy was a bookkeeper, working first for the timber industry, but later hired on with the McIntyre concern which was starting to mine iron ore in that area. He and Mary Ann had three sons while living there. All three went off to the War Between the States. Only Jacob came home. After Mary Ann died, brokenhearted, Abraham moved to Saranac Lake, where he died the following year.

Abraham left few possessions but, being an able woodsman, he had instilled in Jacob a love of the outdoors. It had been more than seventy-five years since Abraham had taken the boys on a three-week trip through the mountains and upper Hudson River Valley, camping and living off the land. Memories of those days had not faded. It was natural for Jacob to turn to the wilderness for his livelihood after returning from the war. Exhausted by death and destruction, and grieving for his two brothers, he embraced the secluded lakes, high peaks, and serene valleys for several months to let his wounded spirit heal.

But adjustment came slower for Kenneth. Jacob had hoped his son would adapt to economic changes on his return from Europe and look for steady work. That he'd seen terrible sights in France wasn't in doubt; Jacob had experienced similar horrors at Gettysburg and in the Valley of Virginia. Like the gnarled birch trunk over which Prissy was running her fingers, a man needed to bend without breaking, and then get on with his life. Thirteen years after returning, Kenneth still had no permanent employment and, due to economic conditions, little few prospects for such. And his drinking was troubling.

"He's no dummy," Jacob said with a sigh. "I've seen him often with a book in his hand, and when he's on the trail, he speaks well to folks about the woods and hills."

"I pray for him every day."

Jacob shaded his eyes to see down past the houses and barn where Abner's land met the lakeshore. The lake was outside the chain of navigable waters and seldom experienced the turbulence of other larger lakes in the Adirondacks. Today, the sunlit water was smooth as glass, rippling only in places where random wind devils teased the surface.

Jacob and Pinky Hunt shared the opinion that Diamond Lake was fortunate to be in an out-of-the-way location. The solitude may have been the reason for the late settlement of Stafford Rest. Most certainly, the abundance of white cedar on surrounding hills was what brought loggers there around the quarter-century mark. Once the trees were cut, many hardy men and women stayed and planted the seeds of the community. Jacob believed the beauty and peacefulness was what held them; the area soil was mostly poor; steep hills, a swamp, and the encirclement of park land would forever limit expansion. That suited him just fine.

He became aware of Prissy's eyes on him. "What is it?" he said.

"Do you pray for Kenneth, too?"

"I pray for all our family. Why would you think I wouldn't?"

She ignored the question. "Jacob, are you ever sorry, you know, about your way of believing?"

It was the threat of a familiar discussion. "No, there's nothing to be sorry over. Why are you asking me that again, Prissy?"

"I worry sometimes. You made some folks at church mad at you."

"That was nearly ten years ago."

"I'm glad you keep going to Sunday services with us, even

21

though people seem to remember that incident."

"That's your imagination. And I go to church because you go. I go to be with you . . . and with Abner and Claire. And, as for the way I believe, me and God are just fine with it."

"Elsie Gobbles thought you went out of your way to insult the preacher."

"Elsie's been dead for seven or eight years. She thought everybody was trying to insult him. What I said to him wasn't an insult, Prissy, because I don't ever mean to insult anybody. I just told him that all the rituals and committee things he was planning had nothing to do with being a Christian."

"You said it in the congregation where everybody could hear. I think he took offense."

"Well, if he did, he didn't mention it. Anyway, he's been gone quite a while now. All that happened a long time ago, and I'm sure folks don't think about it."

"We could go to one of the other churches in the village, the Episcopalian or the Baptist."

"Why on earth would we do that? Abner and Claire . . . all the Ashdowns, they was all Methodists. Even Dad was a Methodist. For goodness sake, he remembered the circuit rider, Freeborn Garrettson, planting churches in the area."

Her expression told him that she still had questions, and he wanted to put her mind at ease. "Listen here, Prissy, I'm not an atheist if that's what you worry about. Not even, what's that word . . . agnostic. But I do think God's ways are bigger than ours, and we ought to stop thinking we have all the answers. Most folks believe in things that don't matter much, and that's all right because they may need to do that. I respect the way people think about God and how they approach him. But I also believe the most important thing is love. We need to love God . . . and love one another."

She laughed. "Oh, I do that. And I love you dearly, Jacob!"

He patted her hand. "I love you too, Prissy, but the love I'm talking about is the kind Jesus spoke of. Like that Samaritan that stopped on the roadside to take care of a Jew. Remember that?"

"Of course, I remember. It's in the Bible. He wanted the Jews to show love to other people different from themselves. And I believe many of them did listen to him about that."

"The problem is that some think it's some long-ago message. I believe it's a message to us right now."

"Jacob, *I know that.* And we *do* love one another. And not just our families. Our church is full of love, and I'm sure the other churches are too."

"Do you remember Rob Dowers?"

"He was here awhile from Utica, wasn't he? He lived in that old house on Clearwater Road."

"He *existed* there. No water. No electricity. Outhouse was fallin' in. He was a pitiful man. He showed up at church one Sunday."

"I remember. People said he smelled, and I think he was drunk."

"I don't think one person greeted him . . . and that includes us. It was a failure on our part. We didn't show love."

"Jacob . . . that's hard."

"It's what being a Christian requires, Prissy. When Tom Brown and me was on the battlefield at Chambersburg, we come on a dying Johnny Reb. Tom gave him the last of his water, even though we was all so thirsty that we couldn't hardly swallow. Tom was like that."

"What I've heard about Tom was that after the war he drank a lot and never kept a job. And he wasn't a church member."

"Yes, and his mouth sometimes got away from him, but my way of thinking is that God'll burn those sins, and others, out of him soon enough. I think God knows what's important in a person."

Prissy appeared thoughtful. "Don't Christians have to do other things, go to church, say our prayers, visit the sick, and tithe our money?"

"We should, but we should do those things because we love God, and love one another, and not because it's a duty of some kind that God demands."

Prissy never seemed at a loss for countering his flights into "divergent views," so he braced himself. She surprised him with a prolonged silence before moving closer and squeezing his hand. "I love *you*, Jacob, my mountain man. I love you more than any earthly thing, even though you do have some strange ideas."

The day was too pleasant to discuss his beliefs, which would probably always be at odds with Prissy's. A breeze brushed his cheek, maybe the tail-end of one above where a red-tailed hawk soared, the whites of its belly flashing in the sunlight.

"I love you, too, Prissy," he said, first to himself, then aloud.

She squeezed his hand again, tighter this time. "I think people might understand you better if they knew about that good thing you do."

"That *we* do, Prissy. It was your decision as much as mine. Nobody needs to know about it except us and those few that have to know."

He expected her to protest, as she usually did, but after a period of silence, he said, "It's hours until time to walk to town. Let's go back to the house for a spell."

She nodded and smiled as she stood. They held hands as they walked across the pasture to pick up the tools. He was amazed that the intensity of his feeling for her had never diminished. Maybe he could show her again how young he was "in all the ways that count."

CHAPTER THREE

November–December 1934

For the second time in the past three days, Obie and his father visited the "old trailhead." Darkness was settling patiently onto the mountain's east side and a chill was descending.

This trip in their ancient Dodge truck had taken nearly an hour; his mother called the vehicle *il rumore delle ossa*. His father had continually shifted grinding gears to coax old "Rattling Bones" over numerous steep grades along the unpaved road. After leaving the truck to start their trek, the unpleasant sounds still echoed in Obie's ears.

Their destination was a half-mile in and over a trail last traveled in daylight, hard to follow even then. Obie had helped his father fasten a block of salt to a tree trunk on the edge of a clearing. He had received no answer to his question of why they were putting it there. The site's isolation, and the secretiveness, made it seem a great adventure.

They were not long on the trail before Obie felt compelled to ask again. He spoke to his father's back, a few yards ahead, "Daddy, what's the salt for?"

"The deer like it and get used to coming here for it. Just don't tell anybody about what we're doing."

"Why can't I tell anybody, Daddy?"

"Because they'll come and take our game away."

"I won't tell anybody, Daddy." He knew, anyway; he'd heard men in Mercer's Store talking about how game limits were too strict. A grizzly-looking fellow had said that large families needed lots of meat to get through long winters. Obie's father had killed one deer already during a with Mr. Hunt. They had smoked the meat. They needed more.

His father said, "You like venison, don't you?"

"A whole lot. So do Mommy and Slobber."

Newly bare trees had allowed the sun to light the way on their last journey over the rough mountain path, but this time darkness had descended, and Obie struggled to keep up. His father had a flashlight but aimed the beam to the front, lighting the trail behind only when there were barriers to avoid.

"Is it much farther, Daddy?"

"You know how far it is. Stop talking." He turned the flashlight off.

"I can't see, Daddy!"

"Your eyes will get used to it. I don't want to scare the game."

Obie's sight adjusted, but the night was still black and frightening. His father's shape stayed just a few steps beyond his reach. He was expected to keep up; that was his father's way. "You can't pamper a boy," he had heard him say to Obie's mother. "He has to learn to depend on himself."

Obie liked being in the woods with his father. The hard things he had to do made him feel proud. He'd even learned to feel at home in the Morass. They'd gone there a few nights last summer to gig frogs. The old rowboat had leaked excessively for a night or two until the boards were soaked through enough to expand and close the cracks. Obie's job was to keep the boat bailed out with a pail brought along for that purpose.

There were no straight waterways in the Morass; navigation consisted of zig-zag routes among fallen trees, stumps, beaver lodges, and stunted bushes. Obie had, at first, found it confusing, especially in the dark. "We're not lost," his father had assured him. "Look up there at the ridge. You can see it even in the dark. See how it dips? And over there on the right side, that's south." He'd pointed out other landmarks as ways of knowing their location. "And back there is the light, Obie. See the glow? You can't see the buildings through the trees, but that's the town. At night, you can always row toward the light." His father's words helped make "the swamp," as many still called it, a friendlier place. He hoped they would go there again next summer.

The difficulty of the trail snatched him back from thoughts about summer. He clenched his teeth and told himself to keep going until his heart stopped beating. His feet crunched in fallen leaves and on occasional patches of early snow crusted over by several days of cold, dry weather. He fell several times. Once, he skinned his knee. He tried to keep from crying, but his knee hurt too much. His father turned on the flashlight and held it close to inspect the injury. "It's just a scratch. Stop crying. You're eight years old, for God's sake."

Just when Obie decided he could go no farther, they stopped. His father placed the flashlight in his hands and told him to turn it on and shine it into the eyes of the first deer they spotted. "I'll tell you when to turn it on. Just keep it steady, and don't let the beam move around too much or you'll scare it away."

They waited a long time; it was worse than walking. Obie's teeth chattered and he was trembling despite wearing a wool sweater and a Mackinaw jacket. He wanted to move around to keep warm, but his father put a firm hand on his arm every time he started to get up. At last, Obie heard the whispered word, "Now!"

He turned the flashlight on and saw a doe close enough to hear her breathing. The animal stood stark still, steam erupting from her nostrils in short bursts. Her eyes seemed to reflect the beacon of light. Obie tried to hold the flashlight steady. His hands shook so much that he was in danger of dropping it. "Daddy . . . please," he whispered.

His father's voice came in a whisper, although it held his usual tone of authority. "Obie, hold it still."

Obie heard the low swish of cloth brushing against cloth and knew his father had raised the rifle. The doe flinched at the sound, then became motionless except for the twitching of her shoulder muscles. Her eyes bored into Obie's as though begging for release from a situation she didn't understand. Obie felt sorry, and the emotion escalated until he was unable to keep his hands still. He dropped the flashlight a second before his father fired the rifle.

"Pick it up, Obie . . . pick it up!"

Obie grappled in the underbrush until he located the flashlight, which had gone out. His father grabbed it from him and pounded it against the palm of his hand until the light came on again. The doe was gone.

"See what happens when you don't follow directions," his father said as he examined the ground. "I hit her, though. She's bleeding."

"Can't we just leave her alone?" Obie begged.

"No, we don't leave a wounded animal to suffer. We'll go after her."

"I'm sorry, Daddy. I'll help you find the deer."

"There's a lot of blood. She won't get far."

A few minutes later, and a couple hundred yards farther into the woods, they caught up with the doe. She lay on her side, not moving. Steam spiraled upward from her body. Obie shined the light into her eyes again. He didn't see a reflection this time.

It took almost an hour to reach the road. Obie held the light to find the path. The doe was heavy, and his father stopped often to rest. Obie was glad he wasn't butchering it in the woods. He'd often helped with that chore but had never gotten used to the smell of guts and blood. His mother had tried to explain death, but it remained a mystery how an animal could be alive one second and lifeless the next. He wondered what happened to make such a change?

His father put the deer in the truck bed and covered it with a tarp. The truck failed to start, and hand-cranking failed. They were parked on a grade. His father made Obie stand to one side and wait while he took the truck out of gear and started pushing it down the hill. Obie knew the routine, for it happened often. When it started rolling, his father jumped in, pushed in the clutch, put it back into gear, and let the clutch out, causing the engine to roar to life. It stopped several yards down the hill amid billows of exhaust smoke as his father pumped the accelerator to keep the motor going. Obie ran to catch up.

Back in Stafford Rest on Cedar Creek Road, the truck went up the steep incline a short distance before the ruts became too deep to go farther. Obie helped drag the deer up to the barn. He'd never been so tired.

His mother met them at the door. "You took a long time," she said. "I did not know where you were." Obie saw that she was annoyed.

* * *

Vi was baking cookies in the woodstove oven. Obie was outside, playing. After a week of "putting affairs in order," which included expanding the woodpile and smoking venison, Ken had gone north to a lumbering job he had been lucky enough to get because of his father's connection to someone there. He would miss Thanksgiving at Abner and Claire's, but she was relieved by his promise to come home for Christmas.

This day after Ken's departure was dark, and signs of fall still clung to the landscape. Obie had said that morning that it was "hanging on with a buckling resolve." She had smiled, for "buckling resolve" was a term Ken had used. She and Obie had looked up those words in the old dictionary kept on the mantel beside Ken's collection of works on geology and mountain floral.

Snow and cold of the winter season loomed so near that Vi could almost feel it. It would be her eleventh winter in the Adirondacks. Winter was not her favorite season, but she had come to love the sights and sounds of her surroundings. The High Peaks, visible on clear days, still had the power to make her gasp. She loved the reds, yellows, purples, and other brilliant hues of fall. Spring was special, too, with ripples on Diamond Lake creating the sparkling condition people said had given it its name. Early summer was often difficult with its swarms of black flies, although the late summer serenity more than compensated.

But now, summer was long gone and autumn was nearly spent. Winter stillness would come rapidly. She shivered at thoughts of the icy blasts to come. Already, cold winds were penetrating cracks in the house's west side, and there was that awful adjustment to early mornings in the drafty outhouse behind the barn. Ken had drained the water pipe from the spring above the house, making it necessary to carry water from the spring itself for household use. Although sheltered with a rough wooden structure, the spring would freeze over, and the ice would have to be broken with a pick left there for that purpose.

The lake would freeze too, and not many weeks later smoke would begin curling up from the tiny portable "Shanties" on the ice where men and boys, and sometimes women and girls, drilled holes to drop in their fishing lines. Obie wanted to "ice fish," and she had considered how it might be accomplished. Ken's father, Jacob, had said he would teach him, but Vi feared that, at ninety-two, he might hurt himself trying to keep up with a young boy. She loved Jacob and Prissy; they were a part of the beauty around her.

She expected that a "closing in," a feeling of isolation, would soon come. It was a time when loneliness, her most feared enemy, appeared. She still missed her family. Her father made infrequent visits, always in summer, and never stayed long. Her sisters had their own families. Her brother had left home, gone to New York, and seldom came back. Vi had been to Albany only a few times in eleven years. One of those times was to attend her mother's funeral.

Ken's absences were concerning, as well. He had been away most of the last winter and, because of her job, she saw little of him even when he was home. The winter before that, he had stayed away for months working in the Lake Placid area during the Winter Olympics. That was an exciting time with people coming from all over the world. Seventeen nations and two hundred fifty-two athletes participated. Even little out-of-the-way Stafford Rest had its share of visitors. Beth Clarington had to hire extra help for her cafe. Ken came home to get Obie and take him to Lake Placid for two days to attend some of the events.

She was reluctant to think about it, but Ken's presence was a mixed blessing. When he was home, he drank too much. Sober, he was as attentive as always, but when drinking he was less affectionate and more distant. During those times, she would look at herself in the mirror, searching for any indication that she was no longer attractive; she was not yet thirty; her face was smooth and unwrinkled; her hair was dark with no trace of gray, and there was no spare fat on her body. Men looked at her. Once, she caught Pinky staring; he had quickly looked away, embarrassed. He was a good man—and even if he felt like that about her, which she was sure he did not, he would never let her know. Were it not for Obie and the daily routine with the Hunts, she might not have borne the loneliness of winters so well.

There was something else: Sabino had reminded her on his last visit. "Violetta, have you forgotten that you are Catholic?"

"No, Papa, I have not forgotten."

"Where do you go to Mass?"

"I do not go. The nearest Catholic church is at Evergreen."

"You have never been there for Mass?"

"I have no way to get there."

"There is the truck."

"It is unreliable. Ken takes it with him when he goes away. Anyway, I cannot drive."

"My daughter, your soul is in danger. You must get Ken to take you. And Obie . . . has he received no instruction?"

"Oh, I have told him of his religious heritage."

"It is not enough. He needs instructions from a priest."

"Yes, Papa, I will see to it."

Her father had not pursued it further. It bothered her, nonetheless. She brought up the subject with Ken, who was unenthused. "I'm not religious like Mama and Claire."

"And Abner?"

"Abner goes to church because Claire does. Papa . . . I'm not sure what he believes in."

"Obie needs to know about such things."

"Well, if it makes you feel better, take him to a church here. You've got your choice of a Baptist, a Methodist, or an Episcopalian."

"Ken, I am required to raise Obie as Catholic. You are a Catholic too, you know. You had to join the Church before our priest in Albany would marry us. You even took lessons. And you promised to raise Obie as a Catholic."

"I did it to satisfy their requirements. I told you that then, and I think the priest knew, as well."

She had been aware of her problem even before discussing it with her father. On one trip to Albany, she had gone to confession. The priest scolded her for such a long absence and told her she was neglecting her child. Despite Ken's reluctance, she *must* go to Evergreen.

She was taking cookies from the oven and considering the unresolved Church issue when Obie came in, followed by Slobber. "Right on time," Vi said.

"We smelled them."

Obie seated himself at the wooden kitchen table. The cookies were hot, and Obie blew on one to cool it. He pinched off a liberal piece and threw it to Slobber, who caught it in his mouth.

Vi stoked the fire and put dirty utensils in the sink before pouring in cold water from one of the buckets lined up against the kitchen wall. Later, after the utensils had soaked, she would add hot water for a final washing.

The kitchen, an open extension of their living area, was not large. Except for the woodstove, the only other heat source in the house was a fireplace on an outside wall. The other room in the modest little house, the adults' bedroom, was often bitterly cold in winter because of its isolation. She wished for more space.

Ken had promised to build another room with an added fireplace. The expense, and the time it would require, ensured that the project was never started. There was some hope, however, for he had searched out four large flat stones for the hearth. They were propped up against the back of the barn, waiting, she hoped, for fireplace warmth. Obie's bunk was crowded against a back wall of the living space. He needed a room of his own.

She gave him another cookie and sat down at the table facing him. It was time for a talk with her son.

* * *

When alone, they usually conversed in Italian, but now she surprised him by speaking in English, "Obie, you are getting to be a big boy now, and there is something we must talk about. Do you remember what I told you about how your Grandfather Petitucci and all his family worship God?"

"Yes, you're Catholics. You believe in Jesus and his mother.

Laura told me she believes in Jesus too."

"The Hunts are Protestants. Protestants believe, but they believe a different way. Most people in Stafford Rest are Protestants."

"Charlie Turner said Catholics are all going to Hell."

He saw that his mother was startled by his words. She smiled that nervous smile he'd seen a lot lately.

"Sometimes," she said, "people say bad things about other people without understanding."

"Am I a Catholic too, Mom?"

"Yes, you are, and I assure you that you are going to Heaven when you die."

"Where is Heaven, Mom?" He'd wondered about that, but this was the first time he'd asked anyone.

"Somewhere up in the sky, I guess, but I do not really know. Obie, I know you have many such questions. That is why I want us to talk. The priests know how to answer those questions. I am going to find us a priest."

"Where?"

"Tupper Lake, or the church closer in Evergreen."

"When will we go?"

"Soon . . . as soon as your father comes back from up north. I will talk to him, and he will take us over there."

"Mom, do we have to be Catholics because Grandfather Petitucci is? Uncle Abner and Aunt Claire aren't Catholic. They go to the Methodist church. And so do Grandpa and Grandma Gainsworthy."

He saw her hesitate before answering. "You can ask the priest about that when we see him."

"Can I have another cookie, Mom?"

"One more."

"And one for Slobber?"

"Yes, one for Slobber also."

He took a bite and held it in his mouth until it dissolved, savoring the sweetness. He liked talking to his mother this way. She never became angry at him the way his father sometimes did.

"Mom, tell me about coming to America when you were a little girl." He'd heard the story many times but never tired of hearing it.

She told it again, this time in Italian, about the voyage, how she had been so seasick, about waiting a long time on Ellis Island before they were allowed to go into New York City.

"Was Italy not a good place to live? Is that why you left?" he asked in English.

"I am not sure. I think the times might have been hard. You should ask your grandfather. I do not remember much, but I do remember olive trees, vineyards, and the pleasant weather. I remember Rome with its grand buildings and many people in the streets." "Once, we stood outside the Vatican, imagining what the Pope was doing inside." She giggled. Obie liked it when she did that.

"Who's the Pope?"

"He is the leader of the Church all over the world. The Pope tells all the priests what to do so the priests can tell us the right things to do."

He wondered how that might work; it was a lot to take in. Anyway, he was growing tired of talking about Catholics. "Did you know anybody else there in Rome . . . in Italy?"

"Yes. There was Maria and Donato." We lost track of them for a time until your Aunt Angie found out they left Rome and live farther north."

He remembered hearing the names but never fully understood the family relationships. "You don't mean your Grandmother Maria?"

"No. Maria is my older sister, even older than Angie. She was named after our grandmother. She married Donato before we left, and they stayed in Italy." Obie noticed tears forming in his mother's eyes.

"Have you ever gone back to visit her?"

"Oh, no. Never. It is too far. We have not seen each other for twenty years. I have letters, but we have not heard from her for a long time. I should write. She and Donato have a family. You have cousins there, Obie."

"Someday, I'll go and see my cousins in Italy."

"Well, I hope you do." She was studying his face. She seemed sad today, as she often did lately. "It is important for families to keep in touch, Obie. The same blood flows through us all. Without being connected, something in us dies."

Except for the blood part, he understood what she meant. "We should have friends too," he said.

"Yes, we should. That is part of being connected."

"Cassie and Laura are my friends. Cassie was my best friend when we were in our class together. Now Laura's my best friend."

"Obie, you should like them equally. I am proud of you for being double-promoted, but being in fourth grade and in Laura's class does not mean you should like her more than Cassie."

"Oh, I don't like her more. It's just different with Laura."

"How is it different, Obie?"

"I love Laura." The words had slipped out.

"Do you not love Cassie also?"

"I love Cassie too and like to be with her, but I'm going to marry Laura."

He hadn't told that secret to anyone before, and hadn't, until recently, thought differently of the sisters. They were part of his earliest memories; they were playmates, forming alliances in all possible combinations. They had been more like his sisters than his friends. The previous fall, when Obie skipped third grade and went into fourth with Laura, he started seeing her differently. He noticed her dark hair, how soft it looked falling over her shoulders, and how sparkling white her teeth were as she smiled at him from her desk two rows away. He talked to her on the playground every chance he found. She seemed not to mind. On the other hand, Cassie had tossed her shaggy blond head angrily and accused him of not liking her anymore. "But I don't really care," she'd added.

His mother took on her "wise expression." "You have lots of time before you need to think about getting married."

The subject was beginning to be embarrassing. They should talk about something else. "Mom, why can't we have a big house like the Hunts?"

"The Hunts are wealthy, Obie."

"Does that mean they're rich?"

"It means they have lots of money to spend and can buy things we cannot afford. The Depression has made it hard on everybody, but they can still have things we cannot."

"That's not fair."

"It is the way it is, Obie. You should not envy what other people have. You must do the best with what God has given you."

He wasn't sure he agreed; it sounded as though she believed they should stay poor. "How do you get to be wealthy?" he asked.

"By hard work and getting an education. Education is the most important. You are smart, Obie. Your teacher told me you are as bright a boy as she has ever taught, that you can be anything you want to be."

"Even wealthy?"

"I guess even that if it is what you want. Just remember, money can do many things, but it must not keep you from doing God's will."

"I'll have to think about what I want to be," Obie said before adding, "I do know I want to marry Laura." The words were hardly out before Cassie's accusing face popped up in his mind like toast from the Hunt's electric toaster.

* * *

Abigail Hunt stood looking out the big bay window of their home on Garnet Point. She was annoyed, but wasn't bothered by that state of mind; dissatisfaction was a part of her personality, a trait in which she took pride. She'd repeatedly reminded Pinky that her tenacious drive and attention to detail were the forces making them rich. Her most recent displeasure had come that morning from having failed to buy a property she'd thought to be "a done deal."

Not long after Cassie's birth, Abigail had realized that buying and selling real estate was what she most wanted to do. Unlike her husband, who seemed content to settle for mere survival during these challenging economic times, she wanted to accumulate real wealth. Thankfully, Pinky had left her to do her own thing, except for the few times he told her she was being unfair to people in her dealings. He didn't understand that everything was fair in business, that a hardened attitude was essential.

Until recently, she'd been buying and selling in her own name, turning property over as swiftly as possible. However, a visit to a large real estate agency in Albany started her thinking about the virtues of having an agency of her own. She would be the paid intermediary between buyers and sellers and still find excellent properties for herself. Already, she had fostered a few deals in which she had demanded, and received, a commission. Although she had yet to obtain a license and take on employees, the planning was underway. She would soon have other people working for her.

The dark early morning clouds had dissipated, and the day had become clear. Abigail's gaze went past the patio with its light skim of late November snow. Diamond Lake, not yet frozen, glimmered in the sun. The lake, however, was not the focus of her attention. She looked across the village to Indian Knob. Her self-trained eyes surveyed homes and lots from the lakeshore and up "the Knob." Several houses there belonged to summer residents, and those people tended to buy and sell through realtors. A place there had recently exchanged hands through her little "mobile agency."

Nevertheless, her plans for birthing a real agency didn't

overshadow her passion for obtaining her own property. The buildings on the Knob were small and often rough, but they held the promise of appreciation because the real value was in the land with its proximity to water. The Depression, as hard as it was on people's lives, had made things cheap—and she would take advantage of that. She already owned three properties on the Knob and wanted more.

The village also held the potential for ownership, although people there often transferred property through private transactions. Everyone in Stafford Rest knew everyone else and knew what was for sale, unlike the more transit Knob population. Her advantage was the increasing ability to attract outside buyers. She clicked off in her mind turnovers she might expect at some point, people who were talking about moving away, families sapped by lack of income, and some who might die soon.

She dreamed about a time when she could open an office in Evergreen, maybe even Tupper Lake. She had talent and know-how, even in little things, like steering the Gibbons family away from White Pine Road. Although she had nothing against Negroes, it was essential to protect property values.

Pinky's attitude toward business puzzled her. His furniture factory had barely managed a profit for years. She'd begged him to fire a few more of his employees, but so far, he'd failed to take her advice. Managing him was not always easy. She shrugged off the morning's disappointment; she would eventually get that property she wanted.

Blackberry Hill, the wooded prominence east of the highway and west of the headwaters of Cedar Creek, was also in her sights. Sparsely populated, it would be the cheapest to develop. Buildings there were modest dwellings with small acreages. Although electricity had come to the village, many, especially on the fringes, still declined to "hook up." They depended instead on oil lamps to light their homes. If she razed the buildings on the hill, such as the Gainsworthy house, constructed a better road, and took electricity there, she could build fine homes with pristine views.

"Mom, what's a subtrahend?" Laura's voice jolted her back from the real estate world. The girls were doing their homework at the dining room table, a Saturday morning ritual performed at Abigail's insistence.

Abigail smiled. Only one thing mattered more than real estate; her daughters came before everything. She asked, "Do you remember opening that package of sweet buns the other day?"

"Yes?" Laura sounded dubious.

"There were six in the package. You ate one. That was the subtrahend."

Laura giggled. "I ate a subtrahend? I don't understand."

"It's a subtraction problem, dear. Six minus one. The number you take away is called the . . ."

"Oh, I understand now."

"I got it right away," Cassie said.

"Oh, shut up, Cassie."

"Stop quarreling," Abigail demanded. "It's childish."

A little later, Cassie asked, "Mom, about our Christmas party in three weeks. Who's coming?"

"Just some of your classmates, dear."

"Can Obie come?"

"No, dear, I think not."

"Why not? He wants to?"

Abigail was irritated by her younger daughter's ability to always come up with an answer that countered her questions. "Cassie, why do you care? Obie's not in your grade anymore. He was removed."

"He wasn't removed," Laura said. "He was double-promoted."

"Obie's smart," Cassie said. "He learned everything in third grade, and that's why they sent him to fourth grade."

Abigail would not show her annoyance. "Anyway," she said, "Obie's not in your class anymore."

"Well, he's in mine," Laura said, "and I want him to come."

An opportunity for a talk she'd long wanted seemed to have presented itself. "Listen, girls, I'm going to tell you something important." She paused a moment, considering how best to start. "I know you've played with Obie since you were little . . ."

"Obie and me were born on the same day," Cassie said. "He was just a few minutes ahead."

"Obie and I, Cassie."

"*What?*"

"I'm correcting your grammar."

Cassie dismissed the chide with a toss of her head. "Being born the same day makes us special. He's my friend."

"Mine, too," Laura said.

This was harder than expected. "Listen, girls, playing with a neighbor boy is all right when you're young, but when you're older, it's time to stop playing with boys so much."

"Stop playing with Obie?" Laura squealed. "Really? Is that

what you want?"

Abigail pushed ahead. "What I mean is . . . well, Obie is Vi's son, and Vi's our servant."

Laura was quick to say, "Calling Vi a servant sounds really strange."

"Yes, but in truth, that's what she is, just a servant."

Laura's eyebrows drew together and her brow wrinkled in her classic anger stance that Abigail knew so well. "Mom, next to our family, and maybe Obie, Vi's the most important person in my life. If you weren't my mother, I'd want her to be. Don't call her *just a servant*. She's a *lot* more."

The talk wasn't going well. "All right," Abigail said, trying to sound conciliatory, "I'll invite Obie . . . this time."

It was disappointing that she hadn't been able to say what needed to be said, but she promised herself that, eventually, she would make her daughters understand their proper place in the world.

CHAPTER FOUR

June 1937

"Stop it, Ernie!"

"Stop it yourself!"

Ernie Boswell had shoved Obie. Obie recovered quickly and pushed back.

They stood toe to toe on a wooden dock, posturing like two gamecocks. The dock, adjacent to the Boswell home and store, was one of four that extended like prongs of a fork into the town end of Diamond Lake. The footing was made slippery by incessant waves whipped by a brisk west wind. Tommy Matthews and Chuck Hinky came running from the big oak beside the store.

"Don't take that, Obie. Sock him good," Tommy said. "Ernie's a bully."

"Knock the tar outa him," Chuck added, fists jabbing and hooking at the empty air in demonstration.

Obie wasn't going to hit Ernie and wondered why they were so angry. Ernie and Obie disagreed on numerous subjects, and they quarreled often, but they always made up. He wouldn't hit Ernie—unless he had to.

Obie had other friends, as well, but these boys gravitated toward one another. Obie was the youngest by about a year. Chuck lived on Main Street in the apartment over the Diamond Inn and Tommy's family lived on the farm at the foot of Blackberry Hill. Ed Baumgartner, a fifth member, was missing today, as he often was. His parents kept a close watch on his activities. "He's a mama's boy," Chuck once said during Ed's absence.

"Yeah, Obie, come on and hit me!" Ernie said, putting both fists in front of his face in a classic prizefighter stance. "Just try it! Just try it and see what happens!"

"I'm not going to hit you, Ernie."

"Obie's afraid," Chuck said.

"You're a troublemaker, Chuck . . . and I'm not afraid of anybody, including you. But I won't hit Ernie. We're friends, aren't we, Ernie?"

Ernie's scrunched-up countenance smoothed, and he dropped

his defensive pose. "Well, don't shove."

"You shoved me first. You tried to push me off the dock."

The blaming game lasted for several minutes with the agitators regularly switching sides to keep things riled up. They were eventually distracted by a rowboat docking. Two men, strangers, accepted their help securing the boat as it was tossed about in the rough water.

Ernie's father owned several rental boats. He also sold ice, bait, and fishing gear in his store. Obie enjoyed being around the docks where something was almost always happening. The men had stringers of lake trout. The boys walked with them to a new model automobile parked by the rough post and plank fence parallel to the lake and dock. Ernie had, the previous summer, instructed them in the advantages of helping fishermen; they sometimes gave the helpers a few coins, or shared their fish. Once, a fat fisherman gave them his whole catch, saying he hated cleaning fish. Today, these men left without even thanking them. When the car was out of sight, they went up to Lake Road and started throwing rocks at trees on the bank above the thoroughfare.

Obie pointed. "I can hit that big knot on the maple."

"You can't even throw that far," Tommy said. "I couldn't, and I'm older than you."

"I *can* do it," Obie declared. "Anyway, I'm as tall as any of you." He picked up a flat stone and fired it across the road toward the tree. To his amazement, it hit the knot, dead center.

Tommy whistled. "If you can do that, I can too." He picked up a stone and wound up to throw.

At that moment, an automobile came around the corner, casting up dust clouds as it sped out toward the main highway. The car arrived at the exact moment that Tommy released the rock. Brakes squealed. The stone barely missed the windshield. A horn blared.

"Run!" Tommy yelled.

The boys scattered. Obie reached the big oak and peered around it to see where the others had gone. He recognized the car. It sat for nearly a minute before moving slowly toward the state road. When it had gone, the others came out of hiding.

"Do you know who that was?" Tommy said to no one in particular.

"Yeah," Chuck said. "The witch. You know . . . Mrs. Hunt. It's a good thing that rock didn't hit her car. She'd of killed you, Tommy."

"My dad says she's crazy," Ernie said. "She tries to buy some of our land here. She keeps coming back even after he's told her it's not for sale."

"I heard she eats snakes and lizards," Chuck said. He followed the words with a gagging noise.

Obie laughed. "She doesn't do that. I know, because my Mom fixes almost all her food."

"That's right," Tommy said. "Your mother works for them. Is she really crazy?"

"She's all right. She's strict, but not dangerous . . . not at all." To say anything bad about Laura and Cassie's mother would feel like he was saying something bad about them.

Chuck said, "My dad works at the factory. He says Mr. Hunt's a regular guy."

"Yeah, I like Pinky," Ernie said, "but I don't want anything to do with her."

Obie hoped it was the end of the talk about Mrs. Hunt. Chuck tapped his shirt pocket. "I've got some cigarettes. Let's go over to the locust grove."

As they walked along a well-worn path, Obie wondered where Chuck's cigarettes came from. His father did part-time cleaning at the Diamond Inn, and Obie remembered seeing Chuck in the back of the building pouring leftover beer from several bottles into one. Chuck's clothes were often dirty—but he was a good friend.

The locust grove was at the beginning of a long narrow strip of woods running north along the lakeshore, an extension of Boswell land that reached the boundary of the town park and beach. Obie had heard grownups discuss it. Mr. Baumgartner, Ed's father, and the mayor, had said, "It's pristine land with a hundred-yard trail all the way through. The trail is situated well behind the road and draws an abundance of nocturnal activity." Obie was unsure what that meant, but the mayor made it plain in a public meeting that he wanted the town to buy the land and make it part of the park, thereby bringing it under better control. Ernie had told Obie that his father wasn't going to sell. The boys knew the area well.

Obie tried not to cough as he puffed on the lit Camel that Chuck was passing around. He'd promised his mother he wouldn't smoke and was careful not to inhale, a way to partially keep his promise. They stopped on a bluff overlooking the water.

Waves were breaking over the rocks below. Where the water was less riled, the bottom was crystal clear. They sat for several minutes watching for fish and other aquatic creatures. Tommy flipped the stub of the shared cigarette over the edge of the bank. "Ernie's got a girlfriend," he announced.

Obie expected Ernie to deny it. Instead, he said, "Frances is pretty. Her family lives in the old Roberts place way up the Knob."

Chuck said, "Ain't you talking about the Gibbons family? They're colored."

Ernie seemed not to have heard. "We talk on the playground, is all."

Obie knew that Hansford Gibbons was a janitor at their school, and Gerdie was a cook in the school lunch program. He repeated what his father said when the family had arrived there from Utica two years before. "They seem like good people."

"But they're colored," Chuck insisted.

Tommy raised his voice, "They're still people, Chuck. You make it sound like you're better than them."

"Well, ain't you a goodie." Chuck shoved Tommy before stating, "My father says we shouldn't associate with their kind."

"What's that mean?" Obie asked.

"You know, colored, Jews, Italians."

Obie didn't care if Chuck saw his anger. A man in Indian Lake had called his mother a name sometimes used for people of Italian descent. His father had hit the man, causing him to stay in jail overnight. His mother later explained to Obie that certain people used terms like that because they didn't know better, or had hate in their hearts. "It is not only Italians they call names. They use derogatory terms about Negros, the Irish, and Polish. They say things against anyone not like themselves."

Obie stood and jerked Chuck up by his arm. He put his face close to Chuck's. "You take it back," he said.

Chuck looked genuinely surprised. "Take back what?"

Tommy said, "You insulted his mother, you fool. She's Italian. I think you'll be sorry if you don't take it back."

Chuck's expression was one of confusion. Obie made a fist. He would plant it right on Chuck's nose if there were no apology. Chuck took a step backward. "I didn't mean nothin,' Obie. I like your mother. I . . ."

"Take it back." Obie needed to hear the words.

"Okay . . . I take it back!"

Things returned to normal after that. Obie hoped he could like Chuck again.

* * *

The following Sunday, Obie sat beside his mother in a pew near the back of Stafford Rest Methodist Church. He had vague memories of being in a church in Albany with his mother and Grandfather Petitucci. He remembered a building much larger than this, with statues and a big cross with Jesus hanging on it. That memory was the extent of his "church" experience. He'd once asked Grandma Prissy if he could go to church with them; she'd said, "You'd better ask your mother."

The service started with singing two hymns from a hymnal taken from a rack on the pew back facing them. Both melodies were familiar, one more so than the other. Occasionally, on Sunday mornings when the air was thick and windows were open, organ music and voices drifted up from the Baptist Church, the closest house of worship to Blackberry Hill. A song, often repeated, had the words "amazing grace." The lyrics were unclear, but Obie soon learned the melody. Now, he saw the words. He leafed through the hymnal and discovered hymns that Miss Bromley, his sixth-grade teacher, had them sing in class.

Obie had asked his mother to let him attend a service. For several years she'd talked about taking him to Mass in Evergreen, which hadn't happened; his father was either not home or was reluctant to go. His mother said she wouldn't go without him.

Cassie motivated Obie to ask his mother about attending the Methodist church. "Don't you like going to church?" she'd asked him one day on the playground.

His answer had caused Cassie to raise her eyebrows in disbelief—or maybe she was teasing. "What? You're eleven years old and have never been to church. What kind of heathen are you?"å

In addition to his relatives, the Hunts were Methodists, which sharped Obie's desire to visit that church. He didn't want to be a "heathen," he told his mother. It was an excellent excuse to see the sisters. He still went with his mother to the Hunt house, although not as often, so he looked for opportunities to see the girls.

Obie could see Abner and Claire sitting near the front, on the left. His grandparents were not in attendance, probably because of his grandfather's failing health. The Hunt family was seated on the right in the first row of pews. Obie couldn't see them without standing.

Had it not been for his relatives' membership here, and wanting closer association with the Hunts, his curiosity might have led him to visit any of the three churches. The Baptist, a white wood-framed unpretentious building, was closest to home, a matter of walking down the hill and across the footbridge over Cedar Creek. Or, he could go across town to the Episcopalian church, the most beautiful of the three buildings. Constructed of gleaming white stone, its steeple was the highest structure in the village. Many of his classmates went there, including Ed Baumgartner, Tommy Matthews, and Ernie Boswell.

The centrally located Methodist church was on White Pine Road, about a city block from Main Street. It was the oldest, and had the largest congregation, according to Mr. Hunt, who knew about such things. It was built of stone and brick in about equal proportion, with an attached wood-frame building on the back that extended perpendicularly, making the whole structure L-shaped. Inside the L, next to the street, sat a small cottage, the parsonage.

Obie had believed that his mother wouldn't allow him to attend a protestant service; she'd said more than once that their religion didn't permit it. She surprised him by not only giving her permission but saying she would go with him. Why she'd changed her mind was a mystery. His mother had been having her "sad spells" more often and was acting in other strange ways. He was concerned—but not today. He was just pleased that she'd come with him.

Cassie had told him about the pastor. Charles Lansing was middle-aged, unmarried, and had come from a pastorate in southern Vermont a few months previously. Her mother had liked him at first but had since changed her opinion. Obie wasn't surprised; Mrs. Hunt found many things to dislike.

Obie watched Reverend Lansing throughout the service, watched everything he did, and listened carefully to his sermon. He didn't understand all the words, nor fully understand the context, but he did wonder what it was like up there. It was strange that the preacher had no robe and wore a dress suit and tie, as did many men in the congregation.

Why was there no Jesus on the big wooden cross? That *was* a mystery. He was fascinated by the church structure, from the polished and sculpted woodwork with meticulous detail to the high stained-glass windows. The sunlit glass cast prisms of color that danced on the backs of people sitting along the sides. He was close enough to read a metal tag under one window. It said, "Donated by," and had a name he didn't recognize.

Near the end of the service, the congregation was invited to go up front for the "Lord's Supper," although it wasn't near suppertime. "All are invited," Lansing said, his long arms sweeping outward in an inclusive motion. Obie rose.

His mother touched his arm. "No, Obie. It is not for us."

As the rest of the congregation went up front, Obie felt conspicuous. He saw Cassie and Laura kneeling at the altar rail and saw Laura's head tilt back as she drank from a tiny glass.

Obie was sure people would avoid them because they hadn't participated in the Lord's Supper. Happily, that didn't happen. After the service, several people shook their hands, including many schoolmates' parents. There were few unfamiliar faces. He guessed it would have been much the same at the other churches. The Hunts shook their hands as though they were meeting for the first time, which felt strange. Mrs. Hunt said to his mother, "Vi, I'm really surprised. I thought . . ."

Pinky cut in. "Vi, Obie, it's good to see you here."

Cassie stuck out her hand toward Obie and then playfully pulled it back. They both laughed at her trick. Laura grasped his hand firmly and leaned close, saying, "It's about time you came. I never really thought you would." He marveled at the smoothness of her hand and savored today's scent, which was lilac.

As the sanctuary emptied, Obie announced to his mother, "I want to go up front to see what it's like."

"All right, for just for a minute."

As they walked down the center aisle, Obie asked, "Do you think anybody would care if I go up there and stand where the preacher stood."

"It's called a pulpit." The voice came from behind Obie and startled him.

The big hand the pastor held out to Obie was not callused like his father's, but strength was in it. The man turned to Obie's mother, giving her a two-handed shake, his hands covering hers like a tarp covering a stack of firewood.

"You are Mrs. Gainsworthy?"

"Yes, how did you know?"

"I try to make it my business knowing everyone in town. It's part of my job, I guess." His head, covered with thick dark hair, bobbed up and down as he talked. Turning to Obie, he said, "And you must be Obadiah?"

Obie gave his usual answer. "My friends call me Obie."

45

"Well, I'd be honored to be your friend. But I do like the name 'Obadiah.' It's right from the Bible, you know. Come on, I'll show you what's up there," he said, motioning toward the pulpit.

He took Obie's arm and led him up the steps. Obie looked out over the sanctuary, which was nearly empty now except for two people putting hymnals back into their places.

"Would you like to ask me any questions, Obadiah?" The pastor articulated his words clearly, as he had during his sermon. It seemed his usual way of speaking.

"I guess not." In truth, he had so many questions that he was at a loss to know where to begin. He leafed through the big Bible, which had slips of paper sticking out, no doubt marking places to read during services. He wanted to see more and was disappointed when his mother said it was time to go.

The pastor walked with them to the narthex door. "I hope you'll come again," he said and made a slight bow and a peculiar head nod as he did so.

Obie thought about the service all the following week. He had, a few times, questioned why people go to church, to the same building week after week, never seeming to tire of doing so. He understood better, now. "I want to go back again," he told his mother.

CHAPTER FIVE

June 1937

Vi and Obie returned to the Methodist church the following Sunday. As they took their places in the same pew they had previously occupied, Vi wondered again if she was doing the right thing. What would a priest say? She believed she could defend her actions. She was not deserting the Church; her disconnection was not her fault.

As Obie leafed through a hymnal, reading softly, she rehearsed an answer to the imaginary priest's inquiry about her sin of attending Protestant services. She would answer with a question: "Is it not better to be with these good people who worship the same God I do than not to attend a church at all?"

Regardless of a priest's probable response, she was doing this for Obie's sake. He needed association with people of faith. Her Grandmother Maria had called it "having God's image stamped on you." The decision to return to Stafford Rest Methodist came only after praying every night the past week, asking for guidance.

She had also prayed about her secret. "God, please show me," she had begged with tears flowing, "when and to whom should my secret be revealed?" On Friday, she had announced to the senior Hunts that she was thinking of going back to their church. Pinky told her, "We look forward to seeing you there, Vi." Abigail, with an eyebrow raised, said nothing.

They lingered after the service, and Vi was surprised and pleased when Reverend Lansing approached them. "Mrs. Gainsworthy, I'd like to speak with you. Perhaps you and Obadiah could come back to my office for a few minutes?"

The pastor gave them a roundabout tour, pointing out the various nooks and crannies and explaining their purposes. Vi was impressed by the fully furnished kitchen in the basement, and Obie asked many questions that the minister seemed pleased to answer.

Eventually, he led them into the open space of the attached building. "This area all seems wasted," he said. "It's a good meeting place for large crowds. Our church is big and growing, and we draw members from a wide area, not only from the village. This is a duplication of space in the sanctuary and is more than we need. I plan to raise funds to turn this whole section into an education wing. Our Sunday school classes for children and adults meet before the regular service, and we gather in odd places around the church. We need comfortable and functional rooms here for that purpose. It will be expensive, so I'm going to work on it with our administrative board and the district." Vi was not sure why he was giving them this information but felt honored that he was doing so.

The office was in the rear, on a south corner with a window overlooking White Pine Road. The Pastor ignored the big oak desk in the center of the room and seated himself in a high-backed chair to face the short couch Obie and Vi occupied.

"I hope you enjoyed the service," The minister said. Vi nodded, hoping that would suffice. He continued, "I wanted to speak to you because it's something I try to do when a visitor comes to service more than once. If you feel I'm intruding on your privacy, say so, because I wouldn't want to do that." He hesitated a moment. "I couldn't help noticing that you aren't taking communion."

Vi experienced a moment of panic. Would it be required? Entering a Protestant church was one thing. She was sure observing the Eucharist here would be a terrible sin. It was best to get things into the open. "We are Catholics, Father."

He looked confused for a moment, and she was relieved when his smile returned. "Oh, that would explain it. And please call me 'Pastor Charles.' This is somewhat unusual, though." He was waiting for her explanation.

Vi tried to still her apprehension. "Father . . . "

"'Pastor Charles,' please."

"Pastor Charles, we have come here because there is no Catholic church in Stafford Rest. Evergreen is too far for us. We have a truck, although it is no longer dependable." She would not mention Ken's indifference to the importance of Catholic education. "I have tried to teach Obie about God, but I know only so much. Maybe he can learn if I bring him here. It is not as good as a Catholic . . . ah . . . I am sorry. I did not mean . . ."

Pastor Charles laughed. "It's okay. Our churches have differing views and rules. That doesn't mean we can't be civil about it." Vi sensed the statement was sincere. "I know the priest at Evergreen quite well. I knew him even before I came here. Father Brennan and I argue, discuss things sometimes, but we get along."

"He might not like it, us coming here."

"Yes, you're probably right."

"We should not come again, perhaps?"

"That is, of course, up to you. You're certainly welcome. Maybe I can help find a way for you to go to Evergreen, if it's what you want. There's also the possibility of your attending the Episcopalian church since their services are more like the Catholic Church than ours."

"Obie wants to come here. If Evergreen is not possible for us, we will come here."

"Maybe Evergreen *is* possible. I really would like to help."

Although this man felt like an ally, accepting his offer meant they might have no further association with this church. Did she want that? She already knew many people here, and the fact that Pastor Charles was kind and understanding was a bonus. She was glad he had invited them to talk. Maybe God had led them here. She had worried about whom to reveal the secret that would change her son's life so drastically. *She had to tell someone.* Pastor Charles seemed a logical choice.

"And something else . . ." She sucked in her breath until the uneasiness in her stomach subsided. She looked at the minister, then toward Obie.

Pastor Charles saw her distress. "Obadiah," he said, "maybe you'd like to look at the big Bible on the pulpit again. I've marked scripture that I've used in my sermons and written some notes to myself. It might be fun for you to look at those." He smiled. "I don't let just anybody do that."

Obie needed no further prompting. When he had gone, Vi sat forward on the couch. It was difficult to hide her nervousness. What she was about to tell this man, she had told no one else, not even her husband. The time would come when she must tell Ken, but not yet.

Nevertheless, she could not blurt it out; she must approach it gradually. She said with hesitation, "I believe we are all children of God, whether we are Catholics or Protestants. I prefer the Catholic way because I was raised that way, but after knowing so many people here, I can see your way of faith is a good way, too, even though it is different from mine. Loving Jesus is not just for Catholics."

"Yes, Mrs. Gainsworthy, I couldn't agree with you more."

"Obie could learn from you, I think."

"Thank you for the trust, but are you not required to raise Obadiah in the Catholic tradition?"

"Yes, but I am in a position where I cannot carry out that requirement. I must make use of the opportunities God gives me. Obie needs association with people of faith. When he is older, he can decide whether to be Catholic or Protestant."

"Well, God does work in mysterious ways, but I can't promise you that our church teachings would bring him to the place where he could make that choice. It's probable that, if he attends our church and Sunday school, he'll become a member of our congregation, or seek membership in another protestant church."

"I see. What I want is for Obie to have a good start, to increase in faith."

"Obadiah seems quite advanced for his age. I think he will easily develop understanding, whomever his teacher is." The preacher seemed determined to use Obie's full given name, maybe his way of showing respect.

She wanted to steer the conversation away from the possibility of their attending Mass at Evergreen. "I do not know Father Brennan. I like it here, and I think you are a good man. I hope you can help Obie."

"I'll do what I can, Vi. Honestly. I'll encourage him as a friend. However, since you are Catholic, I suggest you turn the burden of Christian education over to Father Brennan."

His insistence was troubling—and she had become sidetracked. "And if it is not God's will that we go to Evergreen?"

"I'm sure I can work something out. I said I'd help, and I believe the best plan is to find a way for you and Obadiah to go regularly to the Evergreen church."

She could no longer put off what she must say. "You should know that there will come a time when I will not be able to go to Evergreen."

"What do you mean?"

"Pastor Charles, I am ill. I have a tumor . . . cancer." The words, said aloud for the first time, sounded strange to her ears, an unreal utterance. "The time I have left is uncertain."

"Oh, dear Lord. Vi, I'm sorry."

"Doctor Williamson found it several months ago. He was sure it was too late to cut it out."

"Does Obadiah know?"

"Not yet. Nor does my husband. Besides the doctor, no one else knows except you."

The sadness in his eyes was real. "Is there anything I can do to help?"

She wanted to say that he could forget about Evergreen, but

even with his apparent empathy for her situation, she knew he would not relent.

She said, "If there comes a time when Obie cannot go to Evergreen, please see that he receives guidance." She took a deep breath and swallowed. She wanted a commitment, even if it was short of what she had hoped.

"Of course."

"I have entrusted you with my secret. I do not mean to burden you with this, but if you can steer him toward things that will help him grow in faith, I will be grateful."

He did the head-nod again. "Yes, I will," he said. "I promise."

* * *

After mother and son departed, Charles Lansing sat, subdued by the seriousness of their conversation. She was a beautiful young woman; it was a sad situation. The rumors about her and Pinky Hunt could not be true; she wouldn't be capable of such a thing.

He had given his word to guide Obadiah, but could he keep such a promise? In truth, it was probably out of his hands. Who knew where the boy would go if she died? Charles already knew a lot about the family, having talked with Jacob several times. Ken Gainsworthy's drinking problem ,and long absences, could complicate things; he might not give adequate care to Obadiah. Abner and Claire Gainsworthy would undoubtedly take him in. And Vi had sisters with their own families in Albany and Schenectady. One of them could make room for him.

The situation occupied Charles' mind for days. He finally called Father Gerald Brennan. The line to Evergreen was noisy, further exacerbating the older man's hearing disability.

"Who is she? Whom did you say they are? How old is the boy? Why don't you send them right over?"

"Gerry, that's the problem. I know it's only nine miles, but they don't have transportation."

"Couldn't you bring them?"

"Your Mass begins at ten o'clock, Gerry. We also have services at that time, and our Sunday School is at nine o'clock. I don't have a car and wouldn't have the time even if I did. And it'd be a real imposition to ask one of our members to miss our service. Couldn't someone from your church come over, get them, and take them home again? Wouldn't have to be every Sunday, maybe just once or twice a month."

"What? How often?"

"Just once in a while, Gerry."

"Don't know. Most of my people don't have automobiles."

Out of ideas, Charles played his trump card. "Well, okay. They do like it here. You wouldn't mind if they attended our services, would you? Seems like the simplest solution."

"What? Oh, no. I'll see if I can find someone."

Father Brennan called back the next day with news that one of his parishioners would drive to Stafford Rest every Sunday and pick up Vi and Obadiah at eight-thirty. Another member would take them home after Mass.

Later, as he left his office and walked a dozen steps to the parsonage, Charles gave thanks that it had worked out so well. Still, having them in his congregation could be a good thing. Vi's thinly veiled attempts at steering him away from the Evergreen church spoke volumes about the distress she must be feeling.

He would certainly have no trouble teaching Christian doctrine to the eleven-year-old boy. In truth, turning Obadiah over to the Catholics caused him some remorse for, in his opinion, their way was not the safest way to salvation. Nonetheless, he must avoid arrogance and not assume he came first in line for implementing God's will. Some ministers would consider themselves empowered to go ahead at this point. They might say, "God sent them to me. Therefore, he wants me to counsel them." Charles had long been aware of his inflated ego, and repentant of it, so he always tested such situations. If circumstances brought them back again, he would consider them his responsibility.

That evening he walked up the steep dirt road on Blackberry Hill to deliver the news. Obadiah was helping Vi pick strawberries in the garden above the house. Vi started toward him.

"No," he called, "I haven't picked strawberries for a long time. Please let me help."

The strawberry patch was adjacent to their sizeable fenced-in vegetable garden. They worked nearly an hour. He explained the arrangement he'd made with Father Brennan during that time. He sensed her resignation, a good thing, he believed. She didn't look ill. Obadiah had red lips from eating berries. Charles found it impossible not to sample the succulent fruit himself.

It was growing late by the time they carried the buckets of berries into the kitchen. Ken had come home. He was civil without smiling and informed Charles that he would take Vi and Obie to Evergreen when he could. He then excused himself to change clothing.

"You are welcome to eat with us," Vi told him. "I will not be long in preparing the meal,"

"I really must be going. Perhaps, though, we could have a prayer before I go?"

His prayer, as they stood around the kitchen table, was short, asking for guidance and healing of body and spirit. As Charles left, he told Vi, "I want to make it clear that should something happen to prevent you and Obadiah from going to Evergreen, you're welcome to come back to our services any time regardless of your attendance there. And my door is always open if you wish to talk."

He carried an oatmeal box gifted with berries when he left by the road down the hill. Ken hadn't joined them for his prayer. When would Vi tell him about her illness? It should be soon.

* * *

"Is Ernie here?" Obie asked his friend's father at the marina.

Archie Boswell, a taciturn man by nature, stared at Obie a moment before saying, "Nope."

"Will he be back soon?"

"Don't know."

"Where did . . . "

"Been gone all morning. Said he was going over Indian Knob way. Think it's that little sick girl he's hanging around."

"Frances Gibbons?"

"Yeah, that's her, the colored girl that got out of the hospital yesterday."

"Thank you, Mr. Boswell."

Obie went up Main Street at a trot. He liked Frances and was sad about what had happened to her. Two weeks earlier, she had been diagnosed with infantile paralysis. She wasn't the only one in their area. Amy Castle in Evergreen and Will Dunlow, who lived on the road between Evergreen and Stafford Rest, both about his age, were in the hospital. According to his father, the disease was "sweeping the country." Obie had heard that infected people had to stay in an "iron lung" for a long time to help them breathe. At first, the idea of a sickness that could shrink legs and cripple young people, even kill them as it had Bert Penny in Long Lake, had seemed like something so terrible it could never touch Stafford Rest. When Frances caught it, Obie, along with other village residents, knew fear.

Dr. Williamson was telling people that she had a lighter case than most, which was why they let her come home so soon. He called the disease "polio." Obie's mother said Frances would have painful therapy every day to reduce the crippling effect. "Even so," she said, "She might have trouble walking for the rest of her life."

Obie trotted over the Cedar Creek bridge and turned left up Indian Loop Road. The Gibbons' house was far up the road and on a side path that ascended a steep hill. It was a simple structure with clapboard siding and a tin roof; it looked to have two rooms. Ernie was sitting on a boulder beside the gate.

"Your dad told me you were here," Obie said.

Ernie's eyes were red, and he was subdued. "I come to see for myself that she's okay."

"Mom says she might be crippled."

"I heard that too. I don't think she will be, though."

"Have you seen her?"

"Her mother wouldn't let me go in. That therapy nurse went in a little while ago. I don't know what she did to Frances, but I heard her scream."

"How long you been here, Ernie?"

"Since early this morning. I'm not going away 'til I hear she's doing okay."

"Hasn't her mother or father been out of the house?"

"Nope. I spoke to Mrs. Gibbons at the door, but the nurse is the only one who's gone in or out."

"I'll stay awhile with you."

"Okay, if you want to."

A few minutes passed before the front door opened and a woman in a white uniform emerged, followed by Hansford Gibbons. Although several feet away, Obie heard their conversation. The nurse told Hansford that she'd be back later in the week. In the meantime, he and his wife must administer the treatments she had demonstrated. Finally, she left, passing by the boys without comment.

Hansford turned to go back inside. "Mr. Gibbons," Ernie called, "How's Frances doing?"

The man walked out to the gate, and Obie expected him to tell them to go away. Instead, he said, "Ernie and Obie . . . she's very sick, but she is alive, thanks be to God."

Obie was surprised Hansford knew their names. He was the school janitor, so they saw him every school day, but he couldn't remember them ever exchanging greetings.

Ernie said shyly, "Can I see her?"

Hansford appeared apologetic. "I'm sorry. The nurse says no visitors." When Ernie didn't comment, he said, "I saw you out the window early this morning. Have you been out here all this time?"

"Frances is my friend," Ernie said.

Hansford smiled. His booming voice became soft, "You're a good boy, Ernie. I'll tell Frances you were here and asking about her. Soon as she can have visitors, I'll let you know. Now, you boys run on home. And I pray you'll stay safe from this disease." He went up the walk and into the house without looking back.

"Don't tell Chuck or Tommy I was here," Ernie said. "Not Ed, neither."

"I won't tell anybody." He wouldn't have, anyway. "Want to go up on the ridge?"

"What for?"

"It's where I go when I feel bad about something. Either there or sometimes to the Morass."

"I don't think so."

Ernie said little as they walked down the road toward town, but before reaching the bridge, he said, "Okay, let's go to the Morass. I ain't never been in there."

"Never?"

"Well, once. Me and Chuck took somebody's boat . . . might have been yours. We didn't go very far in, though. Chuck got scared, and we came back out. Even though we could see all the shorelines, it felt like we was lost."

"Yeah, it's like that. Dad and me have been all over it, so I don't get lost. Let's do it."

The boat was old and somewhat waterlogged. It hadn't been used since the previous summer. With Obie rowing and Ernie sitting in the bow, they pushed off into the maze of interlocking waterways, through fallen trees, beaver houses, and mounds of vegetation consisting of brush, water plants, lichen, and small trees that would never become larger. A reddish-brown water snake slithered out from the front of the boat and went below the surface.

Birds were everywhere. Ducks swam not far from the boat and seemed to have little fear of the intruders. Obie spotted an American bittern in the waters ahead with its neck stretched upward trying to look like a weed. A great blue heron took off silently from a pool ahead of them. "He's been fishing, or looking for frogs," Obie said.

"How do you know all this stuff?"

"Dad knows it. I pick it up from him."

"Your dad teaches you a lot. My dad just tells me everything I can and can't do." The was some bitterness in the remark.

"Our dads and moms just want us to be good."

"Dad told me I shouldn't be so friendly with Frances."

"Why?"

"I think it's because she's colored. Chuck says things like that too."

"Chuck's an idiot, sometimes."

"My dad's not an idiot, though."

Ernie was silent as Obie guided the boat into another open space and through a cluster of fallen logs. Minutes passed before he announced, "But I do like Frances a lot. The way you like Laura."

"How'd you . . .?"

"I see how you look at her, that's all."

Obie didn't know how best to respond, so he said, "Frances is real nice. You *should* be her friend."

"I'm going to marry Frances."

Obie felt ashamed. That was what he should have said about Laura.

Two hours later, after traversing a significant portion of the Morass, Obie and Ernie pulled the boat into the shallower water close to the bank where they had embarked. "That wasn't bad," Ernie said, "but it's a real mess."

"You just have to know where you are and where you're going," Obie told him.

"Well, I'm going back up there to see that Frances is all right."

CHAPTER SIX

Summer 1939

Obie's plan was simple. Having finished eighth grade, he would attend Evergreen High School in the fall. Six members of his class of twenty-four were going to Evergreen. In addition to Obie and Laura, Ernie Boswell, Ed Baumgartner, Sarah Van Alstine, and Frances Gibbons were pursuing "higher education." Ernie had wanted to work in the family business, but his mother insisted on "better things for Ernie." He confided to Obie that maybe going to high school was a good thing; it would give him a chance to get closer to Frances. She walked with a cane and had a noticeable limp, the only visible signs of her bout with polio.

For Laura, already speaking wistfully about college, attending high school had never been in doubt. When Obie informed her of his decision, he mentioned that transportation might be a problem. She said her mother would take her in the family car, and he could ride with them. He feared Mrs. Hunt might not be as accommodating as her daughter.

A rumor was circulating that a school bus route to Stafford Rest would be established if the number of students warranted it. He hoped their group, plus the eight previous Stafford Rest graduates already at Evergreen, would be enough.

Obie's status as a student wasn't something he wished to flaunt, particularly in the presence of his peers. However, he was increasingly aware of his desire to "have an education." He'd been unable to suppress a smile when Miss Blessing told his mother it would be a shame if he didn't continue his schooling. "And, it's not only his artistic talent," she'd stated. "He has a strong and curious mind."

As much as he looked forward to high school in the fall, the summer held uncertainty. Other boys in his class would take farm jobs or work with their fathers in their various occupations. There were dozens of federal government Civilian Conservation Corps camps scattered around the Adirondacks; the boys were too young for the CCC, however. Chuck Hinky was taking over his father's part-time janitorial work at the Inn. Over his father's protests that he should stay on the farm, Tommy Matthews was planning to hire on at Stafford Rest Furniture if there was an opening.

Obie's father sought sources of income beyond the odd jobs; During fall and early winter, he led hunting parties. Less frequently, he took groups up the high peaks in spring and summer; Obie hoped to accompany him as he often had in the past. There were forty-nine Adirondack peaks higher than four thousand feet. Obie had already scaled nearly half of them. Call for his father's and grandfather's brand of wilderness work had declined, but some requests still came because of Ken's reputation for knowing the trails and his ability to lecture on flora and wildlife. There had been none this year, however. In slack times Obie envied his friends whose fathers pursued more conventional work.

Despite their many differences, Obie shared a love of the forest with his father. They had the same enthusiasm for the quietness of a trail in the early morning or a far-view from a rocky mountain peak. He respected his father not only for his reverence toward the wilderness but also for his self-learned knowledge of it. Obie had absorbed an encyclopedic amount of history, geology, and biology of the Adirondack mountains by listening to his father as they accompanied numerous school classes and various other groups. His father came alive when he talked about the glaciers that had once covered the area and pointed to striations left on rocky surfaces of mountain peaks.

Obie had learned about mountain birds, their varieties, songs, habits, and migration patterns. There were no flowers or plants, at whatever altitude, that Ken Gainsworthy did not recognize. Those commonalities of interest helped Obie see past their differences; he could even forgive his father's drinking—and what Aunt Claire labeled "neglect."

Recently, however, his father's mood had shifted. "Melancholy" was probably the best way to describe it—and it was troubling. Obie wanted to find out what was bothering him, for he loved their excursions into the mountains and hoped there would be more opportunities.

Obie's passion for the wilderness now had a new dimension. The previous summer, he'd started carrying a sketchpad. While not wholly disapproving, Ken complained that it was often a nuisance. "I have to wait for him to finish, sometimes," he told Jacob one day when he and Obie were working on the farm.

Jacob had meticulously emptied his pipe of ashes by tapping it against a stone in the rock wall below Abner's barn. "Kenneth, these woods are for enjoying, not for racing through," he said. "With all the automobiles and better roads, the park's become a place to explore at leisure." He chuckled. "Even old guides have got to accept that." He placed a leathery hand on top of Obie's head. "Art's a good thing, boy. You keep it up. You draw real good. There's no better place for painting pretty scenes than here in these mountains. No other place like it in the whole country."

His teachers instilled in their students an appreciation for the uniqueness of the Adirondacks. Late in the nineteenth century, the state of New York had set aside the vast northern area known as the Adirondack Park. Boundaries expanded over many years until the park covered ten thousand square miles. Many people, including his grandfather, already owned property there. The solution was to create an entity where parkland and private land could coexist.

All the villages and little towns seeded by hardy pioneer stock continued to exist, peopled by their descendants and newcomers. The number of persons living in proximity to the wilderness was not small. A majority was privately owned, and within the park four thousand square miles was known as the Adirondack Forest Preserve, to be "forever wild." The broad expanse of Park and Preserve, with its mountains and forests of spruce, hemlock, pine, and various hardwoods, was Obie's playground.

He responded to his grandfather's statement with confidence, "I guess we don't need guides at all anymore."

Jacob packed fresh tobacco into his pipe, scratched a match on a stone in the wall, and held the flame over the pipe bowl, puffing until the tobacco glowed and white smoke curled around his head.

His grandfather would not be rushed. "That's pretty much the truth, but the hard-hearted way you just said it don't pay proper respect to all the men and women who made this country what it is. We opened it up and made it so people could come and enjoy it. Us old guides may disappear, but people will keep coming because the mountains will always be here, and people love mountains. Obie, you should show more respect for them who made it possible."

"Oh, I do, Grandpa. I didn't mean . . ."

"It's all right. I just don't want folks to forget."

"Why don't you write it all down, Grandpa? Put it in a book?"

Jacob laughed. "I'm not the book writin' kind. I'll leave that up to you younger folks." He took on his familiar far-away look. "The old-time campers, they come to live in the woods awhile. Over the years, I built me scores of lean-tos all over where I took parties. I wasn't the only one who did it. We had lots of guides . . . and good ones like old Tom Brown over at Evergreen. Him and me served in the war together and worked together awhile after we got back. We took parties all through the lakes. Had a dozen or more in our groups, with them carrying everything they needed. We ported long distances overland. Tom and me always got on famously. I'll get over there to see him soon, but you'll have to take me, Kenneth."

"Papa, Tom's been dead for several years."

Jacob ignored his son's reminder. "Anyway, when they started building so many camps and lodges, it changed how folks looked at it. Rich folks could come here and live pretty much the same as back home. In my opinion, that's what changed it." He threw up a hand as a sign of resignation.

Obie loved listening to his grandfather even if he was sometimes forgetful. He was real, free of pretense. "I wish I could have gone with you on one of those trips, Grandpa."

Jacob's eyes gleamed. "Well, let's do it. And I'll even sit and wait for you to finish a picture. I'm still up to it, boy."

They had climbed a peak together three years earlier. It had been a slow ascent and a labored trip down, but Jacob prevailed.

"I'm sure you could, Grandpa." It was an honest assessment.

Even if Ken were to receive a request to guide a group at this late date, Obie doubted he would take it. He'd been away early that winter before coming home in mid-January. He did odd jobs around town and worked at Abner's, but hadn't returned to his logging job. It was a complete break from his routine. Even more strange was that, on the cusp of summer, his father had not once gone into the woods. He spent hours each day sitting on the front porch staring down at the village—and drinking. Claire came often. Some days there were tears in her eyes. Obie wondered why.

* * *

Days went by swiftly, and mid-summer arrived before Obie had time to lament lost time in the woods. Some days he went to Abner's; there was always work there, although it paid little. Mostly, he worked in the family vegetable garden and mowed lawns for pay with an old lawnmower rescued from a scrap heap behind Mercer's Market. With Abner's help, it had been made serviceable.

Obie worried about his mother. She was often sick, sometimes lying down, even in daytime, and she wasn't working at the Hunt's as much. Even when she did, Pinky brought her home, often by mid-afternoon. Grandfather Petitucci, looking old and tired, came several times, accompanied by Aunt Angie and sometimes Aunt Izzie. It seemed his family worried about her, too. That was natural, however, for they'd taken extra good care of him when he'd had a severe bout with the flu.

One day his mother came home early, slumped into a chair, and closed her eyes. After a few minutes, she sat up with a worried expression. "Obie, I forgot to return a key to Mr. Hunt. It is the key to his tool shed. He will be looking for it. I want you to take it to him."

He left the hill at once with Slobber at his heels. He wouldn't ignore any chance to see Laura. School had been out for several weeks, and he'd seen her only once; there had been little time to talk.

He ran down the hill, over Cedar Creek footbridge, and out Clearwater Road to Main Street. After about a dozen steps along the main thoroughfare, he saw Pastor Charles exiting the hardware store. For anyone else, Obie would have made some excuse to hurry on.

The pastor reached out to pat Slobber's head. "This old guy looks like he's enjoying an outing," he said. Slobber emitted a soft whine at the minister's touch. When the patting stopped, he lay down in the dust at the road's edge and closed his eyes.

"He has rheumatism, but he follows me everywhere if he's invited."

"Are you and your mom still going to Evergreen?"

"Yes, we are. Until lately, we hardly ever missed a Sunday."

"Does your dad go with you?"

"Once or twice when the truck was running. Not in the last year, though. Mom's stopped asking him."

"There are good people there."

"They're really good about coming to get us and bringing us home. Sometimes, someone takes us home with them for a meal."

"That's wonderful. Vi must . . . your mother must enjoy that."

"She does, but we don't go as often now. Mom doesn't feel well sometimes."

Pastor Charles looked ready to ask another question, but said, "I'm sorry about that, Obadiah."

"We try to tell them when we're not coming so they don't make a trip for nothing. If Mom's sick on Saturday night, I go down to the drugstore, and Mr. Carmody lets me use his telephone to call Father Brennan. If she gets sick on Sunday morning, it's harder since the store is closed, and I have to wake him up sometimes."

"Has that been happening a lot, being sick?"

"Lately. I think she's feeling better now. She's been resting, taking it easier."

"Well, tell your mother not to forget what I told her. You can come back to our church anytime you want to. Tell her I haven't forgotten what we talked about. Will you tell her that, Obadiah?"

"I'll tell her, Pastor Charles."

"Maybe I'll go up to see her."

"She'd like that."

"And don't go waking up Miles Carmody on Sunday mornings. If you need to make a call, come here and use my telephone. You can do that anytime."

"All right, I will."

The pastor took White Pine Road toward the church, and Obie and Slobber continued to trot up the highway. Pinky was pulling weeds along his white picket fence. He was surprised to see Obie. "I hadn't missed the key yet. Next time I'm in Evergreen or Tupper Lake, I'll have a duplicate made. Thanks, Obie."

"Are Cassie and Laura home?" Obie asked, hopeful.

"Laura's home. She's on the patio. Do you want me to call her?"

"No, that's okay." He was immediately sorry for the dumb reply? "I thought maybe . . ."

"Laura!" Pinky called. "Laura, come down here! Someone to see you!" Pinkie's eyes twinkled.

Laura glided down the lawn's incline, long dark hair streaming over her shoulders. "Obie," she said, "where have you been for so long?"

He tried to relax. "Oh, just around, here and there."

"Let's go up on the patio and talk."

He cleared the pickets with a perfect scissors jump and fell in beside her. Slobber whined resolutely and lay down outside the fence.

The late afternoon was warm with a breeze stirring leaves of the large red maples on the lake side of the patio. Pinky had trimmed off the bottom branches so that the view of the lake was not obstructed. They sat at a wooden table Obie was sure had been made at the factory. "I'll get us some lemonade," Laura said.

She soon came back with two tall glasses. The drink had ice in it. He liked how the ice clinked in his glass when he swirled the liquid around. The Hunts had a Frigidaire his mother said would make ice in just a few minutes. Their ice supply on Blackberry Hill, wrapped in burlap and stored in a deep root cellar on the hillside, was nearly depleted; not enough had been taken from the lake last winter to get through the hot summer, causing them to cut back on usage. Someday, he'd have a Frigidaire, he vowed. Electricity, too.

"Mom and Cassie have gone up to Saranac Lake today," she said. The breeze caused the hair over her forehead and cheeks to flutter. She brushed it back, and that simple motion, accomplished without apparent deliberation, made his pulse jump. Her eyes were a deep blue. All the Hunt women had blue eyes, but Laura's were the darkest.

"You never come with Vi anymore." Her voice had a melody of its own, one he never tired of hearing.

"Too much to do. Not enough time." It sounded lame.

"You mean you can't find a few minutes to talk to me?" Her tone was teasing. He couldn't help gazing at her full lips as she spoke. What would it be like to kiss those lips? They were knee to knee, creating an incredible and discomforting sensation.

"Well, it's not that I don't want to come and see you . . . and Cassie." He didn't trust his voice, which lately ranged from high to low on its own schedule.

She wore a sleeveless blouse with large arm openings. When she leaned forward, he saw the swell of one of her breasts and glanced away, hoping she hadn't noticed him looking. The feelings he'd been experiencing lately were new, and kind of disturbing. A significant change was taking place in his body—a change others might see. As validation, his mother said one morning after awakening him, "Obie, do not be ashamed of becoming a man. It happens to every boy. It is natural."

Natural or not, he had blushed at his mother's words. Such discussion was not something he wanted with anyone, particularly his mother. In Laura's presence, he tried to focus his mind on other things, but his eyes inevitably went back to her. *She was so beautiful.* Someday he would tell her how much he loved her. Some day they would marry.

"Obie, what are you thinking about?"

Seconds passed as he pondered what to say. He couldn't tell her the truth. It wasn't yet time. Instead, he said, "Just thinking about high school this fall. I'd like to do well there."

She laughed. "Do well? You'll do very well. You're the smartest boy I know. I wouldn't be surprised if you even went on to college."

"Oh no, not me. Soon as I get out of high school, I intend to become a ranger in the park." Although taking up that occupation interested him, he'd made no decision. It seemed that merely talking to Laura made him say stupid things. "Anyway, that's a long way off," he added.

"It's good to plan ahead."

"So, you're already planning what to do after high school?"

"Mom and Dad want me to go to college. She talks about Smith College, which is where she went. Of course, as you say, it's a long time off. I think what I want, eventually, is to marry and have children."

Her words elevated hope; maybe it *was* time to reveal his feelings. He cleared his throat, mustering the courage to speak. She continued, "What about the near future, Obie? What are you going to do, you know, after?"

"After . . .?"

"Will you stay in Stafford Rest? Dad thinks you will. He thinks you'll go to your Uncle Abner's."

"I'm sorry, Laura, but I don't know what you mean."

"You know . . . after Vi goes. You know . . . passes on. You aren't old enough to live by yourself, and your father . . ."

"Passes on? It sounds like you're talking about dying."

"I didn't want to use that word, but yes, it's what I mean, I guess."

"Why would you say that?"

"Well, because of her illness."

A lump formed in his throat, and fear came from some dark place he had experienced only in nightmares. "What do you mean by saying something like that? My mother's not going to die. She's been sickly of late, but she's getting better."

He saw her face pale. She put a hand to her mouth. "Oh, I'm sorry! *You don't know!* Oh, Obie, I'm so sorry . . . I'm so sorry. I thought you knew."

He stood, placed shaky hands on the table, and leaned toward her. "People say she's going to die? Is that what they're saying?"

"Yes, Obie, they do."

"And you believe it's true?"

"Mom and Dad said it." She turned her head away as though afraid of facing him. "They said Vi told them. And Cassie heard people in town talking about it."

Obie felt that he was going to smother. There came anger, too.

"And you've known about this for a while?" he asked, nearly choking on the words.

"Yes."

"Who else knows?"

"About everyone, I guess."

"Well, not me. *I didn't know.* He grabbed her arm and squeezed it. "Laura, tell me what you know."

"Oh, Obie. It's not really my place. It should be Vi or your father who tells you."

"*You* tell me, Laura. Since you know about it . . . you tell me."

She did, and when finished, she clung to him, sobbing.

* * *

When Obie appeared at the parsonage and unburdened himself, Charles was unsure what to do. The distraught boy showed no intention of leaving. Charles eventually left him in his study and walked up the hill with Slobber. Ken was on the small front porch. He was drinking. Vi was resting, so they talked softly with Charles in a rocking chair and Ken on an upended wooden box. A breeze stirred morning glory vines on the latticework that reached from porch floor to porch roof.

"Obadiah can stay with me until he gets ready to come home," Charles said. "He's hurt, and angry too."

"I can understand the hurting part," Ken took a drink from a bottle. "But I don't see why he's mad."

Charles thought what he had to say might rile Ken but plowed ahead. "It feels to him like you and Vi kept him from knowing . . . and I guess you did. He wonders why so many people knew about the seriousness of Vi's illness, and he didn't."

Ken's brow wrinkled, then relaxed. "I guess I can understand that. I felt the same way when she told me, and by the way, it wasn't that long ago that she did, right after Christmas. Several people knew ahead of me, including you, Reverend."

"She didn't want to worry you, Ken. The same as you didn't want to worry Obadiah."

Ken shrugged and looked away. Charles was at a loss about what to say. The man was grieving and trying to deaden the pain with liquor.

"Ken, I know this is hard on all of you."

"How do you know, Reverend? Do you have a wife who's about

to die?"

"Well, no. I didn't mean . . ."

"Sorry. There's no use in taking it out on you."

Charles studied Ken's face. He saw pride there. "I get the impression you're a man who tackles problems head-on."

"I am. If a man can't take care of himself, I say he's not much of a man. I've tried to teach that to Obie."

Charles was blunt. "And I'm sure that works for you, Ken. The thing is, Obadiah's not yet a man. He's still a boy, and he's . . . forgive me, he knows now that he may lose his mother."

Ken stared across the village, taking a long time before responding. "He'll handle it, same as I will. We have to."

"It's going to be awfully hard on Obadiah, Ken. I'll be available for him to talk to, or sit with, or whatever it takes. You too, for that matter."

"Thanks just the same, Reverend, but I have my comforter right here." He held up the bottle. "Anyway, Vi's not dead. She's still working some days, for God's sake."

"Yes, you're right."

They sat until the sun left and a mountain breeze brought a chill. Vi came out on the porch, looking sleepy. Charles was astonished at her appearance. He hated the word "haggard," although nothing else would fit. She spoke to him and smiled before retreating into the house. Ken followed her, and Charles heard him tell her about Obadiah. When he returned, he said, "Vi says it's all right for Obie to stay with you tonight if he wants to, and if it's okay with you."

"That's fine. He can sleep on the couch. I'll send him home tomorrow."

"Thanks for the talk, Reverend."

Except for a sharp edge, Ken's speech was unaffected, which Charles thought remarkable considering the quantity of liquor he had watched him consume.

CHAPTER SEVEN

Summer and Fall 1939

The heat and humidity were oppressive; it was not typical Adirondack weather. Laura considered walking down to the town park where a breeze from the lake was practically assured. Or, she could descend the steep rocky steps below the lake side of the house, cross Lake Road to their private dock and wade in the shallow water. Either way, the return trip would require more effort than she was willing to expend. The reasonable course was to sit still on the patio in the afternoon shade.

Her mother and Cassie had gone to Glens Falls to select wallpaper for a house in the village her mother had just bought. Her father was at the factory, so she was alone. Summer was nearly over. In a couple of weeks, she would start high school at Evergreen. It was exciting. There would be new faces, new friends—and lots of boys.

A fleeting thought came. *Obie was in love with her.* She smiled, remembering the way he pretended indifference. She often caught him staring. She liked Obie, but he was only thirteen, a year and a half younger than she. A boyfriend should be older, or nearer her age.

As fond as she was of Obie, he could never be her boyfriend. She must tell him that—at some point. Why hesitate? Was it to keep from adding to the hurt he was already feeling? She still cringed when she remembered the blunt way she'd revealed Vi's condition. Adding insult to injury, Obie's grandmother died two days after that blunder.

The girls and their father attended Prissy Gainsworthy's funeral at the Methodist church. They walked with the procession behind Abner's horse-drawn wagon that carried her casket to the Ashdown Cemetery above Lake Road. Obie's eyes were red from crying as they gathered around the grave. At present, it would be cruel to tell him they could never be romantically involved.

Vi no longer came to their house, something Laura greatly missed. She'd been twice to Blackberry Hill; both visits were depressing. The vibrant and energetic woman she'd known all her life could hardly walk from her bedroom to the kitchen. So sad. Vi had always taken care of people. Now, she was becoming unable to care for herself.

Previous to those two visits, Laura had never been in the house on Blackberry Hill and was astonished at its small size and starkness. How could people live without electricity and indoor plumbing? Poor Vi. Poor Obie. They deserved better.

Obie wasn't home on her first visit, but the next time she saw him pulling carrots in the vegetable garden above the house. He'd waved and turned back to his work. He might still be angry at her. Maybe he hadn't accepted her explanation that she wasn't at fault, that it was his parents who had withheld the information. Cassie had known, too; Laura had tried to tell him that, but he'd been in no mood to listen.

That last visit had been two weeks previously. Obie's Aunt Angie Temple was there from Albany with three-year-old Cleo, who kept getting into things. Angie announced her intention to stay awhile. Her presence would ease the burden on Claire. Cassie had been more faithful than Laura in visiting Vi; her sister hardly missed a day. According to her, Ken was of little help, and Obie had moved from the house to a room in the barn so Angie and Cleo could have his bed.

She wouldn't go back to Blackberry Hill again. She loved Vi but couldn't bear seeing her thin body and pale face; she was like a different person.

There was another reason to stay away; she wished to avoid a certain man who might be there. Doctor Williamson came regularly and was there on both her visits. The second time, his son came with him. Benjamin Williamson had finished college and was going into medical school. He was accompanying his father on his rounds, so, as Doctor Williamson stated, "He can see what it takes to be a physician in the mountains."

Benjamin drove his father's new automobile up blackberry Hill, parking in front of the house beside the old truck that had sat unused for several weeks. The doctor had recently broken his tradition of eschewing modern transportation and traded his horse and buggy for a new long gray Pontiac with four doors.

During hot afternoons, Angie moved a cot outside to the shady north side of the house. Laura had watched as Doctor Williamson attended her there. Benjamin spoke little during the half-hour the two men were present, but he watched and listened intently to everything his father said and did. The younger man sometimes looked in Laura's direction, his eyes indicating more than casual interest. He was tall with an angular face that in no way distracted from his good looks—although his nose was a little too large. No male, except her father and Obie, had ever given her that much attention. Her mother had told her that she looked older than her age, so maybe Benjamin didn't realize that she was only fifteen. She couldn't help being flattered—and curious. She had waited for him to glance at her again as they left. He did, and she tried to hold his gaze, but he quickly looked away.

Sitting as motionless as she could on the patio and wishing for the arrival of any fresh breeze from the lake, she again experienced misgivings for having encouraged Benjamin Williamson. He was too old for her and not the type for whom she could have romantic feelings. Nevertheless, she spent several more minutes reviewing the incident in her mind.

* * *

Beer and liquor flowed freely at the Diamond Inn, as had been the case all through Prohibition and well before. Since noon, Ken Gainsworthy had occupied a bar stool, only leaving for visits to the outhouse directly behind the venerable brick building.

He returned from one of those trips to find Al Vesner sitting on the stool next to his. The rear end that went with Vesner's nearly three-hundred-pound body extended well beyond the diameter of his seat. Lumberjack and mechanic, Vesner was a gentle giant of a man with hands approaching the size of washbasins.

The two men knew each other well, having worked several jobs together. Ken told Harold Freeman, the bartender, to refill Vesner's beer glass and bring him another whiskey and water.

"Thanks, Ken," Vesner said. "How you doin'?"

"Tolerable. You?" Ken wished at once that he hadn't asked the question. He was in no mood for talk and hoped to head off any chit-chat.

"No use complainin'. Sorry to hear about your mother."

"Thanks."

"How old was she?"

"Seventy-four."

"Must be hard on your dad?"

"Real hard."

In truth, Jacob's grief was almost more than Ken could bear.

Prissy's death had been unexpected. Everyone believed Jacob would die first, for he had often said he would. His mother was gone, and one-hundred-year-old Jacob endured his grief with dignity. His moist eyes appeared to see a past Ken could only imagine. "He won't last a year," Ken told Abner, and his brother had agreed.

"How's your wife?" Vesner asked.

"Well as can be expected."

"She's got a cancer . . . right?"

"Yeah, Al, she has cancer." He wished the questioning would stop.

"She's awfully young for that. How old is she?"

"Thirty-four."

"Don't seem fair with her like that, and us old codgers still goin' strong."

"Life's not always fair, Al."

Vesner was quiet for a long time, for which Ken was thankful. Felix Matthews came in and sat on the other side of Vesner. The three men made small talk for an hour until Felix left. "Milkin' time," he said. His farm was on the flat at the foot of Blackberry Hill.

Ken was finally drunk. He tolerated alcohol well, but the sheer volume had brought him to inebriation. He had trouble holding his head up. Harold appeared like a fuzzy apparition from the jumble of bottles and glasses behind the bar and told him, "Go home, Ken. You've had enough."

Ken was not beyond anger. "Pay attention, Harold!" he said, his voice so high that, for a moment, he thought someone else was speaking. He tried to recover his composure. These fools couldn't imagine his feelings. "I'll have another!" he managed.

He was vaguely aware of pitching forward and banging his chin on the bar top. Someone's arms were around him, lifting him. He focused enough to see Vesner's face next to his and heard him say, "I'll get him home."

The next thing Ken knew, they were outside. The cool lake breeze fanned him back to awareness. What was Vesner doing? He hadn't asked the man for help. "Get away from me!" he said.

"I'm just tryin' to help you home, Ken. If you try to cross the footbridge in your condition, you'll likely fall in the creek and drown."

"No, I won't. I'm fine." No one, even a man as big and strong as Vesner, could make him do something against his will.

"Let me help you, Ken."

"No!" He lost his balance and sat down in the dirt beside the road. He declared with as much bluster as he could manage from that position, "I can take care of myself, and I don't need anybody's help, especially from a big ox like you!"

The gentle Vesner suddenly sounded angry. "Ken, you're not taking care of yourself? You ain't taking care of nothin'. If you cared, you'd be home where you belong giving loving support to your wife. She's up there in that condition, and you're down here drinkin' like the world was going dry tomorrow. God's truth is you're being a poor excuse for a husband."

The insult rocked Ken enough that he managed to gain his feet. "Just leave me alone," he said.

He was aware of Vesner stalking away after muttering, "You're on your own, then!"

There came a revelation at that moment, not a voice, just a crawling together of words in his head, words with bell-ringing truth. He was not at all the man he'd believed he was; *he was a fool.* The anger and fight went out of him like air from a punctured tire. He fell to the ground and things went black.

He knew some time had passed when he awoke but didn't know how much; it was still dark. He crawled a few feet on the concrete pavement, stopped, and sat up. A horn sounded, loud and persistent.

He rubbed his eyes and blinked them clear enough to see the chrome bumper of a black automobile a few feet away. A woman's voice soon replaced the honking horn. "You disgraceful spectacle of a man . . . you get up and go home! You don't deserve Vi. Get up! Get up and get out of my way!"

He struggled to get to his feet but couldn't manage it. The horn honked again. Ken saw the angry face of Abigail Hunt through the windshield. He rolled to the side of the road as fast as he could.

* * *

Abigail was still angry as she parked the Packard in the drive-way. She gripped the steering wheel with nervous hands after turning off the engine. What would she have done if he hadn't moved out of the way? As much as he deserved it, she would not have run over him.

At dinner, she told Pinky and the girls about the encounter. Pinky's reaction irritated her. His propensity, so often trying her patience, was to examine every side of an issue. "Ken has a problem," he said.

"Yes, he certainly does. And your talent for understatement is especially keen today."

"Abigail, It's obvious that Ken has an alcohol addiction. He's handled it a long time, but his troubles may be pushing him to an extreme. He just lost his mother. In addition, the man is grieving for what he knows is ahead."

"I like Mr. Gainsworthy," Cassie said, adding, "When he's sober."

"Hush that talk, Cassie," Abigail responded.

She left the dinner table to bring back an apple pie baked the previous day. She tried to collect her thoughts as she sliced the pie and placed the wedges on dessert plates. It was annoying that the pieces were dry and falling apart. Cooking wasn't for her. It was time to find someone to replace Vi. She was relieved no one complained about the pie, or about the burned pot roast served earlier.

To keep the peace, she should ignore her husband's and Cassie's tolerance for Ken Gainsworthy. That thought lasted only a moment, and her words erupted like fire from a volcano. "That man deserves no praise, none whatsoever. Vi's on her deathbed, and he was down in the village getting drunk."

"He's really not a bad sort," Pinky said as he casually poured himself another glass of lemonade from the pitcher on the table. "Ken and I have hunted every fall together for years. You learn a lot about a man you hunt with. He needs help and understanding."

"Well, not from me." Her family must understand her position.

"Abigail," Pinky said, reaching across the table and patting her hand, "There'll be financial help for them. It's already being arranged. In addition, I expect that you and I will make a substantial contribution."

"Pinky, contributing to any fund giving a cent to that man is a slap in the face to me."

Pinky scrunched his eyes in a rare show of opposition. "This isn't only for Ken," he said. "This is for Vi . . . and for Obie. Have you forgotten the years of faithful service Vi has given us?"

Abigail softened her tone. "Yes, yes. I know. I love Vi too. That's why that man's actions so infuriate me."

"The money will cover funeral expenses and Vi's medical bills. Obie will also be assisted through high school. Those monies probably won't amount to much but will supplement other family income."

"If there is any income," Abigail felt compelled to say.

"We don't even know where Obie will be, or whether he'll continue to stay at home. Even if he goes to live with another family, his uncle or one of his aunts, he'll still need funds."

"That's very generous. I doubt if . . ."

It suddenly occurred to her that if she sounded too reluctant, she might cause her daughters to think ill of her. She wanted them to know that she could be generous, even magnanimous. "How much are we contributing?" she asked.

When Pinky told her, she said, "Oh, it's not enough. We should at least double it."

* * *

Obie worked at a table under the tall, large-paned windows inset into the end of the barnroom facing the house. The windows allowed early morning light into the room with startling intensity. His father had scrounged the windows at Evergreen where a public building was being demolished. Vi had, on her sewing machine, made floor-to-ceiling drapes for the windows. Obie usually kept the drapes tied back to let in light.

Comfortable quarters in the barn had been his mother's idea, and she'd directed each step during an oft-interrupted two-year period. With her keeping watch, Ken, with Obie's help, had reconstructed the large room that had once been a tack room and storage area. The barn had been used for horses, as indicated by the stalls. The loft had been used to store hay. The barn was Dutch style but smaller than most barns of that type. It had mortised, tenoned, and pegged beams throughout. Under Vi's cajoling, it had been transformed into a comfortable room large enough for a small kitchen with a wood stove, a cot, a couple of chairs, and two oak tables. Cool in summer, warm in winter, and with the privacy he wanted, the new rustic room had become Obie's alone. He would never move back to the house.

It was mid-September. There had been wisps of fog around the buildings in the early morning due to a gentle rain during the night, but now the fog was lifting. Obie sat by the window and saw Cleo come through the Arctic entranceway. She played awhile near the woodpile. Aunt Angie's daughter was a pretty child, but she got into things and needed watching. When he stepped outside, she ran to the front of the house. There were no fences on the property, so Obie followed her. There were family problems enough without his young cousin getting hurt. She had found a trowel and was digging in the dirt of one of Vi's neglected flowerbeds. Obie moved to the rocker on the front porch, where he could watch her.

Stafford Rest spread out below like a colorful carpet. There were still patches of fog lying in low spots in town and over the Morass. A larger mass, opaque, formed a white blanket on the lake. Main Street was clear, however, and brilliant under the morning sun. Obie couldn't positively identify individuals going about their morning activities, but their routines were familiar; he knew who they were and what they were doing. Chuck Hinky was picking up trash outside the front of the Diamond Inn, part of his janitorial duties. Old Jerome Stafford, who claimed the town was named for his ancestor, was shuffling toward his hardware store, getting there early to prepare for opening. According to Obie's grandfather, it was a routine that had taken place every workday for the last forty years. People were already going in and out of Mercer's General Store. Tim and Helen Mercer opened at seven o'clock.

A group of people at the corner where Main Street met White Pine Road was what had Obie's attention. He tried to count the distant figures, but they were too far away. Anyway, he knew who was there. Ed Baumgartner, Frances Gibbons, Ernie Boswell, Sarah Van Alstine, and Laura, along with several older students, were waiting for the school bus to take them to Evergreen's High School. He was uncertain about Laura's presence, for her mother sometimes gave her a ride.

Obie had only mild regret about being absent from the group. There was too much on his mind to make it seem of consequence. Nevertheless, he often imagined what it might feel like to wait there each morning anticipating a day in the big school building at Evergreen.

His mother had tried persuading him to go, anyway. Why should he suffer because of her illness, she argued. "Your education is much more important than watching me be sick," she said, sweetening her words with a smile. Pastor Charles had borrowed a car and taken him to Evergreen before the school year started; he explained Obie's situation to the principal. Obie was enrolled and would be allowed to start later, providing it was not much later. In addition, he would have to make up any work he missed. Obie had little hope of entering school that fall.

His grandmother's death had been a shock. He missed her

gentle ways and the love that manifested through her attitude and quiet words. Nevertheless, it had been quick, not like that with his mother. *She was dying; he'd accepted that.* She had talked with frankness about her illness and the outcome. Pastor Charles came often to see her. While there, he always made a point of engaging Obie in conversation. He gave Obie a small Bible and marked several passages he believed would be "useful and comforting." Obie had memorized some.

Something good had happened to his father. Obie was thankful, although he had no idea what had caused the change. Ken was staying home and had moved the cot from the kitchen where he'd been sleeping into the bedroom beside his mother's bed. They talked, and he held her hand. He hadn't been drinking for a month.

Aunt Angie called them for breakfast. Obie was surprised to see his mother in the kitchen. Doctor Williamson had insisted she get up at least once a day for a couple of hours, but that usually happened later. She sat at the table with them while they ate, having nothing herself but a cup of coffee. Obie was delighted. Her voice was stronger, and her eyes held a sparkle he hadn't seen for some time.

"You should eat something," Angie told her.

"Maybe I will have a bit, later."

"The food is warm. It won't be in a few minutes." She took on a tone of incredulity. "I really don't know how you can manage, living like this. We have gas stoves in Albany." Since arriving, Angie had complained about the woodstove and the absence of electricity. "Not even an icebox," she had said.

Despite her complaints, Angie managed to turn out meals equaling his mother's. The Petitucci sisters had learned well from their mother. Vi had long cultivated herbs and vegetables necessary for Italian cuisine and created meals Obie loved. For years, Beth Clarington tried persuading her to cook in her restaurant. Obie forgave Angie's objections about the inconveniences; her coming had removed a terrible responsibility from him and had lifted his spirits. Angie was an angel.

"You're spoiled from living in the city," Ken teased.

"Yes, I do like my comforts," Angie admitted. "Even in Italy, I remember that we had electricity."

"Speaking of Italy, what do you hear from Maria?" Vi asked.

"There was a letter last month. She and her family are doing well, except for Donato. He's been ill."

"What is his illness?" Vi asked.

"Something to do with his liver, I think. He's nearly fifty, you know."

"Mom, are you talking about Aunt Maria, your sister?" Obie asked.

"Yes, Dear. And Donato, her husband."

"Violetta, don't you teach your son about his family?" Angie asked. Her tone was more lighthearted than accusing. "Obie, Maria is our older sister. She wanted to come to America with us. Her husband didn't want to leave. They had four children. I can tell you their names . . ."

"Obie, get some paper and write it down," Vi said.

He'd taken all his notebooks to the barnroom, so he took the little Bible Pastor Charles had given him from the mantel and found a blank page near the back.

"These are in order, with oldest to youngest, as near as I can remember," Angie said. "Martino, Gerardo, Sonia, and Teresa. Is that right, Vi?"

"Yes, that is correct. Teresa, the youngest, is about the same age as you, Obie."

"I'd like to meet them someday," Obie said, hoping the words would please his mother.

Ken asked Angie, "How long has it been since you've seen Maria?"

"Since we came to this country. Over twenty-five years."

"You probably wouldn't recognize each other."

She ignored Ken and said, "Don't you believe that, Obie. I'd recognize my sister any time."

"Anyway," Ken said, "things are pretty rough over there. The political situation, I mean. A lot of upheaval. The Fascists are in control. There's going to be more trouble, lots of trouble all over Europe."

"Angie, did Maria mention anything about that?" Vi asked. "Are they in danger?"

"She didn't mention it. They live in the country now, so maybe they're away from all that."

His mother was up for nearly three hours. Obie went to the garden to pick tomatoes that had escaped the first frost a week earlier. He would pack the green ones in newspaper and put them in the barn loft. With any luck, most would ripen instead of rotting, and there would be fresh tomatoes well into December. He also attended to other garden chores and walked to the village to get groceries for

Angie. Claire came early in the afternoon, soon followed by Pastor Charles, who stayed an hour. Father Brennan, who came from Evergreen about once a week, arrived and prepared to serve the Eucharist. Obie's father excused himself as the priest spread a white cloth over the kitchen table.

Cassie came after school. Obie saw her through the window as she entered the side door. She always visited with Vi before coming to see him. He had paper and pens on a table and was staring at them when she arrived.

"What are you going to draw?" she asked, her yellow curls bouncing up and down as she talked. "Fuzzy head," he often called her.

"Don't know yet. It comes to me after I wait awhile." He wondered what she would think if she knew it had been chiefly sitting lately, not painting.

"Obie, your mother looks better today."

"Yes, I know. She's been talking a lot."

"Obie, I feel so sorry. I love Vi so much."

"Obie!" The voice came from outside.

Obie stepped into the open doorway. Angie stood a few feet away. "Obie . . ." She said again. Her eyes were filled with tears.

"Aunt Angie, what is it?" he asked, although he already knew. Angie engulfed him in her ample arms.

CHAPTER EIGHT

1941

One afternoon in the spring of Obie's second year at Evergreen High, he mustered the courage to walk up the hill with Laura from the bus stop. He intended to reveal his true feelings—finally.

For over a year he'd dreamed of making that declaration of love, even practiced various imagined encounters before the mirror in the barnroom. But Garnet Point and Blackberry Hill were a wide village apart, and there had been little chance to escort her home. He'd often watched with envy as Ernie Boswell strolled up the hill with the sisters to where Lake Road split from the highway.

Cassie's constant presence throughout the current school year was another complication. Today, Cassie and Ernie were absent from school, presenting a rare opportunity.

"Let me carry your books?" Obie said before they had taken a dozen steps from the bus stop.

Her sideways glance and furrowed brow indicated bewilderment. "Why?" she asked. "I'm perfectly capable of carrying my own books."

Her rebuke nearly caused him to turn and flee; he fought the urge. There had been a rain shower during the day, and their erratic path around puddles beside the highway gave him the occasional excuse to take her arm. Neither spoke as they made their way up the hill, and the silence hovered over Obie as ominous as the dark clouds overhead.

Laura still had a puzzled expression as they stood at her gate, but her countenance soon softened. He needed to say something to relieve the tension and make way for his more serious intent. The elm canopy over their heads held new buds beginning to swell; that might rekindle a conversation.

She spoke before he could find suitable words to say about the tree. "Do you want to talk to my father? He might still be at the factory, but I'll go see."

"No, don't bother him."

"Cassie's probably home. She wasn't feeling well this morning."

"I'll see her tomorrow."

"Do you want to come in, Obie?"

He looked away, then back at her several times, to the point of awkwardness. "No, I have to go home." He hated the weakness in his voice. "Lots of things to do."

She smiled. "Obie, why *did* you come home with me?"

"Oh, I'm just killing some time." He knew right away he had said another stupid thing.

She laughed. "You just said you had lots of things to do."

He felt his face burning but was determined to salvage what might be left of this chance to tell her his feelings. "I just thought we could talk. You know, things we can't say when other people are around."

Her smile disappeared as her fingertips settled lightly on his arm. "Obie, what is it you want to say?" After several tense seconds, she urged, "Tell me."

She had invited him to explain, and he wanted perfect words to tell her how much he loved her. He'd say it the graceful way the movie stars did. "Laura, I'm so . . . so . . ." The words stuck in his mouth.

"Yes?"

He'd known Laura all his life. Why couldn't he just come right out and say it, as easily as he might say something to Cassie? But fear won again, and he said, "Maybe later. I really do have to go."

He retreated, castigating himself with every step for his cowardice, but glanced back to see that she was still at the gate, staring after him. *He really was an idiot.* She waved and turned toward the house.

Hope revived when she called out, "Wait, Obie!" She was standing on the steps below the kitchen door. "Dad's here. He wants to talk to you."

His stomach churned; the situation had reached a more serious level. How would he explain his presence to her father? Pinky emerged from the kitchen door as she disappeared within.

"I've been wanting to talk to you, young man."

Obie's knees stopped shaking as Pinky explained that he wanted to hire him for the following Saturday morning to clean a room at the factory. He was expanding his rustic white cedar division, bringing in new equipment consisting of saws, lathes, planners, and other tools with strange-sounding names.

Obie recovered his composure enough to accept the offer. Such a chance was welcomed for the money—and even more for the opportunity to get closer to the Hunt family. He'd long noticed Abigail's coolness and wondered what he might have done to offend her.

She had liked his mother. Abigail had even given them presents at Christmas and sometimes bestowed other favors. His mother had taken leftover food home for years, a real benefit during the cruelest days of the Depression. It was no secret that Abigail disliked his father, so maybe her anger was transferred to Obie. Whatever the reason, he wanted to change her mind. After all, she would be his mother-in-law—if he could just stop being such a fool.

* * *

Obie made excuses to himself for the rest of the week about why he'd been unable to open himself up to Laura. All his explanations led him to one conclusion; he'd simply been a coward. It would be different next time.

On Saturday, Obie listened politely for several minutes to Pinky's explanation about the inner workings of the business: He was adamant about cleanliness; he insisted on sawdust being swept into containers, machinery oiled and repaired, inventories made, and stockpiles replenished. Since he was replacing several existing tools, he felt compelled to give every nook a thorough cleaning. He also wanted windows washed, inside and out, if there was time. "We shut down at noon," Pinky said.

The machinery was loud and incessant. Four people working in the room went about their business, ignoring him. After three hours, with major tasks complete, he attacked the windows. He had to stand on a stepladder to reach ceiling-high panes inside and on a taller ladder outside. By noon, Obie had finished. He put the ladders back in their assigned places and rinsed the wash bucket.

After a brief inspection, Pinky said, "Well, now, I suspected you were a good worker, but I'm impressed."

"Thank you, Mr. Hunt." Obie couldn't help smiling. Maybe he'd say something to his wife.

Pinky lingered. "Obie, you're young . . . fifteen, isn't it?

"That's right, sir, same as Cassie."

"Sure, I should remember that. You used to celebrate your birthdays together. I just want you to know there'll be some work around here for you if you want it, but I don't want to take you away from your studies."

"Oh, I stay caught up at school. I even have time for the newspaper."

"The school newspaper?"

"I'm a reporter." He couldn't hide a grin. "I even get to tell people what I think about things."

Pinky chuckled. "I'm sure you do. You play basketball, too, don't you?"

"This past season, but that's over until next winter. They wanted me to go out for track, run the mile and do the high jump, but I don't have time now that the weather's warmer."

"The girls told me that you work for other folks around here. What kind of work do you do, Obie?"

"Last fall, I helped Rob Nixon and Paul Compton remove their docks from the water before things froze over. I kept snow cleaned off their roofs all winter. I do that for a few other summer residents, too. I rake leaves. I do garden work. I make signs for stores and businesses. I do about anything, really."

"Signs, eh? Like the new sign at Mercer's?"

"I did that just last week. I didn't hang it, though. Mr. Mercer did that."

"It's good work. Artistic. So, you're an artist too?"

"I guess so. Mr. Groves, our art teacher, says I could have a future in some art field if I want it. He gave me some oils and old canvases, too. I like doing that."

Pinky appeared thoughtful. For the first time, Obie realized that Pinky and his grandfather were much alike, despite their age differences. Neither wasted words. "I need signs here. I'll let you know what I want. Just don't lose sight of the fact that your education's the most important thing. Don't let work take away from your books."

"I don't have a problem keeping up."

"How're things at home?"

"Good. We manage okay."

"Who does the cooking, Obie?"

"Usually, Dad, when he's home. Sometimes I do. I make out okay when he's not there. We have a lot of canned things. And I stop at Mercer's Store every day or so."

His father had warned him that questions would be asked. While his mother's estate was being settled, a petition was circulated and presented to the county court. The signers wanted to place Obie in another home because, it was stated, "Kenneth Gainsworthy is unable to adequately care for his son."

His Uncle Abner told the judge, "All this law stuff's unnecessary. My brother's a good father, but Obie can come and live with us anytime he wants."

His mother's sisters had also volunteered to give him a home.

Obie told the judge that he didn't want to live in the city. Such informality was frowned on by the originators of the petition, but Obie was given a choice to live with his father or with Abner and Claire. He chose to stay home. The only inconvenience was that Ken and Obie were required to appear in person before a court representative every six months until Obie reached the age of eighteen.

"We both work at canning fruits and vegetables," Obie said, and added, "We don't have much venison left, but Dad will go hunting again this fall. But, of course, you know that since you go with him . . . most times."

"You'll have plenty of meat." Pinky smiled. "Seems like you have things under control. How's your grandfather doing?"

"He still misses Grandma. He has a good outlook on life, though. Always has. I go see him real often."

"Jacob's a remarkable man." It was said with evident respect.

"Uncle Abner and Aunt Claire fuss at him because he's stopped going to church with them. He says it doesn't feel right without Grandma. Anyway, he has trouble getting around."

"Your grandfather practices Christianity better than some who never miss a service. By the way, I'm glad to see you back in our Sunday services."

"I never really felt at home at Evergreen. Father Brennan was disappointed when I told him I was leaving."

"Well, we're glad to have you back. Pastor Charles is a good, caring man."

"I like him a lot. Mom liked him, too. Even Dad likes him."

Pinky cleared his throat. "I don't mean to pry, Obie, but does Ken still drink?"

Obie knew he must be careful about what he said, but he wanted to be honest. "Some. He stopped completely before Mom died but started up again. It's not nearly as bad as it was. I think he worries about Grandpa."

"He's not abusive, is he? When he drinks, I mean." Pinky's voice trailed off as though he believed he might have gone too far in his questioning.

Obie answered quickly. "Mr. Hunt, my father has never hurt me, never once. He yells at me sometimes, even when he's not drinking. I yell back, too, because we disagree on many things, but we do love each other. You can count on that."

"Yes, I'm sure you do. Ken has many fine qualities, Obie. He's been through a lot. You do know, don't you, that he's a war hero?"

"Uncle Abner mentioned something about that once, but Dad's never talked about it."

"Well, it's a matter of record. He received a high medal for helping save the lives of some men trapped by the Germans. He was awarded other medals too, one I think from the French government."

"I'm not even sure Mom knew about that."

"And your grandpa Gainsworthy was in the Civil War. You're a military family, you know."

"I do know about Grandpa. He's been in the parades here and in some other towns."

"He was a wilderness guide, as well. He's one of the few still left who remembers what the Adirondacks was like in the old days."

"He talks a lot about it."

"Obie, has he ever mentioned the name, 'Bernard Templeton?' Have you heard it mentioned in the family?"

"No, sir. Who is he?"

"He owned a factory in New Hampshire. Made tools and other industrial machinery. During the Civil War, he converted his factory to make parts for guns and other munitions. Later, your grandfather was Templeton's guide every fall when he took three weeks off to come to the Adirondacks. He wouldn't go out with anybody else. You know why that was?"

"No, sir."

"Because Jacob saved his life the first time he came here." Pinky paused as if to let the information sink in.

"What happened?" Even with all his grandfather's stories, he'd never heard that one.

"They were in a canoe on one of the lakes. Indian Lake, I think. A fire was out of control in the woods along one shore, and a deer was swimming away from it. Big buck, the way I heard it. Templeton was a curious man and insisted on paddling right up to the animal. It seems that the buck tried to climb into the canoe. Its hooves knocked a side right out of the boat. It sank so fast that all their supplies and guns went down with it. Templeton couldn't swim, and they were a hundred yards from shore. They nearly drowned, but Jacob finally got the man to safety. Templeton was grateful, and they became close friends. I think Jacob and Prissy even went to New Hampshire once or twice to visit him and his wife."

"Is Mr. Templeton still living? I'd like to meet him."

"Oh, no. That was a long time ago. He's been dead many years. Get Jacob to tell you more about him."

"I will. How come you know all this, Mr. Hunt?"

"I take an interest in local history, that's all."

"Lots of families here go back a hundred years or more. Where are you from, Mr. Hunt?"

"I grew up in White River Junction, Vermont, but I went to Boston in my early twenties. I went to school and practiced law there."

"You make furniture now. Isn't that . . ."

Pinky laughed. "Unusual? Yes, I guess it is. Lawyering didn't fit my personality. Wood's more my style."

Obie wanted to ask more questions about Pinky's personal life but didn't want to appear too forward. "You mentioned Grandpa being in the Civil War . . . and he talks about it. Dad was in the World War but never mentions it. Why do you think that is?"

"I don't know, Obie. Some men hate their war experience so much that they don't want to be reminded. People are different in how they react to past experiences, especially bad ones. I've never been to war, so I don't really know."

"Some people think we'll be in the European war soon. The British are fighting the Germans, and Canada's in it, too. They're all asking for our help. Dad says we'll be in it, too, before long. He says the government knows it, and that's why they've started drafting."

"Yes, men twenty-one to thirty. Perhaps it's just a precaution."

"I hope so. I don't think I could ever kill people."

"Well, let's hope and pray you never have to." Pinky changed the subject. "I told you right after your mother passed away that you'd get an envelope each month. I hope it helps out."

"It comes every month. I'd like to thank whoever sends it . . . and for the bigger gift that paid off our debts after Mom died. Dad's getting more odd jobs now . . . and I've been doing well, so we can do without that money."

"Obie, as I told you, you'll receive it until you finish high school. Just accept it, and use it."

Obie had often wondered about the mysterious source of money and couldn't resist asking, "You know who's sending it, don't you, Mr. Hunt?"

He saw Pinky hesitate a moment before saying, "Yes, Obie, I do know. Fact is, I send the check myself, but the money's not from me. I can't tell you who that is. I can tell you it comes from a special fund. A large gift was donated several years ago to finance the fund. I'm only the administrator."

"I'd sure like to know who set up that fund."

"As I said, I'm not at liberty to tell you at this time. Let's just say I was instructed to see that it goes to worthy causes. I send out other checks from the fund as well. We call it 'the Love Fund.' It's a substantial amount and won't be exhausted for some time, but it won't last forever."

Obie had other questions about the Love Fund, but Pinky walked away for a closer window inspection. "Real fine job," he said. "I'll call on you again. And, someday, when you're in college, if you want a summer job here, you'll have it."

"Thanks, Mr. Hunt. I don't expect to go that far in my schooling, although I might need a job someday."

Pinky's broad smile seemed benevolent. "There'll always be a place for you here, Obie."

Obie fantasized the rest of the day about what important job Pinky Hunt might give his son-in-law.

CHAPTER NINE

1941–1942

Obie saw little of Laura and Cassie, except in church and sometimes within waving distance in the village. He had to be content to worship Laura from afar for the rest of the summer.

At the onset of his junior year at Evergreen, he took Pinky's advice about the importance of schooling and began limiting his "for hire" time to weekends and holidays. There was one exception: With homework complete, he would retreat to the barnroom and meticulously create signs for Stafford Rest and Evergreen local businesses. He used scrounged waste wood from Slim Goodman's lumber yard up the highway, or from wherever he could find suitable wood and sheet metal.

Laura was never far from his thoughts. He dreamed of approaching her again, but fall and winter passed without a chance to pursue romantic intentions. He stayed in Evergreen after school for basketball practice. Ernie, also on the team, had a new driver's license and drove his father's Chevrolet. Ernie's driving was scary on the mountain roads, but riding with him was far better than hitchhiking. Gasoline shortages had forced schools to keep their athletic schedules limited to games nearby, so they usually arrived home at reasonable hours. Even so, on most evenings Obie walked up Blackberry Hill in the dark. Courtship seemed beyond his reach.

Conditions improved after the basketball season ended. He rode the bus again, and daily encounters with Laura increased chances for conversation. The unnerving and unproductive escapade of "walking Laura home" still preyed on his mind. But, after a long session in his "thinking place" on the ridge, he decided he had to stop caring about people's opinions. He wouldn't allow either Ernie or Cassie to dictate the events of his life. So, he walked boldly up the road to Garnet Point beside the sisters two or three times a week.

Obie didn't announce his intentions, believing his actions would be evident to Laura and Cassie. He walked with the girls, touching Laura when he had the chance. Cassie wasn't any help, sometimes positioning herself between them. She was the best of friends, so he knew she wouldn't do that intentionally. She might even aid him in his quest. He resolved to ask her for help.

Beyond thwarted courtship, school work, odd jobs, and mere survival during his father's absences, there was a deepening friendship between Obie and the Reverend Charles Lansing. Obie found conversation easy with the pastor. Their bond had started during his mother's illness. Lancing stood beside him twice in the little cemetery above Abner's farm, once when Grandmother Gainsworthy "entered into eternal rest" and again at his mother's graveside service. Obie's regular attendance at church and Sunday School, combined with frequent invitations to the church office and parsonage, lifted the friendship to new heights.

One day in late May, with lilac bushes blooming all over town and home flower gardens coming to life, Obie knocked at the parsonage door.

"They're saying Clarence Tucker's missing in action," Obie stated as he sat on the couch.

"I've heard. I'll be going to go give comfort to the family."

The war had been a regular topic in their conversations since the Japanese attack on Pearl Harbor the previous December.

"I hate war," Obie said. They were words he'd used before.

"As do I, but there are times when there's no choice but to take up arms. Obadiah, a great evil has been let loose in the world and must be faced."

Pastor Charles went to the kitchen and soon returned with two glasses of orange Kool-Aid. He set one on the low table in front of Obie. "Don't you agree?" he said.

Obie was unsure. Something had nagged him lately. "You're a preacher. Could you kill anybody?"

Obie heard a sigh. "I'm not sure how I'd deal with it. Let's hope neither of us is ever faced with such a choice."

"I just turned sixteen. The war will have to go on for two more years for me to be called up. Pastor Charles, is it wrong for me to wish I won't have to go?"

The preacher's brow furrowed. "No, I don't believe so."

"Some men don't want to kill other men. There's a name for them. Con . . . con . . ."

"Conscientious objectors?"

"That's it. Maybe I'd be one of those."

"You could be, I suppose. There are all kinds of jobs in the military services that don't require carrying a gun."

"I'm not afraid. I don't want you to think that."

"Of course, you're not afraid. I know that, Obadiah."

"How old are you, Pastor Charles?"

"I'm forty-two. And yes, things would have to be pretty dour to call on me."

"What would you do if you were drafted?"

"I'd look to serve in ministry as a chaplain."

"You wouldn't have to kill anybody?"

"No, I wouldn't." There was that sigh again. "But some must lay down their lives. That's the way with war."

"Even if it went on long enough for me to go, I'd probably be too young to become a chaplain."

Pastor Charles gave him a strange look. "Would you like to become a chaplain . . . or a minister?"

"Oh, no. I watch what you do, sometimes. Preaching, and things like that. But I couldn't ever do anything like that."

He wasn't going to tell Pastor Charles about the time right after his mother died when he'd slipped into the sanctuary to stand at the pulpit and pretend he was giving a sermon about why God shouldn't take away parents. It had been a stupid thing to do.

Pastor Charles pursed his lips and made his funny head-jerking motion. "Obadiah, I'm busy today, but we need longer to talk. Could you come back next week after school . . . maybe Thursday."

"Okay, I'll be here." Any excuse to visit with the preacher was a welcome one.

* * *

From the corner window of his office, Charles had a clear view up the road to the intersection of White Pine and Main. He watched the school bus drop off a group of students. The little Negro girl everybody liked and pitied hobbled up the street toward Cedar Creek bridge.

A week had passed since the last conversation with Obadiah. He watched as the boy walked with the Hunt sisters toward Garnet Point. He'd observed that occurrence before—with interest.

He had never spoken about Laura, but Charles could see he was taken with her. Moreover, Cassie was smitten by Obadiah. How the young love triangle might play out would be interesting. It might not go beyond the present stage if Abigail Hunt spotted the interplay— and he had no doubt she would.

Thoughts of Abigail brought conflicting emotions. He was

thankful for the generous Hunt financial support for the church, but the woman was an enigma. She'd long controlled the administrative committees, particularly the Pastor-Parish Committee. Her influence was mainly responsible for bringing him to Stafford Rest; now she was working even harder to move him out. She'd accused him of being too "fundamentalist" in his sermons and Christian counseling. He had dug in his heels, of course. He'd preach the gospel as the Lord gave him utterance.

The only important thing he and Abigail had ever agreed about was his idea of renovating the attached building to make it an education wing. She had, however, never given him the support he needed to get it started, and with their relationship soured, he believed she never would. It was a pity, for the Hunts would have no trouble funding the greater portion of the project. He said a silent prayer for forgiveness for coveting that particular financial support—and a prayer of redemption for Abigail, too, as much in hopes of assuaging his own bitterness as for any good it might accomplish. Obadiah might be better off if he steered clear of the Hunt family.

Charles' promise to Vi Gainsworthy to take Obadiah under his wing was never far from his mind. Taking on such responsibility was a serious, even sacred, matter. He had been the boy's friend and mentored him as opportunities arose. Obadiah had needed it, having lost two critical people in his life in such a short time. Charles was surprised the previous week at his interest in the ministry, however fleeting that interest might be. He must not push. Had he planted the seed? Maybe—through their conversations. If so, his responsibility was to water. "Sow the seeds and let God do the growing" was something he'd heard from his own mentors.

Obadiah arrived at Charles' office half an hour later. They made small talk while Charles considered how best to broach the topic on his mind.

Obadiah brought it up himself. "Being a minister isn't something I'd like to do, but you once talked about being 'called.' I know you were talking about becoming a preacher, but does that mean that God calls us to do certain things in life?"

"I believe that . . . yes."

"And you think our lives are planned out, like blueprints?"

The boy always seemed to ask questions Charles would rather sidestep; his own life had been full of such questions. But he'd feel guilty if he avoided the truth. "Obadiah, I don't really know. We can make guesses about such things, but we can't be sure, not in this life."

"Doesn't the Bible say anything about that?"

"The Bible isn't always clear about that particular subject. It does talk about having gifts for certain Christian duties, but as for having our lives predicted, I don't know."

"I wouldn't like that anyway, having everything all laid out for me, some plan I'm supposed to follow. I'll make my own choices." The words were firm without being defiant.

"Obadiah, for our Christian work, God gives us potential." It felt better to be on solid theological ground. "The Bible calls it 'gifts.' I believe God wants, maybe even expects us to use a particular gift. But he's also given us free will, so we can choose to do . . . or not do. And that's not just in church work. I believe we're inclined to follow our gifts, and when we don't, we feel uneasy."

"My teachers say I have artistic talent. Maybe God wants me to be an artist. I like being in the woods, too. Maybe I could be a forest ranger." He grinned. "Maybe a forest ranger who paints."

"There are many ways of serving God. Cassie Hunt told me that you write."

"I'm a reporter for the school newspaper. One of my articles was picked up and printed in the county newspaper. It was about the Cedar Creek bridge, about its history."

"I read that but didn't notice that it was your story. It was an excellent article."

"I like writing."

"Obadiah, I'm sure you have qualifications in abundance for whatever you do in life." Maybe he was pushing the sixteen-year-old too fast. "Next year when you're a senior will be a better time to consider careers."

Obadiah wasn't ready to stop asking the hard questions. "It's confusing that there are so many ways of believing," he said. "Mom brought me here to this church before Evergreen, and most Catholics think that was a sin. Why do they feel that way?"

Theology discussions were treacherous; he'd need to tread carefully. His own belief was that the Catholic Church was wrong about many things, but it would be best, in this case, to stick to known history. "Catholic and Orthodox Churches sprang from Christianity's very beginning, and we have them to thank for bringing the teachings and traditions down to us. But, as Protestants, we disagree with some of those traditions and teachings. We consider them man-made. And Protestants disagree with one another as well. That's why we have so many denominations. Unfortunately, some people believe so strongly about something that they can't respect other points of view."

"That seems like a bigger sin than going to the wrong church."

"Yes, perhaps it is. I try not to judge other Christians for their beliefs. I'm not saying I shouldn't defend my Methodist traditions, but I try not to be mean-spirited about it."

"Is the Methodist way the best way?"

There it was again, that propensity for asking questions he'd sometimes asked himself. "For me, I believe so. I believe Methodism involves us in our own salvation without burdening us with impossible demands."

"Are you saying we can make our own rules?"

"Oh, no. There's a way to salvation that needs to be followed. We must obey instructions of the Bible, and we can't deviate from them."

"But couldn't the Bible be wrong sometimes?"

They were in dangerous territory. "Absolutely not! The Bible is *never* wrong."

"There must be different ideas about meanings, though?"

"Sometimes the words are unclear, leaving us to speculate on their meaning."

"So, how can we tell the difference between a real truth and one that isn't?"

The boy was trying to pin him down. He was too young to perform an exercise in rhetoric, so he was genuinely searching for meaning. Charles had asked the same questions in his youth, questions that sometimes repeated themselves, even today.

He took a moment to rehearse an answer before saying, "Our little minds can't grasp ultimate truth, Obadiah. I think our best bet is to believe what we've been taught, but with an open mind, realizing that no one can know everything. We should always search for truth, but when we think a truth goes against our teachings, it can be troubling, especially for those who believe they already have all the answers."

"It's pretty confusing."

"To say the least. But there are beliefs that all Christians share, and it's more productive to think about those than about what divides us." That sounded good to his own ears, but in truth, it was difficult to overlook the grievous mistakes of many fellow pastors, some in his denomination.

"Aren't love and forgiveness something we share? Grandpa

talks a lot about that. Don't all Christians do that?"

"They're supposed to."

"Father Brennan said Catholics love God. Don't all Christians love God?"

"Of course. Methodists, Baptists, Presbyterians, Dutch Reformed. They all do. All true Christians love God. We should love one another too, and forgive one another."

There appeared before him an image of Abigail Hunt's accusing face. She'd recently told Helen Mercer that funds were missing from the church bank account to which Charles had access. Some things were difficult to forgive.

"What about Jews? Don't they love God?"

"Of course, they do. You've read the Psalms."

"Some people say bad things about Jews."

"They do, and it's a sin. Jesus was a Jew, and Christianity has its roots in Judaism. They're the chosen race, but they rejected Jesus as the Messiah, and we have to be patient with them as they find their way back to the true path."

He saw the look of doubt on Obadiah's face. He wasn't going to accept things on their face.

"I don't know any Jews except the Reuben family, and they're only around during the summer. I work for them sometimes. I didn't even know they were Jews until Chuck told me."

"I know the Reubens quite well. We worked together last summer raising funds for the area families struck down by polio."

"I'm not going to say bad things about the Jews, or any other group the way some people do."

Charles was pleased with the boy's insight; he recognized ambiguities that needed reflection. "You're right in making that decision, Obadiah."

"But that doesn't mean we have to be close friends . . . since they're different from us?"

"That's a decision you'd have to make, but friendship sometimes chooses us rather than the other way around. I've learned that in my ministry."

"How did you get to be a preacher?"

"I went to college for two years. I also had some theological training, but I didn't go to seminary."

"Seminary?"

"It's a special school for God's workforce. If I had it to do over, I'd go to seminary. The church world's becoming a far different

place. Education is becoming a must if you want to make a difference."

"You've done all right, though."

There came that moment of regret he sometimes experienced
when thinking back on his own education and training. He didn't
regret being where he was; it was a good life and he felt privileged to
serve where God had placed him. Even so, he sometimes wondered
what it would be like serving a large congregation in a city setting
and having a salary that might raise him from poverty.

"God has been good to me."

"I have to go, Pastor Charles. I have some chores and want to
do some drawing."

"That reminds me. I have a gift for you."

Charles went to a closet and took out a cardboard box. He
opened it to show paint tubes, a wooden palette, brushes, and several
other items.

"These are for painting oils." Obadiah's eyes were wide. "Are
you loaning them to me?"

"No, it's a gift."

Charles watched with pleasure as Obadiah removed everything
from the box, his smile becoming broader with each item revealed.
"These are wonderful. Why are you giving them away?" As he asked
the question, he made graceful back and forth strokes with a sable
brush against the palm of his hand.

"Several years ago, I tried painting landscapes but discovered I
have zero artistic talent. Better for you to have them than for them
to sit in the closet. Oh, I almost forgot, I also have an easel." Charles
returned to the closet, pulled out a three-legged stand, and unfolded
it. "And there are some canvases, too," he added.

Charles was happy to see Obadiah leave with full arms and a
broad smile. The boy needed more to smile about.

* * *

Summer came with its hodgepodge of activities. Work on Abner's farm was available anytime, but farm work didn't generate
much excitement. He would have loved to hike the High Peaks trails
again with his father, but Ken told him in early spring, "I'm hanging
it up. That time is past."

From the first day of summer vacation, Obie worked in the village daily, mowing lawns, clearing brush, tending gardens, and

performing odd jobs. Despite that work, he spent most of his time in their vegetable garden and small orchard. Ken had turned their care over to him, and Obie took pride in the vegetables and herbs grown there, some his parents had taught him to cultivate, and some that were new varieties. He spent long hours canning fruits and vegetables the way his mother had, storing them in the hillside cellar between the garden and house.

There was little chance to be alone with Laura that summer, but there was one brief encounter in mid-August. Obie was leaving Mercer's Grocery as she was entering. They stopped on the broad wooden steps leading to Main Street.

"Hello, Obie," she said, her smile the most welcome sight he'd seen since June. She added, "You're really dirty, and you're sweaty."

It was haying season. He'd spent the day at Abner's working alongside three men Abner had hired to get the hay in ahead of expected rain. Rivers of perspiration absorbing dark barn-loft dust had left them all looking like coal miners he'd seen in a book at school.

"I worked at Abner's today," he said. "I haven't been home to take a bath."

"I can tell." Her smile was a sweet sight.

"Haying is dirty work."

"Apparently. I haven't seen much of you all summer."

"I know. I've missed that, seeing you . . . and Cassie."

"You *could* come around to our house."

"I might."

"Well, do it!"

"Okay."

"When?"

"Would tomorrow do?" He knew he was blushing and was suddenly glad for the black on his face.

"Tomorrow I'll be going to Saranac Lake with Mom. Cassie will be home, though."

He drew in a long breath. He must have misread her intentions. Of course, he'd enjoy time with Cassie, but it was with Laura that he wanted time alone. Frustration rose its familiar head.

"I'll see you some other time, then," Obie said, trying not to let his disappointment show.

"Okay, Obie. Maybe I'll see you again before school starts." Turning from the store entrance, she added, "Can you believe it? We'll be seniors."

CHAPTER TEN

Fall 1942

On a Saturday afternoon halfway through the fall season, Laura sat at the Hunt kitchen table adding small pieces of aluminum foil to a sphere that had grown to the size of a soccer ball. For several months, she had saved the metal foil of gum and candy wrappers and other packaging materials, most rescued from village trash cans.

It was her contribution to the nationwide war support effort. Her father and sister saved foil too, but it was Laura who put it all together. Her mother, while not impeding, voiced the opinion that rummaging through trash was belittling. Her father bought savings bonds for their parents and encouraged the girls to buy stamps at school.

Laura eventually tired of the endeavor and went to the bay window in the living room. Cassie had told her that Obie would be raking leaves at the Whitmore house a hundred yards down the hill. She stood patiently at the window until she saw him. Half-a-dozen families relied on Obie for keeping their lawns mowed and cleaned. Several businesses in the area had his signs in their windows or hanging over their doors. Her father had been praising him since he helped clean a room at the factory; he still performed occasional "little chores" there. Pinky had said he wouldn't "overwork the boy," suggesting that Obie needed time to study.

Even at a distance, she could see the rhythmic motions of his arms and shoulders as he raked. An audible sigh escaped. Sitting across the room, her mother glanced in her direction and then pretended to look elsewhere.

What was she to do about Obie? She'd tried to enjoy the company of other young men and thus "widen her social horizons," as her mother often said. A few boys, like Norman Harrison, also a senior, had piqued Laura's interest. Norman, who lived in the village of Evergreen, was one of a few with her mother's approval. His father was a successful businessman. Norm had asked her to a dance at the high school last year and even came to pick her up in his family's roadster. The evening had been enjoyable—at least the first part. She allowed Norman to kiss her but pushed him away when he tried to put his hand between her knees. He had not asked her for a date again, and she had no wish that he would.

Her world felt limited. She'd seen more of Ernie Boswell than any other male outside her family simply because he lived nearby. Ernie was her friend even though there was a certain unrefined quality about him that annoyed her. And, he never seemed to tire of talking about Frances Gibbons. He confided in Laura that he wanted to court Frances; Laura told her mother, an unwise move, for Abigail had declared it "scandalous."

The attention from Ben Williamson was another matter; he came to town infrequently on short holidays from medical school and summer work in clinics. He never approached her directly, but she knew he often came near, watching her; it happened far more often than chance allowed. She admitted to some secret corner of her mind that admiration from an older man, especially a soon-to-be professional, was exciting.

Without actually saying so, her mother was encouraging her to favor men of good financial standing; she might be right. It would be appealing to think of a future without money worries. She knew her own family was well off, but such things were seldom discussed, or if they were, not in the girls' presence. She sensed in Ben an element of danger, and it had surprised her that it didn't seem a bad thing. Nevertheless, if he would come into the open and talk, she'd simply put an end to it.

Reluctantly, her thoughts came back to Obie. He was usually lingering near, not obtrusive, just not far away. He was too young, although he looked older than his age. She was intrigued, for he was no longer the little boy she and Cassie had played with as they were growing up. He could be called "handsome." And he was gentle with her and Cassie, unlike some boys at school. Mature—that was the word. He had rough edges, understandably so considering how he lived, but that would be nothing hard to correct.

He was in love with her. He hadn't told her, but she knew, nonetheless. She experienced mild frustration in that knowledge, for there was no one she liked or admired more.

What might happen if they could ever be alone—really alone? Opportunities had been few. Shortly after her interesting encounter with Obie at Mercer's, he'd overcome his shyness to ask her if she wanted to go to a movie. His Aunt Angie Temple was driving up from Albany and taking him to Glens Falls to buy clothing. He and Angie often went to movies during her once-a-month visits, or she went shopping while he attended a movie alone. Laura had asked her father for permission, not wanting to take the chance that her mother would forbid her. She'd hoped to find private time with Obie, but Cassie insisted on going too, and six-year-old Cleo was always in the way. Cassie grabbed the seat next to Obie at the "Blondie" movie. Whether that was intentional or not, Laura was unsure.

The school held dances and other socializing events that Obie might ask her to attend. But he had no automobile, and she blanched at the prospects of asking her mother to transport them; that wasn't a possibility. She had twice attended basketball games the past winter to watch him play. The attention he received from other girls disturbed her, though he seemed oblivious about it.

Her mother disliked Obie despite his having been around their family longer than she could remember. When Vi was alive, the three children had celebrated their birthdays together. Vi would bake a cake and set things up. Obie was always there, helping his mother. She sighed. She missed Vi, even after three years.

Her attention was drawn to another figure at the Whitmore fence. Cassie was there, gesturing to Obie. Laura leaned closer to the window. The way Cassie acted around Obie was beginning to annoy her? Cassie and Obie were good friends—but might she have feelings beyond friendship? Laura quickly dismissed that idea; Cassie would scream it to the mountaintops if she had designs on Obie.

* * *

"What do you want?" Obie said as he stomped toward Cassie. He looked impatient.

"I was down at Mercer's and brought you something to drink." She thrust an open bottle of Coca-Cola toward him. "You look like you could use it."

"Thanks." He wiped the sweat from his face with a bare arm before taking the bottle. "I'm trying to finish up here so I won't have to come back Monday after school. These leaves will lay here until spring if we get early snow."

Obie's arms, she observed, looked strong without being heavily muscled. *What would it feel like to have those arms around her?* She'd attended all the home basketball games last spring and even learned the rules so she could talk basketball intelligently with him—if the chance ever came. It hadn't, because he was so busy, but she'd enjoyed watching him play. He was a "forward" but played "center" a couple of times when Zack Hamilton was injured. The new basketball season would soon start, although there had been some discussion about canceling it because of gas rationing. This would be Obie's last basketball season—and his final year at Evergreen High. Her senior year looked bleak, indeed.

Obie handed back the empty bottle. "You really were thirsty," she said.

"I've been here since noon." He laughed.

"What's so funny?"

"Your hair. It sticks out all over like corkscrews, and it bounces when you walk. I could see that as you came up the road."

He'd used similar words before, and although she believed it was said with affection, it hurt. Her mother had given her permanents on several occasions, but in a few days her hair would again be a troublesome mess. She envied Laura's more manageable locks.

Hair wasn't the only thing about Laura that she envied. When the three were together, Obie seemed unable to see Cassie. It hadn't been like that when they were younger and in the same classroom. Obie had always found a way to move his desk close to hers. After he was double-promoted and went into Laura's class, his attention was always on her. *Why did he have to be so bright?*

"Thanks, Cassie. I really have to go back to work now."

"Will you be in church tomorrow?"

"Aren't I always in church on Sundays?"

"Maybe you could sit with us for a change."

"I'd like that, but maybe you'd better ask your mother first."

"Okay, I will. And I'll save a seat for you."

She noticed his peculiar expression. He shrugged, turned, and walked away.

* * *

Abigail walked from the house and down the steps to the enclosed and heated portion of the patio. She sat where she could see both daughters; Laura was still inside looking out the window, and Cassie had just left the Whitmore fence after talking to Obie.

Their interest in Obie was unhealthy—an obsession. Young girls having crushes on boys was expected, but this had gone on far too long and with the wrong boy. She should have acted sooner. *She would put an end to it today.*

When Laura had a date with Malcolm Harrison's son, she had

approved, for the Harrison family was a good one although not as wealthy as the Hunts. Malcolm was becoming involved in politics. She'd hidden her disappointment that nothing came of their one date. And there was that handsome medical student, Doctor Williamson's son, who would soon be a doctor. She tried to understand why Laura didn't see his interest. He was a bit older but could be an excellent match someday.

Abigail sometimes tried to picture Obie more compassionately. After all, he was Vi's son. Nevertheless, she faced facts. Although intelligent enough and well-behaved, he'd never have the opportunity to excel. The undertaking of people in the community to help him, however well-intentioned, was a wasted effort. Unlike her daughters, Obie would never see inside a college or university. Pinky believed he'd be a good factory worker. That would probably be his highest achievement.

She would act today to divert her daughers' interests in Obie. Laura would have no great difficulty with it, for she was levelheaded. Cassie, on the other hand, might need guidance.

A few minutes later after Cassie came home, Abigail asked the girls to join her in the living room. Pinky wasn't home, which was just as well. She steeled herself for the undertaking.

"What did we do, Mom?" Cassie asked.

"Oh, no, dear. It's just something I've been meaning to talk to you about."

Laura appeared anxious. "Are you sick, Mom?"

"No . . . no. I'm sorry. I didn't mean to make you think that."

"It's just that after what happened to Vi, it's just . . ."

"It's nothing like that, girls. I simply want to remind you about our place in the community, what it means. You're nearly grown, and even though we've touched on this before, I thought we should go over it again."

"Okay," Cassie said. "Tell us. I have homework to do."

"This is important, Cassie."

"I have a question first, Mom. This is important, too."

"What is it, Cassie?"

"Can Obie sit with us in church tomorrow? His father doesn't come to service and he sits alone."

Abigail was taken aback. Who could know such a request concerning Obie would come from her daughter just as she was about to take steps to remove his threat from their lives. For a moment, she considered postponing the discussion. No—it wasn't a discussion, anyway. She meant to make it a decree. She had to go through with it to make them understand.

"No, Cassie, he can't sit with us."

"Why not, Mom?" Laura asked.

"How would it look to other church members?"

"Just fine, I'd think," Cassie said.

Abigail ignored the remark. "Listen, girls, I need you to understand. Our family is a leader in Stafford Rest, and even in the larger township and county. As such, we must maintain a certain social level. We discussed this once, concerning Vi."

Laura's voice rose. "Mom, I remember what you said then. You called Vi 'a servant.' There's nothing wrong with serving people, but I felt as though you were belittling her. To Cassie and me, Vi was part of our family."

Abigail surged ahead. "We all cared for Vi, but you're both old enough to understand that she wasn't really the same as us. Anyway, it's not Vi I want to talk about. It's Obie."

Cassie's wide eyes revealed her displeasure. "I guess you're going to tell us Obie's not the same as us, either?"

"That family's a disaster. His father can't keep a job. They depend on community help just to . . ."

"That's not true, Mom." Laura's face was red. "Mr. Gainsworthy works at a lot of different things. He chooses to do that. And Obie works hard, too, more than he should have to. Anyway, what does it have to do with the kind of person Obie is?"

"Laura, I'm not saying Obie's not a good person."

"What *are* you saying, Mom?"

"You and Cassie are seeing too much of him."

Cassie's retort was quick. "You don't want us to associate with Obie at all, isn't that it?" Not waiting for an answer, she added, "Well, I won't stop being friends with him."

"Neither will I," Laura said.

Abigail couldn't contain her anger. "Understand this, girls . . . you're not to associate with Obie, not now, not in the future. And I'm writing a letter to Ken Gainsworthy stating that he's to keep his son away from the two of you. It's time you accepted the truth of the matter." She hesitated to put words to thoughts she should keep private, but her outrage loosened her tongue. "He's the son of an immigrant and a drunk. He's beneath us."

* * *

Cassie was in no mood to wait. She rushed to the back of the church right after Sunday morning service and pressed a note into Obie's hand.

> *Meet Laura and me at 2:00 p.m. at the park. We have something important to tell you.*

Later at home, she told Laura what she'd done. She was unsure how her sister would react, but she didn't care. If Laura didn't want to go with her, she'd go alone. Obie should learn of the conversation with their mother before her letter reached Blackberry Hill; he must know that the sisters had nothing to do with it. Nevertheless, she was relieved when Laura approved Cassie's bold move.

A stiffening breeze was blowing off the lake when they arrived at the park. Obie was already there, sitting at a picnic table by the beach with a puzzled expression. "What's going on?" he asked, rising to face them.

They told him everything, alternating between Laura's calm and deliberate explanation and Cassie's more animated one. Cassie didn't try to rein in her anger. "I hate my mother for this. She thinks she's better than everyone else."

Obie looked down at the ground during the girl's explanations. When he finally spoke, his voice was subdued. "Cassie, hating your mother isn't a good idea."

Cassie ignored his remark and said, "I can't ever feel the same about her after this. I want you to know, Obie, no matter what Mom says, I'll always be your friend."

"That goes for me, too," Laura added.

"Does she know you're with me now?" Obie asked as he looked toward the house on the hill.

"She knows we're in the village. We told her we were going to see Tillie Monroe. She's a very old teacher who retired years and years ago. We sometimes visit Miss Monroe for 'tea.'"

Obie's expression was one Cassie knew well. He had the right to be angry but spoke in his usual measured and logical manner. "I don't know why she doesn't like me, but I'm not going to hold it against her. I pick up the mail, so Dad won't see the letter. I'm not going to let it bother me."

His conciliatory manner angered Cassie further. "Well, it

bothers me. Laura, doesn't it bother you?"

"Yes, it does, but Obie's right that hating her may not be the right thing to do. She *is* our mother. We have to live with her."

"I'm going to go right on being your friend, Obie, if that's all right with you. What about you, Laura?" Cassie was determined to hear a more substantial commitment from her sister.

Laura put her hand on Obie's arm. "Obie, you've been my friend for as long as I can remember. That's not going to change."

Obie looked from one girl to the other. "Are you sure you want to risk getting in trouble with her?"

"Of course, I want to risk it," Cassie said. She was never surer of anything.

"I guess it means I can't walk from the bus stop with you anymore."

"She told us we have to drop out of Sunday school class," Cassie said.

"Because I'm in the class? You don't need to do that. Tell her I'm not in the class anymore. It'll be the truth."

"Are you sure?"

"I'm sure."

It was a significant concession, and Cassie wanted to soothe his feelings. "She can't see us on the school bus or in school."

"Or at other times, either," Laura added. "We'll find other times and ways."

Cassie saw his expression and recognized the onslaught of the methodical way he put his thoughts into words. She was unwilling to wait. "What are you thinking?" she urged.

"I'm trying to envision those 'other times and ways.'"

"Well, I know one. If you can't come to our house, we'll come to yours."

"That makes sense," Laura said.

"I don't know," Obie said. "My father might not like it . . . although you might come when he's not there."

"He's away a lot, isn't he?"

"He'll be logging up north during January and February, which could extend beyond that. He usually comes home Saturday night and stays until Sunday afternoon."

Cassie was heartened. "Friends find a way. It'll work out. You'll see."

They moved closer together as the breeze from the lake picked up.

"Do you think she's watching us?" Cassie asked.

"It's too far to recognize anyone," Laura said. "Obie, if she asks who we were with, we'll tell her you're Tillie Monroe." She laughed.

"What's so funny?" Cassie asked.

"I can't think of anyone more unlike Tillie Monroe."

CHAPTER ELEVEN

Fall 1942

Obie slept fitfully that Sunday night. The conversation with the Hunt sisters in the park replayed relentlessly; it had been difficult to hide his anger. Now, he fought down the growing bitterness toward their mother. He'd done nothing to deserve such treatment. On Monday, he went to school irritable and sat alone on the school bus. That evening, after dinner, he said goodnight to his father, who was home for a few days, and retreated to the barnroom where he'd been sleeping since his mother's death.

It was impossible to concentrate on homework. He lay on his bunk, hands behind his head, staring at the beams overhead. Dimmed-down light from the kerosene lamp cast flickering reflections on the rough wallboards. He tried to focus on what the girls had told him. What should he do? Their disclosure had jolted him. He should not have been surprised, for he'd long sensed Abigail Hunt's dislike and knew it would become an issue at some point. The sisters had assured him that it made no difference in their feelings, and he'd accepted that with relief and gratitude. He believed their friendship was strong enough to overcome any obstacle.

Nevertheless, after turning off the lamp, he considered more objective questions. Could Mrs. Hunt be right about not wanting her daughters to associate with him? He seldom thought about social or economic disparity. On deeper reflection, the truth seemed obvious. Obie was poor; his father was poor; all his relatives worked hard to make do. The Hunts would never have to worry about such hardship. The girls would go to college; Laura still talked about Smith College, and Cassie said she wanted to be a teacher. For him, college was a dream not often entertained. In addition, the Hunts knew important people. Local and state politicians visited them regularly. Pinky had, more than once, been asked to run for a county office. The Hunts were sought after and looked up to.

Abigail might be right. He hated the cruel way she'd gone about it, but wouldn't he want the best for his children if he were in her place? She was smart. She must see where his interest in Laura might lead if she failed to step in. Her statement about his being "beneath" them was true, in a sense. He could never live up to Pinky and Abigail Hunt's expectations for their daughters, at least not in the near future. He slept little the rest of the night.

He arose early, went to the house, and packed his knapsack with sandwiches, dried fruit and nuts, and other essentials for a day in the woods. As he packed, his father got up and prepared to leave for Abner's. Ken wasn't pleased with his son's plan.

"You're going up to the MacIntyre Range alone? Why?"

"I have to think something through, Dad."

"Why can't you do your thinking here? There's snow up there already. There'll be more soon. It's no time of year to go up there alone."

"I need to be by myself awhile. I needn't go above the snow line. Anyway, the weather's been warm and will probably stay that way all day."

"It can change fast. Are you prepared to stay overnight if you have to?"

"I'll take a bedroll, but I'm sure I'll be back by suppertime."

"Do you have all the supplies you need?"

"I know what to pack, Dad."

"Where are you headed, specifically?"

"Algonquin."

As he expected, his father's advice to "Stay on the lower slopes" was brief and to the point. As Obie was getting ready to leave, Ken asked, "Couldn't you find somebody to go with you? What about Ed Baumgartner or Ernie Boswell?"

"Ed's not much for hiking, and Ernie talks too much. Anyway, I need to be alone."

His father's tone became softer. "What is it that requires so much thought?"

"Just things."

"It's about Laura Hunt, isn't it?"

The question surprised him. He'd told no one of his feelings for Laura—not even Laura. How did his father know? Was it right on his face for everyone to see?

"That's part of it," he admitted.

"She's not for you, you know."

A surge of anger caused Obie to turn his back on his father. There was no other way to avoid firing back words of denial—or maybe words to cover his frustration at their truth.

"The Hunts pretty much run things around here," his father

said. "And Abigail's a cold, calculating woman. They aren't about to put up with people like us."

"You like Pinky."

"He's likable enough, but I doubt he'd want you in their family, or me by extension."

"They treated Mom well."

"She was valuable to them. You're not." The hard edge of his father's words hurt.

"Laura and Cassie aren't like that."

"I might agree with you about Cassie, but if you're putting any hopes on Laura, you're looking for heartbreak."

Obie couldn't trust himself to answer. He slipped into his jacket, grabbed his pack, and headed for the door.

His father called after him, "Look here, Obie, you're just as good as anybody . . . and better than most. Laura's no better than you. She just thinks she is."

"I've got to go."

"How're you getting there?"

"I'm taking the school bus to Evergreen and hitchhiking the rest of the way." Without turning, he said, "I'll be back before supper."

He sat by himself again on the bus, ignoring quizzical looks Laura and Cassie sent in his direction. He was surprised that no one questioned his knapsack with the bedroll lashed on top,

When the bus parked in front of the high school, Obie exited and walked toward the main highway. He'd hitchhiked before; someone would give him a ride.

"Obie!" Cassie caught up and tugged at his arm. "Obie, are you mad at us?"

"No."

"Where are you going?"

"Up in the mountains."

"Why?"

"I need a day by myself, Cassie. I'll get back to Evergreen in time to catch the bus home. If I miss it, I'll catch a ride."

"You shouldn't go by yourself."

He patted her hand. "Cassie, I know what I'm doing. I'll be okay."

He saw that she wasn't convinced. She surprised him. "I'll go with you. Give me a minute to catch up with Laura and tell her."

He grabbed her arms and swung her around to face him. "No! I don't want you going with me. You go on into school." He shoved her toward the building.

She resisted. "Why not? I have the same right to go climbing the peaks as you do." The corkscrew strands of her hair stood out. He imagined that the condition became more pronounced when she was angry.

"I told you I want to be alone. I can't take you with me and still be alone, can I? Besides, Pinky would kill me if your mother didn't get to me first."

Cassie sighed. "Maybe it's not a good idea at that. I'm not dressed for it. It's going to cost you, though. I won't tell anybody if you promise to take me up there sometime. The nearest I've ever been to the high peaks was traveling on the highway over to Keene."

As usual, Cassie had been difficult to outmaneuver. "All right. I promise."

"I don't take promises lightly, Obie."

"Neither do I. You should know that by now."

He watched her until she entered the school. It took five minutes for a northbound automobile to stop for him. The driver let him out at Saranac Lake, where he quickly caught another ride through Lake Placid and east to the Adirondack Loj Road. He was prepared to walk the total distance to the Loj where the trails began, but a supply truck came along before he had gone half a mile. Within three hours of leaving home, he was on the Van Hoevenberg Trail, climbing into the mountains.

*　*　*

Algonquin, in the MacIntyre Range, was the second highest mountain in the Adirondacks, and his favorite of all the high peaks. He'd been there several times with his father, but it had been with Grandpa Jacob that he'd first climbed to the rocky summit on one of Jacob's "magical days."

That memory caused Obie to look back at Heart Lake. Jacob told good stories. The descriptions of Civil War battles brought goosebumps, no matter how many times they were repeated, and his tales of adventures in the mountains were classics. Heart Lake and the Adirondack Lodge story was one of Obie's favorites.

In the late 1870s, Henry Van Hoevenberg and Josephine Scofield, engaged and much in love, had stood on top of Mt. Marcy and picked out Heart Lake, the place they chose to build their wilderness home. Sadly, Jo died soon after. In 1890, as a memorial to his lost love, Henry built the Adirondack Lodge on the shores of Heart Lake and near Mount Jo. The lodge was strategically located, an ideal jumping-off place to several high peaks, including the highest, Mt. Marcy. The Lake Placid Club took it over in 1900 and, during an outbreak of forest fires in 1903, the Lodge burned down.

"It nearly killed him," Jacob had said. "Mr. Van came back, though. He did a heap of good. He worked with the Adirondack Camp and Trail Club developing trails and building huts and lean-tos. I'm glad to say I helped on many of them projects myself. The Preserve wouldn't be what it is today if it hadn't been for Mr. Van."

Obie recalled the story every time he came this way. Today, Henry and Jo felt closer than usual, maybe because Laura was so much on his mind. She wasn't dead, of course, but maybe she was lost to him. What memorial could he possibly build for her?

The trail led to a cutoff to Algonquin, where he considered continuing toward the Marcy trail. Old "Cloud Splitter" was only eight miles away. It wasn't even noon. And, he didn't have to return today; his father would understand. He could stay overnight partway up Marcy and make the top tomorrow if he chose to go on.

Reason prevailed; he'd told his father he'd be on Algonquin. Doing what he'd said he'd do was important. Bad things did happen, and it would be doing a disservice to anyone trying to find him if he weren't where he said he'd be.

He climbed quickly. He could, if he wished, reach the summit of Algonquin by mid-afternoon and then come down in time to either go home or make camp. Or, he could let events play out as they would; there was no urgent reason for going to the top. That wasn't why he was there.

Conifers and hardwoods were present in about equal numbers. He stopped often, resting on soft needle carpets beneath Balsam Firs, white or red pines, or one of another dozen evergreen varieties. He ate some of his sandwiches on a brief stop and refilled his canteen from a cold stream.

In a random start-stop travel mode, he stayed on the trail and finally came to the tree line. From there, the ascent through the dwarf tree and alpine zones would be steeper and the trail rougher. Without further consideration, he started for the top. Might not the cascade of rugged peaks seen from there generate a plan for the course of his life?

Six years earlier, he'd been up there with Grandfather Jacob. Resting after a strenuous climb, Jacob told him, "Mountains lift us up to God." The words had not made much sense to his ten-year-old mind, but he remembered them today as wise and appropriate.

He encountered areas of snow accumulations as he climbed, especially in shaded ravines, but they didn't impede travel. The wind was harsh, however. Obie pulled a sweater from his knapsack to layer against the cold.

A half-mile from the summit, he stowed his knapsack behind a boulder; no use carrying extra weight. He'd be back in an hour or two. He'd seen no other hikers, nor had he expected to. There was satisfaction in believing he was alone on the mountain.

He held a steady pace up the ever-steepening incline, through and past stunted scrub, and over matted dwarf fir carpets. His breath, coming in short bursts, sounded to his ears like the bellows in Kyle Rudnick's blacksmith shop beside Cedar Creek.

The summit approach was windblown with sublime alpine meadows containing vegetation that his father said was "more suited to the Arctic." The soil there, which had accumulated over the ages throughout the rocky outcroppings, supported mountain sandwort, heath, and numerous slow-growing perennials. Those varieties, and many more, formed a hardy mat that covered all but the rockiest surfaces.

After reaching the top, he stood still on a vast expanse of solid stone until his breathing slowed. It was much colder there, and as his body temperature dropped, he wished he had brought the extra shirt and the toboggan hat from his knapsack. The afternoon sun had disappeared and he could see a weather system approaching from the southwest. No worry, though; going down would be much faster.

Visibility in the other direction was still good and he marveled once more at the layers of magnificent peaks stretching in all directions. He could locate and name them all: Marcy, Skylight, Wallace, Colden, Iroquois, Street, and Nye. Ken had taught him well. Lakes twinkled in random locations in the valleys; a hundred or so were within eyesight. Heart Lake, where he had started, was still visible.

Obie found a rock formation suitable as a windbreak. He shivered as he sat still, using the panoramic view before him to focus his attention.

Pastor Charles had encouraged him to pray and instructed him in ways to do so. He'd memorized Psalms as prayers, and the minister applauded him for it but suggested using more personal prayers. He had said, "Giving God your gratitude and telling him about your joys and your problems should be like talking to a good friend."

That way of praying had remained something of a mystery. *God was God and not someone to be buddies with.* Under Father Brennan's tutorage, Obie had learned Catholic Church rituals. He still used his rosary beads and made the sign of the cross when it seemed appropriate. Hanging onto those practices made him feel like he was paying respects without getting too close. But, in truth, he was unsure who or what God was.

One night, not long after his mother died, he'd ventured a question. "Just who are you, anyway, God?" He asked it aloud and waited. When no answer came, he concluded that God was too busy to bother with such trivial matters. He had neither need nor inclination to tell anyone who he was.

If God had compassion for fundamental problems in human lives, as Pastor Charles had said, maybe he would guide Obie in the situation that was bothering him. Perhaps he would show him what to do about Laura Hunt. "She's not for you," his father had said. *Was it true?*

He glanced into the distance to the eastern peaks. It was no longer clear. Clouds were moving in. He decided to ignore that and concentrate. He'd pray as the preacher suggested. He sat back against the stone with sharp edges rubbing against his back.

"Dear God," he said, hoping it was a good way to begin, like starting a letter. "This is my problem, and it may not be very important to you with so many bad things going on in the world, but it's brought me to where I can't think of anything else. Laura Hunt's the girl I love and want to marry . . . someday, of course. Her mother hates me and will try to keep us apart. My dad says Laura's not for me."

Obie paused. What would Pastor Charles say next? "Lord . . . what is your will in this? Are you telling me through Mrs. Hunt and my father that I must give her up? I hope it isn't the case, for I love her. Pastor Charles says you always answer our prayers. If that's true, then please help me." He paused again, feeling even more confused. "Maybe I'm asking the wrong things. Maybe we have to make our own decisions. Or, maybe the decisions are already made for us. I do know that I need help with this problem that keeps me from thinking about anything else."

Obie sat still for a long time with closed eyes. He hoped that, if he waited, he might receive an answer. The preacher said God's answers might not come in a flash of light or a booming voice, but in unexpected ways, in inspiration, or sometimes in "a still small voice, hardly tickling your ear." Obie was unsure what God's voice might be like if he chose to speak, so he readied himself for whatever meaning might be revealed—and in whatever form it came.

Stinging pecks on his face could no longer be ignored. He opened his eyes and realized he'd been oblivious to what was happening around him. The valley had disappeared and the mountaintop was encased in white. Objects a few feet away were no longer visible.

In five minutes, the scene had changed so drastically that Obie rose in wonderment. He wasn't fearful; such squalls often came at that time of year. A few hundred feet down the trail the sun was probably shining. In any event, it was time to go. An answer to his prayer, if one ever came, would have to wait.

He loped down what he hoped was the path he'd followed going up. Snow was falling so fast that it covered the landscape and obscured familiar landmarks. He was aware of the sun's position and tried to detect deviance in light that might guide him. He hurried, hoping any moment to break from the squall and get his bearings. There was no panic yet, only the feeling of urgency to get down where he could see.

Sudden bitter cold, bourn on the snow-laden wind, whipped his face so hard it lost feeling. His eyelashes froze. His hands were numb, and his ears had lost feeling. Three layers of clothing on his upper body were inadequate. He needed to find the knapsack. There he had a hat, gloves, and an extra shirt.

When his boots crunched into thick growth, he realized he was off the trail and in trouble. How had it happened so quickly? He'd made all the wrong decisions; the first was coming here alone. He had two of the best teachers in the Adirondacks concerning wilderness survival. Forgetting their teaching had brought him to a situation he'd believed impossible—confusion and disorientation in the woods. What a fool he was.

He paused and leaned against a boulder, forcing himself to think. He was still above the tree line. Staying there with inadequate clothing meant he could freeze to death. Farther down, evergreens would provide shelter. He hesitated because he was desperate to find his knapsack. Matches would mean having a fire, and his bedroll could mean survival if the storm continued. He considered going right and left, zigzagging to find the trail.

Visibility was still near zero. He believed he was near the tree line but worried about where he was in relation to the trail. His location mattered because if he descended the wrong side toward Iroquois Peak, he would go farther into the wilderness. Darkness would come soon. His flashlight, so easily slipped into a pocket, was still in his pack. He swore at his stupidity.

Flat and expansive rock faces were covered by several inches of new snow. The usually slick surfaces that made walking difficult even in good weather, were now treacherous. Obie slid numerous times, once skidding on his hip. One pant leg had a rip, and he felt blood oozing through the seat of his trousers.

His hasty new plan was to travel down and to the left to find the trail. "Keep moving," he forced himself to say repeatedly. He watched for something familiar within his limited vision that indicated he was going in the right direction.

He slipped and fell again. This time he sat still. He accepted the reality; if he were to survive the night, he must locate a shelter. Why was this happening? *It appeared there was no answer to his prayer.* Did that mean that he had no future? "Is that it, Lord?" he said aloud.

He looked up, half expecting to glimpse an angel somewhere in the white; there was nothing. It was disheartening, and he reacted with a dispirited burst of anger. "If you do answer prayers, and I get off this mountain alive, I'll take that to mean you approve of me marrying Laura." He added, wanting to be sure God understood, "If you let me live, I'll keep all your commandments. I'll serve you however you wish."

He waited a while before struggling to his feet. *He was going to find that dammed trail.* Asking God for help was one thing, but he had to do his part. He plowed ahead, each step taking him onto terrain that became less rocky and more level.

Minutes later, though the still-blowing snow, he saw a sight he'd almost given up on. He rubbed ice from his eyelids. His snow-covered knapsack lay against the boulder where he had left it.

* * *

Cassie knocked on the windowpane for the third time; Ken Gainsworthy might be drunk. By the light from the fireplace, she could see him sitting in his rocker by the kitchen table. When he reached for the bottle on the table, she pounded harder on the glass. Slobber, inside, was barking. She was not about to give up. She had struggled up the road in the dark, having neglected to bring a flashlight. No light from the barnroom heightened her anxiety.

Ken finally turned in her direction. "What? Who's that?" he called.

"Mr. Gainsworthy. It's me, Cassie Hunt. Please come to the door."

She saw him rise and walk toward her. The door creaked open. "Come in, Cassie," he said. If he was inebriated, his voice didn't reveal it.

"I'm all muddy."

"Don't worry about it."

She followed him into the kitchen. Slobber licked her hand. Ken removed a pan from a hook without looking at her and started filling it with water from the faucet over the sink. "Want some tea?" he asked.

"No, thank you, Mr. Gainsworthy. I'm here to ask you about Obie."

"He's not here."

"Yes, sir, I know that. He told me where he was going this morning, but he wasn't on the bus coming home. Laura and I are worried because we've watched from across town for his light in the barn-room, and it hasn't been on. We thought you might know where he is."

"He went hiking in the Macintyres." He slurred the last word, revealing for the first time a degree of intoxication. "He went up Algonquin."

"He told me this morning he was going for the day. Did he tell you when he was coming back?"

"Soon, soon now. He said he'd be back for supper. He'll be home soon."

"It's nearly ten o'clock, Mr. Gainsworthy."

"Oh . . .!" Ken looked concerned. "He should've been home by now."

"Mr. Gainsworthy, did you know that it's raining . . . raining real hard? They said on the radio that it's snowing at higher elevations."

Worry showed on Ken's face. "No, I didn't know. Obie's not equipped for that weather. I'll have to get Abner and go look for him." He turned toward the coat rack near the side entrance. "I'll throw a few things together." He stumbled and nearly fell, catching himself on the sewing machine beside the doorway.

"No, Mr. Gainsworthy. It's all right. Dad and Laura are in the car down at the foot of your road. They're waiting for me. Dad already has a plan."

Ken cleared his throat. "I can take care of it."

"Please, Obie's our friend. We want to help."

Ken hesitated. "What kind of plan?"

"Dad has already talked to Pastor Charles who will alert some men in case they're needed. We're going to drive on the road as far as we can. If Obie hasn't shown up there, we'll call Pastor Charles to send searchers." She had a burning sensation in the pit of her stomach. Could it really be happening that Obie's life might be in danger?

"I'll go with you," Ken said.

"We need you to stay here in case Obie comes home. We could miss him on the way."

She wasn't sure how Ken would respond. He stared at her a few seconds before saying, "All right. I'll wait here."

"Thank you, Mr. Gainsworthy. If he shows up, send him down to Pastor Charles, and he'll get in touch with us."

Ken nodded. He wasn't too drunk to see the logic in the plan.

She made her way back to the car and they left at once. Cassie had never known her father to drive so fast. She tried to see inside every car they met on the road as they traveled, but darkness and constant rain obscured her vision. Laura was crying.

They found him on the Loj road, a hundred yards short of the state highway. With his knapsack slung over one shoulder, he plodded along with a dazed expression. Cassie shed tears of joy at seeing him. Laura jumped from the car ahead of her and put her arms around him. He was soaked and shivering when he got in the car.

He sat between the girls on the way home, stealing heat from their bodies. Cassie didn't mind at all. Through chattering teeth, he told them of his walk down the mountain trail through the snow, slush, and finally mud. He had failed to find anybody at the Loj and kept going.

"Guess I wasn't thinking too clearly."

"We're just glad you're okay, youngster," Pinky said over his shoulder.

"It was stupid going up there alone. I should've known better."

"If it's any consolation, you're not the first experienced mountaineer to get caught like that."

Cassie sensed Laura snuggling up to Obie. "I was so worried about you," her sister said in a soft voice. "I'd die if anything happened to you."

Cassie felt him relax into a heap, emitting an audible sigh. She wanted to be angry with Laura but was so glad Obie was safe that the effort failed.

"Tell us everything that happened," Cassie said.

Obie was quiet for a long time. She repeated her question, thinking he might not have heard.

"It was quite an experience."

"Well, tell us." She tried not to show impatience. Sometimes, talking to Obie was exasperating.

"Maybe later."

Something had happened on the mountain, something he was reluctant to discuss. Nevertheless, she was confident about getting the whole story from him later. Her mother had left for Boston earlier in the week to visit a sister? What would she say when she found out they'd helped Obie—as she most certainly would?

CHAPTER TWELVE

Winter 1943

After four games, the rest of the Evergreen High School basketball season was canceled. Gasoline rationing made team travel unseemly to school administrators, even for short distances. In addition, four senior players had already left to join the military services. There was disappointment bordering on outrage among the remaining players because not all regional high schools had taken such drastic steps.

Nevertheless, the cancellation affected Obie positively; he could be home more. The period following Christmas took on a quiet, slow pace. His father had taken a carpentry job in Lake Placid and was coming home once a week. He'd been home a whole week at Christmas.

Dreams came to Obie some nights—primarily pleasant ones carrying him away to warm, sunlit villages where everyone spoke kindly and offered him delicious food and drink; others took him to mountaintops reached without effort, peaks that afforded him a view far beyond any mountain he'd ever climbed.

One dream, however, caused some disquiet: He was in the barnroom painting a portrait of Laura; bush strokes came effortlessly, almost magically laying down layers of paint in just the right hews, shades, and proportions. He was pleased with the results and rushed to show Laura. She asked him why he had painted a portrait of Cassie. He looked at it from every angle, but it was always Laura he saw on the canvas. She stalked away in anger.

Did dreams have meaning? His mother had thought they did. She liked telling Obie about dreams that she believed foretold future events in her life. He'd listened attentively when he was small, but as he grew older, he began expressing doubts.

Now, he remembered a conversation shortly before her death. She had said, "You are right to have questions, Obie. Not all dreams have meaning. Some are just our minds turning over things we heard or thought about during the day. Your father has bad dreams when he eats too much cabbage for dinner. But, maybe some dreams do have meaning. Maybe we will not know that until later when something happens that makes us remember the dream."

His dream about the painting nagged at him for days. *Was God telling him something? Was such a thing even possible?* Pastor Charles also seemed to believe in the power of dreams.; he pointed out several places in the Bible where dreams were prophetic and meaningful.

What could his crazy dream possibly mean? It defied logic. But so did prayer—and he believed sincerely in that.

Some of Obie's friends were not blessed with the tranquility he enjoyed. Tommy Matthews had agreed to stay on the family farm and brooded over that decision. Ed Baumgartner was applying to colleges in the East; he wanted to major in history and never tired of talking about it, worrying that no good school would accept him because of his erratic high school grades. His father, longtime mayor of Stafford Rest, was applying pressure. Ed told Obie his father believed being in college might be a way to avoid or delay the draft.

Chuck Hinky, who'd long since dropped out of school, was awaiting a county court appearance about some items he'd "picked up" near a house in Evergreen. "I thought they'd been abandoned," Chuck told Obie. "Wasn't worth much, anyway . . . just some old pipes and fittings. Anyway, I'm joining the Marines. They'll let me go when I tell them that."

Ernie Boswell's amorous nature had landed him in a thorny predicament. Cora Stringer, a girl he'd been dating in Evergreen, was pregnant. "I'm in big trouble!" Ernie told his friends one night after they gathered in his hideaway, a storage building adjoining his father's store. They sat in old overstuffed chairs in a semicircle. Several small boats wintering in the warm place surrounded the little group.

"What're you going to do?" Ed asked.

"What can I do? I have to marry her." Ernie picked nervously at a cotton segment on a tear in his chair arm before getting up and going to a Hoosier cabinet a few steps away.

"There's other ways," Chuck said. "There's doctors down in Albany or New York who can take care of the problem."

"It's too late for that. Our parents know." Ernie paused long enough to remove several Baby Ruth candy bars from the cabinet and pass them out, along with bottles of warm root beer, items that Obie guessed were filched from the store. "Mr. Stringer said he'd shoot me if I don't marry his little girl, and Dad said he'd pump in a second bullet."

Chuck was insistent. "I'd take her to a doctor in Albany, anyway, if I was you."

"Getting married is the right thing to do, I guess." Obie had never seen Ernie look so beaten down.

"Be glad it wasn't that other girl you knocked up . . . that Frances Gibbons?" Chuck said.

Ernie's countenance changed, and for a few seconds Obie thought he might hit Chuck, but Ernie said, "I've never touched Frances. She wouldn't let me. She let me kiss her once or twice, that's all." Ernie stalked off a few feet, looking miserable.

After that, the subject seemed forgotten. But Obie knew Ernie; he worried about his friend's state of mind.

Obie's tranquility had limits. In addition to schoolwork, he cleared snow from roofs of a dozen summer residences on Indian Knob and performed routine chores at Abner's farm. While he felt little pressure from those activities, he tried without much success to ignore a hovering uncertainty about conditions over which he had no control. America was deep into the war. His father brought home a radio with a large battery to power it. Obie listened to war news, marking the progress of armies on a wall map given to him by one of his teachers.

Even with the Allies entrenched in Africa, the Russians driving the Germans from their country, and the initial bombing of Germany, a quick victory wasn't assured. Success in the vast Pacific seemed even more elusive. Boys and men he knew had died, and the wounded were starting to return with tales about the fighting and the conditions in the battle zones. Lem Venturi had been home for a month, the stub of his left leg covered by pinned-up trousers. Lem spent hours each day in the Diamond Inn with his crutches leaning against the bar.

Obie's days were not all engrossed in school, work, or in thinking about the war. Since his ill-fated mountain hike the previous fall, Laura had been much friendlier. She even saved a seat for him on the bus. As opportunities came, he made awkward attempts to get closer to her and to find ways to express his feelings.

Although that goal was elusive, his confidence grew. They were in the same study hall at school and had been sitting together since the Christmas break. Once, at the big library table, his bare arm contacted hers. Obie had an open book before him and Laura was writing in her notebook. He sat still to see what she'd do. She moved her arm a little, brushing lightly against the hairs of his arm. It caused a tingling throughout his body. Glancing at her, he could see that her eyes were half-closed and she was smiling. Obie resolved to find opportunities to be alone with her.

He'd expected a reaction from her mother after the Algonquin experience. None came. Abigail must know about it since the whole town knew. Locals had kidded Obie about being rescued by two girls. If the sisters had endured Abigail's anger for the part they played, they hadn't told him. He saw Abigail in Mercer's General Store and made a point to speak. She glanced away, pretending not to have heard.

The dead of winter brought cold that persisted. Obie planned Saturday ski excursions into the woods. When Laura and Cassie found out, they asked to go along. On a few Saturdays, the trio traveled around the ridge circling the town, engrossed in a world of their own creation, knowing their laughter would likely be heard by no humans but themselves.

They usually started their journey above Obie's house, skied the nearly two miles around the ridge, and emerged at the highway above the Hunt house. Obie always left the girls there and skied back along the trail alone.

On one particularly frigid Saturday afternoon, Laura begged off, and Obie was ready to put his skis away when Cassie challenged him to make the trek, anyway. They stopped to rest at about the halfway point over the high cliffs at the back end of the Morass. They were breathing hard after the quarter-mile gradual climb to the highest point on the east ridge. Wisps of white vapor shimmered about their heads.

Cassie laughed. "We made good time, didn't we, Obie? Laura would have held us back."

"Oh, I don't know about that. Laura's good at this, too," he said, feeling he should defend her even though he knew Cassie was probably right.

"She's not tough, like you and me."

"She's tough enough. Cassie, you shouldn't denigrate your sister."

"*Denigrate?* You're showing off, using big words?"

She was right. He'd used the word in a school newspaper article but had never said it aloud. *Why would he try impressing Cassie that way?* "Sorry," he said.

"It's okay. I already know you're smarter than me. What's it mean, anyway . . . make fun of her?"

"Something like that."

"Laura's my sister, and I love her. I wouldn't *denigrate* her except in fun."

As their breathing returned to normal, Cassie asked, "Obie, we're really good friends, aren't we, the three of us?"

"Of course we are?"

"And you and me?"

"Good friends, yes."

"And we all three love one another?"

"Yes."

He pounded the sides of his skis against a rock to rid them of accumulated ice and prepared to go. She said, "What is love, Obie? What do you think it is?"

He started to give a quick reply of the kind he knew she'd appreciate, but her expression told him that this wasn't her usual Cassie-type question; she was looking for a serious answer. He'd discussed this very subject with Pastor Charles.

"The Apostle Paul said that love is kind and isn't puffed up. He said it believes . . . and hopes."

"What else?"

"Well, let's see, I think Paul said it endures and is patient."

She looked away and he thought he heard her say, "I've been patient." Turning back, she asked, "Obie, who do you love more, Laura or me?"

The conversation had turned awkward. "Cassie, you shouldn't ask me a question like that. I love you both. There's more than one kind of love, you know. I love my friends, and there's the love a boy feels for a girl . . . you know what I mean."

She stood a long time, her eyes never leaving his face. Her mouth moved, trying to form words. They finally came. "Obie, I'd like you to kiss me."

Her request startled him, and he tried to think of ways he could change the subject. She stepped close, her upturned face near his, expectant. He kissed her cheek.

"No," she said, "like this." Her mouth found his. Her eyes were closed. He started to pull away but didn't. Despite the weather, her lips were warm. Finally, he stepped back, a little dizzy. Why would he kiss Cassie when it should be Laura he was kissing?

She was smiling. "I never kissed a boy before, except Ben Quackenbush when we played 'spin the bottle' at Katie Hanover's party. That doesn't count, though. I was in sixth grade."

"Well, I never kissed a girl before . . . ever."

"Really?"

"Never."

"Didn't you like it?

"Sure, it was okay."

She squeezed his arm. "Let's do it again."

Without asking himself why, he pulled her close. Her breath was sweet, and her lips moved eagerly against his. This time, her eyes were open, and her pale blue irises seemed to engulf him. For an instant, he felt he was falling into a yawning blue hole.

Cassie broke the spell. She pushed him away and laughed. "I can't wait to tell Laura about this."

"Cassie, *please* don't do that. Promise me."

"Why should I promise? Are you ashamed of kissing me?"

"Ashamed, no. But we wouldn't want her thinking we were in love or something like that and not just friends."

Cassie stared down at the windblown rock surface. "No, I guess we wouldn't want her to think that."

They skied the rest of the way in relative silence. Later, as he followed their tracks back along the trail alone, he wondered why kissing Cassie had made him feel that way; she was just pranking him; that was her way. He must straighten out his thinking. *It was Laura he loved.*

* * *

"You haven't been attending Sunday school. Why not?"

Pastor Charles was pretending anger. Obie had recently become a full-fledged member of Stafford Rest Methodist Church. The preacher had told him the day after Christmas that he should "make a choice." He'd not attended church in Evergreen since the Mass following his mother's death. Father Brennan had twice come to Stafford Rest to tell him he needed to be confirmed, a process that would require him to finish his study and pass an examination.

Obie made a quick decision. The distance to Evergreen was a factor, but he'd also concluded that Catholicism, a suitable choice for many people including his mother's family, was not the way for him. In addition, he had a compelling desire to attend services with Stafford Rest people.

Pastor Charles probed again. "Why aren't you attending? I sat in last Sunday, and Miss Bell said you hadn't been there for some time. What's going on?"

Obie hesitated. Abigail Hunt's hand was on everything in the church, and saying something against her was a sure way of heaping trouble on his own head. And he suspected that Pastor Charles would defend her.

"I just decided to quit."

The preacher stared him down. "I don't believe that at all. You enjoyed the class too much to just up and leave it. Tell me the truth, Obadiah."

Lying was a way out. The promise made on Algonquin about lying and about other things had proved impossible to keep. He'd told no one about it and regretted having made such vows.

"Pastor, Charles, I . . ."

"It has something to do with Laura Hunt, doesn't it?"

There it was again. His father had known. Maybe the whole world knew his business.

"I'd rather not talk about it," he said, unsuccessful in keeping a defiant edge from his voice.

"It's nothing to be ashamed of. She's a lovely young lady."

"How did you know?"

"That's not hard. I see the way you look at her."

"Pastor Charles, I know you mean to help, and I appreciate all you've done for me, but I'd rather not discuss *this.*"

Pastor Charles's expression was one of compassion. "Obadiah, I'm not at liberty to tell you the source, but I do know a little about this situation. I know Mrs. Hunt doesn't want her daughters to be, how do I say this without offending . . . quite so friendly with you."

"Cassie told you, didn't she?"

The preacher ignored the question. "Mrs. Hunt worries that the three of you might be getting too close, isn't that it?"

"Worse. She doesn't want me anywhere near them. She hates me."

"'Hate' is a strong word, Obadiah, and Christians should use it sparingly. Nevertheless, I realize there's some animosity. Have you done something to cause it?"

"No! Never."

"Obadiah, I ask you this as your pastor, and it'll go no further. Have you ever made improper advances toward either Cassie or Laura or even done anything that might be interpreted as improper?"

"No, I haven't." He wondered, briefly, if kissing Cassie last week had been improper. It had been her doing, anyway. "Never," he added.

"I believe you. And I believe you do care for Laura. Don't be ashamed of it. Young love happens to most of us."

Pastor Charles inspired confidence. "I do love her," Obie said, his voice unsteady. "I love Cassie too, but not in the same way I love Laura. Mom worked for the Hunts for years, and the three of us practically grew up together. We've been best friends all our lives."

"I hope you're not confusing love and lust?" Not knowing how to answer, Obie remained silent. The preacher continued. "If you had to guess, why do you think Mrs. Hunt feels the way she does?"

Obie had shared too much to back away from the truth. "Laura and Cassie told me she thinks my family is beneath hers. 'Beneath' is the word she used."

Pastor Charles tapped a pencil against his chin. Maybe he'd not believe it. His words followed a sigh. "What a terrible thing to say about anyone, much less about a young boy. Obadiah, is that why you're not attending Sunday school? Is it because you feel you have to avoid the girls?"

"They said their mother wanted them to drop out because I was in the class. I told them I would, instead."

"I see. That's generous of you. I'll speak to Mrs. Hunt."

"Please don't. It'll only make it worse. I see them at school, and other times, too. Don't make her mad at you."

"I can handle Mrs. Hunt, Obadiah. Now, do you want to talk about what else is bothering you? For the last three months, you've had something on your mind . . . ever since you were lost on the mountain."

"I wasn't lost. Just turned around."

"That's beside the point. *What happened up there?* You know I'll keep at you until you tell me." He smiled.

"You're pretty smart, Pastor Charles."

"Not smart, Obadiah, just observant. It's part of my job to know what's going on in my flock."

Once again, Obie found himself willing to pour out his secrets to this man. "Something did happen," he said. Obie told him about thinking he might die and about making promises to God before finding his way off the mountain.

"And you feel like you were trapped into making a promise you can't keep?"

"Yes, that's it. It's exactly how I feel. How did you know?"

The preacher laughed. "When I was twelve years old, I nearly drowned. As I was going down for what was surely the last time, I cried out to God the same way you did. My father reached in and pulled me up just in time. My earthly father, that is."

"Is that why you became a minister?"

"Oh, no, not at all. I did go through a guilt phase, the same kind you're going through, but it was years before I felt the call to ministry. There's something you should know, Obadiah. Your experience isn't uncommon. Most folks get into situations where they make such promises. Those promises are usually broken. I believe God expects that to happen."

"You mean God wants us to break promises?"

"No, he doesn't want that, but he understands when we promise out of fear. He doesn't hold us accountable for such a human failing. The important thing is that we call on him. It shows our faith, our belief in him, and in his ability to help us."

"So, I don't have to worry about going to Hell because I can't keep my promise?"

Pastor Charles laughed again. "No, Obadiah, you're not going to Hell because of it. I must warn you, though, that some promises to God are not to be taken lightly."

"Not the ones I made on Algonquin, though?" Obie wanted to understand with certainty that he was in the clear.

"You're absolved," the pastor said as he waved an airy hand over Obie's head. "The promise I'm talking about is one you've thought about, and prayed about, not one you make under duress. And keep in mind that the experience you had might be an indication that God wants to lead you into his plans. How do you feel about the things you promised, especially about your promise to serve him as he wishes . . . and to keep his commandments?"

"I want to do those things if I can. But is anybody ever good enough?"

"We can be good enough to try. John Wesley, the founder of our Methodist faith, talked about 'going on to perfection.' Wesley knew nobody ever gets there, not in this life."

"Thanks for telling me all this, Pastor Charles. I feel better about it."

"I'll pray for you, Obadiah, not only for your relationship with the Hunt family but also that you may be led into a field of service to God and his kingdom."

"Thank you. I believe in prayer."

"Did anything else happen up there on the mountain?"

Obie hadn't mentioned anything about Laura being the reason for most of his promises to God. He'd keep that to himself.

"No, nothing else."

"Everyone has a purpose in this life. God wants you for something, Obadiah. Keep your heart and mind open for what it might be."

CHAPTER THIRTEEN

Winter 1943

Bitterly cold air rolled in on an overnight snowstorm. Obie was out early breaking a path across frozen Diamond Lake, the shortest winter route to Abner's. The clear sky was brightest in the east, waiting for the sun to peak the hills. Portable shanties sat scattered and silent on both sides of his path, white hoods hanging from their roofs. Fishermen would be out later in the day to clear snow off the shanties and reopen frozen fishing holes.

He climbed off the lakebed at Abner's dock and lifted his boots high to traverse the unbroken path leading up to the house. Once there, he stood in front of the big fireplace recovering the feeling on his face. Abner was at the barn. Grandfather Jacob sat in a rocking chair near the stone hearth, a shawl around his thin shoulders. Claire offered Obie breakfast. He declined but accepted a mug of hot chocolate.

"I thought you'd be shoveling off rooves this morning," Claire said.

"I'll get to it later. I wanted to come and see Grandpa first."

Jacob heard and motioned Obie to a chair beside him. Obie kissed his cheek before sitting.

"How are you today, Grandpa?"

"Better, I guess."

For months following Prissy Gainsworthy's death, Jacob had appeared to waste away, eating little and maintaining an uncharacteristic silence. Gradually, over nearly four years, he had regained an interest in life and people. Claire had told Obie that Jacob looked forward to his visits, so he tried to get there at least twice a week. During those visits, Obie gained new insight into his grandfather's thinking. Underneath a rough exterior accented by old-fashioned ways, there lay deep insight and intelligence. Jacob had the heart of a poet, and Obie fed that at every opportunity.

"Grandpa, the lake's beautiful today."

"Um . . . tell me what it's like."

"The snow sparkles with the morning light on it, and little puffs of wind stir up crystals on top. And, it's awfully quiet, except sometimes you can hear crows cawing in the distance and hear an occasional hawk whistle."

Jacob closed his eyes and was quiet. "Is it awfully cold?" he finally asked.

"So cold that my nostrils stuck together when I breathed hard. And the wind made my eyeballs hurt." Obie wondered if he might be overdoing the word pictures.

Jacob shivered as though experiencing the conditions that Obie described. "Obie, you're a good boy. You'll go far."

"What do you mean Grandpa . . . go far?"

Claire moved off to a corner, but Obie knew she was listening. She loved her father-in-law and protected him from conversations she considered stressful.

Today, Jacob appeared anxious to talk. "Most folks would think it meant making a heap of money or being some big-shot in politics. It's not that at all. It means having a family to love and to love you. It means being able to help out somebody that needs help. That's the life that'll make you happy."

"Money's not a bad thing, though, is it?"

"Depends. They call it a medium of exchange. Just be careful what you exchange it for. You can buy things for yourself, and you can buy things for other folks." He paused. "Which do you figure is better, Obie?"

"If I had money, I'd use it to make my life easier. But I'm sure there's satisfaction in helping others worse off." Obie felt a ping of guilt at giving those two positions equal weight? He had no compelling wish to give money away.

Jacob said, "You've got the right idea, only more of the 'helping' part than the 'getting.'"

"Grandpa, are you saying that the less we have, the better? If that's the case, I should be really, really happy."

Obie heard Claire's soft laughter. Jacob grinned. "No, we need some things, and certain comforts are good, but we shouldn't want much more than we need."

"Is that the way you've lived, Grandpa?"

"Pretty much. Prissy, your grandma, she insisted on having a way to wash clothes. She cried when we came here because she was so happy that Abner had put electricity in the houses and she could have a clothes washer."

"I understand how Grandma must have felt." He did understand; heating water on the stove, pouring it into a washtub, and using a washboard to scrub out the dirt was his Monday evening ritual.

Jacob sighed. "I should have done more to make her life easier. Maybe doing good to others can be overdone when it affects the ones you love. I should have spent less time traipsing through the woods and more with her."

His grandfather's reference to his occupation brought to mind a conversation with Pinky Hunt. Obie searched his memory until he found a name. "Grandpa, tell me about a man named Templeton. Pinky Hunt told me you saved his life. Is that true?"

"Bernard Templeton . . . a long time ago."

The soft light from the fireplace flickered against Jacob's aged face as he told the story about a deer kicking the side out of their canoe and how the two men nearly drowned before they reached shore. The narrative didn't differ substantially from how Pinky had told it, except that Jacob downplayed his part. "He'd likely of made it to shore anyway," he said.

"Were you friends a long time?"

"We was. He was rich, but he was the kind of man I like, doing what he could to help other people. We talked about that a lot. Me and him, we got along real good." Jacob appeared pensive before saying, "Obie, I've got a question for you."

"Yes, sir."

"If somebody was to give you a whole big pile of money . . . money you hadn't earned by your own sweat, what would you do with it?"

Obie was intrigued by the question. Had Templeton given Jacob money that he'd then given away? Was his grandfather testing him?

"Grandpa, you're not going to give me a whole big pile of money, are you?"

Jacob tilted his head back and laughed. "No, sir! I am not! Even if I had it to give, I wouldn't. I'm a believer that everybody ought to make their own way if they can. I was just curious about what you thought."

"I suppose I'd give some of it to needy people. I'd be generous." He had a troubling thought that his grandfather's idea of "generous" might differ from his own.

Jacob hadn't finished probing. "How would you know how much to give?"

Since he had no real money except the two dollars in his billfold, answering the question felt as meaningless as trying to explain how much water ran down Cedar Creek every day. Pleasing his grandfather was important, however. "Pastor Charles talks about tithing. That's ten percent. He says the Bible teaches that." Obie had become uncomfortable with the subject and hoped that would be the end of it.

Jacob smiled, sat back in his chair, and said, "I heard that you're going regularly to the Methodist church." Obie had given his grandfather that information several times. Jacob was getting more forgetful. At nearly one-hundred-one years of age, he could be forgiven.

"Yes, I have been, for three years." He told Jacob the story again, of his friendship with Pastor Charles and how it had come about.

"So, he took you under his wing, did he?"

"He's been really good to me. Taught me a lot, too."

"What's he taught you, Obie?"

"Church stuff, planning out my life course, things like that."

"What's that life course look like?" Obie detected a hint of rare sarcasm in Jacob's tone.

"Oh, he doesn't try to push me into things I don't want or that I'm not suited for, but he does think I'm suited for religious service of some kind."

"Um . . . you don't say. Like being a minister?"

"Oh, no. Nothing like that. Grandpa, I haven't settled on my life's work. How I serve God doesn't have to be connected to how I earn a living."

"I figured you'd be a painter . . . artist that makes pictures."

"Yes, I'm interested in that."

"You're a smart boy. I guess you have lots of choices."

The mention of painting reminded him of his troubling dream. He wondered what Jacob would think about it. It was a chance to get an opinion from someone who'd experienced many dreams. "Grandpa, do you think dreams mean something?"

"You mean like telling the future?"

"Something like that. Or warnings, maybe?"

Jacob was quiet so long that Obie thought he wasn't going to answer. Finally, he said, "I think God works in any and every way he chooses. I don't put any limit on what God can do. I think a dream would be a good way he'd choose to tell us something. Fact is, he's done just that in the scriptures, and more than once."

"Paster Charles said the Bible of full of people having dreams."

"Did you have a dream like that?

Obie considered giving Jacob the details of his dream, something he'd revealed to no one, but then decided that it was too personal to share. "Oh, I have dreams all the time. Nothing important, though."

Jacob pulled his shawl tighter around his shoulders. Claire rose and went behind him. "Papa, do you want to move closer to the fire?"

"No, I'm all right."

"Maybe you should lie down and rest awhile?"

"No, Obie and me are having us a good discussion. Keeps his mind growin' and mine goin'." He laughed at his own play on words and waved Claire off. "Obie, I'm just happy that you want to serve God."

"Mom told me that it's the best way to live."

"Vi was a wonder for this family. I'm glad that you don't want to be a preacher."

"Why is that, Grandpa?"

"Because they all get to be narrow-minded."

"Narrow-minded? I don't know what . . ."

"What's the opposite of 'narrow,' Obie?" Jacob had a knack for keeping him off balance.

"'Wide,' I guess."

"Well, I'm all for wide churches, wide preachers, wide Christians, for that matter."

Obie had already gleaned random knowledge about Jacob's divergent religious views. The family seemed embarrassed about it. He wanted to know more. "Do you disagree with the doctrine of the church? Is that it?"

"I have my differences with some church people. And I don't go to church anymore, but that's because Prissy's not here to go with me." He paused, looking a little confused. "And I never was much of a church-goer. But not going to church don't make me an unbeliever. Me and God talk together a lot. Our best talks are in the woods. At least they used to be when I could get there." Jacob sighed. "Now we can talk as we enjoy the mountains through that window yonder." He pointed to a window on the north side by the stairway entrance. Obie had found Jacob there several times.

"Are you saying you don't like churches, Grandpa?"

"Oh, no, sir, I'm *not* saying that. Churches are good. The idea of being together with other believing folks is Jim Dandy. Christians have been getting together since the early days. I used to enjoy that part of it, and I've made heaps of friends in church." Jacob's voice took on a somber tone. "But there's a danger that creeps in on cougar feet." He paused.

"And what is that, Grandpa?"

"Folks become drawn-in, come to believe certain ways . . . doctrine that gets too important in their own eyes. Thinking like that builds up walls that keep out folks who might believe another way . . . or keep people in who'd benefit by associating with someone outside their own barricades. Churches build walls. They ought to take down most of them walls."

"I don't think Methodists are like that?"

Jacob's voice rose and had an uncharacteristic bite to it. "Of course they are! Just like Baptists, Episcopalians, Dutch Reformed, and all the other denominations all over these Adirondacks."

"Pastor Charles says we need to follow God's rules. "Defend the faith," he says."

"I know what he says. He's been coming over here. We discuss . . . and argue about things sometimes. What he's defending is church doctrine, not faith. He's not as bad as some, though. He don't think he has all the answers. The thing is, he still don't try to see beyond."

"See beyond?"

"Beyond, to something that's more important."

"What's that, Grandpa?"

Jacob chuckled. "The fact is, I don't really know . . . and that's my point. It's beyond my knowing and everybody's knowing. I do know that there's something there and that it's bigger than you and me . . . bigger than anything. Sometimes I can feel it, something grand. I figure I'll know more about it soon enough."

"Grandpa, you're doing just fine. You'll be with us a long time yet."

If Jacob had heard, he gave no indication. The topic seemed to have invigorated him. He said, "I think what you call 'defending the faith' is a waste of time. What some folks call faith, ain't. They confuse faith with 'knowing.' They think they need to know everything about God to have faith in him, so they build up a whole set of rules about how they have to live and act. It becomes a way of looking at God and becomes their way of understanding him. Real faith's simpler. It's believing God is here, there, and everywhere and that he loves us. We don't need doctrine for that. It's what we can feel without knowing a whole heap about it. I believe love is what it is. *Love's what matters, Obie.* It's not about following made-up rules."

His grandfather's words rubbed elbows with truth, as though hearing something already known, but something he couldn't quite remember, much less understand. Nevertheless, he wasn't going to toss away all he'd learned from Father Brennan and Pastor Charles.

"I don't know, Grandpa. I think strict rules are important. They're like bookends keeping things in their proper place."

"There might be some truth in that, but the trouble with bookends is they only keep a little bunch of things together, like the pretty little things Prissy kept in boxes. I took some of them out recently and put them on the shelf in the dining room where we can see them. They remind me of her." He stopped, looking confused, before continuing. "Churches keep God in a box. The Methodist box, the Catholic box, the Lutheran box. They all have rules that make people see God in ways that keeps him small. Jews, they have their boxes, too."

"But wouldn't everything fall apart without rules? We need rules, don't we?"

Jacob shrugged and looked exasperated by Obie's ignorance. "There are certain beliefs Christians ought to have, but there's not near as many as preachers try to make you think. All that stuff stands in the way of us being *real* children of God. People spend too much time defending their doctrines instead of loving and caring for one another."

"You might be right, but I think people at church would be upset if you suggested changing their ways of thinking."

Jacob laughed. "I did that once, and I bore the scars for a mite spell. Now I'm careful who hears my views." He became quiet for a moment before saying with renewed vigor, "Look here, Obie, I know that some folks need that kind of religion. Without it, they'd not be practicing their Christian faith. So, for them, it's okay. I don't judge."

Jacob slumped and appeared to have finally tired of the subject. The conversation had taken on more depth than any he'd ever had with Jacob—or with anyone. He hoped he'd have another opportunity to talk like this with his grandfather.

After briefly staring into the fire, Jacob said, "Obie, you have a long life ahead of you. I just want the best for you. You'll do well."

"Thank you, Grandpa. *You've* had a long life. Why do you think you've lived so long?"

Jacob scratched his beard. "Because God has let me. Well now, that's true, but there's more to it. I think it's because I make wine." He stopped, seemingly to let the words sink in. Claire was shaking her head and smiling.

Obie said, "I didn't know you drank wine, Grandpa, let alone make it."

"He don't," Claire whispered. "Neither one."

Jacob tossed his head, indicating he'd heard. "It's symbolic. That's the way I meant it."

"Wine takes a long time. Is that what you mean?"

"In a manner of speaking. When you make wine, you're planning for the future. What's the big word people use . . . optimism? Making wine is being optimistic. You've got something good out there. It might take a little time to get to it, but you've got the hopes of it. You're patient."

"So, having good things to look forward to has allowed you to live a long time?"

"It sure has helped. You have to have hope, even if you never get to drink the wine. It's the belief that you will that counts. It's a choice, boy . . . you have to decide whether or not to make wine."

"Are you still making wine, Grandpa?"

"The fact is, I've had my time in life to enjoy my wine. Prissy was my excellent wine. For me, there'll never be a vintage like her." He stared into the fireplace for a few seconds before saying, "There *are* other wines, though. I'd like to see how you turn out." He grinned, showing his few remaining front teeth.

"Our teachers talk about goal-setting. Is that like making wine?"

"I suppose it is, but you have to do more than *set* goals. You have to work to reach your goals. You'll need to do more than think about it to make it real. Same with wine. Lots of work between the vine and the table." He stopped a moment. "Do you have a girl yet?"

The question startled Obie. "Oh, I don't know," he stammered. "I know some girls."

"The one with the yellow hair I've seen you with, Pinky's daughter. She reminds me of Prissy . . . your grandmother. Maybe she'll be your wine."

"She's a good friend, Grandpa, that's all." He felt that his words were true, but in his imagination, he saw Cassie's upturned face and felt her soft lips against his.

Jacob studied his face. "Don't ever give up on your dreams, Obie, whatever they are. Be a winemaker."

His grandfather slumped in his chair and his watchdog came forward. "Papa, you should rest awhile."

"And I should be going," Obie said as he reached for his parka. "I have lots to do, Aunt Claire. Tell Uncle Abner I was here. Grandpa, I'll see you again soon."

"You're a good boy, Obie. We had us a real good talk."

Obie took the Lake Road back to town, walking in the tracks of a few vehicles that had already passed that way. He pondered his conversation with Jacob.

He admired Jacob's spirit, the way he'd bounced back from great loss. Nevertheless, his views on religion were strange, too simplistic, loose, and undisciplined. There was, however, the ring of truth in some of Jacob's arguments. Someone who'd been alive a hundred years would have gained a great deal of wisdom. Obie was glad that such questions were not anything he'd likely have to deal with—or even think about. Still, he was already looking forward to his next conversation with Jacob.

CHAPTER FOURTEEN

June 1943

On a warm Saturday morning in June, Obie climbed to the ridge above his home to paint. Lake and village dominated the middle ground from where he set up his easel. The high peaks were behind him and not visible; he went less often to the other side of the ridge for that northern view. Smaller mountains rose in the east, revealing shadows and highlights which would change throughout the day. Views along the ridge varied, not only day-to-day but from month to month and season to season An artist could paint here for a lifetime; *maybe that was what he would do.*

The fact that his grandfather's land bordered state land was convenient. According to his father, Jacob's ten acres on Blackberry Hill had once been pasture land for horses. The property, which extended to the hilltop, had been acquired twenty years earlier. Jacob and Prissy never used it for anything but a place to live quiet lives. Obie's parents, after moving there, cleared a quarter acre on the gentle slope above the house for a vegetable garden and pruned a small orchard of long-neglected McIntosh and Northern Spy apple trees. Higher still, on the steeper grade, profusely-growing blackberry bushes produced sizeable sweet fruit. Ken speculated that someone had planted the bushes; whether before or after the resident horses was unclear.

The berry patch recognized no artificial boundaries and had gradually invaded state land. No one cared, and the Gainsworthys treated it all as their own. Blackberries grew in other locations, particularly on the ridge and behind the Morass by the cliffs, but they were smaller and of a mouth-puckering quality. Blackberry Hill berries rivaled any commercial variety. Villagers went there in July and early August. On nearly any sunny day during that time Obie saw people of all ages walking up and down the path with pails in their hands. He'd picked enough every summer for his mother to make pints of jam to last through the year and even some to give away. His father had asked Jacob if he wanted to keep people off the land.

"Let them have their berries," Jacob said. "Folks have been going up there a long time. They don't hurt anything."

Obie's chosen location for painting this day was not one previously used. After laying down a light undercoat on his canvas, he roughed in the scene with charcoal and was mixing paint on his palette when he heard movement behind him. He whirled as two figures closed in, one from either side. Cassie reached him first, snarling in imitation of some wild animal. Her arm hit his palette, and it went flying. Laura came from the other side, grabbed his arms, and pinned them to his sides. All three rolled in the grass, their laughter loud enough to upset crows along the ridge a hundred yards away.

"Now, look what you've done," Obie growled after disengaging himself from the chaos. "Serves you both right if you got paint on you."

Laura stood and looked down to ensure she'd escaped such a mishap. "We tried to sneak up on you," she said.

"Well, you succeeded."

"We stopped by the house," Laura said. "I looked in the barn-room and saw that your painting materials were gone, so I thought you'd be up here."

Cassie picked up the palette. "Sorry, the paint has dirt in it."

"It's okay. I have more paint." He scraped the ruined paint onto the remnant of an old shirt. "But I don't have enough yellow ochre for what I want to do. I guess you're not going to let me do any painting today, anyway."

Laura turned to Cassie. "Why don't you go down to the barn-room and get Obie the paint he needs?"

"Why don't *you* go, Laura?"

"You're the one who knocked it out of his hands. You should go. What do you need, Obie?"

"Yellow ochre. But you don't have to do that, Cassie." He'd already convinced himself that today's painting session was a lost cause. "I'll paint another time."

Cassie looked uncertain. "Did I make you spill it, Obie? I don't remember. But if I did, I'll go get you some more."

Opportunities to be alone with Laura seldom came. It would take at least twenty minutes to go down, find the paint, and walk back. Twenty minutes alone with Laura would be a gift from Heaven. The temptation was too great. "I'm afraid so, Cassie."

"All right. Give me instructions." Her scrunched-up mouth indicated her reluctance to leave.

"The tube of yellow ochre is in the black box under my bed. If it's not there, look in the burlap bag that hangs on the nail by the window." Another bit of deception; the paint *was* in the bag, but the misdirection would buy him another minute or so with Laura. "I could use some more white, too," he added. "It's in one of those places."

When Cassie had left, Laura turned to Obie. "Let's go sit," she said, pointing to a large flat stone formation near the rocky cliff that extended below them.

He took her hand to help her onto the rock. She wore shorts, which was unwise, considering the black fly population. Up here, though, the breeze helped clear them out. He couldn't help staring at her shapely legs.

They sat, making small talk about school and the coming graduation. "You know I'm enrolled at Smith College for this fall," she said.

"You've told me several times."

"Have *you* decided yet what you're going to do? You can probably still get into college somewhere."

"Laura, I'm going to get a job as soon as I graduate high school. I'll be drafted like all the other boys if this war isn't over in a year. College isn't for me, especially at this time."

"That's too bad. You're a good student."

"I'll make my way."

"I don't doubt you will."

"If you go off to college, I won't see much of you."

"Would that bother you, Obie?"

"You know it would."

"I'll try to come home often. And you could come and see me." She laughed. "We wouldn't have to hide from my mother."

"You'll make new friends. You'll forget all of us here."

"Obie! Never!"

He didn't like the direction of their conversation. That she might meet another boy was something he didn't want to contemplate.

She said, "Is it true that Ernie Boswell's marrying Cora Stringer?"

"Yes, he is."

"I'm surprised. "I always thought it was Frances Gibbons he wanted to date."

"He did. I think Ernie was really in love with Francis. Maybe he still is."

"So why didn't he date her? She's a nice girl. She wants to be a teacher or a librarian."

"His dad told him he'd disown him if he married a negro."

"That's horrible. Poor Ernie! But Cora's nice, too. I hear she dropped out of school. There's a rumor that she's pregnant. On second thought, maybe she's not so nice. Do you think Ernie might be to blame for that?"

He hesitated to comment on a situation not yet public knowledge. He was relieved when she added, "Still, I feel bad for Ernie about Frances. I think you should marry the one you love."

Obie studied her face; she was so beautiful. "So do I."

"Ernie seems sad. He still walks with us as far as Lake Road. I think he knows about us."

"Knows *what* about us?"

"Our feelings about each other."

What was she saying? Their eyes met and held. Her expression indicated he'd not misunderstood her meaning.

He stammered. "Laura, does that mean . . . is that what . . ."

She laughed as she reached out to take his hand. It was warm and soft. "Obie, haven't you ever wondered why I've never dated anyone?"

"You had a date with Norm Harrison." That had caused him considerable pain.

"Once. It didn't mean a thing. He won't even speak to me now. You and I are seniors in high school, about to graduate in two weeks, and neither of us has ever looked seriously at anyone else. Doesn't that mean something?"

He entwined her fingers with his. "It does for me." *The time had arrived, at last.* "I love you, Laura. I've always loved you." He'd finally said it.

"I know."

"You do? I've never told you."

"Girls know those sorts of things, Obie. And you must know that I've fought with my feelings about you?"

"Laura, I've never been sure how you felt."

She squeezed his fingers harder and moved closer until their knees touched. "I was hoping we could talk like this. It's why I sent Cassie away."

"She'll be back soon."

"Then we must talk faster," she said with a smile. "Obie, for the longest time, I've had a problem with your being younger than me. Now you're six feet tall and seem like the most mature boy in school, so I can't use that as an excuse. When we were little, we were like brother and sister. It's a feeling that's taken time to get over . . . but I'm over it."

"And you feel differently about me?"

"Yes, Obie. I don't want to use the word 'love' yet. It's not that I don't have that in my heart. I just don't want to put it into actual words. Do you understand?"

"I guess so." He was sure his disappointment was showing. He needed to define their relationship. "Can we be sweethearts, then? Go together?"

"I'd like that very much."

He wondered for a moment if he had died and was actually in Heaven. Reality crept back. "Your mother might have something to say about it."

"I'm sure she would if she found out."

"She might. People *will* talk."

"We'll deal with it when it happens, and it will happen sometime, you know."

"You're going to be away at college. How will that work?"

"We have all summer. After that, we'll write, and I'll come home as often as I can. We'll find a way if you're willing."

Willing? He said a little prayer of thanks while putting an arm around her shoulder. Her long dark hair covered her shoulders. She turned toward him so that their faces were only inches apart. He moved closer until his lips touched hers. They held the kiss for lengthening seconds as he breathed in her familiar lavender scent.

Obie was reluctant to break away. When she finally did, he said, "We've wasted a lot of time, haven't we?"

"I regret to say that we have. But it'll be different now."

She lay back on the rock, apparently oblivious to the hard rough surface. He leaned toward her, balancing himself by placing his hands on the stone surface beside her. They kissed again, and this time it seemed more urgent. Several seconds passed before she pushed him away and sat up.

"What's the matter?"

"Nothing at all. It's just that Cassie'll be back any minute."

Her words caused him to look toward the trail. Cassie was standing by his easel. How long had she been there? Even at a distance, he saw the gleam from her tears. She threw the paint tubes onto the pile of rags beside his easel and fled down the path, her blond hair bouncing as she ran.

* * *

That evening, Laura secluded herself in her bedroom. She and Cassie had shared a room until two years earlier when their mother separated them after a spat. Although the disagreement was long forgotten, the girls had concluded that having separate rooms was a good idea. Today, she was glad for the privacy.

Laura had gone down Blackberry Hill after Cassie but could not find her. Their parents weren't home, and Laura ate lunch alone. Worried, she went into town to ask people if they'd seen her sister. A few had but were vague as to her whereabouts. It was dark when Cassie finally came home and went straight to her room without saying anything. As much as Laura wanted to talk, she decided to wait until morning.

Laura tried, unsuccessfully, to read a textbook assignment. Her emotions were mixed. Even as she worried about Cassie, she was relieved that Obie had finally expressed his feelings. She already knew that he loved her. Hearing him say it was satisfying.

She'd told him that she wasn't yet ready to speak of love. Nevertheless, when he held her in his arms, she'd wanted to tell the whole world that she was truly in love.

Often, in the quiet of nights, especially during the past year, she had imagined how Obie's kisses might feel—and of even more intimate things. She'd been surprised by the intensity of the actual experience. She touched her mouth and tried to remember the exact sensation. The tenderness of their encounter had frightened her, and even now made her feel flushed. If Cassie's return hadn't been expected, what might have happened?

And what about Cassie? She'd seen them kissing—and her reaction was unexpected. Laura searched her memory to recall any time she and her sister had ever talked about Obie in any serious way other than friendship. Laura had assumed Cassie would understand. How could she not have noticed Obie's attention? Anyway, Cassie was assertive; she would have said something if she'd had such feelings for Obie. Regardless, Cassie had been upset. Apparently, there were layers to her sister's personality not yet revealed. They must talk.

There came a knock at her door, and Cassie called softly. How timely. Their parents were unaware of what had transpired and were in bed. The sisters could have a quiet talk and maybe resolve a misunderstanding.

Cassie had no such intentions. As soon as she closed the door behind her, her voice rose. "You sent me away so you could be alone with Obie, didn't you?"

"Cassie, I . . ."

"Yes or no?"

"Yes, but I needed desperately to talk to him."

"You could've told me what you wanted to do. I'd have left you alone. It was embarrassing to find you doing that."

"We were only kissing."

"Do you think I want to watch you kissing?"

"I'm sorry, Cassie. I really am."

Cassie gradually calmed, and Laura recognized a new quality in her manner. Her eyes were red from crying, but she stood taller and straighter than usual. It was like the day Laura looked at her mother and realized Abigail had aged, instantly, like a chunk of time had been lost. Cassie, her little sister, had suddenly grown up. That observation, with the still fresh images of what had taken place on the ridge that afternoon, hurt. "I should have been more thoughtful," she said.

Awkward seconds passed. "Maybe I shouldn't have run away like that. I was angry, and disappointed."

"Where *did* you go? I looked for you."

"I walked along Lake Road by the farms, way past the cemetery, then went back to the park. I stayed there, and around town, until it got dark."

"Come here and sit on the bed with me."

Cassie complied. Laura waited until their eyes met. "I knew you liked Obie, but when I saw your face today up on Blackberry Hill, it made me think that your feelings go deeper than I imagined."

"It's always been you he looked at. I'd be a fool not to know it. My one hope was that you wouldn't care for him the way I do. I'd hoped you'd fall for Ben Williamson instead."

"I've never been that interested in Ben."

"Well, he's certainly interested in you. It's plain to see. And didn't you spend an afternoon with him after the May Day parade? What was that all about?"

"We just sat in the park and talked about families and such." Laura was glad for the dim bedroom light; it would hide her vexation. Ben had, in fact, asked her for a date and made suggestions that indicated a more than casual interest. "I told him, politely but firmly, that I wouldn't date him."

Cassie hadn't finished venting. "When I saw you kissing Obie and seeing how you looked at each other, I couldn't stand it." She picked at the pillow between them before saying, "He loves you, doesn't he?"

"He told me that he does."

"And did you tell him that you love him?"

Laura hesitated before saying, "I told him I didn't want to say the words yet."

"And *do* you love him?" Cassie's unruly hair bobbed as she nodded her head. She was expecting an answer.

"I believe I do. I don't want to say those exact words, though. Not yet."

Cassie let an audible sigh escape. "Sister, dear, no one in the world is closer to me than you, but I'm giving you fair warning. You won't tell Obie that you love him . . . but I *would*. And if you wait very long, *I will.*"

* * *

Abigail could see Pinky's knuckles turning white because he was holding so tightly to the steering wheel of their new Cadillac Sixty Special. They were on their way down to Long Lake to visit friends.

"I've never seen her so cheerful," Pinky said.

"Laura has a good head on her shoulders. She's coming around to our way of thinking."

"*Your* way of thinking, Abigail. You shouldn't have interfered."

"Well, see, she's forgotten him. I knew she would."

"You're sure about it, are you?"

"Yes, I'm sure. She's come to her senses. She's studying hard. She goes nearly every day to study with those other girls. She's already enrolled at Smith. I'm taking her there next week to see the campus."

"Is that what she wants?"

"I'm sure it is."

"You're sure about many things, Abigail. I wish I could be so sure all the time." He glanced sideways at her. "I'd like to ask you a question."

"Go ahead."

"You told me you didn't like the way Obie and Laura looked at each other and that you'd asked her, both girls really, to stay away from him. Tell me, Abigail, what is your objection to Obie?"

"Watch the road, Pinky!"

"Is it Obie, or do you think you can protect her . . . them, from all your perceived dangers . . . boys in this case? Laura's practically a woman, and Cassie will be soon. You can't keep on protecting them. They need to make their own decisions and live their own lives."

"That's nonsense, Pinky, and you know it. Until I stepped in, Laura was about to make a huge mistake. She was about to fall for that . . . that . . ."

"That good and decent young man whose mother served us faithfully for so many years?"

Abigail tried to keep from screeching. "Vi working for us has absolutely nothing to do with it. It's a matter of blood. Vi was Italian, from Italy. We don't know what situation her family had there."

"She could be descended from emperors for all we know. What difference does it make, anyway? And Laura's not about to get married. Young people flirt. It's natural. Didn't you do the same when you were her age?"

She ignored the question. "And what about the Gainsworthys? That family has been stuck here in the mountains for generations, steeped in ignorance. None of them has ever amounted to a thing."

"Abigail, it's a good family. Abner's an excellent farmer, and farming's not easy here in the Adirondacks. Old Jacob is a Civil War veteran, attained the rank of corporal in the Union Army, and was decorated for bravery. There are other things, if you knew . . ."

"Corporal? Corporal? My grandfather was a colonel. Yours was a captain. And, what about Ken? There's a fine example of manhood."

"Ken's a victim, Abigail. It's true he drinks, but he's a decent man. He lost the person he loved the most and can't seem to get over it."

"He was a drunk while Vi was still alive."

"Yes, he's had a drinking problem for a long time. Jacob thinks his war experience causes it. As for Jacob, he was an Adirondack guide, a highly respected profession here. His father before him helped open up this area. They're pioneer stock, backbone of our country. We've raised our daughters here too, so you might say they're also pioneer stock."

"Our daughters will have educations from the best schools. They'll have professions in Albany, Boston, or New York. Women can do that now. They'll live someplace that values culture. You'll see. And they'll marry accordingly."

"And what about you, Abigail? Would you like to live someplace else? Stafford Rest's not a center of culture, and never will be."

Abigail hesitated. This was unlike Pinky; he was usually easily convinced. She should defuse their disagreement. She placed her hand on his arm. "Dear, dear, Pinky, you know I stay here with you because of my love. You know, 'whither thou goest, I will go; and where thou lodgest, I will lodge.' You have your factory, your hunting, and your love for the mountains. I'd never take you away from that."

She could feel the tension flowing from him. The strategy never failed.

"Well, not even for culture?"

"Not even for culture."

Pinky wasn't finished. "You quote scripture quite well, but you forgot what comes after that part. You forgot 'thy people shall be my people.' These people here are our friends. My employees are my friends. I have to say that you've never treated them with much respect. And, I still believe you're doing Obie an injustice."

As much as she wanted to respond, it wasn't the right time. Eventually, she would bring him around to her view. With or without him, she wouldn't be deterred from protecting her daughters. That was what it meant to be a good mother.

She put her head back and closed her eyes. Pinky needed her. He was too careful in everything. He failed to appreciate her efforts, as did the girls. The truth was, they could never manage without her. Who else could redirect Cassie's touch of wildness or maneuver Pinky into making the right financial and domestic decisions?

It went even beyond that. Her real estate business and her property acquisition through that medium had given her great power in the community and county. She was acting behind the scenes to get Pinky recognized as a prospect for county government, maybe even the state legislature. Getting him interested was another matter. She was making progress, however. It would be interesting to see how far they might go.

As much as she wanted to propel herself into the political world, she had to be realistic. A woman's chance of success in politics was dismal. Getting behind her husband and pushing was a logical second choice. She would accelerate her efforts. Stafford Rest Methodist was an excellent place to start; she already had a robust base of influence there. Was it not she who maneuvered the vote to get

Charles Lansing appointed? True, that choice had not been the best, but her skill in swaying individuals was evident.

Her influence could even extend beyond the local level; her letter and petition had won Bernadette Simon the job of Stafford Rest postmistress after Jack Schermerhorn was drafted. Although Bernadette was not a clever nor intellectual person, she was faithful in her friendship and could be counted on to back Abigail in whatever venture was proposed. It was a loyalty that could be exploited if the need ever arose.

She and Pinky belonged to the right political party. She was already whispering in certain ears at church, and around the area, paving the way so the name "Pinkerton Hunt" would be a logical choice for whatever opportunities might arise.

Pinky would come to appreciate her. Because of her, their family would be rich, powerful, and well known. Her daughters would marry men of substance.

CHAPTER FIFTEEN

June 1943

Cassie remained calm, not an easy task considering the frustration of talking reason to Laura. It was mid-afternoon, and the sisters were on the shady portion of the patio. Cassie sat on large tie-down cushions in an Adirondack Chair. She faced Laura, who sat in a metal glider that emitted a high-pitched squeak with each back-and-forth movement.

Laura had been single-minded for the past week, so Cassie was not optimistic when she tried a second time to penetrate her sister's irrational mindset. "Mom will blow her stack when she finds out you're meeting Obie."

"And I don't care. I'm nearly nineteen. I can do as I like."

Cassie was sure age would not deter their mother from trying to run her daughters' lives. "Do you think that'll make your life any easier?"

When Laura didn't answer, Cassie said, "She *will* find out, you know. When has either of us been able to keep anything from her?"

"I have so far, with your help . . . and I do thank you, Cassie."

"Frankly, I'm getting tired of lying. I can't blame you for meeting Obie, but you must find another way."

"We're careful. I go to his house when his father's not there."

In Cassie's mind, Laura had always been levelheaded, the leader. Now she wasn't thinking straight. If she were, she would realize that, eventually, the mother of one of the girls with whom she was supposedly studying would reveal the truth to Abigail. Anyway, school would be out in less than two weeks, and Laura would be forced to create some new excuse.

Cassie had helped when Laura asked, although not without resentment. Their trio had broken up; Laura and Obie were in love, and Cassie was left out. If she believed in divine powers, she might think she was being punished for some sin. There was nothing she considered a serious sin in her life unless wanting Obie for herself was a sin.

There had been times at night, especially in the past year, when she lay awake letting imagination carry her to the most intimate of situations. Some of what might happen between a man and a woman had been revealed by listening to conversations of older girls. Details, however, were still shrouded in mystery. Right or wrong, it had been Obie with whom she wanted to learn about such things.

She tried not to burn with jealousy about what Laura and Obie might be doing when alone. A part of her didn't want to know; another part needed confirmation. The latter need won as she leaned forward and asked, "What do you do at Obie's house?" The words were out, and she held her breath.

"We talk a lot . . . and make love."

"Make love?"

"We hug and kiss."

Cassie stared down at the patio's flagstone surface. "Nothing else?"

"No, we don't." Laura sounded annoyed. "Obie's a perfect gentleman. Always." She put down the magazine she'd been using for swatting flying insects and turned to face Cassie. "Why do you want to know?"

"Just curious."

The glider stopped moving. "I think it's more than curiosity. I think you're jealous. You don't want to let go of your own feelings for Obie."

"As though I ever had any hold on him."

"I'm talking about *your* feelings, Cassie, not his. I'm sorry you're hurt, but you need to stop thinking about him like that and go on to other things."

Cassie wanted to say that she would become an old maid if Obie were lost to her. She said instead, "Are you going to marry him?"

"I expect to, someday. He hasn't asked me."

"Have you told him yet that you love him?"

"No, not yet."

Cassie turned her head and couldn't help mumbling, "She just wants to be sure."

"Look here, Sister. I do love Obie, but so many things are uncertain at this point. Don't forget, he's only seventeen, although he looks and acts older. I'm entering Smith in the fall. We have several weeks to make decisions."

"Okay, it may be too soon to think about marriage, but you shouldn't go off to college without letting him know how you feel."

Laura was staring at her, a question in her eyes. She said, "You've made no secret about your feelings for Obie, so I don't understand why you're concerned about *me?*"

"You might not believe it, but it's because I want you both to be happy." Cassie tried to believe that she hadn't uttered a lie.

Laura's countenance softened. "We are happy. So very happy." She was pensive a moment before continuing. "Can I tell you something very private?"

"Of course."

"I'm having a hard time not wanting us to do more. Do you know what I mean?"

Cassie said softly, "I think so." Laura's admission did nothing to soothe her anxiety. There was some relief that things hadn't gone as far as she'd imagined they might have. Still, what sounded like her sister's wish to speed things up was disturbing. "Why haven't you let him know you feel like that?" Cassie asked.

"He doesn't want that. Anyway, it wouldn't be the right thing to do."

Cassie remembered something Clara Kelly had said during gym class, and Clara was a rumored expert in boy-girl things. "It's what he wants," Cassie said. "All men want that. It's natural." She wasn't sure about the absolute truth of the borrowed pronouncement, but it did make her point clear.

"Not Obie. He's different."

"Maybe. But yes, you could be right. Obie does take religion seriously." Laura stopped moving the glider and said without looking at Cassie, "I'm sure he believes, as I do, that couples should wait until they marry to be intimate."

Cassie was confident that Laura was right, but an opportunity to shock her was something she couldn't let pass even though it wouldn't advance her cause. "I bet most people don't believe that way. I'll bet Obie could be persuaded. I bet I could talk him into it."

Laura gave her a scorching look. "Watch your dirty mouth!"

Cassie smiled, enjoying the knowledge that she'd made Laura uncomfortable. For a moment, she considered telling her about the time on the ridge when Obie had kissed her. She resisted because Obie had asked her to remain silent about the incident. She asked, "When are you seeing him again?"

"Tonight, for a little while. Will you back me up with Mom?"

"I don't know . . ."

"Please, Cassie!"

"I guess so . . . this time."

"Thanks, Sister, dear."

Cassie tried hard to love Laura as she always had. Her success was limited.

* * *

Obie hurried through routine chores after arriving home from school. It was a pleasant day, and there had been little time that spring for tapping the ready supply of panfish lurking near the town end of the lake. Usually, he would have launched the old boat his father kept in the weeds up Cedar Creek and rowed out along the rocky northern shore. Since he'd be meeting Laura in three hours, there wasn't time to take the boat.

He took nightcrawlers from his cache behind the barn, grabbed fishing line and stringer, and headed for the highway bridge over Cedar Creek. The creek widened and flowed into the lake a few yards beyond the bridge. It was a favorite spot for village residents; a dozen people might be seen with lines dangling over the railing on a nice day.

Today, however, only one other person occupied the bridge. Pastor Charles was in the process of baiting a hook. He already had two good-sized rock bass and a perch on his stringer.

"I see they're biting," Obie said.

"Indeed. I have nearly enough, and I've only been here fifteen minutes."

Obie baited a hook and dropped his line to the water. A few days earlier, he avoided talking to Pastor Charles because he was hurrying to see Laura. He hoped the slight had gone unnoticed.

"How's the fund drive for the education wing coming along?" Obie said to start a conversation on a subject he knew was important to the pastor.

A worried expression crossed Pastor Charles' face. "Not so good, not good at all." He turned his back to Obie. The minister had worked hard on the project that hadn't generated much interest in the congregation. It was clear he'd rather not talk about it.

Obie soon had several fish on his stringer. The pastor announced that he'd had enough. As he prepared to leave, he turned to Obie. "How is everything with you, Obadiah?"

"Couldn't be better." Obie smiled. *He would soon see Laura.*

"You and Laura are seeing quite a bit of each other, aren't you?" Obie was startled and couldn't hide it. Pastor Charles laughed. "Now, don't get angry at Cassie. It came up in casual conversation, and she didn't say much. I just put two and two together."

"We're going together." The words, articulated for the first time, sounded strange to his ears.

"I haven't seen you together around town."

"We try not to be obvious."

"Obadiah, where do you meet?"

"We see each other at school and sit together on the bus." Obie hesitated before adding, "We meet at my house."

"Is your father at home during that time?"

"No, he hasn't been."

The older man hung his stringer of fish back over the metal bridge railing. Obie feared that a serious discussion was coming, perhaps a sermon. "Obadiah, I have to be frank. That's somewhat troubling."

Obie felt defensive. "We haven't done anything we shouldn't. I respect Laura." Wasn't controlling his passion proof of it?

"Here's the problem, Obadiah. Your attraction for each other can be like a whirlpool in water. Everything can appear calm at the edges and then suck you into swirling water so quickly you can't stop yourself."

Obie couldn't stop a chuckle. "You make it sound like drowning."

If Pastor Charles saw the humor, he failed to show it. "God gave us the joys of intimacy with one another, but there's a right time for everything."

"Like when we're married?"

"Yes, exactly. You should be faithful to that ideal. But meeting Laura alone at your house is not a brilliant idea, is it? It would be best if you met in public places. It would look bad if Laura's observed going to your house without Ken being present. You should be thinking of your young lady, of her reputation."

"We haven't done anything we're ashamed of."

The pastor took on a serious tone. "Please don't meet with her at your house, Obadiah. Always take her someplace public."

"Her mother's going to find out if we're seen together."

"She's going to know sometime, and maybe that's not such a bad thing . . . get it over with."

"She'll kill me."

* * *

With Pastor Charles's words still fresh in his ears, Obie ate a hurried supper, stacked dirty dishes in the sink, and went out the door with the intention of meeting Laura at the footbridge over Cedar Creek. Instead, he found her just outside the door on the path from the road.

"I was able to get away early," she said while hugging him.

He was worried about her reaction to altering their routine but wanted to get it over with. "I have something important to tell you," he said.

"Let's go to the barnroom. You can tell me there." She tugged at his arm. "Come on."

He followed her. The room was warm. Obie opened the window.

Their meetings were always in the barnroom. Sometimes, she watched him paint, and this time she went straight to his studio area.

"You haven't done a thing since I was here yesterday." Her tone was teasing.

"I'll have more time now that our tests are all finished. And school will be out at the end of next week. Big changes for everybody, good and bad."

"Some of the boys are joining the service. Norman Harrison is going into the Navy the day after graduation. He's already eighteen."

"I heard."

"Is this war going to end soon?"

"The one in Europe will be over in a few months. The Pacific war could last longer."

"I hope and pray you won't have to go. I couldn't stand it."

"They won't call me for another year. It may all be over by then. Anyway, I think I'd register as a conscientious objector."

"What's that mean?"

"I'd tell them I don't want to kill people. They'd give me a job where I wouldn't have the carry a gun."

"They do that, even in wartime?"

"I think so."

"I didn't know you felt that way."

"I think the war's focused my attention on how I feel. I wouldn't have the stomach for shooting a man."

"If everybody felt that way, there wouldn't be any more wars.

You're pretty special, Obadiah Gainsworthy."

"Some folks will think I'm cowardly."

"Well, not me. I think you're swell for standing up for what you believe in."

She ignored the chairs and sat on the bed, patting a spot beside her. He got up to join her, then hesitated. Sitting on the bed was inviting trouble. She'd slapped his hand once when he let it rest on her knee. "Don't," she'd whispered and followed that with, "Not yet." He'd been left to speculate about what "not yet" meant.

There came a nudge of shame at such thoughts. Pastor Charles' words about "swirling waters" came to mind. He needed to tell her about altering their meeting plans. He went quickly to sit in the rocking chair. "Laura, there's something we need to discuss."

Laura turned sideways, and her skirt lifted over her knees, making her white thighs visible. He was unable to look away. She brushed down the folds of her skirt and came to sit on the arm of the rocker.

"It's about where we meet," he said, his voice feeling weak.

Without responding, she bent to kiss him. He didn't resist, and she slid down to sit on his lap. He was acutely aware of the need to change direction. "Laura, we shouldn't be doing this. We said . . ."

She arose at his words, appearing to be annoyed, and went to sit on the bench beside the table. He waited. She said, "Yes, I know. We do need boundaries, but I decided last night that there's nothing wrong with two people who love each other having the freedom for some things."

"Some things?"

"Not everything. You know . . . some things." Even with the distance between them, he could see her blushing.

"And you said 'two people who love each other.' Does that mean . . .?"

"Yes, you silly boy. *I do love you.* There, I've said it. Isn't it what you've been waiting to hear? Obie, I love you. I really do.!"

"Please say it again!"

"I love you! I love you! I love you!"

They stood simultaneously, and he took her in his arms and held her so close he could feel her heart beating. "Laura, I love you more than anything or anyone. Believe me . . . I do." With an urgency, helpless to divert, he said, "Let's get married."

She stepped back. He wasn't sure if her expression signaled surprise or apprehension. "We're too young," she said.

"We're not."

"Mom would kill us."

On past occasions when he'd let himself believe this day might come, he had created scenarios for how events might play out. Now, he drew on a likely one. "We can run away. We'll go over to Massachusetts. I'll get a job, and you can still go to college. Your mother wouldn't even have to know."

She laughed. "It wouldn't work, Obie. Anyway, I don't think Smith allows married students. But your proposal of marriage doesn't go unnoticed or unanswered. Yes, my darling, I will marry you as soon as the circumstances are right. You'll have to be patient, however. Can you wait awhile?"

He drew her close again. "If I have to."

She held onto him with an intensity that surprised him and said in a whisper, "Obie, have you ever seen a girl without . . . you know?"

"Naked, you mean?"

"Yes."

"I haven't. Have you?" Boys, I mean."

"No, never, unless you count the time when I was four and our mothers put all three of us in the bathtub together."

He laughed. "I don't remember that."

"You wouldn't. You were two and a half."

He knew he should steer the conversation into a safer area but said, "Well, if we want to see each other naked, we could go skinny-dipping. There's a water hole I know in Garnet Creek not far from your house." He knew it was an impossible suggestion for many reasons.

"Be serious, Obie. That's for kids. We're adults and shouldn't have to slip around. We have our privacy right here."

Her words presented an opening to restart the interrupted conservation. However, he was overwhelmed by the fact that the girl he'd adored since childhood and about whom he'd fantasized for years was actually saying these things to him. He hesitated, searching for words to steer them back to a safer path. Instead, he held her again, savoring her scent and the feel of her body pressed against his.

She removed the red ribbon holding back her hair, allowing it to flow over her shoulders. His fingers moved along the contours of her face. He kissed her forehead, cheeks, nose, and finally, her lips. She took his hand, laid it on one breast, and then the other. "I won't break," she said.

Her blouse was already unbuttoned partway from the top. His trembling fingers continued the process. At the same time, she unbuttoned his shirt and he slipped out of it. They stood with their bodies pressed together, unmoving. Laura had her head tilted back. Her eyes were closed. He could hear her breathing.

After a few moments, she said with her mouth close to his ear, "Do you ever think about us together, how it'll be when we're together and . . . you know?"

"I think about it all the time." Reason had become a formidable enemy, but he forced himself to say, "But we're going to wait until we're married, aren't we?"

"Do you want to wait?"

His chest was about to burst. "I don't know."

"Is that the truth?"

"I want it to be, but I love you so much."

"And I love you."

Reason went down in defeat and resolve fled the battlefield. "No, Laura . . . I don't really want to wait."

"We don't have to, Obie." She took his hand, and he followed her toward the bunk. They tossed garments mindlessly to the floor. His heart pounded so hard he thought it might explode. She lay on the bed, and he knelt beside her. She tugged at his arm.

He pulled back. "Laura, I want this more than I've ever wanted anything, but are you sure it's what *you* want."

"Yes, Obie! It's what I want, too."

There was a sensation of swirling, of spinning helplessly in a whirlpool against which he was powerless.

CHAPTER SIXTEEN

June 1943

The sun had already slipped behind the hills at the far end of Diamond Lake. Obie expected Laura, but Cassie stood at the barnroom door, her face contorted in anger.

They hadn't talked since her flight down Blackberry Hill the previous week. On the bus and during chance encounters in school hallways, she'd avoided looking at him. He could tell she was hurt. Laura dismissed it as indignation for having been duped into going after his painting supplies, which made sense at the time. He was sorry for his part in that, but her mood now was something more serious. He braced himself.

She stared straight at him, her eyes red, possibly from crying. He was surprised that her voice was calm. "Laura sent me to tell you that she'll be about an hour late."

"Thanks for telling me."

"I know what you've been doing up here."

"Doing?"

"You and Laura, the past three evenings."

Obie studied her face, searching for confirmation that she might have discovered his and Laura's secret. Laura would never have told her. Cassie was being herself, guessing, hoping to hear a confession—or a denial. He'd give neither. He would give her a truth. "Cassie, Laura and I are in love."

The words brought up images from the past three evenings. Their lovemaking had been a time of abandonment of everything but themselves. Other commitments, ideals, and responsibilities disappeared within seconds of Laura's arrival on Blackberry Hill. During their time together no one else existed. When they were apart, he could think of little else.

Cassie stepped into the room and straightened to her full height. She was taller than Laura despite their age difference. Her grimace caused Obie to brace himself, for he recognized the look. Unlike her sister, Cassie seldom turned from confrontation.

"You may be in love, but somebody's going to get hurt."

"I'd never hurt Laura. We're going to get married."

"No, you're not. Not for a while, anyway. She's going to college. Will you take that away from her? What if you go into the military service? The war could last for years. *You could be killed!*"

He felt defensive, for Cassie was naming the very things he had mulled over in Laura's absence, but which were soon forgotten on her return. "The war's going to be over before I'm drafted . . . and I didn't mean we'd be married right away. We can wait. Laura can have her education. The war will end. We'll wait until then to get married." He searched her face for evidence that she understood.

"I don't think Laura will want to wait. I know my sister. Yes, she loves you, but she's crazy-in-love. She'll throw everything away for you." Cassie's voice took on a softer tone. "Obie, I love you both and want the best for you. But you're the strong one. At least I hope you are. *You* have to take control."

No matter what defenses he might raise, she was right. It was up to him. *How did Cassie become so wise?* His intimacy with Laura had complicated things. He'd been wrong to let it happen. There wasn't any way to change that, but he could bring it under control. More than anything in life, he wanted to marry Laura, but at the proper time.

He wanted Cassie to understand. "You're a good friend, a good sister, too. And you're right. Laura and I must wait to marry."

"I knew you'd want to do what's right."

He had to make amends on another matter. "I'm sorry, Cassie, about my part in what we did to you last week. I wasn't acting like a good friend. I'm sorry. Please forgive me."

Her eyes seemed to bore right through him. She said, as much to herself as to him, "Yes, I forgive you, Obie . . . for everything."

* * *

Abigail fumed while she pushed the carpet sweeper persistently into all four corners of the living room. Several "maids" employed over the years had failed in their attempts to meet her standards of cleanliness. Edith Taylor, the present maid, was no exception. On Monday, she would look for someone new.

While returning the sweeper to its appointed place in a hallway closet, she concluded that Edith's inefficiency was not the most urgent problem. Her genuine concern was caused by her suspicion that something clandestine was happening. Cassie had returned home a few minutes ago, and she and Laura had gone out again. A pattern had become recognizable.

She said to Pinky, who sat at the dining room table, "It's late. Why are they going out so late? Tomorrow's a school day."

Pinky seemed little concerned. He placed his pipe in a cigarette tray on the table. "Did they say where they're going?"

"Beth Nellis' house. Cassie said some of the girls are getting together."

"They're celebrating graduation."

"That's three days away. Pinky, do you realize they've gone out every night this past week? At least Laura has."

"So what? Girls do that, you know. Leave them alone. Cassie has another year in high school. Laura's all but finished. You know, just as I do, that things will never be the same. She'll never see some of her classmates again. People scatter. Let her have this time."

"I don't think that's where she's going."

Pinky looked exasperated. "Abigail, you've got to let go of our daughters, let them live their own lives."

She was getting nowhere trying to reason with Pinky. She walked to the window. The girls had reached town. It was getting dark, but she could make out Cassie's bright red blouse. She watched them walk up Main Street toward the bridge. The Nellis residence was across Cedar Creek Bridge on the left. Abigail strained to see.

"I could swear only Cassie crossed the bridge," she announced. She could be imagining things, but she had to check it out. "The Nellis' have a telephone. I'm going to call them."

"Abigail, you're impossible."

"I don't care. I'm going to get to the bottom of this," she said as she removed the mouthpiece from the telephone on the kitchen wall.

* * *

Laura was out of breath when she entered the barnroom. "Have you been running?" Obie asked.

"A little. I can only stay an hour, and I don't want to waste a minute." She threw her arms around him. "Kiss me quick."

He complied, holding her close. "Why the rush?" he asked after stepping back.

"I'm supposed to be at Beth's house, so I need to go back there in case Mom should talk to Mrs. Nellis. Cassie's already there. Mom's suspicious. She's starting to ask questions. We may have to make other arrangements."

"Yes, you're right, Laura. We need to discuss this."

"A discussion? Okay." She smiled as she stroked his bare arm. "What shall we discuss?"

"Us! We need to talk about *us."*

"What? You're tired of me already?" Her smile faded as she appeared to realize he was serious. "What is it, Obie? What's the matter?"

"I talked to Cassie earlier. She said things that made me realize I may not be doing the right thing by you. I . . ."

"What did she say?"

"She pointed out, or at least hinted, that we might have expectations that aren't realistic. We need to talk about what we really should do. I've asked you to marry me. Laura, for as long as I can remember, that idea's been in my head. I was eight years old when I told my mother that I was going to marry you. It's been an obsession, I admit. When I asked you to marry me, I was thinking about us getting married as soon as possible. That was selfish. We have to wait longer."

"And I was the one who said we had to wait. But this . . . what we're doing, it changes things."

"I agree that it bonds us together, but we have other things to do first. Laura, I've thought this through." He wouldn't tell her that the "thinking" had occurred during the past hour. "I want you to go to college. I'll get myself established in some occupation. In four years, we can marry and be together the rest of our lives."

He tried to assure himself that four years was not a long time, but it suddenly loomed before him as foreboding as a trip to the Milky Way.

She confirmed the feeling. "Four years? That's an eternity. I don't want to wait, Obie. I want us to be together now."

Cassie had said to take control. "Laura, we have to do the responsible thing."

Her expression revealed hesitancy. She sighed. "Would we see each other?"

"Every chance we get."

"I don't think I can give this up."

He searched for suitable words. "Maybe it's not the right time."

"Do you want to stop?"

He wanted to say, "Never!" He said instead, "It might be for the best."

After a moment, she replied, "All this because of a talk you had with Cassie?"

"I was already thinking along those lines, Laura. Cassie helped me get my thoughts in order."

Laura smirked. "Cassie has a purpose in saying what she did. Did she ask you what we were doing?"

"Sort of. She was fishing. I didn't tell her anything."

"She asked me, straight out. But she doesn't know anything. She's guessing."

"She's concerned about you."

"You don't really know Cassie very well, do you, Obie?"

"How can you say that? We've been friends forever."

"Yes, but you don't know her deeper feelings."

A haunting image of Cassie on the ridge on a cold and blustery winter day came without invitation. He'd remembered that encounter more often than he should have. They'd kissed, and there was a moment when he was glimpsing a part of Cassie and himself that he'd never seen before.

He tried to push the memory from his head. "Well, tell me, what deep feelings does she have?"

"Even I don't have a complete answer. I know one thing though . . . she'd like to see us break up."

"Why would she want that?"

She's deeply in love with you, Obie."

"That's crazy!"

Laura placed a palm against his chest. "Maybe. On the other hand, I guess it's for you to figure out. Anyway, as much as I love my sister, I'm the one who has you, and I'm going to keep you."

She was wrong about Cassie. What concerned him more was that he and Laura must change course. "Sweetheart, we need to think seriously about what we're doing."

She backed away. "Maybe you've stopped loving me."

"Laura, I love you more than life. All I'm saying is that maybe we should have restraint until we're married."

"Four years, is it? Maybe you can switch your emotions on and off. I'm not sure I can. I doubt you can, either." She placed herself squarely in front of him. Her voice rose higher, and her eyes were like daggers piercing his resolve. "I know you want me as much as I want you." He watched, powerless to object, as she unbuttoned her blouse, removed it, and stepped out of her skirt. She tossed her head defiantly as she touched his arms, inviting his embrace.

Obie stood, transfixed. Her body was a wonderful and beautiful thing. How could he deny her—or himself? Nevertheless, he must. *He must take charge.*

He became aware of Slobber barking. It was a normal sound, for many animals inhabited the nearby woods, especially at night. Slobber was doing his job.

Obie put his hands on her shoulders and pushed her away, gently but firmly. They were standing like that when the door opened. Abigail Hunt stood framed in the doorway, disbelief on her face.

CHAPTER SEVENTEEN

June 1943

Laura shrieked and snatched her blouse from the floor. Obie took several steps backward, stumbled, and nearly fell over the rocker. His heart felt like it was going to leap out of his chest. What was going to happen? *What would Abigail do?*

She came through the doorway and advanced toward them in quick little steps that signaled serious intent. He glanced at Laura. She was crying.

Abigail's calmness surprised him. "Laura, put your clothes on and go down the hill to the car. I have business to attend to here. I'll join you shortly."

"Mom, please . . . it's not what it looks like."

Abigail snorted. "Of course, it is."

"We love each other." She was pleading.

"We'll talk about it later."

Laura dressed quickly while Obie glanced alternately at the floor and the ceiling beams. Still in disarray as she brushed past him, she said, "This won't keep us apart. Nothing can do that."

Abigail grabbed her arm and shoved her toward the door. "Go down the hill and get in the car . . . right now!"

"Mom, what are you going to do?"

"What I have to do. What any mother would do. Now, go!"

As soon as Laura was through the door, Abigail turned to Obie. Shadows cast by the oil lamp on the table flickered on one side of her face creating a grotesque appearance. "So, this is the kind of person you are. I knew it."

"I'm sorry, Mrs. Hunt. I'm sorry about everything."

"If you had a gun here, I'd likely use it on you."

"I guess you'd be justified." *Anything to gain her mercy.* He was trembling in cadence with his voice. "I'm sorry," he said again.

"*Sorry!* I don't want to hear it."

"Mrs. Hunt, please. I've been in love with Laura since third grade. We'll be married . . . someday."

Abigail stepped closer until her face was inches from his. "Get this straight, Obie Gainsworthy. Not you, nor the likes of you, will ever marry a daughter of mine. Never! Never! Never!"

His fear faded, replaced by escalating anger. He understood her concern for Laura but wouldn't stand still for her insults.

"The likes of me? What do you mean by that, Mrs. Hunt?" When she didn't answer, he said, "I know, though, what you mean." He struggled to keep a steady voice. "My family's poor, but my relatives are good people. I've been wrong, and I don't blame you for being angry about it. But I don't like being insulted."

The sound from her mouth resembled the low growl a wounded badger had made as it turned on his father. "It doesn't matter what you like or don't like. You are never going to come near either of my daughters again."

"Isn't that up to them?"

"No, and I'm going to tell you why."

Her frigid words nearly cowered him into silence. He recovered. "Mrs. Hunt, I won't always be poor. I'm young, but I have ambition."

"You'll never amount to a thing."

He ignored the remark. "I'll provide for Laura . . . more than provide." She made that snorting noise again, and he summoned courage. "I'm going to marry her, no matter what you think."

He was momentarily surprised to see her face soften, but then he saw the sinister look in her eyes telling him she was just getting started.

"Sit down, Obie," she said, with a motion of her hand toward the rough oak table as casually as if she were entertaining a guest in her own home.

He sat, and she seated herself across from him. "I don't care in the least what you might become or be, but we do need to come to an understanding. You'd better pay attention to what I have to say to you . . . and you'd better grasp my full meaning."

"I'm not giving up Laura."

"We'll see. First things first. I see you in church every Sunday. Do you consider yourself a pious person?"

"I consider myself a Christian."

"In light of your recent endeavors, I'd say you have some work to do in that respect."

About that, at least, she was right. "I try, Mrs. Hunt."

"Do you take an oath seriously, Obie?"

"Oath?"

"It means keeping your word. I'm sure you're smart enough to understand that."

The insinuation angered him further, but he controlled himself. "I do take an oath seriously," he said. "Very seriously."

"I'm going to tell you something, then, and I want your word that you'll never tell anyone what I've said."

"I'd have to know . . ."

"No, you don't. I want your promise."

A horrible thought came—one he could never imagine surfacing were she not pressing him. *Pinky Hunt and his mother.* His mother had been fond of Pinky and him of her. He'd already concluded she would have left the Hunts years before her death had it not been for Pinky. He balked at the image of his mother being unfaithful. In truth, his parents' marriage had its troubles. When he was younger, such assessments hadn't occurred to him, but recent reflections had brought the insight. Was Abigail about to tell him that Pinky Hunt was his father, and Laura and Cassie were his sisters? He felt light-headed.

She left him no choice. "All right, I promise," he said, subdued.

"It's an oath."

"I understand."

She opened her purse. The fading light through the high window panes revealed a roll of bills held together by a wide rubber band. "You know what these are, don't you?"

"Of course, it's money, paper money." He was relieved that Laura wasn't a blood relative but was appalled that Abigail might be attempting to bribe him.

She held a bill toward him. "Take it," she urged, placing it in front of him on the table.

It was a one-hundred-dollar bill. He'd seen one once at the bank in Tupper Lake. She really was offering him money. He was repulsed and shoved it back at her. "I don't want your money, Mrs. Hunt. You can't buy me off, no matter how many of those you show me."

She laughed as she picked up the bill. "Buy you off! Getting a dollar of Hunt money is about as likely as your marrying Laura."

"Then, why are you showing me this money?"

She leaned forward. "So you'll know that I have the power of money behind me . . . Hunt money. And this is but the tiniest portion of what I have." She thumbed the stack of bills once as though shuffling a deck of cards, then secured it with the rubber band and shoved it back into her purse.

As she snapped the purse shut, she said, "Money will buy about anything, Obie. It buys security, it buys friends, and it buys power." Her voice had risen to a level that revealed the true extent of her anger—anger she'd been repressing. She added, "And it can also buy people to do unpleasant things that I don't know how to do."

"I don't understand what you're saying."

"You will in a moment. How old is your drunk of a father?"

"He's fifty-six, and I don't like . . ."

"Would you like him to get older?"

He stammered. "I don't know what you mean."

She rose from her chair and leaned across the table. "Obie, by tomorrow evening, you will be out of Stafford Rest. I don't give a damn where you go or what you do. Just be gone from here. If you don't go, your father won't live to be fifty-seven, and your own life will be in doubt."

Obie played the words over in his head before he could believe she'd said them. He recovered. "You're threatening me, Mrs. Hunt!"

"You bet I am, and you're to take it very seriously. I have resources to people who don't value human life, people who'll do anything for money. And I have money. I'll use it. Let me be clear. You've violated my daughter. There's a thing called justice, and I'm calling down my justice on you. I'm not a violent woman, but I'm justified in doing whatever is necessary to protect my daughters. That's why I'll have no trouble getting someone to carry out justice if you don't do as I say."

"I can report you to the state police."

"Have you forgotten your oath about keeping this between us?"

"I didn't give my word not to fight back against threats toward my father or me. I'll report you."

"You can, but consider that I know all the law enforcement people within twenty miles of here. They'd laugh at you."

He slumped in his chair, trapped. "You'd really have my father murdered?"

"And you too." The words had the feel of truth.

"What do I have to do?"

"Simple. Pack up and leave. Be gone by this time tomorrow and don't come back. That's what you *must* do."

Her words seared. Near panic, he saw the hopelessness of his predicament but couldn't help making one last counterattack. "I want to see Laura before I go."

"No, you're never to see her again."

The last thing he wanted was to plead, but he did. "Mrs. Hunt, we love each other."

"You'll get over it. She'll get over it."

"Just once . . . before I go."

"*No.*"

He bluffed. "Then I won't go."

"You know the consequences." She rose and started for the door.

"Laura will never forgive you if you don't let her see me."

She stopped and stood still. When she turned, he saw a slight change in her face, slightly less confidence. Maybe he'd stumbled onto a weakness.

"All right," she said. "One time. Tomorrow evening at eight o'clock I'll drive Laura to the foot of Blackberry Hill and give you a few minutes alone. Half an hour. No . . . twenty minutes. No more than that! It'll be your last time together . . . your absolute last time. Do you agree?"

He nodded.

"I'm doing it for Laura, and there are some rules. You're not to tell her about any of this. Nothing, Obie. She'll be told you volunteered to leave for a time so things can cool down and to protect her reputation. *Is that understood?* Agree, or forget meeting with her at all."

"What choice do I have?"

"None. And remember . . . be gone by dark tomorrow and don't return. You'll be sorry if you do."

* * *

Obie was in turmoil, and there was no relief. His lifestyle had given him competence in handling complexities efficiently. Still, the present bombardment of anger, fear, and humiliation caused him to lie awake, making minute-by-minute changes in his future course of action. There seemed a thousand things he must plan and do.

Anger came in waves that momentarily washed aside fear. Who was Abigail Hunt to threaten him? He would defy her. Then, he would remember the threat toward his father, and his fear returned. If it were only himself in danger, he'd tell her to go to Hell—where she belonged.

There were also moments when he considered the possibility that she might never do what she threatened. How could she? After all, she was Laura and Cassie's mother. He attempted to believe he'd misjudged her, until he remembered her merciless eyes. The one time he dropped off to sleep, those eyes dominated the nightmare that woke him.

He heard his father come home late. Obie listened for the kitchen door closing. His father was innocent in all this. Obie could not take a chance that Abigail was bluffing. He couldn't put his father in danger. The solution seemed to do as she ordered. The rest of the night was spent putting together a plan.

Obie was up at first light but not in time to catch his father before he left for Abner's, which probably was fortunate since he'd not decided what to tell him. If everything went as planned, they could talk later in the day.

He was soon on the road, hitchhiking. Rides were plentiful that time of day with people going to work in various locations. He soon caught a ride to Amsterdam, and another down the Mohawk River to Schenectady, arriving downtown well before noon. He called his Aunt Izzie from a public telephone. "Can I stay with you and Uncle John for a few days?" he asked.

"You know you're always welcome. Your grandfather has been asking about you. We'll all be glad to see you."

"I need to take care of some business here, Aunt Izzie, and I have to return home this afternoon. I'll come back sometime tonight. I may be really late. Is that okay?"

"Just let yourself in. The door is unlocked. I'll make up the cot on the porch for you."

He'd arrived in Schenectady with some uncertainty about accomplishing his mission and had been ready to stay another day. Therefore, he was surprised to find himself on the way back to Stafford Rest by mid-afternoon with the proper papers in hand. In addition to emotional fatigue, he worried he wouldn't get home in time to do all the necessary things before meeting Laura. Seeing her was the most important, even if he left town with nothing except what he was wearing.

A Utica Club beer truck picked him up in Amsterdam. After brief stops in Gloversville and Broadalbin, he got out in Northville and started walking up the highway along the Sacandaga River. He'd gone only a few hundred yards when Pinky Hunt's delivery truck picked him up and dropped him on Clearwater Road at the Cedar Creek footbridge. He recognized the irony.

His father wasn't home and probably wouldn't be until well

after dark. Obie couldn't wait that long. In less than three hours, he would meet with Laura. Then he'd go to Abner's, for he must tell his father something, at least a partial truth.

On his way up Main Street, Obie looked toward the Methodist church down White Pine Road. He wished he could see Pastor Charles, but there wasn't enough time. He stopped a moment, taking in the contours of the church building, and considered the memories. He'd tried to be a good Christian. He sighed; his actions had likely removed him from God's sphere.

He was relieved when he met his father on Lake Road by the Boswell Marina. Ken looked tired. As they walked through town, Obie casually announced that he was going away, but said nothing about his activities of the day. He felt bad about the cavalier manner of delivering the news; he would write a letter later, telling him the truth—or at least some of it.

"When?" Ken asked.

"Tonight."

"Why?"

"I'm just looking for an opportunity." Obie hoped it would suffice.

"For how long?"

"Awhile." He felt guilty because he had no idea when, if ever, he could return. "I have to do this, Dad."

"Why? We've been able to get along just fine. I could stop you, you know. You're still underage. You can find work right here. If your mother was alive, it'd break her heart."

"Dad, Mom would want me to do the right thing as I see it."

Ken didn't comment. When they were in front of the Diamond Inn, he stopped. "Where, exactly, are you going? Schenectady? Albany? Saratoga?"

"Dad, I have a job lined up. That's what this is all about."

"What kind of job?"

"I honestly don't know much about it yet. I don't even know where it is. I'll be given all the details." The half-truth rubbed up against his conscience but was necessary. If his father knew the full extent of his plan, he'd attempt to derail it.

"You'll write when you get where you're going, won't you?"

"Of course."

"Don't take the dog with you. He's too old to travel."

"I can't take Slobber. Maybe he can go to Abner's during times you're away."

"I'm stopping here for a quick drink," Ken said, nodding toward the Diamond Inn doorway. "I'll see you later tonight. I want to talk some more about this."

That wouldn't happen; Ken would have more than one drink, and Obie would be gone when he came home. He had the urge to hug his father but shook his hand instead. That was the way it was with them.

"Thanks, Dad, for treating me like a man in this."

Ken nodded and turned toward the Inn. Obie watched him until he entered the front door. For a moment, he considered visiting Uncle Abner, Aunt Claire, and Jacob. Jacob's quiet calm and insight would be helpful. He concluded that there wasn't enough time and started toward Blackberry Hill. He must pack and say goodbye to Slobber.

* * *

From the weeds along Cedar Creek where it flowed down the hill and curved toward the lake, Obie watched the black Cadillac turn around. He went up alongside. It had been a night and day unlike any in his life, all leading to this moment.

Abigail opened the door and got out. "You may sit here," she said, sounding like she was doing him a great favor. "You have exactly twenty minutes." She pointed. "I will go there, across the foot-bridge, and wait."

Habit nearly caused him to thank her, but he caught himself and remained silent. She disappeared into the dusk as he slid under the steering wheel. Laura's eyes were red with dark circles underneath.

"Oh, Obie," she said as she slid close and took one of his hands in hers. "Our world has been torn apart."

Despite the lump in his throat, he got the words out. "Laura, I have to go away." She would demand an explanation; he couldn't utter it yet.

He kissed her forehead, caressed her cheek, and held her in his arms. They sat like that for several minutes. Obie savored her light lavender scent.

She looked up at him. "This isn't the end, you know. I'm of age. I'm not going to college. I'll meet you wherever you are, wherever you wish, and we'll be together. Please, Obie . . . tell me it'll work."

He was silent. She continued. "I despise her. Once I leave, I'll never come back. I hate doing that to Daddy, but she's just too awful. And you don't have to do what she wants, you know. You don't have to go away at all."

"Laura . . ."

"What *did* you two talk about, anyway? She told me that you want to protect me by leaving for a while, that you think your presence would cause public gossip because we couldn't stay away from each other. Well, she's right about that part, but you were foolish to agree to go away somewhere. Why did you let her talk you into it?"

He ached to tell her that her mother was a devil. He softened it. "She suggested, although 'suggest' might not be a strong enough word."

"It sounds like her. I'm sorry, Obie. If you insist on going, I guess we'll have to put up with it for a while, for a couple of months, then I'll come to you."

"No, Laura. That won't work."

"Why not? Where *are* you going? You're not going far away, are you?"

"I don't know yet. It may not be close by."

In the growing darkness, wrinkles of frustration formed on her forehead. He understood why. He must tell her.

"Laura, today I enlisted in the United States Army."

She pushed him away and sat up straight. *"You what?"*

"I'll be leaving out of Albany in three days after I take some tests and get processed. I have no idea where they'll send me. It'll be somewhere for basic training. They said it would probably be in the south."

"Obie! This is the worst . . .! *How could you do this?"* She pounded his chest. "It's bad enough you let my mother talk you into leaving town, but then you went and did something stupid like this that'll make it impossible for us to be together for years, maybe never. You could be killed if you go to war. What were you thinking? *Why did you do it?"*

He lied. "I'll have to go some time, anyway. I thought it better to go ahead and get it over with."

"You're not eighteen yet. Why did they let you join?"

"I forged a letter of consent from my father. They never questioned it."

"Of course, they didn't. They don't question anything. They just want bodies to go do the fighting."

"Maybe. Anyway, I'm going. There's no turning back. I want

you to go ahead and go to college. The recruiter told me basic training would last thirteen weeks, and after that I'll get a furlough for a
week or two. I'll come to Northampton in September. We can be
together awhile without your mother finding out."

"Do you care if she finds out? I don't."

How could he tell her that if her mother suspected they were
seeing each other, it would place his father in danger? He hated lying
to Laura, but there seemed no other way. It might be years before
their relationship could come into the open.

"She's concerned for your reputation." It was a truth with serious reservations.

"Oh, Obie, of course I want to see you in Northampton. It's so
frustrating that all this has happened. I wish you hadn't joined the
Army, but we'll have to make the most of it. I'll go to Smith, and you
and I will be married as soon as the opportunity presents itself. We'll
keep it a secret. Smith won't know. My mother won't know."

He pulled her close and kissed her. He wanted to sit quietly and
hold her in his arms, but time was running out for him to say everything he must. "We'll have to wait a little longer. I'd like to finish the
Army duty first, unless some things change."

Her answer was a long time coming. "All right, whatever you
want, Obie. I'm ready, though, whenever you are."

"Your mother will be back soon. We need to set up a way to
communicate. Will Cassie help us?"

"I'm sure she would, but the best way is for you to send mail in
care of Beth Nellis. She'll get it to me."

"Does Beth know about us?"

"I've told her some things."

"All right . . . if you're sure."

"Once I go away to school, we won't have to worry about it. I'll
send you my address as soon as I get there in late August. Oh, Obie,
I can't wait for us to be together again, if only for a few days, or even
hours. I think about you all the time."

He drew her close again and said, "There'll come a time when
all this is behind us. Then, we can spend our lives together."

"Obie, let's make a pact."

"All right. What kind of pact?"

"Give me your hands." She intertwined her fingers with his.
"Obie, I promise you that I'll be yours forever. I'll bear your children, as many as you want, and I'll love you until the day I die. Now,
you tell me."

"My dear Laura, my only love . . . I'll never forsake you. I'll protect and love you as long as I live."

"And our children, too? Obie, I'll give you a son."

"And our children . . . I swear it."

"And I swear it too."

Abigail had returned. Obie squeezed Laura's hand before getting out. Abigail entered the car, saying nothing. She closed the door without looking at Obie and drove away. He watched the lights of the Cadillac until it crossed the bridge over Cedar Creek and disappeared from his sight.

CHAPTER EIGHTEEN

June-August 1943

A recruiting sergeant in Schenectady had told Obie that coping with Army life was simply a matter of learning discipline. On the troop train bound for South Carolina, he constantly assured himself that he was capable of such discipline.

A convoy of brown buses met the train. There quickly came hastily barked orders from foulmouthed sergeants, and even more foulmouthed corporals, all of whom seemed angry and in a hurry. They were separated into groups. "Line up! Fall in! Get on the bus! Get off!"

Even the bus driver was possessed by some unknown urgency, rounding curves on the gravel road at a frightful rate of speed and making lightning-like shifts of gears on the grades as they moved from the train depot toward some destination that was yet a mystery. Notwithstanding such hustle, they had to wait once they arrived.

The sun was blistering, even early in the day. They stood in the middle of a city of identical long and low wooden buildings, all sitting in perfect alignment, maybe predicting the orderliness of Army life. Shimmers of heat rose in spiraling columns from the roadway and black tarpaper roofs distorting the outlines of the few pine trees standing in the background. They were herded into a scraggy formation of men still in civilian clothing carrying valises, handbags, paper bags, and cardboard boxes. One man had a bulging burlap sack slung over his shoulder.

A mentally deranged sergeant and his assistants soon convinced Obie of the unlikeliness of his quick adjustment to Army life. His resolve to rise above the difficulties was severely tested as he tried not to flinch from the escalating volume of spittle erupting from the mouth of the sergeant who "explained" from ten inches away, the proper way to stand at attention. He wasn't the only one singled out. No one in the group of thirty or so seemed to have "the intelligence to scratch a cat's ass."

Once the unnamed interim sergeant finished his introduction to Army ways, a bull of a man in his mid-thirties introduced himself as Staff Sergeant Wallace and his aide as Corporal Leon. In his early twenties, Leon possessed an air of self-importance all the way from his starched and ironed cap to his spit-shined boots. Wallace was less "neat" but exhibited a depth of character not evident in the younger man. Wallace pointed out the building that would be their "home" and clicked off the rules they were to follow in living together. Without pausing, he informed them of what was expected, collectively and individually.

Wallace was exacting and graphic, ending his speech with, "I'm your Technical Instructor. You're mine for the next three months. I'll tell you when to get up. I'll tell you when to lay down. I'll tell you when you can eat and when you have to go hungry. You'll do whatever I tell you, and you'll do it double-time. You'll not complain. You'll not bitch. It's my job to turn you from the weak, sniveling, spineless dredge of humanity your parents have sent me into maybe, just maybe, the semblance of a soldier that won't get his ass shot off the second he faces the enemy."

The day was one of "hurry up and wait." There were medical examinations, shots, paperwork, haircuts, issue of clothing, and intimidation. Obie was yelled at, shoved, and verbally abused so often he came to expect it. He tried to tell himself that it was all part of the training, a regime meant to make them good soldiers. He steeled himself to handle whatever they threw at him.

A few men had difficulty adjusting to their new lives. In formation, while waiting to march to lunch, a young man next to Obie was caught with his cap on crooked. "What's your name, Rookie?" Corporal Leon bellowed.

"Burroughs."

Leon said with a Brooklyn accent, "Well, Burroughs, did you not hear what Sergeant Wallace told you about how we expect to see this cap sitting on your head?" At the same time, he grabbed Burroughs' cap and swung it from side to side, striking him on both cheeks. Burroughs was a small man, but his larger-than-life attitude made Obie think Leon's approach might not be the best choice.

"Do I have to repeat myself?" Leon said.

Burroughs snapped to attention. Obie saw his anger. His face was almost as red as his hair, and his eyes flashed a warning. Nevertheless, he said, "No, I do know how to wear my cap."

"Don't forget it!" Leon shoved the cap onto Burroughs' head and pulled it down until it bent his ears out of shape. "Fix it," he snapped as he walked away.

Burroughs muttered loud enough for Obie to hear, "You ever

hit me again, you cocky bastard, and not even your mother will recognize you."

Leon heard, too, maybe not the words, but the tone. He whirled and came back, putting his face almost against Burroughs's face.

"Would you like to repeat that, recruit?"

"Sure . . . I said you can kiss my ass!"

By that time, Sergeant Wallace had arrived on the scene. He grabbed Burroughs by the belt and did a series of hops with him toward a quartermaster building not far away. Several men laughed.

"On your faces!" shouted Leon. Obie hit the dirt, along with the other platoon members. "Give me twenty pushups! One! Two! Three . . ." He continued to twenty.

"Now," Leon said, "Does anyone else see any humor in this?"

There came a resounding "No!" from the group. One or two voices from the back uttered something else. Obie couldn't tell if there were words of disrespect or an innocent response had not been clearly articulated. In any event, the perceived dissension was unacceptable to Leon.

"On your faces!" he roared again. "Give me fifty!"

Obie's arms ached, but he made the fifty. He took pride in the achievement.

That night, after finally being allowed to lie on the bunk he'd been forced to make up, tear apart, and remake until the "hospital corners" were just right, Obie concluded it had been anything but a fun-filled day. He longed for the peace and quiet of Blackberry Hill. Even his hatred of Abigail Hunt was muted.

Obie heard Burroughs reappear shortly before midnight, filthy from head to toe and drained of energy. He fell onto the bare mattress of the bunk next to Obie's without bothering to remove his clothing. No one disturbed him, not even Leon.

When the loudspeakers blared out reveille the following morning, Obie found it hard to believe he'd slept. Leon went down one side of the barracks and Wallace down the other pounding on the metal bunks with small wooden bats. They reversed direction, and any man without both feet on the floor received a rap on his toes. Daylight came by the time they finished dressing and making up their bunks; it was already hot.

They were to "fall out" in five minutes. Obie's muscles were sore. Burroughs groaned a lot. His pants legs were still caked with dried mud, and his palms and fingers were red and covered with blisters. Obie sympathized but wanted to appear casual.

"Where are you from, Burroughs?"

"Virginia, by Roanoke. It'd be a nice place to be right now."

"I know what you mean."

"And you?"

"Upstate New York. Stafford Rest. It's a little town in the Adirondacks."

"You're a long way from home."

Burroughs hobbled as they took their already assigned positions in the formation. They had new fatigue uniforms, clean except for Burroughs' filthy one. After being assailed several minutes for their inadequacies, which seemed to be many, they were eventually marched off to the chow hall for breakfast. Wallace walked several paces to the side, calling cadence in loud and unintelligible utterances, sounding like, "Laugh, life, laugh!" Most of his other commands were likewise incoherent.

While seated at one of the dining hall's long wooden tables, Obie heard many whispered complaints about the food. He found it satisfactory—and someone else was fixing it for him.

Back at the barracks, they were ordered to shave and shower. Wallace gave Burroughs a scrub brush and a bar of brown soap and told him to wash his fatigues.

"How do I get them dry, Sergeant?" Burroughs asked.

"The sun will dry 'em soon enough."

"Where do I hang them?"

"On your frame! Gawd Almighty, do I have to tell you everything?"

"What frame?"

"Why, son, you hang em on your own boney-assed frame."

There was no privacy. Showers held dozens of men at once, and the air was thick with steam and obscenities. A new way of life had begun, and Obie was determined to make the most of it. Hating Abigail Hunt hardened his resolve.

* * *

Obie, exhausted, stretched out on his bunk. It was nearly time for the lights to go out. He would sleep uncovered because extreme heat, trapped within the low wooden building, would not dissipate until early morning, if then; that had been the daily conditions the entire week since their arrival. Throughout the room men were bedding down. Some were already snoring.

Obie turned on his side toward Matt, with whom he'd wasted little time in becoming friends. Matt was sitting on his footlocker with an empty C-ration can between his feet where he could flip ashes from his cigarette. His hands still had areas of peeling skin from blisters accumulated on the day of arrival. Matt hadn't told him how the damage had been inflicted; he wasn't a complainer.

"You don't smoke?" Matt said as he crushed out his cigarette inside the can.

"No. Dad never smoked. He thought it would interfere with his climbing mountain peaks. Anyway, I promised my mother. She said it was bad for the health."

"No doubt it is. I guess I'm hooked on them, like about everybody else in this outfit. I hear war's bad for your health, too, so I'm not worried about what puffing on a cigarette will do."

Soon after Matt collapsed onto his bunk, the barracks went dark except for a dim glow from telephone pole lights filtering through the open windows. Obie wished for a breeze to cool the building's interior and carry away the scent of stale sweat.

Matt said in a not too subtle voice, "Gainsworthy, isn't this the damnedest place to have to live?"

A voice Obie recognized as Leon's roared from one of two small rooms at the end of the barracks. "Burroughs, I know it's you talking! Lights are out! I'll be seeing you in the morning!"

"Yes," Obie whispered, "It sure is."

* * *

The weeks went by quickly, and Obie adjusted to Army ways, as most men did. He became proficient in several activities: He could field strip, clean, and reassemble an M1 while blindfolded as fast as anyone in his platoon; his father had taught him well. He hated the hand-to-hand combat drills, but endured; his size and strength served him well.

Long hikes were conditioning and endurance challenges. Troops were forced to carry packs with blankets, raincoats, towels, toilet articles, gas masks, mess kits, bayonets, and shovels. Some items were stuffed in packs and others were attached to them. In addition, their belts held cups, canteens, first aid kits, and miscellaneous items, adding pounds that became grueling burdens. Other items were added depending on the purpose of the maneuver.

In addition to mastering skills required for converting them into combat soldiers, there were constant interruptions by company duties, including guard duty, KP, and working in the pits at the rifle range. They marched everywhere. Voices from many directions persuaded them that they were no longer individuals but one big entity with a single purpose—killing a yet unseen enemy.

Obie kept perspective, or something resembling it. Such conditioning produced well-trained soldiers, but he refused to lose sight of the fact that he would never use those "killing skills." He'd spoken to Sergeant Wallace three days after arrival about applying for conscientious objector status. The sergeant had stared at him with an expression Obie had trouble interpreting before saying, "Ask me about it again later." Thus far, Obie hadn't pursued the matter.

Their only free time came late at night. Even when he was so tired that all he wanted was to lie down and sleep, his thoughts turned to Laura. He managed at least one letter a week. Hers came twice in the same period, sometimes more often. They were his lifeblood. He told no one about her. A few men talked about their girlfriends or wives; some shared information that Obie thought demeaning.

Laura was articulate, so he wasn't surprised that she also wrote good letters filled with community news and accounts of her activities. Her promises of a future together gave him comfort. One letter, in particular, coming two-thirds of the way through basic training, filled his eyes with tears and reinforced his belief that he could endure anything.

Dearest One,   *August 6, 1943*

I cannot begin to tell you how much I have missed you in the weeks since you left. I think of you every minute of every day. I know from what I have heard some people say that the Army is not easy, and I fear it may get harder since, in all likelihood, you will go overseas to where the fighting is. You said you were going to register as a conscientious objector. Have you done that? Please don't delay.

Oh, my dear Obie! I dread the time when you will have to go into danger. I hope and pray every day that this terrible war will soon be over. However, in spite of my fears, I know you will come home safely to me. It cannot be any other way. We have dreamed and planned a life together, and we <u>will</u> have it. Do you remember that we talked about having children? I want a son, a son just like you.

Can't you just see us in our little house near the lake with the white picket fence keeping the children in? (I know we didn't talk about that, but it's something I've been dreaming about.)

People ... and you know who, have tried to keep us apart, but we will be together someday, and no one will keep us apart. I love you so much, Obie, and I know you love me. I will be yours forever and forever.

Do you know yet about your furlough after you finish basic training? The time is rapidly approaching when I'll leave for college. Why can't I get excited about it? I ache to have you hold me in your arms again.

Yours forever, Laura

Obie read the letter through often. Yes, he would go to Northampton. And someday, he'd return to Stafford Rest, despite Abigail Hunt's threats. He'd stand up to her; he and Laura would be together on their own terms.

He remembered exactly how it felt to hold her, her skin soft to his touch and her breath sweet on his face. As pleasant as those images were, the letter lifted him to heights never felt before. She loved him—more than anything—more than anyone. She would be his, forever. She had pledged it.

* * *

Laura kissed the envelope. It was a ritual that had started with her first letter. She dropped it into a mail slot beside the post office window, hoping to avoid Bernadette Simon. Bernadette, the postmistress, was a friend of her Mother's and was inclined to ask questions. The woman was busy, so Laura quickly got away from the tiny wooden building scrunched between the Diamond Inn and Mercers. She went into Mercers.

Her real reason for walking into town was to mail the letter, but she'd volunteered to pick up grocery items to ensure that her mother didn't suspect. Mercers carried nearly everything suitable for a home, but many things were scarce. The federal government had issued stamp books to regulate the usage and prices of gasoline and many food items. Her friends bemoaned the shortages, especially sugar, although Abigail seemed to find it without much trouble. Nevertheless, the term "black market" was one she didn't allow family members to use.

Laura picked up canned fruit and vegetables and a loaf of bread. Helen Mercer engaged her in conversation while she paid for the items. Once on the street, she wished she had chosen lighter groceries to carry up the hill. It looked as if it was going to rain at any moment. Just past the bridge over Garnet Creek, the paper bag ripped. A can fell out. While putting it back in, the bag tore open from top to bottom and spilled all its contents. A couple of cans rolled into the ditch.

Laura started retrieving and putting everything in a pile beside the road. The bag was useless. She'd leave the groceries there and go home to get a more substantial container—or maybe her mother was still home and would drive her down to pick them up.

From behind came a gentle toot of an automobile horn. She didn't recognize the stopped car, a new and expensive model of something unfamiliar. A quick breath escaped when Benjamin Williamson stepped out—Doctor Benjamin Williamson.

"Bad luck, the bag tearing open like that," he said, seeming to measure his words. He was wearing a white shirt with a dark tie. He was handsome, even with his too slicked-down hair. He bent to pick up the cans. "Can I give you a ride home?" It sounded more like a statement of intent than a question.

She was flustered. "Oh, that's all right, Doctor Williamson. I live up the hill. My mom . . ."

"It's not any trouble. And I know exactly where you live."

She'd probably given him that information last May during their extended conversation in the park. He knew anyway, for he'd been with his father last year when the older doctor came to treat her mother's high fever. Laura had concealed herself in her room with the door ajar enough to hear everything. Ben had asked questions during the examination that impressed her with their complexity. He must be brilliant. In truth, she felt intimidated by the young physician. He'd been watching her for years and had all but admitted it the afternoon they sat together in the park.

She should refuse, but it had started to rain, and his offer was reasonable. She would seem a fool not to accept, and appearing a fool to Ben Williamson was something she wished to avoid, although she wasn't sure why.

"All right," she said.

He placed the cans on the back seat and opened the passenger side door for her. After they were inside, the rain became torrential. He turned on the windshield wipers.

When they pulled into the driveway beside the gate, it was still raining heavily. "I'll go inside and get a bag," she said, nervous beyond reason.

"Laura, you can't get out in this. Wait until it stops."

"Mom needs these things right away," she said, latching onto an excuse she recognized as implausible, but one she hoped would suffice.

"Her car isn't here, so she must be out." He had a quick mind—which wasn't a surprise. "Give it a few minutes. It'll stop, and then we can carry your groceries in."

"It'll probably let up soon," she muttered.

She felt trapped and confused. She desperately wanted to place significance on his having spied on her for so long, and to find some imminent danger in him, but the man sitting beside her had a benign quality. In truth, she liked him—and she liked the attention. Admiration from an older man, a professional man at that, held an appeal.

She glanced sideways at him. He looked about as dangerous as her easygoing father. His voice was gentle, and he used perfect English. His intelligence was evident in his eyes. His lips were full, often turning up at the corners in what was almost, but not quite a smile. She attempted to think rationally.

"You're going into practice with your father, aren't you?"

"Yes, I am. Dad wants to retire. He's been a physician in Stafford Rest since before I was born."

"Where did you go to school? To become a doctor, I mean?" He'd told her before, but she needed something to say.

"Johns-Hopkins. Dad went there too."

"It must be fulfilling, Doctor Williamson, being able to heal sick people." She was overly conscious of her words, wondering if she sounded condescending.

"Laura, please call me 'Ben.'"

"Oh, I couldn't . . ."

"Of course, you can." He smiled, the first real one. "I'd like it if you would."

"All right . . . Ben."

"That's better. So, tell me about your plans. I hear you're going away to school. Smith, isn't it?"

Had he been snooping? No, to think so was silly. Many people knew she was going to Smith. The rain hadn't let up, and with the wipers turned off, the space inside the car felt closed-in. "I'm enrolled for this fall. I'll be leaving soon."

"Smith is a good women's college."

"My mom went there."

"Looks like the apples haven't fallen far from the trees in both our cases."

"What? Oh, you mean going to school where our parents went?" Something occurred to her. "You're older than me. I should remember you when I was younger and you were in your teens. For some reason, I don't."

"That's because I wasn't here. My parents divorced soon after my birth, and I lived with my mother in Boston. Sadly, she died during my third year of college. That's when I started coming here. Dad talked me into applying to med school. So, here I am."

"I'm sure you'll be a good doctor. Lots of folks were worried there'd be nobody to take your father's place."

He turned to face her. "Laura, there's something I want to tell you." She heard him suck in his breath. Moisture covered his forehead. She was surprised; *he was shy.*

"What?" Her one-word utterance sounded harsh to her own ears.

"You must know by this time that I like you . . . that I like you a lot." He exhaled with an audible burst of air; he'd been holding his breath.

"Well, it's hard not to suspect you of thinking something about me, although I'm not sure what that is."

"I should have talked to you sooner."

It was time to confront him. "You've watched me, even followed me sometimes, haven't you?"

He blushed. "I apologize for that, Laura. Let me explain. I've been very busy and couldn't spend much time in Stafford Rest, so I tried to look in on you, so to speak, during the time I did have. It wasn't my intention to stalk. You were in high school and had your own group of friends. I thought maybe you'd have a boyfriend, and if I saw evidence of it, I'd just turn away. You've never had a serious boyfriend that I could see. You and your sister were with the Gainsworthy fellow a lot. But that didn't look like a romance."

"Ben, I . . ."

"Let me finish, Laura. I've thought a lot about how I would tell you all this, and if I don't get it out, I may not be able to." His eyes pleaded.

"All right . . ."

"I'm older than you, that's true, but I'm only thirty, so I'm not that much older, although it might seem like it to you. Some women might think I'm a good catch."

She wanted to head off what she believed was coming. It was hard to keep her voice steady. "Ben, I hope you're not going to declare romantic intentions, because if you are . . ."

"Please let me finish, Laura. This is hard for me, you know. I haven't talked to any other girl . . . woman like this."

She believed him. The car's interior was warm but not enough to account for the beads of perspiration on his forehead. "Ben, I can't be your girlfriend. I . . ."

"Be my girlfriend?" A look of confusion appeared. "I'm not asking you to be my girlfriend."

It was her turn to be confused and further embarrassed. "I thought . . ."

"I'm asking you to be my wife, Laura. I want you to marry me."

She was stunned by his words. Her astonishment materialized as hoarse laughter. She watched his countenance change and knew she'd hurt him. She must be kinder. She said, "For all practical purposes, we've not spent more than two hours together."

"For you, that may be true. As for me, I've loved you for a long time."

"This is impossible. There are things you don't know about me."

He appeared not to hear. "I believe I can convince you, Laura. I believe we were meant to be together."

"Ben, listen to me . . ."

He raised a finger and continued. "I can make you happy. Not only am I in a position to earn more money than the general population, I have no siblings, so I'm also going to inherit a sizable amount of property and money from my father." The way he emphasized "property" and "money" sounded like something her mother would say.

"Ben, there's more to life than money." Even as she spoke, she couldn't deny that wealth had significance. As annoying as her mother was, she was probably right in preaching the importance of money.

"I know that," he said, "but there's security, too." He grabbed her hand. "I'll care for your every need. You won't have to go to college. You'll never want for anything. Please, Laura, say I have a chance to win your heart."

For a moment, she struggled to prevent being overpowered by

thoughts of the changes in her life in the past few weeks. First, there had been Obie's declaration of love, wondrous by any measure. Now this, a proposal from a man she hardly knew but who was offering her the world. Was there any way she should take this seriously? She loved Obie—loved him so much she could hardly stand it. Was that not what counted in the long run?

How could this be happening? Half an hour ago, she was buying groceries. She wanted to remove her hand from his but didn't. In just a few minutes, she'd gone from being put off by Ben Williamson to being intrigued. Nevertheless, she had to tell him that it was impossible—and end this madness.

"Ben, I must tell you something. You said I'd never had a boyfriend. That's not true. I'm in love with someone. Deeply in love."

"Who?"

"I'd rather not say. I can see that you're a nice man, and under other circumstances, I might consider more. But, I'm sorry."

The rain had stopped. Williamson's half-smile faded, and he slouched back into his seat with a sigh. He failed to release her hand. There was determination in his eyes and his voice. "Laura, I'm not socially adept, and Dad says I have to improve my bedside manner. I want you to know, though, that I have one great strength. I'm persistent. I never give up. I've fallen in love with you and, somehow, I'll convince you to marry me. Now, let's get these groceries into the house."

It was the infliction in his speech that convinced her of his sincerity. Nothing was decided, he was saying. A shiver climbed her spine.

CHAPTER NINETEEN

August-September 1943

Obie's friendship with Matt Burroughs blossomed. Matt had grown up on a farm, although his father was more a "country gentleman" farmer than the dairy and subsistence farmers Obie knew at home. The farm bordered a small town where his father was mayor. Mervin Burroughs had been in the state legislature and still enjoyed some prestige, power, and political connections that came from it.

"Papa's a rounder, all right," Matt stated when the family topic came up again one Sunday near the end of basic. They were sitting on a shaded rock wall below the chapel after attending a required church service. "He's got his 'good old boy' connections. I have to admit that they do get things done."

Obie loosened his tie, as Matt had, and asked, "You going back there after the war?"

"You bet. Where else would I go?"

"Well, college, maybe?"

"College? I wasn't much of a student."

"You're smart, and you speak well."

"I'll farm, more than likely. Papa doesn't do much with our acres. I can turn it into something better."

"Dairy?"

"A possibility, but I think I'd rather raise horses. Believe I'd be good at it. We already have some riding stock and a couple of Stand-ardbreds."

"Do you have a girl back home?" Obie asked. Matt had been close-mouthed about his love life and Obie had never spoken to him of Laura. Maybe it was time.

Matt laughed. "Sure. Lots of them."

"Any special girl?"

"Not yet. I'll find her, though. You've got a girl, haven't you, Obie? I see all the letters you get. They're not all from your father, are they?"

"Her name's Laura."

"Are you going to get married?"

"We're going to wait until after the war."

"I think that when two people are in love they should grab everything they can, while they can. It's what I'd do if I found the right girl . . . which I haven't. I have plenty of time, though. I just turned nineteen."

Obie had carefully guarded his age secret. The bogus letter had gotten him in, but he wasn't sure what would happen if they found out he'd written it. He hadn't been challenged and believed that unlikely if he kept quiet for nine more months.

"I get your point," Obie said, "but we've decided to wait."

"You mentioned college. What about you? You're pretty sharp. What'll you do after the war?"

"College isn't in the cards for me. Marrying Laura is the most important thing, and I'll have to go to work to make us a living."

Matt hopped off the wall. "But given a chance, what would you study?"

"I'm interested in forestry and art. Journalism would be another possibility."

"I bet you'd do well in whatever you decide on. By the way, I see you reading that little book every night. What . . ."

"It's a Bible. My minister gave it to me."

Matt's expression never changed. "You're religious, then?"

I try to be. It's hard in this environment."

"What kind of church?"

"I'm Methodist." He thought it best not to describe the diverse road he'd taken to that destination.

"My uncle's a Presbyterian minister in Roanoke, and my Aunt Ruth on my mother's side tries to convert us to her Baptist faith, but I guess I'm not much of anything. Mama goes to church, and Papa goes when it suits him, but I quit going when I was thirteen." He fanned away a fly. "How about we go to the PX and get some ice cream?"

They left the pine tree shade and sauntered along the road between the rows of barracks.

"You think we'll stay together after basic?" Matt asked.

"I sure hope so. Troops usually go as a unit, so we'll probably stay with this group."

"If they ever give us choices about things to do and places to go, let's you and me try to stay together."

"Absolutely."

"We're probably going overseas."

"We could go somewhere for further training first, but lately, they've been shipping troops overseas right after basic and training them after they get to wherever they're going."

Matt paused before saying, "I was reading a newspaper in the dayroom last night. Causalities are high."

"Yeah, I know."

"Where would you rather we go, Europe or the Pacific?"

"Europe, I think."

"Me, too."

Obie sucked in his breath before asking, "Have you ever considered conscientious objector status?"

"Naw. Have you?"

"I'm considering it. Guess I'll have to do it soon, though."

"May already be too late. You should've declared that when you first enlisted." Matt appeared thoughtful before asking, "Are you scared to fight, Obie?"

Obie tried to judge the question as being without accusation. "I don't want to be killed if that's what you mean, but I'm not afraid. I don't want to kill another human being."

"I understand that, but I just want to go and get the job done . . . get this war over."

They said no more on the subject, but Obie was sure Matt also felt the uncertainty that loomed over them all—a specter on a horizon not yet clear. Sergeant Wallace forced it into reality one day as they stood in formation. "Look at the man on each side of you. Look at the man afore and aft. At least one of em won't be coming home in one piece, or not at all. And look at the one in the middle. That's you. If you don't learn what we're trying to teach you . . . well, there's no sure thing."

* * *

The absence of mail from Laura for nearly two weeks disturbed Obie. It wasn't a long time, but he'd become accustomed to her two-a-week messages and was lost without them. *Could she be sick? Had her mother discovered their correspondence?*

With three weeks left in basic training, he wrote a letter expressing concern. When no answer came, he wrote another short message, pleading for an explanation. Another week went by as he worried and fretted.

Efforts to maintain his peace of mind proved impossible. Matt listened to his frustrations and offered his explanations of what might have gone wrong. Obie was grateful for Matt's concern but decided he had to think it through himself. He reread her last letter several times, looking for clues to what she was thinking. He finally concluded that she was unable to mail a letter, but that she still loved him. He had to know, however; he would make a telephone call, regardless of the consequences.

He arranged for a call at the post telephone exchange and was assigned a time for the following evening. Wallace approved it without asking for personal details.

Obie knew he was taking a chance. If Abigail answered, he would hang up. If Pinky answered, it would be awkward but not impossible. There was, at least, a fifty-fifty chance of getting either Laura or Cassie.

The Hunts had one of the few private lines in Stafford Rest, and the ring was steady, unlike the more familiar ring of a party line. Several seconds passed before someone answered. He exhaled as a female voice said, "Hunt residence, Cassie Hunt speaking."

"Cassie, it's Obie."

"Oh, Obie. It's so good to hear your voice."

He could waste no time. "Cassie, is Laura there? I need to speak to her."

"No, I'm sorry. She's off somewhere with Mom. I'm not sure where."

"She's all right then? I haven't heard from her for a few days."

"She had a summer fever a couple of weeks ago, but she's over it." Cassie seemed to hesitate. "She's been acting a little strange, like she has a lot on her mind. Maybe she's just feeling nervous about leaving home. She's scheduled to go away to college in a just few days."

"Yes, I know. Cassie, do you know if she's been receiving my letters?"

"As far as I know, she has. I've seen her reading letters and hiding them from Mom. She doesn't tell me much, you know. Are you worried about her, Obie?"

"Not now that I know she's not sick."

"Do you want me to tell her you called?"

"Yes, please. No, on second thought, don't tell her. She might think I have doubts about her feelings for me."

"Do you have doubts, Obie?"

"No . . . none."

"That's good because I'm sure she loves you."

"And I love her. But don't tell her I called. And please don't tell your mother."

"As if I would." She laughed. "Well, we finally have a secret, you and I."

"You're a good friend, Cassie. I don't know what I'd do without you."

Her pause was longer than expected. "Yes . . . we are good friends."

Later, he wished he'd told Cassie to inform Laura of his call. Laura should know he was concerned. He was relieved she was simply busy and maybe upset about leaving home. She lived a sheltered life. It was going to be a big move for her. He would be patient.

In the days following, he often reminded himself that she was getting settled at Smith, which was why she wasn't writing.

Wallace called Obie into his office two days before graduation and handed him a form. "You wanted to declare yourself a conscientious objector. Do you still want that?"

"Yes, I do," Obie said, taking the sheet of paper.

"Fill it out and turn it in at company headquarters. I should have gotten it to you earlier, but I'm sure the Army will find some safe job for you, wherever you end up."

"Thank you, Sergeant Wallace."

Wallace waved his hand in dismissal, then cleared his throat. "You know, Gainsworthy, I've seen several men do what you're doing. I try not to judge. Every man has to decide those things for himself, but I think you'd of been a fine soldier. Good luck, anyway."

Obie believed he meant it, the "good luck" part.

* * *

Basic training ended on an early September day as hot as the one on which they started. Orders were cut for furloughs. Wallace shook hands with all of them. Even Leon dismounted from his high horse to offer congratulations and best wishes. Most men, including Obie and Matt, were to report to Newport News in ten days to prepare for shipping out. Rumor was that they were going to the African Theatre.

Obie was ecstatic at the prospect of soon seeing Laura. He'd already bought a bus ticket to Northampton. He'd written a letter to her shortly before she was scheduled to leave home, telling her of his travel plans, including his arrival time in Northampton. She would be there at the bus station to meet him. *He must have faith that she would be there.*

A truck was scheduled to transport several men into town that morning. Obie had his duffle bag and satchel on the barracks steps waiting when Matt arrived from company headquarters waving an envelope and smiling. Obie experienced a happy moment, for it must be a letter from Laura.

The writing on the envelope was Cassie's. A lump in his throat felt as big as a house. He fought his fear. What if something had happened to Laura? No . . . God would not be so cruel. He tore open the letter.

> *Dear Obie,*   *September 6, 1943*
> *I'm sorry to have to give you this news. I know it will be hard for you, and I'm sorry. I really am. Laura was married today to Ben Williamson. You know him. He's the son of the older Dr. Williamson, and he became a doctor himself not long ago. She wouldn't tell me if something had happened between you except to say that it was over. She didn't seem like she wanted to talk about it with me. I thought maybe something was wrong when you called our house. You didn't tell me anything then, and I won't ask you now unless you want to talk about it. How she acted has hurt me deeply because she always told me everything.*
>
> *I really don't understand why she changed her mind. Benjamin is nice enough, but he's older and not the type I thought Laura could feel that way about. He didn't want a traditional church wedding, and she went along with it. They were married by Pastor Charles on our patio with only our family present. I hope she hasn't made a big mistake. They left right away to live in Boston. His father, the old doctor, is very angry with him for leaving. I hope you get to come home and I hope I can see you then.*
>
> *Your good friend,*
> *Cassie*

Tears blinded Obie as he stuffed the letter into his pocket. He was beyond words; his head was spinning. He sat on the barracks steps for a long time. Matt sat beside him, concerned.

Obie took out the letter and reread it. The pain was just as bad the second time. He handed it to Matt before removing the bus ticket from his wallet and tearing it in half. He fumbled in his bag to find and remove the form Wallace had given him. He ripped it into several pieces.

Matt handed back the letter. Its shreds soon joined the pile of ruined paper on the steps.

"Will you take your leave at home?" Matt asked, "Back in Stafford Rest?"

"Damn Stafford Rest! I'll never go back there. Never!"

"Come home with me," Matt said, and Obie nodded.

Part Two

1943–1945

Nightmares

CHAPTER TWENTY

October 1943

In the harbor at Algiers, Obie and Matt stood at the rail of their troopship and watched the frenzied activity on the docks and in the avenues leading away from the water. Familiar odors of the sea and rotting fish mingled with foreign scents wafting up from nearby streets. Military vehicles were parked along the docks among carts and local vendors' wagons selling an endless variety of goods. Service members of several nations, American, British, and some wearing uniforms neither recognized, milled about, shouting orders at the disembarking men. What appeared to be a chaotic situation would eventually resemble order; it was the Army way. He looked forward to walking on land and exploring the exotic African city.

The ocean crossing had been a horrible experience accentuated by incessant rolling, pitching, and vomit smells that permeated the close quarters. They learned their destination after they slipped into the Mediterranean, although speculation had been rampant. Many believed they were going to Italy, the new front after the Allies defeated Rommel in Africa and chased the Germans out of Sicily. "The last phase of the Mediterranean Campaign!" declared a major on board who was within Obie's hearing. "Where can the Krauts go? North to the Alps is their only refuge. It'll take two months at the most."

There was mixed reaction when their destination was leaked, then confirmed. Matt said, "Pushing a pencil or guarding prisoners may not be glamorous, but it's sure as hell safer."

Obie and Matt had privately speculated about their roles in the Allied-occupied city and how long they might be there. The Italian front was expected to advance rapidly. The Russians were destroying masses of German troops, and another front against Germany itself was undoubtedly planned. The war could be over in a few months. They might never be near a battle.

Their musing at the ship's rail ended when they were called into formation on the deck. Obie became anxious when one hundred men, Obie and Matt among them, were separated from the rest and placed in charge of a first lieutenant in his mid-twenties who had recently come aboard.

The officer spoke to the group as they stood in a relaxed formation. "I'm Lieutenant Howard. We'll be transferring to another ship shortly. It will carry us to the mainland of Italy. I don't know where, as yet. I do know we'll be replacements in the 34th Division. The Red Bulls saw plenty of action here in Africa and Sicily. We'll be further assigned to regiments and companies once we arrive in Italy. This is much different than what you may have expected, but we must follow orders. I'll be your commander for the rest of this trip. Unless I'm ordered to secrecy, you'll know what I know."

Unloading troops took most of the day. After the docks were cleared of military vehicles and soldiers, the one hundred were allowed to exit the ship. Obie's time on the soil of Africa amounted to a brisk walk from gangplank to gangplank as they transferred to a smaller cargo vessel.

That evening, they assembled on the deck as the freighter left the harbor. "Our destination is Naples," Howard told the group. "The city has just been captured and is being stabilized. That said, it's still a very dangerous place. From what I've learned, the Jerrys have left it booby-trapped and wasted, and they come back every day to bomb and strafe. The harbor's filled with sunken vessels, but we're clearing it. Most supplies and troops have been going through Salerno, Castellammare, or other port cities, but Naples is now the closest port to the front and has a harbor that can handle large troop and supply vessels. Our group will be among the first contingents entering through Naples."

In convoy with several other vessels, the voyage from Algiers was relatively uneventful. They made several "diversionary" maneuvers because of reported German submarines, but there was no sight of the enemy. Eventually, they anchored late at night, nearly a mile offshore.

A landing craft materialized early the following morning. To reach them, it made a meandrous trip through a gauntlet of partially submerged vessels, some sunk by Germans, some by the Allies.

Howard's troops made their "landing" near the city. On the fringe of a crowded beach, duffle bags were thrown onto idling trucks of various makes and ages. The midmorning sky cleared, and the sun was warm on Obie's shoulders, unexpected because the rainy season had already started, and he'd imagined a downpour without letup. After two weeks on the water, he was ready to plant his feet on any solid ground, wet or dry.

"Pile onto the trucks," ordered a staff sergeant whose long face had already become familiar. He'd greeted Lieutenant Howard with a smart salute before directing the activities of the new arrivals. The sergeant's fatigues were worn but clean. A bandage covered his left ear; he went deliberately about his business. Once he'd finished supervising the loading of baggage and troops, he climbed into the back of their half-track and sat beside Matt. Obie, sitting across from him, saw that he was younger than first thought. The name on the tag over a pocket of his fatigue jacket said "Silverman."

Matt asked, "Sergeant, do you think we'll stay in Naples?"

"No, Private Burroughs, you'll be up at the front pretty soon." The accent was Massachusetts, bordering on Boston.

"How soon?"

"Probably a week or two at the most. A new assault is shaping up."

"Have you been out there . . . to the front?" Obie asked, eying the bandage.

"I have," Silverman responded, but I'm on special duty here now, and you'll be seeing a lot of me for a few days anyway." He cocked his head, presumably to see Obie's nametag. "Welcome to Italy, Gainsworthy."

"You were wounded?"

"At Benevento, several days ago. It's nothing," he said, touching the bandage. "Only a scratch. They gave me a choice of sitting around the company or coming back here to pick up new troops, so I came here. I'll be escorting your group back to my unit in a few days."

"What unit is that?" Matt asked.

"34th Infantry." Howard had been right.

Silverman continued, "I've been with the division since before we trained in Ireland. Mostly Iowa men at first. There's been a lot of turnover since. We were in Africa first, crossed into Sicily after finishing that job, and finally came through the mountains from Salerno." Obie was sure he detected pride in the words.

Silverman, tall and slender, had smooth hands with long fingers that looked more like those of a piano player than a battle-hardened noncom. His forehead was high, giving his head an elongated look, distinctive but not distracting. He said, "There's a notion that the Italian campaign will be a short one. Forget that. It'll take months to rout out the Jerrys. They're disciplined and determined, and they'll throw up every obstacle they can find."

While on the freighter to Naples, Obie had heard similar opinions from a contingent of African Campaign veterans. One of their officers was so firm in his declaration that Obie gave credence to their conviction that it could be a more protracted war than he'd expected.

"Where, exactly, are we headed?" Obie asked.

"I left the regiment at Benevento a couple of days ago. I hear they've since moved farther west. Eventually, we'll all be up at the Volturno River. That's an uneducated guess, however. They might even keep you near Naples for a couple of weeks of training. More than likely, though, you'll receive your training closer to the front."

"Where are we going today?" Matt asked.

"We're assigned to a small temporary company in the city. Regiment sent me here solely for the job of picking up your group of replacements. Others will be arriving also. Traffic into this port has picked up tremendously in the last few days. It's not my decision who goes with me, however. Lieutenant Howard is your commander. I'm only the escort."

"I'm hoping for a chance to see some of Naples," Matt said.

"Not the best idea. The city's unsecured, and most of it's off-limits to military personnel. Too dangerous. Jerrys left scads of booby traps when they pulled out. You can take a quick look as we're riding through, though."

Obie's father had predicted they would end up in Italy. While crossing the Atlantic, Obie tried to read everything he could find about the country. He wished he'd listened more closely to the stories his mother told. He couldn't remember the name of her village, only that it was in the hills near Rome.

Obie asked, "How do the Italians feel about us being here?"

"They like us . . . most of them. The German occupation has worn them down, so they see us as liberators. Mussolini still has his supporters, though, and some citizens just want to come down on the winners' side. It's an unstable situation. I doubt anybody will stop you if you go sightseeing, but your best bet is to stay right in the company. If you don't, all I can tell you is, be careful."

"What about the girls?" Matt asked. "Are they . . ."

"Burroughs, you'd be better off staying away from these Señoritas. You'll have enough to worry about without that kind of involvement."

Involvement. Laura. Even without reminders, thoughts of her betrayal came frequently and at unexpected times.

"If you have a girlfriend at home," Silverman said to Matt. "I'm sure she wouldn't like you being with somebody else."

"No girlfriend. I don't attract women the way Obie does." His smile faded as he glanced at Obie, apparently embarrassed for forgetting.

"Gainsworthy, do you have a girl at home?" Silverman asked.

"No." He almost added, "not anymore," but let the lone negative stand.

Silverman seemed to realize that he'd hit on a sensitive subject. "That's actually good," he said. "Where we're going, you'll need to keep your mind on your business."

Obie bit his lip to keep from venting an avalanche of pent-up adjectives that expressed his opinions of Laura and her mother—some quite unholy.

* * *

They quartered in a confiscated public building in a downtown section not far from a train station. The Germans had done their best to destroy the city before leaving. Businesses, even whole industries, were in ruins. Army engineers were at work everywhere. Roads were being cleared with bulldozers. The city had no electricity and little water. Before the war, Naples had a million inhabitants. Half that many remained and the majority struggled to survive. Even so, the city had a unique vibrancy, an unexpected life. Street vendors were moving about, avoiding the wreckage. Many shops were open.

Lieutenant Howard put sergeants in charge of smaller units to ensure that military discipline was followed. Before the first day was over weapons cleaning, boot shining, and cleanup of living quarters were all part of a "spit and polish" atmosphere. As Howard made inspections that evening, Obie heard him say, "Good for morale."

They were issued folding canvas cots, a luxury after living so long in ships' cramped sleeping quarters. Obie slept well that first night on the soil of Italy.

He wrote two letters the following day. The one to his father was short and to the point; without saying where he was, he indicated that he had ended up where Ken had predicted. He promised to follow with a longer letter once they were settled.

He also wrote to Cassie, his second letter. She'd initiated correspondence with a short letter forwarded from South Carolina. It had reached him while they were waiting to embark on the Atlantic voyage. He'd answered at once. Other mail caught up with them in Algiers and was delivered to their boat the morning of their departure for Naples. Among letters from his father and other relatives was the one from Cassie that he reread several times during the voyage.

Her letter was full of local news: Tim Bullock had been killed in the Pacific; the Blake home in Evergreen had burned, her father had given the family help from the Love Fund, and Charles Lansing was staying in Stafford Rest. Obie knew the Methodist Church Conference moved their pastors around, and Pastor Charles had told him it could soon happen to him, but it seemed he'd been spared. Construction had finally begun on the new education wing of the church. Cassie was a senior and would be going to college next year. She was having a difficult time living with her mother.

"I have the feeling," she wrote, "that I'll never come back once I leave."

He took great care in composing his letter to Cassie. He remembered what the liar Laura had said about Cassie's feelings for him. He didn't believe it but would avoid writing anything that might give her the wrong idea. He wanted no such relationship with anyone. Nevertheless, Cassie was a special friend. Obie often wondered what it would be like to have a sister. He imagined she would be like Cassie, easy to talk to and free with advice and demands. Such a sister would stomp her foot in anger at him, as Cassie often had. He smiled at the thought.

Dear Cassie,   *October 8, 1943*

We arrived yesterday. I got your letter a few days ago. I was delighted to get it. If you want to know where I am, I think you should talk to my father. On second thought, I'll just plain out tell you that I'm in Italy. If the censors want to take that part out, they can.

We are staying in a big old building right in Naples, which is by the sea. We are close to the Piazza Garibaldi. (Hope I spelled it right.) There are a hundred or more of us, although they say more men will be joining us soon. They call us replacement troops. Things are sort of makeshift since the Allies got here. We are sleeping in the basement of this public building and have a small chow hall, but we ate outside this morning since it's not raining. It rains a lot here at this time of year. I don't know exactly when we'll be going up to the front. Some of the men think it might be soon.

Matt and I (I told you all about Matt in my previous letter) will try to see part of Naples tonight. The Germans occupied the city before we chased them out, and they left booby traps to blow people up, so we have to be careful. They're still clearing the harbor but have already done a fairly decent job.

When we first arrived yesterday morning, I talked with a staff sergeant named Silverman who's been in several campaigns. I've seen him around today. He's a nice fellow, friendlier than some noncoms, and relatively young, about 21 or 22. He's been in the Army for a little over two years. There's a rumor that he led a patrol out of a bad situation in the mountains where they were surrounded. For that, they promoted him, and I believe he's up for a medal of some sort.

Cassie, I want you to say hello to Pastor Charles for me and tell him I'll write soon. You stay well and study hard. I know you'll be a teacher someday, as we talked about. I'm sure you'll be a really good one, too.

Your friend always, Obie

He fought melancholy after posting the letters, but nothing compared to the previous joyless weeks. Ten days at Matt's home in Virginia had been a luxurious hell. Matt's parents showered on Obie the same attention they gave their son. His sister, fourteen-year-old Tina, fell in love with Obie at first sight. Nevertheless, Obie was in agony that alternated between anger and grief. Matt had a couple of dates and wanted to "fix up" Obie with his cousin, Opal, who was pretty. Obie begged off. "I'm hardly fit to be with myself, let alone anyone else."

He'd gone for long walks around the farm and into the village, trying to sort out the warring demons in his head. By the time they said goodbye to Matt's wet-eyed parents and sister, he'd recovered a measure of normalcy but was acutely aware of a vacuum in his life with nothing to fill it. Obie's prayers had gone unanswered, and his dreams had been stripped away. *Like Laura, God had deserted him.*

A question, coming often, always threw him into an abyss. *Why did she do it?* She'd not even had the decency to give him an explanation. All his discussions with Pastor Charles about love and forgiveness as the foremost Christian ideal meant nothing now; *he wasn't going to forgive.* She had fled and taken with her all his feelings for her. He doubted he'd ever feel love of that kind again—and he had no desire that he would.

* * *

They'd been advised, but not ordered, to stay within company confines. Nevertheless, Obie and Matt set off that evening to see as much of the famous city as possible—even in its brokenness. MPs were everywhere; they would not be allowed to stray into restricted areas.

Obie was appalled at the conditions. Trash was piled head-high on nearly every curb. The odors that assaulted Obie's nostrils were not unlike that of Abner's bait bucket with its "cured" tidbits. He'd been able to avoid the bucket for cleaner air, but the sights, sounds, and scents here were overpowering in many places. Despite such annoyance, he caught an occasional whiff of baking bread and garlic, familiar smells that brought a cleansing effect to his nostrils; they would be coming from restaurants still open for business.

Numerous shops were open, even in damaged buildings with broken window glass. Most patrons were servicemen: British, Australian, Canadian, and Indian military clustered, as did groups of local women and girls. Occasionally, he saw couples walking with their heads together.

Matt said, "Maybe we can hook up with a couple of girls." His meaning was clear.

Obie was silent on that matter. He was glad he was with Matt, for no reason other than to keep his friend out of trouble.

The rain had stopped and the air had cooled; he was glad for his fatigue jacket. They wandered into a section that looked more residential than the streets near their company site. From there, they could see the bay. The low sun cast a red glow on the city landscape between them and the sea. Mount Vesuvius dominated the southern view, emitting spurts of ugly smoke and saying, "I'm quiet right now, but I'm not dead."

Obie realized they were about to stray from approved territory, so they retraced their steps until they were back within a few blocks of their quarters. By then, the sun had set and it was getting dark. The streets were filling. Candlelight was the dominant interior lighting source, with an occasional kerosene lamp casting stronger glows on windows facing the streets. Military orders to keep the city dark at night had its dissenters.

As if by magic, a girl appeared from the dark; one moment they were alone, and the next she stood beside them. Obie thought she might have come from one of the three-story damaged buildings lining the walkway on either side. She was young, maybe sixteen, thin to an extreme, and pretty, although unkempt. The gingham dress she wore had rose patterns on a blue background. Her dark hair was long. Obie suspected that her thinness resulted from malnutrition, a condition evident in many on the streets.

Matt spoke to her. "How are you, Miss? You're sure pretty."

She shrugged her shoulders, indicating she didn't understand. In Italian, Obie said, "Good evening to you, Señorita."

Matt looked puzzled. "You speak Italian?"

"I *did* tell you that my mother was Italian."

"Well, that's good. You can ask her some questions."

"What is your name?" Obie asked.

"Rosa," the girl said. She fingered a crucifix on a chain around her neck. "I am Rosa Rizzetti." There was pride in the utterance. "What is your name, GI?"

"I'm Obie, and this is Matt. He wants to meet you. He doesn't speak Italian, so I'll talk for him."

Obie hadn't used his mother's language for a long time and had stumbled over some words. This girl's dialect was slightly different, but he was confident they could correspond without difficulty.

"I like you, GI Obie. I can talk with you."

"What's she saying?" Matt asked as he moved closer.

Obie raised his hand. "Give me a minute." To Rosa, he said, "Matt thinks you are very good to look at."

She stared at Matt for a moment. "All right, GI Obie. He is good to look at, too. I will be a friend with GI Matt, also. Are you rich?"

He laughed and said in English, "If only you knew."

Obie noticed a boy about Rosa's age standing fifteen feet away beside the nearest building. His trousers were several sizes too large and had holes in the knees. It was obvious he was listening to their conversation. "Who is that?" Obie asked her.

"Beppe, my cousin. He sometimes looks out for me . . . or he thinks he does." She swirled toward the youth. "Beppe, go home. It is all right." She turned back to Obie. "We will go to a restaurant? Yes?"

Obie waited until Beppe had disappeared into the shadows. "Yes, we'll go to a restaurant, but you'll be Matt's friend," he said dismissively and saw at once that she had taken offense.

Rosa studied his face. Her voice rose as she said, "I think you do not want to be my friend. Why are you mean to me? I have done nothing to you. Maybe you do not like women?"

Obie had, at first, believed that her words were part of an act meant to seduce. He might have misjudged. She was just a young girl, a victim of the war trying to survive.

"I'm sorry, Rosa. I just wanted you to know that it's Matt who decided that we are going to a restaurant." He was confident that was the truth.

"What's she saying?" Matt asked as he leaned across Obie's shoulder.

"She wants something to eat."

"Well, let's feed her."

"I told her that you'd be her date."

Matt smiled. "All right. Let's find a restaurant. After we eat, you can go find your own girl if you want to."

Rosa led them to the *Ristorante di Giuseppe,* which was on one of the side streets. It was a small one-story stone structure among two and three-story buildings that had suffered bombardment of the severest kind. The tiny establishment had been spared. The sidewalk in front was primarily clear of rubble, although broken concrete and bricks had been thrown into a narrow space between it and one of the other buildings. The odors remained.

Curtains covered the restaurant window. Like in most of the city, there was no electricity. Several patrons were Army men. Some had women with them. Tables, about a dozen in a space where there should have been half that many, were covered by stained tablecloths. A lighted candle sat on each table.

They seated themselves at a table in a corner. A man wearing an apron appeared. "Good evening, Seniors," he said in broken English. "I am Giuseppe. I am here to serve you."

"Good evening," Obie replied in Italian. "And we are two hungry Americans . . . and one very hungry girl."

"How will you pay?" Giuseppe asked, seeming not embarrassed about his forthrightness.

"Dollars."

"Have you no goods?"

"Goods?"

"Cigarettes? Coffee? Sugar? Chocolate? Condoms?"

"No. We don't have those things."

Giuseppe looked disappointed but took their order. Obie had heard that the sale and trade of stolen American goods was an ongoing activity. Troops were warned against being caught up in it. "A court-martial offense," they were told.

The food was simple fare. The pasta, with highly seasoned tomato sauce accompanied by half a loaf of bread, was good, although inferior to his mother's or Angie's. The red wine was excellent, a fact not surprising. The Germans had confiscated all they could use and destroyed much more as they left, but the quantity of wine in the country was great. Obie had heard that many homes had their wine cellars.

Rosa was silent except for the noises she made while eating. She gulped her food, washed it down with wine, and licked her fingers. That she was enjoying the meal was apparent.

"Slow down, Rosa. We have enough time," Obie said.

Her large eyes took on an unfathomable expression, making him wish to retrieve his words. She set her glass down after taking a drink. "GI Obie, have you ever been hungry?"

"Well, no. Not really."

"My family . . . I have a mother, and two brothers, and two sisters. They are hungry, always. My father . . . I do not know if he is alive or dead. The Nazis took him north before the surrender to do their hard labor. Yes, I eat swiftly because any second you or GI Matt may say, 'That is enough.'" The fire lighting her eyes diminished as she laid her fork down and leaned back with her arms crossed.

"Is she mad at us?" Matt asked.

Obie translated. Matt peered at Rosa with compassion and reached out to take her hand. Obie watched their eyes meet and wondered what was evolving.

"Tell her she won't be hungry again as long as I'm around," Matt said.

"Are you sure you want to tell her that? You won't be around long. Not here anyway."

"Tell her!"

Obie translated and watched the two become even more engrossed in each other. Language seemed not to matter.

Nevertheless, he had to warn Matt. "You met her less than an hour ago."

"That doesn't seem important right now." He continued to hold her hand.

At that moment, a soldier whom Obie recognized, a company cook, entered the restaurant. Maxwell Burke had not come with the group from Algiers; he was already in the Naples' company. He nodded to them before going to the open kitchen door where he passed a large bag to Giuseppe, a thinly disguised action. The paper bag split, and coffee tins became visible.

"You see that?" Obie said.

"Don't say anything. He's a tough guy. Let it be. It's none of our business."

"Maybe we should tell an MP."

"You want to get us killed?"

The thought was sobering. "Guess not."

They finished their meal. Rosa looked satisfied. She clutched Matt's arm with both hands.

"I'm going back to the post," Obie said when they were outside again.

"It's early, Obie. You can hook up with some girl real easy with your Italian."

"I'm not interested."

"What's the matter with you?" Matt's expression was one of consternation. "Don't you realize this could be our last chance for a long time to do this?"

"Maybe."

"You're still thinking about *her,* aren't you?"

"No!"

"Sure . . . you are. Man, you've got to forget that bitch."

For a moment, Matt's words angered him, but he recovered. "I've put all that behind me."

"Of course, you have." There was sarcasm in the words. "Well, you go on back and get a good night's sleep. I'm going to enjoy myself."

An hour later, Obie was back on his cot, quietly contemplating whether or not he'd finally put Laura out of mind. He slept but heard Matt come in much later, muttering to himself. Obie knew why; the NCO in charge of quarters was informing everyone in their group that they would be moving out within forty-eight hours.

CHAPTER TWENTY–ONE

October 1943

The following morning Obie's group received official confirmation of their assignment to the 34th Infantry Division. They were scheduled to move up within twenty-four hours.

Obie was curious about Silverman. He'd gleaned some facts about the sergeant from two Sicily campaign veterans awaiting reassignment. While applying a shine to his boots, Ted Clemons told him, "We were in different platoons, but I saw what he did at Fondouk Pass. He charged a pillbox practically by himself. Went in there with mortar and small arms fire all around him. He's up for a Silver Star, but that's for something he did recently at Benevento."

Paul Aimes, a quiet and thoughtful Tennessean sitting to one side but listening, quickly observed, "There are more dead heroes than live ones. I wish Silverman the best, but sometimes your luck just runs out."

Later that day, Silverman approached Obie. "You and Burroughs are right out of basic training, so you'll need some looking after. I'm going to take you into my squad. I hope that meets with your approval." Obie detected irony in the statement; it wasn't a choice.

"Well, yeah, it's okay with me, and I'm sure Matt too, but don't you already have a squad?"

"I'll be assigned new men. My old squad, what's left, was absorbed by other squads after I was wounded. Our regimental commander told me I could pick my men, and I'm making up a list of names right from this group since I already know several of them. Lieutenant Howard knows and approves."

"You talk to regiment commanders?"

Silverman laughed. "Once. The colonel visited our medic tents after we took Benevento." His smile faded. "We had lots of causalities up there."

Silverman's "what's left" statement bothered Obie. "Did you lose many . . . from your squad, I mean?"

Silverman looked away. "We did. Of eleven men, including me, we had nine causalities. Four died."

"I heard that you're up for a medal."

Silverman shrugged. "I didn't do anything any squad leader wouldn't do under the circumstances."

"Some of the men here think differently." Obie couldn't help asking, "What happened, anyway?"

"Two squads, mine and Miles Robertson's, were pinned down in a draw by the river. We were getting fire you wouldn't believe . . . mortar, artillery, small arms, and machinegun at close quarters. We were being annihilated. Robertson was killed, and I pulled the two squads together. I provided some cover while the rest retreated. It was somewhat of a disaster; too many dead. When I got word from the regiment that I'd been recommended for a medal, I told them I didn't deserve it. They said I was getting it anyway. I told the colonel that, rather than a medal, I'd like the option of hand-picking my next squad."

"And he agreed to that?"

"He laughed at me and said he'd never had such a request, but he gave his permission right then and there. My company commander was there too and acknowledged my request. About the medal, I don't know. I haven't heard anything. Maybe he took the swap seriously, and I won't get it. That's okay because, as I said, I don't deserve it."

"It would be nice to have, though."

"I don't need another one."

"You already have one?"

"Bronze Star. I'm proud of that. I deserved that one."

"What happened?"

"Gainsworthy, I've already told you more about myself than any other soldier in Italy." He paused a moment. "Sometime, though, I'll tell you all about it if you're still interested. It's more likely you'll be sick of me. I'm a hard-ass."

"That's hard to believe."

"Some of you won't like what I'll be doing. I'll grind what I know into you, and the grinding might be painful. Maybe you'll want to think it over about joining my squad."

"Do I have a choice?"

"Hell, no! But you should know that once we get to division, you might be assigned to a different company or platoon than mine. So, consider all this temporary."

"But we *could* stay together?" Obie said, hopefully,"

"Yes, that might happen."

"About this 'maybe' temporary squad you're organizing here, won't we all be new men?"

"No. Clemons, Aimes, Deboise, and Burke are combat veterans who've been with the division since we landed at Salerno. They're in Naples for various reasons but will go back with us. Burke's been in combat as long as me. He's been behind the lines for a few weeks because of some disciplinary action. Don't know what . . . don't want to know. He was busted down from sergeant, but he's still a good soldier."

Obie considered telling Silverman about what Burke was doing in the restaurant the night before but decided against it. It was none of his business. He asked, "Where's the regiment now?"

"They don't share much information with noncoms, but our destination tomorrow is likely Montesarchio. That's a few miles west of Benevento. I'm guessing the whole division will assemble there."

"Is that the front . . . Montesarchio?"

"No. Except for some small pockets of the enemy left to harass us, the front's moved to the Volturno River. I believe the whole Fifth Army's massing there."

"And that's where we're going?"

"It is." Silverman raised a finger, a clear indication to curtail the questioning. "Gainsworthy, you don't need to see the bigger picture. Nor do I. That's the job of generals. Just keep your mind on your business and your head down. Do what I tell you, and you'll stay alive."

Should he doubt Silverman's words? He'd just admitted losing three-quarters of a squad in a recent battle. Paul Aimes' comment, "sometimes, your luck just runs out," came to mind. But he liked Silverman, who, for some unknown reason had taken him and Matt under his wing. He'd give the man his trust.

Obie joined Matt, who was sitting on the steps of a nearby building, looking miserable. "I liked her," he said.

"There'll be others, you know."

"She liked me too. We kissed."

"Is that all?"

"Yeah, but if I could've seen her tonight, things would've moved forward."

"Listen, Buddy, Rosa's simply after a meal ticket. You do know that, don't you?"

Matt took his time answering. "Yeah, I guess so. Anyway, I got her address and let her know I'd write."

"How's she going to read your letters?"

"She introduced me to her cousin, Beppe. He speaks English. And maybe you can help me."

"Sorry. I speak some Italian. I don't write it."

"Obie, I know you think I'm crazy, all this happening so quick. But she's a pitiful little thing. I wouldn't mind helping her and her family out."

"They're all pitiful. We can't help them all. The best thing we can do for these people is to drive out the Germans. That's how they'll get their lives back."

Silverman oversaw their packing and, in many instances, demanded repacking. He was exacting in what he wanted them to have. He told Obie, "We're short on many things. The divisions haven't even received heavy clothing for winter, and some basic items were even left in Sicily. I'm scrounging things and not just leaving it up to what the company clerks give us. You don't get it if you don't ask. I don't have the rank or authority to demand, but I can pester."

They left in a large convoy midmorning the following day. Light rain fell. Their contingent was a small part of the replacements heading toward the front. In addition to Maxwell Burke, Theodore Clemons, Paul Aimes, and Leander Deboise, all combat experienced men, Silverman had rounded out his squad with newcomers Obie, Matt, Timothy Copland, Thomas Rivera, Edward Grugs, Harold Perkins, and Christian Meinard, making a total of twelve, including Silverman. All the new men had come in on the ship with Obie, but he knew only Perkins and Grugs, and them not well.

For two days, Obie had observed the massive volume of traffic. Convoy after convoy passed through the city from the port toward some unknown destination. Along with an increased troop presence, there were vehicles of many kinds, trucks, tanks, half-tracks, cannons, and jeeps, all presumably on the way to the front. *Was it normal traffic or something more significant?* Their group hooked onto the end of one of the convoys.

They had two weapons carriers, three-quarter-tons for carrying duffle bags and supplies, and several trucks for moving troops. Traffic out of Naples was heavy, although it moved with reasonable speed. Italy was a land of farms and small villages, which became evident soon after leaving. He should have known, for his mother had told him stories about the land numerous times.

Vegetable gardens, vineyards, and olive trees were scattered over the coastal plain, and as the convoy skirted hills and low mountains, he saw that they also covered terraced slopes as far up as there was tillable soil. Many villages showed heavy damage, and villagers often stood on the roadside watching them pass. What were they thinking?

Their route took them northeast, skirting the mountains, and then east into them. Once in the hills, the procession slowed to a crawl. MPs made them pull over several times to allow strings of armored vehicles, tanks, and other heavy equipment to pass through.

"Something big's going on," Silverman observed.

To the east were the Apennines, much higher mountains with clouds around their tops. Two stuck up through the clouds creating the illusion of being even farther-away mountains that stood above a hazy plain. Obie's artist eye detailed how he would lay out the scene on canvas.

He was anxious, he told himself, not frightened. He glanced at the men on the other side of the truck bed, trying to discern what they might be thinking. There was little talk. Each man appeared lost in his own thoughts. Silverman had used straightforward language as they left, "We'll likely be in combat in a few days." It was said without a trace of emotion. Words in Obie's head kept repeating; *I'm going to war. I'm going to war.*

They'd been forewarned about travel conditions and, eventually the road became so bad they were forced to walk; several times they had to push their trucks. The wind turned harsh and rain fell all day, worsening the avenue of mud. It was a condition far more distressing than anything he'd experienced in the Adirondacks.

Trucks became helplessly mired numerous times. Angry sludge sucked at Obie's feet. Hours passed, as did the difficult miles. Moving up the boot of Italy, even without enemy contact, was proving a Herculean task. The highway had probably been a good road at one time, but the treads of German tanks and the weight of other heavy equipment, followed by vehicles of the Allies, had shredded it into the mess under their feet and into the distance ahead.

"Sarge, when are we going to get there?" Matt asked.

"We get there when we get there," Silverman replied with an annoyed edge to his voice. "Don't be in such a damn hurry. I doubt you'll like it any better after we arrive."

At one location, they walked single file. Silverman led, with Obie and Matt behind him. Rivera and Copland followed. Rivera, a tall thin Californian, told Obie that he was a doctor's son. Copland, from Ohio, was thickset and muscular, a blowhard and tiring to listen to, especially as the day wore on. Matt muttered under his breath every time Copland spoke.

In time, they emerged onto a mile-wide plain. They had come, at last, to the bivouac of the 34th Division just west of the town of Montesarchio.

* * *

Obie took his turn standing guard at a knoll on the staging area perimeter. From there, he could see everything. Montesarchio was on the other side of the valley, and Mt. Taburno stood north of it. On the broad plain before him was a single division consisting of three infantry regiments with their supporting companies and battalions.

For the first time, Obie saw what a gigantic beast their army was. Row after row of tents of varying sizes served as living quarters, hospital, supply, and headquarters; they covered the valley floor in a patchwork of grays. Occasional stone buildings, and more colorful framed ones confiscated for headquarters or other uses, broke the monotony. Men were everywhere, moving like ants through the jumble. Machinery, in long rows, stood off to the side. The low rumble of engines and vapor curling upward in the humid air provided evidence that the division was alive and ready.

To Obie's relief, Silverman's squad had been attached, intact, to one of the battalion platoons. He was also surprised to learn that Lieutenant Howard would be their platoon commander. Silverman told him that Howard had been wounded in Africa and was just now returning to the front.

Disregarding Silverman's advice, Obie made an effort to understand the military situation. Aimes was helpful; the corporal, older than most of the soldiers, had been a history teacher in civilian life. Although looking tired and exhibiting tenseness, he might have a broader vision of what was happening.

Aimes explained that there would soon be three American divisions along the Volturno River, making up General John P. Lucas' VI Corps. To the west, on the left flank, where the Volturno flowed onto the coastal plain, the British 10 Corps was assembling. Together, they made up the bulk of General Mark W. Clark's Fifth Army, poised to strike at "some of Hitler's best troops."

Howard told the men that the impending attack was no secret, even to the Germans, but when and where was known only to top

Allied brass. One of their regiments was already moving north to relieve part of the 3rd Division on the river. Although slowed by rain, mud, and enemy fire from north of the stream, the exchange proceeded. All units were on alert.

That afternoon Silverman came into their tent. "We're moving up," he announced. "Get your packs on!"

Obie's confidence, if it could be rightly called such, evaporated. A feeling of dread swept over him.

* * *

Silverman and his squad caught occasional rides but walked most of the way, twenty miles or more. Roads were barely recognizable. Some vehicles were so bogged down that bulldozers were required to push them free.

They went into an area adjacent to the valley during the night and camped against a black mountain. The other two regiments occupied the most forward positions. All through the night, artillery and supporting battalions joined them. The rain continued, sustaining the level of misery. Obie huddled under his poncho, shivering from the cold.

Although well back, they heard firing all night from across the river. Early in the morning heavy gun sounds came from farther down the river. Their artillery soon joined in. The barrage lasted an hour.

Lieutenant Howard called his squads together. During the previous twenty-four hours, the nearly seventy platoon members had functioned as a group, and Obie was able to match names with most faces and the functions for which each man was responsible. Everyone appeared bedraggled. They gathered around Howard, who had just come from a staff meeting composed of officers up to the divisional level. His platoon sergeant, Tech Sergeant Smith, was with him.

"Men, here's what I know," Howard said. "We're at the Volturno River, and sitting right across from us is Hitler's Tenth Army. They're comprised of several Panzer divisions under General Marshal Kesselring. Make no mistake about it; these are some of the Germans' best troops. We've pushed them back to this point, and they're making a stand. The 34th is in a central position to drive them back even farther. On our left flank is the 3rd Division, and on our right will be the 145th. The Brits are on the far left, to the sea. This won't be easy, but it's a job that we have to do."

"Damn right," yelled Copland.

"Shut up, Copland," Silverman said calmly but sternly.

Howard continued, "All the divisions will attack at the same time. Two regiments of the 34ᵗʰ Division will make the advance crossing. Our regiment will be in reserve."

Groans could be heard throughout the group. "Sir," said a soldier from another squad, "how long will our regiment be in reserve?"

"Not long. We'll be in the fight as soon as a bridgehead is established, or even sooner if we're needed."

"When will the attack start?" The question came from Paul Aimes.

"I don't know, though I can say with some certainty that it will be at night. I suspect it will be as early as tonight."

After a pause, Smith signaled the end of the briefing with, "Thank you, sir!"

Howard said, "Sergeant Smith's going to see if he can get some dry socks for us."

* * *

Matt and Deboise had hung a tarp over a line strung between two trees, making a lean-to-like habitat that did an acceptable job of turning rainwater. Nothing could be done about the soggy earth; if they sat at all, it was on their helmets.

Obie and Meinard returned from a mess detail and were invited to join them. Obie passed out C-ration chocolate bars he'd confiscated.

"I hate this weather," Matt muttered.

Deboise said, "What I hate is Germans."

A moment of silence passed before Meinard spoke. "I'm German."

"What's that mean?" Deboise asked, looking puzzled.

"Both my parents are from Berlin. I was born in the United States, but my first language was German."

"Well, I'll be . . . How'd you . . ."

"My parents became citizens, and I was born an American citizen."

Darkness was descending, and Obie could see neither man's face. The tension needed relief. Before he could speak, Matt said, "Obie's mother was Italian. He speaks Italian. Meinard speaks

214

German. It'll be handy for us to have people who can do that."

Deboise cleared his throat. "Hell, I didn't mean . . ."

"It's okay," Meinard said. "I'm prepared to give everything I have for my country, even my life if I have to."

A voice Obie recognized as Burke's came from another make-shift shelter several feet away. "I hope we don't have to listen to any more of that patriotic crap."

Deboise, seeming to have recovered his composure, said, "You can bet your sweet ass we'll be in the thick of it quicker than a squir-rel can crack a hickory nut." When his words received no reply, he continued, "We might even be goin' the other way."

Deboise's comment had a sobering effect. Although Obie had long abandoned becoming a conscientious objector, he didn't like to think about taking the life of another human being. However, he'd tried cultivating the idea that he shouldn't care about his own life since he had nothing to live for. But now, on the eve of battle, he realized that he had abundant fear. *He wanted to live.*

How bad would their situation be? Meinard's fervor was ex-treme, and Deboise's attitude, probably due to battle fatigue, was a further worry. Would they jeopardize the safety of the other men, including himself? Silverman said their survival depended on their taking care of one another. How would Meinard and Deboise stand up in battle? How would he? It appeared he would soon know.

CHAPTER TWENTY–TWO

October 1943

Howard's assessment was correct; the Fifth Army assault against the Volturno River German defenses began that night. Obie's regiment waited in the rear, not patiently but resigned. The rain let up, and a full moon lit the valley. Groups of soldiers clustered, waiting for news from their attacking forces. It trickled in at first and faster as communications were established.

Through Howard's frequent updates a clearer picture emerged. The Allies had faked the main assault around midnight at Triflisco, through the narrow gap leading onto the coastal plain, hoping to fool the Germans into moving in more troops there; the main assault was through the middle of the forty-mile front. That became evident at one o'clock when heavy shelling started and lasted an hour. Forward troops of the 3rd and 34th Divisions began crossing the river.

The crossing was hard. Word filtered back to the waiting regiment that there were heavy causalities, even after extensive reconnaissance. Nevertheless, both divisions advanced taking hills and towns as they went, some with ease, others hard-won. When daylight came, artillery fire blasted the German fortifications. Tanks were held from crossing the river because of heavy enemy fire. Rain fell again in the afternoon. Within twenty-four hours the divisions had a bridgehead established north of the river.

The two attacking 34th Division regiments drove as far as Caiazzo, and within forty-eight hours the 45th Division on the far right, made contact. The weakened German air force strafed but couldn't halt the Allied advance. The Germans had no choice but to pull back from the river. It became imperative for the Allies to build bridges so that supplies and equipment could cross and catch up with the troops.

Howard said to his waiting platoon, "Be ready to move out!"

* * *

Burke's stubby forefinger pointed out on a map that the Volturno, flowing from the north, followed a course shaped like a backward L. They were crossing the bottom of the L, but would soon be going north along the river's west side. Bridges were finally in place; some were laid on rubber pontoons. The order came for the regiment and the 100th Battalion to follow the rest of the division north.

The area north of the river was cleared except for small pockets of enemy troops left behind to harass the Allies. Obie heard occasional gunfire. He saw groups of German prisoners escorted to the rear, some defiant, most looking scared. Many were wounded, some walking and some on stretchers.

They camped two miles east of Alvignano to await orders. Obie was exhausted, but there would be no time for rest; the regiment was soon ordered to take Dragoni, but then almost immediately received a new assignment. They were to march northeast, cross the Volturno again, and establish a bridgehead on the road to Piedimonte d'Alife. They were to capture both a highway bridge and a railroad bridge, keeping them intact. Enemy tanks had been reported in that area.

The countryside was dotted with farms and vineyards. Small buildings and geographical diversity gave the enemy numerous places to hide, but there was no sign of them except for scattered sniper fire.

Battalions of the regiment advanced on separate paths. Forward platoons received fire around midnight as they entered the valley of the south-flowing river. Artillery shells exploded on the flanks, lighting up the night sky. Machinegun clatter from the river was constant.

Obie fought anxiety. *Would he be brave or so scared he couldn't function?* He concluded that he was already afraid—even terrified. His hands, holding his M1, shook. He recoiled each time an explosion rocked the ground under his feet. His greatest desire was to find some shelter, a hole to crawl into.

They ran, walked, and jogged until near the water's edge. Other platoons were already crossing the swift-moving stream. Firing across the river continued. Mortar shells exploded around them. Men near Obie and on the river were yelling. The noise became constant; he wished he could stuff his ears with something to block it.

On the left, a man screamed, groaned, and screamed again. Someone yelled, "Medic! Medic!"

Matt, right behind him, moved up close. "God, Obie! Do we have to wade into this?"

There wasn't time to answer. Silverman spoke with some

urgency, "Down the bank! Stay in single file and grab a rope! Keep your weapons dry! Come on! Move!" He led the way.

Obie hadn't been "dry" since the first crossing. The water came up to his waist as he entered it and momentarily shocked him. He heard Matt gasp. He glanced back and saw his friend struggling to stay upright. His shorter frame brought water up to his chest. Matt held up his M1 but lost his grip on the rope strung across the river. Obie grasped him by the collar and pulled him back into position to grab the rope again.

"I don't know if I can do this," Matt said, his despair evident.

From the back, a voice Obie recognized as Burke's bellowed, "Keep 'em moving! Get under that far bank!"

Obie lost track of the other squad members. Firing persisted as he reached the steep bank and scrambled up holding his M1 in one hand while grabbing roots and protruding brush with the other. He extended an arm to help Copland scale the embankment. There was enough light to reveal the man's wide smile. Copland appeared to have found his element. Obie was far from his.

The bank was high and offered temporary shelter. The squad members climbed out one by one and bunched up on a small rock shelf. Judging by voices on either side, other squads were doing much the same.

"We all here?" Silverman said. "Perkins! Where's Perkins?"

"I'm here, Sarge!"

"Sarge, I've been hit," someone said.

"Who's that?"

"Grugs!"

"Where you hit?"

"In the arm."

"You want a corpsman?"

"It's only a scratch."

"Burke, take a look at Grugs."

Less than a minute passed before Burke pronounced Grugs fit to continue. Grugs offered no protest.

Howard sent word that they were to stay in place for the present. Sounds of firing lessened and then all but ceased. After a few minutes, the order came to advance. They'd expected to meet more resistance, but as nervous men spread out word came from another battalion that the Germans had withdrawn. A little later, Howard told them, "Krauts blew both bridges. Nothing left but rubble."

They were finally allowed to rest. The 100th Battalion arrived not much later, uniting the regiment. Men bedded down wherever they could without finding any real comfort. Everyone was wet and cold. C-Rations were distributed, but there were no hot meals.

"Never thought I'd like this stuff," Rivera said.

Grugs' wound was minor; a piece of shrapnel had penetrated his left arm above his elbow. A corpsman pulled it out with tweezers and applied a white salve to the injury before covering it with a bandage. "Nothing to worry about," he told Grugs.

"Did it bleed?" Silverman asked.

"Yeah, a little."

"Then you have yourself a purple heart," Silverman responded, smiling.

The following morning the valley was filled with fog. Obie's clothing was still wet; his boots sloshed when he walked. He ached all over, but his sore feet gave him the most trouble. He saw many bodies, primarily German. American dead were also being recovered by what Burke called "the goon patrol." Obie tried not to look.

Howard, looked fatigued as he called his squads together. "Here's what I know," was his familiar refrain. "The 135th has cleared Route 135 to Alife and is advancing on the town right now. They're meeting some resistance but getting the job done. The 45th Division has closed in from the east and has taken Piedimonte d'Alife. They're a tired outfit, and our division is relieving them. Our next objectives are north of here, the towns of Sant' Angelo d'Alife, Raviscanina, and Ailano." He stopped and looked toward Obie. "Did I get those names right, Gainsworthy?"

Obie was surprised. Howard had never shown that he recognized Obie's existence, certainly not his name.

Howard continued without waiting for an answer. "We've had our first contact with the enemy, but we've missed most of the real action so far. That's about to change. They'll start making stands, which means we'll have to root them out. It's going to get harder."

"Will the division stay together?" Obie asked Silverman.

"We may get broken up into smaller units."

Copland sounded displeased. "What about the Japs? You think they'll hold up their end?"

Obie knew he spoke of the 100th Battalion which consisted of native-born Americans of Japanese descent. They'd been attached to the Fifth Army since September and had been on the left flank in the advance from the river to the bridges.

Silverman said. "They're good soldiers. They did well at

Salerno."

Clemons spoke up. "I talked to one of them. It sounds like they wiped out several pockets of Krauts on the way up here."

"Seems funny," Grugs said. "Our troops are fighting against them in the Pacific, and here we are fighting together."

"They're Americans, just like us," Obie stated.

"I still don't trust them," Copland said.

"Who do you trust, Copland?" Silverman asked. He gave the private no time to answer. "Look around you. No! Really look! Who do you see? There's Deboise from Arkansas. 'Hillbilly,' you call him, and you don't say it with respect. Gainsworthy, he's a hillbilly too, just different hills. His mother was Italian. Think he might be partial to Mussolini? What about Meinard? His ancestry is German."

Copland was staring at his feet. "Well, of course . . ."

Silverman wasn't finished. "And me . . . a Jew. Surely you have some thoughts about that. Look around you, Copland. There are people here from Chicago, New York, Iowa, Tennessee, Arkansas, Kentucky, Boston. Look at their faces."

Copland continued to stare at his boots. His face was red.

"You rely on these men, Copland . . . and they rely on you. We're in this together. If we're going to survive, it's because we look out for one another."

Copland stood a moment longer before he whirled and walked away from the group. Silverman's face was red, too. This was no mere pep talk contrived to whip them into action. Silverman had previously shown little emotion. The sergeant was human, after all. *And he's a Jew.* About that, Obie was surprised.

* * *

Orders came for the regiment to move out at eighteen hundred hours, about the time it would get dark. Artillery was blasting known enemy positions in the hills and along roads. Theirs was the first regiment to advance. They did so quickly, traveling a mile east of the river and parallel to it. Silverman judged that their first objective, Sant' Angelo d'Alife, was three or four miles north.

"You'll meet strong opposition tonight," A regimental officer warned. "Just don't get caught in the open flats after daylight."

Their anticipated route was along the valley floor and into the foothills of the Matese mountain range. The 125th and 151st Field Artillery Battalions were supposed to come up behind them for support. The main road from Alife to Ailano ran up the valley west of the hills. Side roads led to objective villages. Those roads were interlocking, creating strategic points that required capture.

Their battalion, with alternating platoons leading their wedge, made good progress until they reached the first road junction. "That's the upper road to Sant' Angelo d'Alife," Howard informed them after consulting a map. "There's another junction about a mile farther along, about halfway to our objective."

Darkness had already fallen. They heard sporadic firing on their left. The whole platoon was in an indentation under the highway, three hundred yards south of the junction.

"Silverman," shouted Lieutenant Howard. "Send a four-man patrol beyond the intersection and up the road. I want to make sure there are no entrenchments to the northeast."

"Yes, sir! Burke, Aimes, Clemons, Gainsworthy!" Obie felt like the breath had been knocked from him.

"Burke, you're in charge," Silverman said. "Do not go into the intersection. Go up the slip on the right and onto higher ground past the vineyard. It looks like there might be two or three farmhouses. Check each before you move to the next. If it's all clear, come back down the other side of the road. Got it?"

"Got it," Burke said.

They moved off, crossed the road above, and entered a wide ditch on the other side. Burke led the way. He stopped often to listen. Obie's heart pounded far more than the exertion warranted. He was glad to be with three experienced infantrymen. He wondered why Silverman had chosen him to go instead of Deboise, an experienced soldier.

They moved slowly, listening, watching, moving again. The first farmhouse had three occupants, a woman and two young children, all terrified.

"Have the Germans been here?" Obie asked the woman.

"Yes, but they have gone," she said, sheltering the children with arms around each.

There was no one in the next house. They crossed the road a quarter-mile beyond the intersection and walked back to the waiting platoon without incident. Obie was drenched with sweat.

He sat on a rock that extended from the bank, hands shaking. What kind of soldier was he, scared out of his wits even with no enemy present? Matt sat beside him for a while, not saying anything.

They moved on. It was dark, but Obie could see the black

outline of hills on the right. As they edged into them, he remembered playing cowboy and Indian games in such terrain with Ernie Boswell and Chuck Hinky. *This was no game.* Skilled enemy soldiers with cover and the advantage were hiding here.

The sound of Machinegun fire came. "Down!" shouted Silverman. Obie needed no such warning. The firing increased from a low hill on the right and flatter terrain on the left.

Platoon sergeant Smith was a few feet to Obie's left. He was on the phone, probably with Regiment. "We're in crossfire! Yes, we can see where it's coming from. Any chance of getting artillery? Damn! Yes, sir." A moment later, he yelled, "Squad leaders!"

Obie couldn't hear the hurried conversation. Silverman came back and squatted in the middle of his group.

"We're under crossfire from two positions," he told them. Artillery's not in place yet, so we're on our own. Lieutenant Howard is sending a squad to take out the one below the road. Our squad will silence the one up the hill to our right."

Obie saw a faint outline where the top of the rise met the sky. Below that, the hill was pitch black.

"Ready your weapons," Silverman said.

The brush was high, and they made noise trashing through it. Gunfire came from above. Everyone dove for cover.

Silverman spoke in a soft voice. "We're about fifty yards below their position. They have us pretty well pinpointed. While you draw their fire, I'm going up there, and I need two men to go with me."

Burke said, "That'll be tough, Silverman. Can't see your hand in front of your face. There's no telling what the terrain's like between here and there."

"You have a better idea, Burke?"

"No."

Copland said, "I'm with you, sarge."

"All right, I'm in," Clemons said.

"Okay, let's move out. Burke, while I'm gone, you're in charge. See if you can draw their fire without losing cover."

Time passed slowly. A cloud moved from over the moon and Obie could see the men around him. Gunfire from above became more sporadic. He kept his head down. He had grudging admiration for Copland and Clemons. How could anyone volunteer to walk into such an unknown situation?

Abruptly from above there came the sound of two grenade explosions, seconds apart. Rifle shots followed. The machinegun

222

stopped firing.

"They got 'em," Deboise said.

After a few more rifle shots, it became silent.

"Get ready to move out," Burke said.

Wild thrashing in the brush startled Obie. Copland ran into their enclosure. "God! God! God!" he kept repeating.

Obie grabbed his arm. "What happened?"

"He's dead!"

"Silverman?"

"No, Clemons! He got shot. I saw it."

"Did you get the Krauts?" Burke asked.

"Half his head was gone!"

"Did you get the damned Krauts?" Burke shouted. Copland was crying. Burke slapped him.

"He doesn't know," Deboise said. "He ran away, didn't you, Copland?"

Burke took charge. "Three men, go see what happened and help out." Not waiting for volunteers, he called out, "Burroughs, Gainsworthy, and Perkins! Get up there on the double! Deboise, you go too. You're in charge . . . and find a corpsman to take along."

They wasted no time. Obie listened for the machinegun to start firing again, but it remained silent. They were soon on top of the rise. A figure rose in front of them. Deboise raised his rifle.

Obie put a warning hand on his arm. "It's Silverman." Although breathing hard, Silverman appeared unhurt.

"You get the Krauts?" Deboise asked.

"Yes, but they got Clemons. He ran up and dropped a grenade right in the bunker. Took out the gun and all except one of the Germans. That one got him. I got the Jerry." He paused a second. "Clemons died instantly."

"Hell!" Deboise said. "He was a good man."

"I can't find Copland."

"Man, he ran like a deer with its ass on fire."

"He's safe, then?" Silverman sounded relieved.

"Back down there with his tail between his legs."

Obie followed Silverman to the bunker's edge. He could see Clemons draped over the rock wall, inches from the protruding barrel of the machinegun. Obie touched the gun. It was hot. The side of Clemons' head was a mass of red. Blood was everywhere. The corpsman brought a stretcher, and Silverman helped him lift Clemon's body. Perkins stepped up, ready to help the corpsman carry the stretcher. Silverman pushed him aside.

"My job. I brought him up here. I'll carry him back."

Obie looked into the bunker again. Four men were lying in varying positions, none moving. Matt, standing beside him, said, "God awful!"

Deboise appeared. "Yeah, war's hell, as they say. But there's spoils too." He jumped across the wall and started going through the dead men's pockets.

"What're you doing?" Matt asked.

"Takin' from them what won't have any more use for these things," Deboise replied.

"Ghoulish," Matt said.

"Look here, Burroughs. I didn't ask to get sent to this hellhole, but since I'm here, I'm taking everything I can get. This kraut's an officer, and he's got a Lugar on him. I'll get a hundred bucks for it. If you're smart, you'll hop the fence and see what you can find for your own selves."

Matt, with a look of disgust, whirled and walked away. Obie followed. The sounds of firing guns across the valley made it difficult to think.

CHAPTER TWENTY–THREE

October 1943

"Why is he writing to you?" Abigail asked while handing Cassie the V-Mail letter.

Cassie's snide tone matched her mother's. "I asked him to!"

"Who wrote first?"

"I did."

Cassie's plan had been to pick up the mail to keep Abigail from discovering their correspondence. They'd been found out, but she didn't care.

Abigail's demeanor softened. "Cassie, sweet, he's not interested in you. It's Laura he wants to contact. He's using you to . . ."

"He knows Laura's married. He wouldn't do that."

"I wouldn't put anything past him."

"Mom, I don't want to talk about it. Obie and I are friends. Neither of us want that to change."

She hurried to her bedroom, closed the door, and tore open the envelope. Weeks had passed without hearing anything. Although parts of the letter had been censored, she had little trouble figuring out where he was. "Italy," she said aloud.

She read the letter through again, studying every word. Eventually, she put it aside to write an answer.

> Dear Obie,
>
> You don't know how happy I was to get your letter. Your dad told me where you might go, so I had already looked up Italy in my encyclopedia and read all about it, weather, mountains, and cities. It's been in all the newspapers here too. I went with Dad and Mom down to Glens Falls to a movie. We saw the fighting in Italy on a newsreel. I feel so sorry for what all you boys have to go through.
>
> Dad didn't want to drive to Glens Falls because of the gas rationing, but Mom insisted. She said she knew where to get gas if we have to. We have shortages of many things. We have to do without to get this war over quicker.
>
> Many boys at school are not waiting for the draft. Some are joining up before they finish. They go into all the branches. Several

are joining the Marines now. Dave Madora, Chris Bradlowski, and Chuck Hinky just went into the Navy. Chuck tried to join the marines several months ago but was turned down for some reason. Obie, some of them will not be coming home. Greer Adams was killed over there where you are. I don't know exactly where, except it was on a river. I still don't know if God is real, but to be on the safe side, I pray every night to keep you safe. No, I pray for you a lot more, so often that God may be tired of hearing from me.

I'll talk to Pastor Charles as you requested. He's such a good man. The last time I saw him, he said he would write to you. I haven't seen much of your father lately. I believe he's working as a carpenter somewhere.

Please take care of yourself, my dear friend, and write when you get time. I'll send you a Christmas present and hope it arrives in time.

Love, Cassie

She'd tried to keep it proper, without the sentiment she felt. It had to be that way—for the present. She'd written nothing about Laura, either; that would upset Obie—and herself. She still couldn't understand or forgive the callous way her sister had treated Obie.

Later that night, she burrowed her head into her pillow and whispered, "Obie, dear Obie. Be safe and come home to me. I love you so."

* * *

Clemons' death was a shock, and the squad mood was somber, but there wasn't time for grief or reflection. They were soon ordered to move on toward their next objective.

As they neared the slopes of the Matese Hills, the intensity of enemy fire increased. The Germans were well fortified, challenging to locate, and could easily observe the Americans.

Morning came, and with it increased vulnerability to fire from the hills. The whole battalion was at risk and elements of it resorted to taking cover at various times and locations. Howard's platoon took shelter along a streambed lined with mature trees. The 125th and 151st Field Artillery caught up mid-morning and started shelling enemy positions. The fierce barrage continued for an hour. Word came for their platoon to move out.

Howard continued his habit of orienting his men. "The 100th

226

on our left flank is putting up one hell of a fight. They've destroyed several tanks."

The presence of tanks was not welcome news. "We don't have tank destroyer weaponry up here," Burke complained.

Perkins sounded hopeful. "I've heard it's pretty easy to jump up there and drop a grenade down the hatch."

Burke dragged out syllables in his most sarcastic artistry. "Well . . . that's good news. When we have to look down the turret of one of Hitler's Panthers, I know just which expert to call on."

Perkins usually wore his gullibility as conspicuously as a top hat at a picnic, an innocence that made him likable. This time, he understood the putdown and turned red. Many men, including Perkins, looked up to Burke; few stood up to him. Perkins, whom Obie suspected was even younger than himself was no exception.

Obie checked and rechecked his equipment. Although they'd been under a barrage for hours, he had yet to fire a round.

Silverman called them together. "Stay with me," he said, "and do what I tell you. I don't want to lose anyone else."

Within minutes, two enemy positions opened up from the higher ground on their right. Obie heard bullets striking bushes all around them. Someone cried out in pain. Howard ordered two squads to "go silence those damned guns." Obie's squad lay in a muddy ditch and listened to grenades exploding. The machineguns stopped.

They moved on, from bush to bush and vineyard to vineyard. The whole platoon was scattered across wide swaths on both sides of the road. Two company supply trucks followed, well to the rear. Matt moved in close to Obie.

Deboise, behind them, said, "It's like leapin' from turd to turd . . . a dirty, smelly business."

The desperation in Deboise's speech and demeanor bothered Obie. He was a veteran fighter, a proven good soldier, but maybe there was a limit to a man's combat endurance.

Progress was slow. Obie was alternately hot and cold, forever wet, and presently hungry and thirsty. Tanks were reported somewhere to their left.

"How many and where?" Howard asked.

"Don't know how many," said a youthful voice from a neighboring squad. "I'm on the radio, sir. Wait a second." After a pause, "Sir, battalion says they count fourteen tanks by the river, and they're coming our way."

"Oh, hell!" Does regiment know?"

"Yes, sir, they do. They've called out a recon aircraft to get the coordinates so our artillery can zero in."

"Good. Let's get these troops to the wooded section ahead for better cover."

From the rear, Allied artillery soon opened up on the tanks. Obie heard shells fly over their heads and explode down by the river. It took the platoon the better part of an hour to clear out three bunkers blocking their path. One, well-fortified, remained in front of a stone farmhouse. Silverman's squad was assigned the job of clearing it.

They moved up toward the farmhouse, taking cover when the enemy machineguns opened up. Mortar came from somewhere on the right. Howard sent another squad to silence it.

Silverman crouched beside them cradling a Thompson submachine gun in his arms as he rapidly dispensed orders. Obie was once again in the grip of fear. The trembling he'd previously experienced returned as he lay waiting for orders to move. *What was he expected to do?* All the training hadn't prepared him; that make-believe had little to do with reality.

Was he about to die? The image of Clemon's body, limp as they picked it up, still haunted him. *What was it like to die?* Would his spirit still be aware of what was happening on this battlefield, or would he be transported somewhere peaceful, someplace away from this horror? Maybe it would just be oblivion—the end of everything. His most crushing thought was that he would die without knowing why Laura had betrayed him.

He hadn't prayed since leaving South Carolina—and he wasn't going to. God, if he existed, had let him down. He said softly, "I'm not going to be afraid."

He glanced at the other men. Matt appeared calm, but Obie knew that he was experiencing his own internal war. Meinard had a determined countenance; there was no fear there. Deboise rested his head on the top of his M1, waiting. Silverman seemed focused, as usual.

Mortar fire ceased after a series of explosions on their right flank. Fire from the entrenchment in front of the house was spasmodic, erupting when the Germans detected movement. Silverman cautioned them to keep their heads down. Obie needed no reminder. Minutes passed.

"Dammit, let's get on with it," Deboise said.

"Now!" Silverman yelled as he leaped from the ditch and ran forward with his machinegun blazing. Obie followed Silverman, dodging right and left. He heard other men behind him.

Obie caught up with Silverman. The wall was built of stones stacked several feet high with sandbags on top. Obie leaped high and landed on top. At least a half-dozen Germans were in the pit. Three turned toward him, faces frozen in surprise.

Obie fired at the closest man and saw him fall. Another tried to swing a machinegun toward Obie. Silverman took him down, along with a third man who couldn't get his weapon into position. Burke, Rivera, and Aimes poured in a torrent of fire, killing three others. One remaining German threw his hands over his head in surrender. Men behind Obie and Silverman stormed over the wall and into the house, making it secure. The fight was over in seconds.

Obie sat on a sandbag, needing to get his breath. *He'd killed a man—taken a life.* He put his head in his hands.

Matt came and sat beside him. "You okay?" he asked.

"Yeah, I'm fine."

"Don't know if what you did was brave or stupid. You nearly ran over Silverman."

"It was stupid! I wanted us to get it over as quick as we could. Silverman will be on me about it . . . you can bet on it."

The family had been in the cellar. They came up, a middle-aged couple accompanied by three younger people, a boy and two girls. "Gainsworthy!" Silverman called. "Get over here and find out if they can tell us anything useful."

The father explained that the Germans had confiscated their house but let them go about their farm chores. They'd not been allowed to leave the property. "They ate all our food," the youngest girl said.

Meinard quizzed the scared German prisoner and told Silverman, "He doesn't know anything. He's only an infantryman."

"How much he knows isn't for us to decide," Silverman said. "We'll send him behind the lines. Copland! You escort him back."

Perkins spoke up. "Sergeant, Copland's not here."

"Well, where the hell is he?"

"Don't know," Perkins said. "He wasn't with us when we charged the house."

Silverman was angry. "Burroughs, I want you and Rivera to go back and find him . . . and drag his ass up here to me. And take this prisoner with you. Give him to the MPs. What're you waiting for?

Move out!" In what sounded like an afterthought, he added. "Don't mention anything about Copland . . . not now, at least."

The platoon suffered one causality but no deaths. They reached the wooded grove without further difficulty. Support troops and supplies eventually caught up. Water had been delivered periodically the past twenty-four hours, but there had been no food. Company cooks glanced nervously over their shoulders as they unloaded items from their trucks and dispensed k-rations and coffee. No hot food was available. Obie gulped down a can of cold beans even as the order came to "move out." Matt and Rivera hadn't returned.

The enemy fire intensified from the hills and from straight ahead. Tanks were again approaching from the south. Things became disorganized in a hurry. Howard had called for tank destroyers and bazooka squads which hadn't arrived. Divisional artillery blasted enemy tanks, but several were still advancing toward them. They were taking fire from three sides. He heard Howard on the phone.

"Should we fall back? Yes, sir. Yes, sir. Yes, sir, we will hold on." Obie didn't need to hear the other side of the conversation; there would be no retreat.

As they moved forward, enemy fire increased, and their squad became separated from the rest of the platoon. Shells landed nearby, their explosions sending shrapnel and stones flying in all directions. From the far left, Obie heard men calling for medics.

"Hell . . . we have to get out of this," Silverman said.

He sent out Burke and Aimes to locate enemy bunkers. On their return, they reported three well-fortified entrenchments a thousand feet directly ahead. They were in a nearly straight line about three hundred feet apart. A vineyard occupied the space in front of the bunkers. "Maybe we could call down artillery on them," Obie heard Silverman suggest.

Howard's voice, several yards away, held frustration. "I've been trying. I can't get through. We need to go ahead and do it ourselves before those tanks overrun us."

"Yes, sir. Do you want my squad to advance on the bunkers?"

"Affirmative. Take the one on the right. I'll throw two other squads at the other positions."

"Yes, sir."

"Tucker's a causality. I'll lead his squad myself."

"Negative, sir. Too dangerous. Let Sergeant Smith do it."

"Sergeant, I give the orders!"

After a momentary pause, Silverman asked, "Should we go at once?"

"No. On my signal."

Silverman gathered his group. "I didn't tell the lieutenant that our squad is light. With Copland, Burroughs, and Rivera on detail . . . and Clemons gone. Well, everyone needs to give it a little extra."

Obie checked his rifle, ammunition belt, and grenades. Silverman told him, "Let the more experienced men lead, Gainsworthy. Your bravery's not questioned. Your judgment is."

"Sorry. It was stupid, jumping ahead of you like that. I got nervous."

"It turned out all right this time. There's always the next time, however."

A few minutes later, Howard sent word to "advance at once."

Obie's heart raced and he felt the veins in his neck pulsate. Would he never get over the fear? Silverman had called him brave. If only he knew.

Unlike the conditions of the previous charge, there was more cover, but also a longer distance to travel. Obie let Silverman, Aimes, and Burke get ahead of him. Deboise hung back. Meinard pushed ahead until he was right behind Silverman. They ran short distances in between bursts from the enemy machineguns.

Obie could hear troops from the other squads advancing on their left. The enemy on the hills had spotted them, as evidenced by heavier mortar fire from there. Artillery from the north had bombarded them sporadically all day—and they seemed to have the range. One shell exploded ahead of Silverman, enveloping them in a cloud of smoke.

Obie was reeling from the noise. Another explosion on the right threw him down so violently that his M1 went flying. Dizzy, he got up to retrieve it and fell again with his nose in the dirt. He lay for a moment, smelling the rich black soil and trying to remember where he was. A beetle crawled a few inches from his face. He watched it creep onto a leaf, fall off the other side, and lay on its back. He wanted to help it, to turn it upright.

"Get up!"

Had he said that? He struggled to make sense of what was happening. Get up, beetle! Get up and live!

"Get up!" Grugs was kneeling beside him. "Gainsworthy . . . you all right?"

Obie got to his feet and was able to stay up. He grabbed his weapon and moved forward, still feeling unsteady. Grugs stayed close. Smoke and explosions increased. Obie lost sight of the bunkers. He heard men shouting; he couldn't determine the direction. He could see no one except Grugs, who also appeared disoriented.

"What's happening, Gainsworthy?" Grugs said.

"Don't know. Everything's all mixed up."

"It's confusing."

"Let's keep close together."

"Where do we go? Which way?"

"Keep moving the way we're facing. Stay together."

Obie stumbled over a body. It wasn't anyone he knew. He kept going. As his head cleared, he heard the clatter of machineguns ahead. Bullets struck the trunk of an olive tree nearby.

"Where is everybody?" Grugs asked, his voice sounding choked.

"Ahead! Keep going."

The artillery fire increased. Obie kept running. Grugs stayed close. They broke out of the smoke. Ahead, twenty yards across a span of open ground was a bunker with American soldiers swarming over it. Obie saw Silverman standing on top of a wall firing his Thompson into the enemy den. Other men were there too, but Silverman dominated the scene.

The gunfire ceased except for intermittent firing on the left. The other two bunkers had also been captured. Obie climbed up and stood beside Silverman. The bunker interior was a mess. Bloody lumps that had been men were everywhere. Burke was already going through pockets. Aimes sat on a boulder, looking lost. Obie expected to see Deboise competing with Burke for souvenirs, but he was being sick behind the bunker.

"You get lost, Gainsworthy?" Silverman asked.

"What?" His ears were still ringing.

"When I told you to hang back, I didn't mean for you not to show up."

Obie was at a loss for words. Silverman was dressing him down without waiting for an explanation. Angry, he turned and walked away.

Silverman assembled the squad, and they rejoined the platoon. The tanks had been stopped, it appeared. Two platoon members had been killed, and two wounded were sent back behind the lines. One, Smith said, would probably not survive.

A jeep came up the road behind them. Matt and Rivera hopped out. The MP driver did a quick U-turn and left. Lieutenant Howard, fifty feet away, motioned the two men toward him.

Silverman hailed him. "I can take care of it, sir."

Howard nodded and turned back to his session with another squad. There was little doubt that he had a lot on his mind.

"Copland's wounded," Matt told Silverman. "He's going back to Alife."

"What happened?"

"Says he got hit as we were about to attack the farmhouse."

"You talked to him?"

"Yeah. He took a shot through the hand. Lots of blood."

Burke stood a few feet away, listening. "Which hand?" he asked.

Obie thought the question strange. "What difference does it make?"

Burke laughed. "Still a newbie, I see."

"Well, if it makes any difference, it's his left hand," Matt said.

Burke laughed again. "See, Silverman. I told you so."

"Burke," Silverman said, "I'll take care of this. You can have your suspicions, and you might even be right, but there's no proof. Keep it to yourself. I'll do the reporting to Howard."

Obie was still confused about the exchange.

Aimes explained. "Some men shoot themselves to avoid battle. They've been doing that since guns were invented. They probably used arrows or swords before that. Are you right-handed or left-handed?"

"Right."

"So's Copland. Tell me, which hand would you take a chance on ruining?"

"Aw, I see what you mean. Would Copland really do that?"

"He ran off and left Silverman and Clemons, didn't he? Even so, I'm not judging a man for trying to save his own neck, even if he did it . . . and we don't know that for sure."

"Well, I know," Burke said. "He's a damn coward."

"Everybody has limits," Deboise said from the spot he occupied well back from the others.

CHAPTER TWENTY–FOUR

November–December 1943

They stopped on the southeastern slope of a hill overlooking Sant' Angelo d'Alife. To a man, they were hungry, wet, and exhausted beyond caring. Obie managed some often interrupted but much-needed sleep under the shade of a small sycamore.

Early the following day their battalion attacked and took the hill northeast of the town. The 100th managed to drive off tanks and fight their way from the valley to a strategic knoll. The battalions moved through morning fog into Sant' Angelo d'Alife proper, which was secured with little effort.

There was little letup in their forward movement, slow as it was. It took several days to advance through, Raviscanna, Ailano, and Pratella, villages that had been wrestled from the enemy by other division units. It seemed a milestone when they entered the Sava River Valley.

When support elements of the division caught up, there was a mail call, but nothing for Obie. He found time to write to Pastor Charles.

> *Dear Pastor Charles,*   *November 1, 1943*
>
> *I hope everything is okay with you. I know you know my where-abouts through Dad and Cassie Hunt, so I won't bore you with those details. I've been in the battle zone for several days and have been in a few skirmishes. I remember our discussions about going to war and my reluctance to do that. Well, things don't always turn out as expected, do they? I'm here, and I want you to know I'll make the most of it.*
>
> *We've crossed the Volturno River twice and have made steady progress up the Valley. It's been rainy and cool most of the time. I just dried out today, except for my boots, which are still soaked. They give us dry socks, <u>sometimes.</u> Most of my friends' feet hurt because we don't get enough rest and are always wet. We all smell pretty bad, as you might guess.*
>
> *I heard that you are going to stay in Stafford Rest for at least another year. That's good. Stafford Rest Methodist would not be the*

same without you.

We often talked about spiritual matters, and you've given me good advice. I need that again, for I'm having what I'm sure you would call a" spiritual crisis." I've come to terms with the fighting and killing thing, so that's not an issue. The truth is, I've lost my faith ... and it's something I miss. Some of the men here go to services when the chaplains catch up with us, and they seem to be in touch with God, but it's hard for me to see God anywhere on these battlefields. I can't even believe He exists, at least the same kind of God we talked about. I do try to believe, though, and I've even tried to pray again, but it's like a big brick wall has been thrown up between God and me. You've told me that God is good. Pastor Charles, maybe you could answer this question for me. Why would God take away from me the person I loved the most? "I'm sorry for venting. And that's enough self-pity.

We'll leave here (vicinity of Amandia) any hour now and keep pushing the Germans north. I was scared at first. Not as much anymore. Maybe I'll live to see the end of all this madness. "Madness" is what Aimes, one of my squad members, calls war. He's smart.

Please write as soon as you can.

Your friend, Obadiah Gainsworthy

Obie put the letter in his pocket; he'd consider whether or not to mail it. He'd downplayed the extent of his spiritual void but had said things the minister would feel compelled to address. Would he understand? Could anyone understand? It seemed a paradox that, although surrounded by thousands of men living in the same conditions as himself, he felt utterly alone.

The Armies pushed on with apparent disregard for any individual's thoughts on the matter. Obie respected and feared the Germans. They occupied the best defensive positions, often on higher ground where they could see Allied troop movement. They were well-equipped, brave, and anticipated Allied military tactics. Even when pushed back they launched counter-attacks that were effective and deadly; they stayed as long as they could in defensive positions before retreating in an orderly and efficient manner, leaving mines in the exact places men were most likely to step.

War news at the divisional level was reasonably accurate. Otherwise, the truth about what was really going on was evasive. Some war correspondents and divisional reporters were the best sources. There was confirmation that all three divisions, and the British 10th, had crossed the Volturno and pushed well beyond. It was slow progress, however, for enemy withdrawals were calculated and timely.

Obie trusted Aimes' opinions; the history teacher was a quiet man, but knowledgeable. "What's happening," he said, "is that while we're back here grubbing out these mobile pockets of resistance, they're up there somewhere preparing a solid defensive line."

Silverman said, "If Aimes is right, and I believe he is, it's going to get a good deal harder. There are five or six divisions over there waiting for us."

Deboise, with his voice several decibels softer than usual, said, "I wonder if we're ready for such?"

* * *

Obie waded quickly. On this, the third Volturno crossing, he found the braided headwaters swifter and colder, even if not as deep. Obie's squad traversed several sand and gravel bars barren of vegetation except for small twisted willow trees. Men tried to be quiet. After a fierce barrage of artillery fire laid down by the Allies for two hours, the light gurgling sound of the flowing stream was just a notch above dead silence. However, that was an illusion, for the sounds of battle continued farther away, both up and down the river.

Obie's ears still rang from the big guns whose recent booming had reverberated off the hills, as Deboise said, "like thunder in a holler." They'd been well back when the artillery started at ten o'clock in the evening, but hadn't moved out for the crossing until nearly midnight. Obie both cursed and blessed the darkness as they stumbled up the low river banks toward brush-covered hills to the north.

It was a major divisional movement. Their next objectives were the villages of Santa Maria Oliveto and Roccaravindola, some three or four miles away. Resistance wasn't severe and artillery strikes were spasmodic. They eliminated random machinegun nests, a chore slowing forward progress. Two explosions occurred not far beyond the river, seconds apart, one on either side of Silverman's squad. Men were calling for medics.

"Dammit!" Silverman said. "Mines!"

He'd no sooner made the pronouncement than more explosions occurred along the line and to both right and left.

"Sarge, what are we gonna do?" Perkins asked. "I'm afraid of stepping on one of them things."

Squad members had discussed land mines with dread. Stories

about victims with their legs and genitals blown away had been told and retold with graphic clarity.

Silverman ordered them into a single file. They would take turns leading; he went first. Obie took his turn after Silverman and experienced the terror of taking the next step. Matt took Obie's place ten minutes later, his hard breathing audible. Explosions continued all around them, accompanied by cries for corpsmen.

They were still harassed by well-concealed positions equipped with machineguns, mortar, and self-propelled guns. They stopped often while Howard called on squads to silence enemy entrenchments and secure prisoners.

Mortar fire increased. Deboise had been last in line when they started; when his turn came, he took hesitant steps into the lead. A massive explosion occurred on the right that jarred the earth. Each man tried to step exactly where the man in front of him had stepped.

A blinding flash in front of Silverman threw the sergeant back into Matt, who tumbled into Obie and sent him sprawling. Just when they thought they might have left the mines behind, Deboise had found one.

"God, oh God, oh God, help me!" The voice was Deboise's.

"Corpsman!" Silverman called several times.

Caution was forgotten as the squad gathered around Deboise. Burke swore softly. Silverman produced a small flashlight, which he covered with an article of clothing from his pack. He held it so that the light illuminated a small area near the ground, enough to see what injuries Deboise had sustained. Apparently in great pain, Deboise lay back with his M1 still in his arms. Burke gently took it from him.

"How's it look?" Aimes asked.

"Not good," Silverman said. "His leg is gone. Perkins, go find a corpsman. Make it quick!"

"Where? Where do I look?"

Silverman was out of patience. "I don't know. Just get going."

"What if I step on one of them mines?"

"Get going, damn it!"

Deboise had grown quiet. Silverman put the beam of his light on his ashen face. His eyes were closed.

"He's passing out," Rivera said.

Perkins returned with a medic who put a tourniquet on the stump of Deboise's severed leg and gave him an injection of morphine. The corpsman was soon called away to tend to another man.

Silverman and Obie lifted Deboise onto a stretcher.

Silverman said, "Rivera and Grugs . . . you carry Deboise back to wherever you can find someone to relieve you. Don't leave him until he's in someone's care. Do you hear?"

"Loud and clear," Grugs answered.

Silverman regrouped the squad. "We've lost a man . . . a good man," he whispered. "But we have to keep going."

"Sarge, is Deboise going to be okay?" Perkins asked.

"He'll be fine. He's done his part, and now he's out of it. He'll be fine." Obie hoped he was right.

They met fierce resistance as they approached the high embankment under Highway 85. Howard called artillery down on the road, and, for a few minutes, shells fell closer to the Americans than to the enemy. Bazooka teams came up, and frontal attacks captured several positions. Silverman's squad became separated from the platoon and Meinard and Perkins were lost in the dark for a time. Perkins was yelling for Silverman.

Burke yelled back. "Perkins, shut up. The Krauts have big ears."

To validate Burke's statement, a stream of tracers poured toward the two men who were fifty yards on the right. "Get over here!" yelled Silverman.

"Where are you?"

"Over here! Over here!" Silverman repeated.

Perkins soon stumbled back to the group with Meinard following him. "I thought you'd gone off and left us," Perkins said, his voice trembling.

"Are you all right?" Silverman asked.

"We're okay," Meinard said. "I tried to tell him where you were. He was scared."

"I wasn't scared," Perkins said.

Obie understood Perkins' fear. It had been their most brutal fight yet, and it was far from over. Nevertheless, they methodically pushed beyond the highway. It was daylight when they entered the hills near Santa Maria Oliveto. Other battalions had taken strategic hills in the west. There were still Germans in the town.

Silverman's squad was ordered to silence a machinegun nest in the south section where a two-story stone building overlooked the road that weaved up the hill from the south. Three men were to approach from the rear, a blind area for the Germans, they hoped. Obie, Matt, and Meinard were assigned that job.

"Gainsworthy's in charge," Silverman said.

The trio approached the building from behind while the rest of the squad attacked from the front. They had almost reached one of the building's entrances when a sniper's bullet found Meinard. He went down without a sound. Obie and Matt secured the structure and took two prisoners. With that accomplished, Obie ran back to where Meinard had fallen.

Silverman was already there, bent over Meinard. "He's gone," he said.

Obie sat on the ground by Meinard's body. Burke and Perkins herded the two prisoners out onto the street. One was wounded and limping.

Tears welled up in Obie's eyes. "It's my fault," he said, finding it difficult to breathe. "I should have double-checked all the windows."

"It wasn't your fault." Silverman's voice held a tone of authority. "Get that out of your head. This is war. He's not the last friend you'll lose before it's over."

Burke was swearing and threatening to shoot the prisoners; Silverman stopped him. Guns continued firing throughout the village for over an hour.

From there, the division moved into higher mountains, a situation making daily life even more trying because of the cold and the sluggish supply lines. Knowledge that the Germans were being pushed backward was all that kept morale from crashing. Allied aerial bombing ahead of the troops continued up the valley, but it was less effective because weather and topography prevented pilots from clearly seeing their targets.

The troops moved from hill to hill while enduring fire from pockets of the enemy occupying higher ground. Obie moved around like a zombie, never escaping the deprivation of sleep and rest. Attacking and fighting off the enemy became a daily routine, deadening to mind and body.

"I don't feel human," Obie said to Silverman. "Killing hardly bothers me anymore."

"Put it out of your mind. Don't dwell on it."

Men lived in unwashed clothing with hardly a break from rain, sleet, and cold. Streams were flooded, and mud made roads difficult, sometimes impossible. Supplies reaching them were meager, carried by mules or on the backs of men. Hot meals were dream fantasies. Foot disease was rampant. Obie caught a cold which turned into a cough that persisted. The other men were no better off.

CHAPTER TWENTY–FIVE

December 1943

The 34th Division was given a break away from the front in early December. Rain was falling the day they arrived at St. Angelo de Alife. Thick mud was underfoot everywhere. The luxury of tents, cots, and hot meals overrode all such inconveniences. Obie slept for thirty-six hours, arising only once to visit the latrine.

Nevertheless, adjustment came slowly as the days passed. Visions of Monte Marrone, dubbed "Old Sawtooth," had haunted him since the regiment left its slopes; it had nearly done him in. No one from the squad had been lost, a fact hard to believe. He had nightmares about that ordeal—and other battles. It was usually Matt who shook him awake. Other men had nightmares, too.

An odd mix of relaxation and "training" took place in the division. Men in the camp found their levels of peace. Even Burke was more sociable. Some drank, often to excess. Others read books from boxes that had magically arrived in the battle zone. Poker and dice games were continually in progress. Both company and division held events and programs men were required to attend but often found ways to avoid. Silverman believed they would be there through Christmas, maybe into the new year.

The division held an award ceremony and a parade of sorts. Silverman's squad marched in front of their platoon and stood at attention as he was awarded the Silver Star. Other medals were awarded as well. There was one each, posthumously, for Clemons and Meinard.

Obie was surprised when Silverman approached him after breakfast the following morning. "That time I yelled at you, Gainsworthy . . . you didn't deserve it."

Obie lied. "I'd forgotten all about it."

"You seem to stay away from the drinking crowd."

"My dad drinks." He said it without embarrassment, which would have been impossible a few months earlier.

"I thought it might be because it's against your religion. Burroughs told me that you're religious."

No, that's a thing of the past."

"Religious faith's important."

"For some, it seems." He remembered, then, that Silverman was a Jew.

"My family's religious . . . at least some are. My grandfather was a rabbi. Father . . . that's another matter." He laughed and added, "Even if I were a good Jew, it'd be impossible to live like that out here. But, God forgives, I hear."

"So, I've been told."

"You sound bitter, Gainsworthy."

"It's just that I no longer believe in anything like that." It was the first time he'd said those words aloud.

"Why is that?" Silverman cocked his head. The man expected an answer.

It was the first time he'd been asked to defend his position; he proceeded with caution. "It's a comfort to some people, I guess. I see Grugs reading his Bible, and Aimes has a Bible, too." He took a breath. "The truth is that I've come to doubt that God, if he even exists, has any interest at all in us."

"I'm sorry to hear that. You're pretty young for such weighty theology."

Why would Silverman be saying that? His religion was nothing like Obie's.

"I have reasons for the way I feel," Obie said.

"I'd be happy to hear about that."

"And maybe I don't want to talk about it."

"Suit yourself, but I think you might feel better about it if you did." The man was as relentless in conversation as he was in combat.

"Silverman . . . I've had it with religion. It was ground into me by both Catholics and Protestants with their ideas about grace and love . . . and forgiveness. None of that is true, it seems. I'm done with it."

"Okay, I get that. Yet, you seem like a good person."

"Well, I *am* a good person. What's *that* got to do with religion? Even a man like Burke has moral lines that he tries not to cross."

"Maybe there's a little bit of God in all of us."

Obie was uncomfortable with the direction of the conversation and said, "Well, that's how I feel." When Silverman remained quiet, he added, "I'd like to hear more about your family."

"Sometime, I might bore you with my story," Silverman said, dismissing the subject with a wave of his hand. "Will you go to college after the war?"

"Probably not. Too expensive."

"There'll likely be money for veterans for schooling."

"That's about the only way I could afford it."

"I was in college for two years. Boston University."

"Will you go back there?"

"Don't know. I might go somewhere else. We need to get through this war first to even think about such matters." He hesitated a moment, then asked, "I don't mean to pry, but what about that girl back home . . . the one Burroughs mentioned? Is she part of your plans?"

Obie felt his face flush. He was surprised that Silverman remembered. How might he circumvent the question? Perhaps he could dismiss it as something unimportant or trivial. No—he couldn't do that. It was the most burning issue in his life, always on his mind, even in war. Matt had suggested that he talk to people about it; maybe he should; maybe the sergeant would listen and understand.

"Silverman, she's certainly not a part of my future, but it hurts to discuss it."

"We've all got things in our lives that are hard to talk about . . . but I've got time to listen if you're up to it."

After giving Silverman a condensed version of events in Stafford Rest that led to his enlistment, Obie said, "Before I left, we promised each other . . . gave pledges to each other that we'd marry when the war was over. I was still in basic training when her sister wrote to tell me that she'd married one of Stafford Rest's doctors. Just like that . . . no warning. They went to live in Boston. Tell me, Silverman, how would that make you feel?"

"It's certainly a sad story, Gainsworthy. Are you still in love with her?"

"No! *Hell no!* How could you even think that?"

Silverman seemed thoughtful before saying, "My take on it is that you need to get her out of your head. You won't forget, but you can't dwell on it. What's done is done. The present is where we live . . . and we can control the present to some extent. And we can certainly plan the future. You can plan your future by staying alive, and when this war's over you can go and get an education and do whatever your heart tells you to do. Forget her. There are plenty of women out there who won't treat you like that."

The possibility of ever having those feelings for anyone else was not something he could comprehend, much less speak of. "How about you?" he asked. "Do you have a girlfriend?"

"No . . . I don't. I'm not at all sure I'm the marrying kind. My mom was forever trying to fix me up with a good Jewish girl.' None of her choices worked out. I'm sure she'd still be trying if she were alive."

"Maybe you'll find someone when the war's over."

"That's what it all depends on, Gainsworthy . . . the war being over?"

* * *

Mail came to Alife with a letter from Cassie. Her words evoked vivid images, bringing Stafford Rest closer. He composed his reply, staying positive and avoiding anything about Laura or his state of mind.

Dear Cassie,   *Dec. 15, 1943*

Your letter was really welcome. We're resting at a place called St. Angelo de Alife. You'll be glad to know we are away from the battle zones and will likely spend Christmas here at Alife. I knew Greer Adams but didn't know he was over here. I'm sorry he was killed.

We're being fed well, and I'm getting fat. They show us movies quite often. I saw "How Green was My Valley" the other night. It's awfully muddy everywhere here, but I'm getting used to it.

I'm getting to know several of the men quite well. I know the ones in our squad the best. They're a good group of men, especially Sgt. Silverman. He was just awarded a medal for bravery. I don't think I'm very brave.

Matt is in good health, except for a cough, like many of us. I let him read your last letter. He said to say hello. I worry about him sometimes. He talks a lot about a girl he met in Naples. Her name is Rosa. He says he's in love with her even though he's only been with her for about five hours altogether. Do you think that's possible? I'm sure he'll never see her again, but he insists he will.

Silverman has been telling me that I should go to college. I always try to keep some goal before me for when this is over. It's not always easy.

Merry Christmas, Cassie. You're my best friend, even more than Matt, and that's saying something.

Your friend, Obie

Obie received letters from his father, Angie, and Charles Lansing two days before Christmas. Ken Gainsworthy's letter was characteristically brief.

Dear Obie,

I have been helping in a building project up north since October. I thought of going to Schenectady to find work. The General Electric company is hiring and pays well, but it's too far from home. This job will be finished in March. I won't be back in Stafford Rest until then. Abner has been watching the place. He took Slobber over to the farm to stay until I get back. I hope you are careful. I tried to teach you some things about survival that I hope you won't forget. Your mom was from a small town not too far from Rome. I don't remember the name, but I told your Aunt Angie to write and give you the details. She might be slow in doing that. Andrew Temple, her husband, was killed last month in the Pacific.

Dad

Although Obie had never known Andrew Temple's well, his death was a shock. Full of family news, the letter from Angie was obviously written before she knew. He must write to her.

The letter from the minister was thick. His beautiful cursive style with large swirling strokes covered several pages.

Dear Obadiah,

Young man, you don't know how overjoyed I was to receive your letter. It was wonderful to know you are still safe. We've been getting news from the fronts, and although I believe we are winning the war, it is a hard struggle. I have never been in war, having been too young for the last one and too old for this one, so I guess I cannot really understand the hardships you boys have to endure. Nevertheless, I think of you every day and pray for you. The church has a prayer circle that meets once a week (this is in addition to our regular prayer meetings on Wednesday nights.) We make one another accountable for praying, specifically for Stafford Rest boys and boys from neighboring towns that we know. Some have been killed, and I have tried to visit those families even if they are not members of our church.

Let's get to some concerns you raised in your letter. First, know that those concerns have bothered Christians over the centuries. I hope it might give some comfort in knowing you are not alone. I could write down the words of some of them, but this letter would become overly long. Therefore, I'll try to condense what I believe to be a consensus opinion, realizing there are always dissenting voices.

Know that this war is not your doing. It is the result of evil people with evil minds. Christians must fight evil until God's Kingdom has come to Earth. Only then will there be no more wars. You are probably confused by God's commandment, "Thou shalt not kill." Taken literally, it does confuse. God has given us commandments, and we need those. He has also given us judgment and the ability to use logic. I once rejected such ideas, thinking all the answers were in place. Age and experience sometimes make adjustments to our thinking. It would be much easier if everything were black and white, good and evil. We are often presented with situations where we must compromise and choose "the lesser of evils." That's not only in wars, either. I know this because I've made compromises that caused me pain and doubt, but I won't go into that.

Here's an example where Jesus was involved. One of God's commandments is to honor the Sabbath. The Jews were strict about it. Jesus, however, softened it by telling stories and by example. He showed us that we must sometimes see justice done by approaching the Law from another angle. Hitler and his armies have ravaged Europe, murdering innocent people and destroying institutions, some set up by God Himself. That's what the Allies are fighting. It's what you are fighting, Obadiah. You have no choice but to do what you must do because the great evil cannot be destroyed without it.

You say it is hard for you to see God on the battlefield. Remember what I told you once: God does not follow you around checking up or protecting you from the calamities that can befall us. Neither will He interfere with your free will. He will not stop nor deter the bullet headed for you. You have to get yourself out of the way. I believe God has life courses ("possibilities" might be a better word) laid out for us, which we attain with His guidance and help. But God can intervene. Prayer brings intervention about, I believe. It's God's universe, and we are all subject to natural laws. But don't forget that those laws are His, and He can override them at His will.

Many Germans in the trenches across from you are innocent, too, caught up in something they cannot control. The war is not their doing either. You probably already know that, and it may bother you, whether you realize it or not. Many enemy men are Christians too. However, you must do what you have to do. It cannot be helped, *and you will have no blood on your hands.*

God is there, Obadiah. He does exist. I can see that you are struggling in your belief, but know that you carry Him with you. You say you try to pray. You must pray. Go off by yourself when you can. Yes, talk to the chaplains. Your faith will be restored. From the time you were small, I have believed that you are destined for a life of service of some kind. He has His plans for you that are known only to Him. We pray for you here. He will intervene. He will keep you safe.

The building project, the new education wing, is in full swing, and it is happening much quicker than I ever imagined it would. You know how long I have worked to see it happen. I am happy about it, but I am also sad, for the cost has been more than I might have imagined, and not only in dollars. Enough said about that.

Now, I speak of your question in your letter: "Why would God take away from me the person I loved the most?" You didn't use her name, but I know you speak of Laura Hunt, now Laura Williamson. You confided in me about Laura, and I do keep confidences. You both were so young, and you were doing and thinking grown-up things with too high expectations. You cannot lay any blame on Him for that. You must force yourself to give her up. I don't use "forget her" because I know you cannot do that, and it wouldn't be a good thing anyway. You must steel yourself to realize that she is married and is lost to you for anything beyond friendship. Forgive her. It will make your life so much better. God will help you through the process. God has someone in mind for you to love, and in time you will find her.

Obadiah, God bless and keep you. We'll see each other again.

Charles

* * *

Even from a distance, Cassie could tell that Abigail was more than a little annoyed. "You don't take it seriously enough, Pinky. She had another letter from that boy yesterday."

"Abigail, stop thinking about it. If you can't do that, then for goodness sake, stop talking about it."

Cassie hadn't been quick enough, allowing Abigail to intercept Obie's letter. She'd torn it from her mother's hand, undaunted by the consequences. Now, Cassie was on the enclosed and heated porch within hearing distance of her parents, who were sitting at the kitchen table and apparently unaware of her presence. She removed the envelope from between the pages of her algebra textbook where she had carried it all day through all her classes. She pressed it over her heart and continued to listen.

"It's obvious he's using Cassie to get to Laura. Doesn't it bother you?"

"He and Cassie have always liked each other. I don't see that their correspondence has anything to do with Laura. He's not the kind to break up marriages. If, as you told me, Laura simply chose Ben over Obie, he'll get over it."

"You're wrong about him."

"To be honest, Abigail, I feel sorry for Obie. I suspect it hurt him deeply when Laura married Ben. I think Obie loved our daughter."

Abigail responded with anger. "Pinky, you sound like she did something wrong."

"No, I didn't mean it like that, but you have to admit, the whole thing was sudden . . . and strange."

"Not really. She thought highly of Ben. It was natural for her to turn to him when her good senses came into play."

"Except for the day last spring after the parade, I don't ever remember seeing Ben and Laura together."

"You don't see a lot. Open your eyes, Pinky. Obie will break Cassie's heart."

"You don't know that. Anyway, he's overseas, in Italy."

"He'll be back."

"God grant it. They're all young, Abigail. Leave it alone. Their friendship . . . or something more, will be what it will be."

Cassie leaned forward and strained to hear. She expected her mother to respond in anger but her voice, although pointed, was remarkably controlled. "Obie isn't good enough for my girls. He'll probably turn out just like his father."

"No, he won't. He's a smart boy. He could even end up being our son-in-law. Have you thought of that?" Cassie wanted to scream "Yes!" but smothered that impulse.

"The likes of Obie Gainsworthy will never marry either of my girls."

"Laura's already married."

"Yes, and to a good man. Benjamin Williamson is going places."

"That may be, but if Laura was having trouble with Obie, as

you said, it seems she could have made more of an effort to reconcile." He sighed. "I hope she'll be happy in this marriage."

"She came to her senses, that's all. She saw Obie for what he is and chose a man with whom she can have a future."

"Maybe they *were* having trouble. Obie enlisted before school was out. That seems like an act of a desperate person." In the pause, Cassie imagined she could hear her father thinking. He said, "Abigail, did *you* have anything to do with that situation?"

"No, I did not, beyond encouraging her after discovering Ben had asked for her hand in marriage."

"Well, I felt bad for Obie."

"Don't waste your time with pity for such as him."

"Abigail, stop it!"

"No, I won't stop. Don't you know Cassie's in love with him? We have to put an end to it before it's too late."

Cassie gripped the arms of her chair. Pinky, for once, was quick to answer. "What do you wish for him . . . to die in Italy?"

"It would certainly solve a problem."

Tears streamed down Cassie's cheeks. She was trembling, and her stomach churned. She wanted to storm the kitchen and swear at her mother. Instead, fearing the murder in her heart might become a reality, she gathered her books and crept up the back stairs to her bedroom.

CHAPTER TWENTY–SIX

December 1943–February 1944

A cardboard box, crushed and leaking cookie crumbs, came in the mail two days after Christmas. Obie shared the hard, dry treats with his squad. The gift resurrected memories of his mother teaching Cassie, Laura, and Obie to bake cookies in the Hunts' big oven. Cassie would have baked these in that same oven.

In early January, the respite at Alife ended. The regiment moved out over mountains and through a succession of villages, passes, and rivers, all with names he could never forget: Migano Gap, Camino, Radicosa, Purple Heart Valley, Carper.

They pushed on, their killing machine against the enemy killing machine—on beyond the Volturno Valley, across the divide to the Garigliano and Rapido Valleys. The destination on every man's lips was "Cassino," a formidable fortress that blocked the way to the Liri Valley and the road to Rome.

As Aimes predicted, the Germans had set up a long line of defense the breadth of Italy. The "Gustav Line," they called it. Cassino was the master key for breaking that line, the teacher informed them.

The Abbey, a centuries-old monastery, sat high on a mountainside overlooking and dominating the valley and the town of Cassino. The Germans declared a hands-off policy for the religious and historical site, but the Allies suspected them of using it for cover. Hundreds of enemy guns and rocket launchers were situated in impregnable positions on the steep mountain face. Concrete bunkers, pillboxes, minefields, and teams of enemy soldiers guarded all the approaches from the valley and the mountains.

Crossing the Rapido River required a Herculean effort by the Allies. The 36th Division suffered horrendous losses. Attacks were hurled back until, at last, a bridgehead was established and several Allied divisions had converged on the area around Cassino. The 34th Division approached across heavily defended ridges northeast of Cassino, then punched across the river in concentrated attacks on enemy entrenchments. For the most part, supplies stayed just out of reach. Along with the others, Obie remained cold, wet, tired, and hungry.

Copland's injured hand healed and he was declared fit to return to his squad. He said little. He seemed nothing like the Copland who had come to Italy. He was watched closely by the other squad members.

Their squad had received three replacements, green troops fresh out of basic. Delbert Keanan was twenty years old, a cocky Irishman from Connecticut whose huge size was startling. John Chadlowski was from Buffalo, New York. He was a couple of years older and diminutive next to Keanan. He bragged about being a boxer, a flyweight. He appeared eager to experience battle. Silverman took him aside for a reality discussion. Carl Marcum from Nevada was quiet, standoffish, and scared. He was killed during one failed attempt to cross the Rapido.

By late January their division was in the hills with the 142d Regiment attached as a special task force combat team. The higher-up commanders complained to still higher-ups that the men were exhausted after a month of fighting through the mountains and should be relieved. They were told, in essence, to "suck it up and go do your job." There was groaning, but resignation. Obie had learned to expect little, forestalling disappointment.

Orders were not long coming. While other regiments were to attack and hold critical positions northwest of Cassino, Obie's regiment was to leave the mountains and proceed south onto the town itself. Support from three tank battalions was promised. The opening maneuver would take place the following morning. They were ordered to rest.

Obie often longed for solitude, for a time and place to think about something besides war. On this eve of battle they were in a relatively sheltered position behind a hill cleared of the enemy, so he judged it safe to slip from his group and sit beneath an undamaged cluster of grapevines on a terraced hillside. Guards patrolled the perimeters.

He wrapped himself in a robe taken from a destroyed German bunker and took out his small Bible—the one Pastor Charles had given him. He had the book with him because he'd always appreciated the poetic beauty of the Psalms. Aside from any religious intent, he acknowledged that they had inspired people for thousands of years. In the fading light, he sought verses to give him courage for the coming battle.

He was surprised by a desire to pray. Even so, he wasn't deluded; the faith in prayer he'd possessed on finding his way off

Algonquin wasn't present—and wouldn't be again. Any perceived benefit from prayer was an illusion. God, if he even existed, was indifferent. Nonetheless, if for no other reason than to tell Pastor Charles he'd followed the pastor's advice, he would try.

Obie's prayer, predictable in its content, was uttered aloud in a soft voice and without emotion. It seemed appropriate to give thanks for victories and survival. He asked for protection for his friends, father, relatives, Pastor Charles, and Cassie.

After a moment's hesitation, he said, "About Laura . . ." He found no other words. "Amen," he managed.

"Amen." The voice came from behind him.

Obie turned to see an officer with a cross on his helmet—a chaplain. The man was smiling. He'd seen this chaplain around, but they had never spoken. If a man in his squad had startled him in such a manner, he would have felt violated, but this man had a quiet dignity about him that let Obie relax.

"I'm sorry, soldier," the chaplain said. His voice was soft. "I didn't mean to listen, but I came on you unexpectedly and didn't want to say anything until you finished."

"It's okay, sir."

"I'm Chaplain Jim Forrester. I guess I'm doing the same thing you're doing, sneaking away for a few minutes alone. Well, not alone, apparently, but to be with God at a little more comfortable level."

"Yes, sir."

"What's your name?"

"Gainsworthy, sir. Obadiah Gainsworthy." Obie had little experience talking to officers except for recent short conversations with Lieutenant Howard, who was friendly anyway.

"That's a mouthful. What do your friends call you?"

"Obie."

"Do you mind if I call you 'Obie?'"

"No, sir,"

"Tomorrow's the big push, eh?"

"Yes, sir. We have to take the town to get past the Abbey and through to the Liri Valley." It was common knowledge, but he felt compelled to say something.

"It'll be quite a task, won't it?"

"It sure will. The Germans are holed up in there. We'll have to blast them out a house at a time. We won't finish tomorrow." They were phrases borrowed from his comrades.

"Lives will be lost," Forrester said.

"Yes sir . . . ours and theirs."

The chaplain studied his face. "I'm holding a service at regiment in about half an hour. I'd like to have you attend."

Obie searched for excuses. Finding none, he said, "Yes, sir. I'll try to be there."

* * *

Even with tank support, it took the regiment over a day to clear the area north of Cassino, a prerequisite for proceeding against the town itself. Confidence was shaken when they came under heavy antitank guns, necessitating a retreat.

That night Obie wrapped himself in his bedroll and slept fitfully. The following morning brought gloomy wet weather. In addition, he was cold and sick. Another dismal task ahead didn't help morale. Lieutenant Howard alerted his men that the next push would come shortly before dark.

Obie tried eating K-rations but couldn't get them down. A stomach bug was going around, he was told.

"Go on sick call," Silverman told him. We'll have enough to deal with without taking care of you."

"I'll be fine, Sarge."

Tanks and troops moved out at five-thirty that evening. At first, they faced little enemy fire, and Howard was jubilant when they entered the town. Resistance soon increased and they fell back. They'd gained ground, but that progress came with a price; causalities increased, and the Germans captured two of their tanks and damaged several others.

Obie was ill. Silverman sent him to a first-aid station where he was given some foul-tasting medicine and sent back to his unit. Even with the thunder of guns from the mountain ridges in the northwest, he slept that night.

They resumed the attack early the following morning. Entering Cassino was like marching into Hell. Fire erupted from every building. Creaking tanks with their tracks clanging against concrete and cobblestones crept ahead. Straight ahead was Castle Hill, an extension of the ridge running up to the Abbey. The enemy was firmly entrenched in vertical cliffs on the north side from where they reigned destruction on everything below. A bullet ricocheted off Obie's helmet during one attempt to advance. Despite difficulties, they managed gains.

Later, after they drew back to consolidate, Obie knew he couldn't continue. He sat on a ruined section of concrete wall and dropped his head between his legs to keep from passing out. Matt and Perkins were assigned to escort him to the rear. His temperature was high, and he lay on a cot in a hospital tent hardly knowing where he was.

Three days passed before he was well enough to get up, but he was so weak he could walk only a few feet before becoming exhausted. The following day he was taking enough interest to note that the noise of battle had increased.

When he returned to his battalion, debilitated and pounds lighter, he felt out of place, as though he'd let his friends down. Men were haggard and unshaven. They were having a difficult time.

Matt filled him in. "Company L came up to strengthen our regiment, and it's helped, but we're a long way from breaking through. Can't get by Castle Hill. Even if we did, there's still the monastery."

"How're they doing up there?"

"Taking ground. One squad even got near a wall. It's an impossible job, though. I don't know how they can do it. Probably won't. Causalities are high, even worse than our regiment. We've lost a lot of men. Last I heard, our platoon had four killed and seven wounded."

"And our squad?"

"The new guy, Keanan, took one in the arm. Looks bad. He'll probably be going home. Other than that, we're okay."

"Let's hope it stays that way."

"Obie, are we going to get through this war? Sometimes I don't think I'll make it. We've had so many close calls. Sooner or later, something's bound to happen."

"We'll make it. After all, you have Rosa to live for. Have you heard from her?"

"No, and it worries me. What's it been, six weeks since you helped me write that letter?"

"Something like that. Remember that I told you not to get your hopes up. A lot can happen." He resisted adding, *"As it did to me."*

"What's that they say? Love will win out? Rosa and me are destined for each other. Don't you believe in love, Obie?"

The silence became awkward as he considered how to answer. He managed, "Not the way I used to."

"You must believe in destiny, or in something more than the

here and now. You told me once that you were a Christian . . . or maybe you said 'church member.' Anyway, you probably pray. And you must believe that your prayers will be answered."

"Matt, I . . ." He wished he'd told Matt his true feelings earlier.

"I'd like to have faith that Rosa and I will live through this war and be together when it's over."

"I'm sure you'll make it."

"Will you pray for us? For Rosa and me?"

How could he tell Matt that prayer was useless? With a feeling of guilt, he said, "I guess . . . if you really want me to."

"I do. I'm not much on prayer, myself. You probably have a better connection to God than I do."

Obie wanted to deny that possibility but remained quiet.

CHAPTER TWENTY-SEVEN

February–March 1944

Cassie eavesdropped on the conversation in the living room while trying to complete her homework at the kitchen table. "Why go to Boston now?" Pinky asked Abigail. "The baby's not due for more than three months."

Laura's pregnancy had shocked Cassie initially, but she'd grown used to the idea that her sister would be a mother. A little niece or nephew would be a wonderful thing.

"Our daughter's going to need me," Abigail said. "Ben's too busy to help. I'm needed there more than here."

"Have you considered you might be an intrusion rather than a help? Did either of them ask you to come?"

"Not in so many words, but I know they'll appreciate it."

"What about your business?"

"Angela Goodwin can take care of it. She knows the ropes. Any major decisions can be made over the telephone."

Although Abigail involved herself in Cassie's life in various ways, she wasn't often forthcoming about her own activities. Cassie learned more by listening to her parents' conversations than by what either told her. She'd had no idea her mother planned to go to Boston again.

Cassie detected concern in her father's voice. "How long will you be gone this time, Abigail?"

"I'll stay a few weeks after the baby is born. I won't rush to get back."

Cassie smiled at speculation about what her mother's long absence would mean. Living with Abigail wasn't easy. Laura and Cassie had, for the most part, escaped her ire by simply giving in. Their father's easygoing manner of acquiescing to Abigail's wishes may have inspired the girls to do likewise. But things had changed; Laura was gone, and her big loving bear of a father was not someone with whom she wanted to discuss the matter. It wasn't likely that he'd take a stand against Abigail.

There had been another incident between mother and daughter the week before. Coming home early, Cassie found Abigail sitting at the kitchen table reading Obie's letter that had arrived that day. Her mother made no effort to hide her actions.

"Mom, that's unforgivable. How could you?" Cassie had snatched the pages from Abigail's hand.

Abigail was unrepentant. "It's my duty to protect you from people like Obie. I wanted to see what filth he's writing to you."

"It's not filth. Obie is good and honorable."

"Your sister could tell you something about that."

The remark brought questions. Had Abigail discovered the depths of Laura and Obie's relationship despite their attempts to keep it from her? What *had* happened to cause Laura to change her mind and marry Ben? Laura had always seemed strong, but maybe there was some instability in how she approached problems.

Cassie said, "Lots of people around here can tell you the kind of person Obie is."

"I can't imagine what good things that might reveal." The sarcasm was evident.

"Mom, why don't you ask Pastor Charles what he thinks of Obie? Obie might have made a few mistakes, as we all . . ."

"I don't trust the Reverend Lansing's judgment in this matter. Those two were close."

"Well, I do trust his judgment. You used to like Pastor Charles. What changed your mind?"

"I'm looking out for our church. He's been here five years and told he'll have to move on soon. Not this year, but maybe the next."

"I think it's mainly you trying to get rid of him."

"We decided that he deserved at least another year. He'd already started the education wing project, and we believed he should have the chance to finish it. He'll go next year, however. He's not suited for Stafford Rest. A family man would be better for our church."

Cassie hadn't been able to hold her anger in check. "You interfere in people's lives, Mom, and half the time you have no idea what you're talking about."

Abigail's face had grown scarlet. "How dare you? How dare you speak to me like that?"

"I'm sorry, Mom, but it's how I feel. You seldom have anything good to say about people. Obie's my friend, and I intend it to stay that way."

"No, Cassie. I'm going to end this infatuation you have for Obie. I've told you several times that he's not for you. I told Laura too, and she listened. He's garbage."

"You may have convinced Laura of that, but you'll never convince me. And I'm tired of hearing it . . . that lie!" Cassie hit the table with a clenched fist.

Abigail, eyes flashing, had grabbed Cassie's head, a hand on either side of her face. She shook her daughter until Cassie was dizzy. "You will not ever, at any time, have any more contact with him. Do you hear me?"

Cassie had pulled away. She'd wanted to hit her mother. That moment had changed the mother-daughter relationship that Cassie thought might never be retrieved; she wasn't sorry. She rejoiced at the prospect of three months from under her mother's tyranny.

* * *

Laura Williamson examined her profile in a full-length bedroom mirror. She better understood the Biblical term "great with child." Her mother, already with them for two weeks, thought Laura was carrying a boy.

Laura hoped it would be a girl simply because she'd promised Obie that she'd bear him a son; she wanted to avoid any reminders of that relationship or the conflicting emotions endured the past few months. *That part of her life was over.* She'd made her choices and would move on. She had a husband, a good man who had proven his love for her and whom she believed would be a good father.

Ben did have some strange ways, not necessarily bad, just different. They'd both been forced to make concessions, and their financial situation had, at first, been stressful. They rushed out of Stafford Rest and settled in Boston with little preparation and no furniture. His father, Doctor Lloyd Williamson, had been furious, having expected Ben to join him in his Stafford Rest practice. Blindsided by the news that his son was marrying and moving to Boston, he swore the Adirondack Mountains would crumble to dust before he'd ever give Ben any help.

The couple had struggled for several weeks until Ben entered practice with a friend, Doctor Theodore Emmons, who had recently finished his residency in Cambridge. Ted gave Ben a loan, and things were going well; Ben was a good physician, as was Ted, and their practice was swelling.

An improved financial situation didn't mean there were no personal problems. Ben was often stoic. On the day last summer when he'd taken her home in the rain, she'd thought him simply shy. Now, he often avoided conversation. She'd been in the office several times and noticed he was brisk, even dismissive with patients and strangers. He excelled in medicine, which probably saved him from suffering the consequences of a questionable bedside manner. She accepted it as a part of his personality, something to which she would adjust. In love matters, he was passionate and affectionate, although sometimes controlling.

He bought her expensive clothing and insisted she visit the beauty parlor weekly. He took offense when she lightheartedly accused him of treating her like his showcase but later apologized. They attended dances, dinners, and fundraisers for the war effort. Laura loved that part; she was well-suited for Boston social life.

He would be late that evening, as he often was. She sat on their bed and reread Cassie's letter, one section for the third time.

> *I've been writing to Obie and he to me. He's in Italy. They are having a tough time of it. So far, he's safe. I hope and pray this war will be over soon.*
>
> *I miss you. It's been so long since we've seen each other. You and Ben must be so happy about your pregnancy. Mom says it's a boy. She's guessed correctly several times in Stafford Rest. Maybe he'll be as handsome as Ben. Please don't tell Ben I said that.*
>
> *I need to say something, and I hope you won't take it the wrong way. You gave Obie up to marry Ben, and we never talked about it. I won't try to second-guess your reasons because it's your business. You once accused me of being in love with Obie. You were right, and if my memory serves me correctly, I confessed that I did. I still do. I've loved him for as long as I can remember. I might be preparing myself for heartbreak, but I intend to continue our friendship with the hope that it can become something more. I hope I have your blessings in that.*

Tears suddenly filled Laura's eyes and overflowed, spotting the page. She hugged herself and rocked back and forth for several minutes. A sigh came from unknown depths. She said aloud, "I will forget him . . . I will!"

* * *

Members of the 34th Division, exhausted in mind and body, rested again at Alife. Many, who had occupied the ridges by the monastery, needed help walking or had to be carried from the mountain areas. The division was severely depleted, and replacements started arriving—men with different levels of expectation. Obie wrote to his father, to Charles, and to Cassie, recounting his experiences, although downplaying the terrible conditions they'd endured.

Obie, Matt, and Rivera were promoted to private first class. Aimes became a staff sergeant. Speculation was that he'd be assigned his own squad when there was an opening. He wouldn't accept it, he said. Burke stormed around swearing at anyone within hearing because he'd been thwarted in starting a climb back up the ranks. Sergeant Smith moved up to regiment. Silverman was expected to become the new platoon sergeant, but Tech Sergeant Permine was assigned the job. Silverman expressed relief. Permine was a nervous man with bulging eyes and protruding Adam's apple. Some men called him "the chicken" behind his back.

With little warning, they moved from Alife to San Giorgio near Benevento, even farther from the front. One day Obie found Silverman alone. The sergeant was sitting on a truck's running board, shuffling through papers. He'd been assigned, along with several other seasoned NCOs and officers, to train new arrivals. "Want to assist me?" he asked Obie.

"I'm not qualified."

"Gainsworthy," Silverman said with his best Boston accent, "don't you realize you've been through some of the worst combat conditions any army has been asked to endure? Nothing could be worse than Cassino."

"Thanks for asking, but I'd like to get as far away from it as possible while we're here." When Silverman didn't respond, Obie asked, "Do you think we'll go back to Cassino?"

"No. We'll go to Anzio."

There had been speculation about Anzio. A large body of Allied troops had landed at the seaport city south of Rome. The plan was to push inland from there and join forces coming up from Cassino and the coast. Together, they'd sweep north to capture Rome. The Anzio front, however, had turned into a nightmare. Allied divisions were stopped cold after being unable to move more than a few miles. New German troops were rushing in with the intent of pushing them back into the sea. Additional Allied divisions would be landing there in preparation for a drive to break out of the trap. Their division, rested, would be a logical choice.

A few days later, in mid-March, news came that the town of Cassino and the Abbey had been bombed beyond recognition. Most men cheered at the news. Obie had mixed feelings. During the struggle for the town he had gazed up at the fortress many times. The Allied armies could now push on to the Liri Valley and begin the trek to Rome. Nevertheless, the cost was great. The Abbey, a Christian icon, was historically linked to ancient defenders of the faith. The German occupation of the monastery was immaterial; they were a temporary blight that could have been removed without destroying priceless treasures. No one seemed to share his objection.

Two days later, the regiment moved to a staging area near Naples. Lieutenant Howard told them they were headed for the Anzio Beachhead.

* * *

Ash from Vesuvius covered everything in the Naples area. Eruptions continued from the great mountain across the Bay, one more worry for civilians who had already borne terrible burdens. Some Allied airfields in the area were being moved to locations where engines and equipment would not be damaged. After months of misery in the mountains of Italy, the annoyance of ash and confusion in the staging area near Naples seemed of little consequence.

Other feelings absorbed Matt. He brooded because they were to ship out in a day or two, and passes were not being issued. "I have to see Rosa, one way or another," he declared.

Against Obie's advice, he sneaked out the evening of their third night in the area. Obie worried and kept listening for his return. What if he failed to come back? The skinny little Rosa had a punishing headlock on him—and Obie was convinced it would end in heartbreak. If, in a peaceful environment, a girl could prove so callous in feeling toward someone she had pledged to love forever, what chances did Matt have with Rosa in this war zone?

Matt returned sometime after three o'clock in the morning. Obie was relieved to hear him slip into the tent and settle into his bedroll. He wanted to hear his friend's story but knew it would have to wait until morning.

Matt was still sleeping when Silverman called on Obie to

accompany him to the city. They were to pick up replacement officers at the harbor. Silverman drove the truck. The two men chatted
about various things during the drive into the city. It felt strange;
after several months under enemy surveillance or fire, they were now
simply two men in a truck carrying on a conversation having little to
do with battle or war.

They made their way without incident though city streets still
being cleared of debris from bombing and German sabotage. Im-
provement was noticeable; more stores and businesses were open.

They arrived at the docks in the late morning. Obie was struck
by the buildup of troops, mostly outgoing. Five young infantry second lieutenants who had come in on a freighter threw their bags into
the back of the truck and climbed in. When Obie offered someone
the front seat, they all declined, saying they wanted a good view of
the city. Their banter and celebratory attitude indicated they didn't
realize what they were in for.

Later that evening, to Obie's consternation, Matt managed another rendezvous with Rosa. "Has she heard anything from her father?" Obie asked the sleepy-eyed Matt the following day.

"Not *from* him. They had word that he was with the Germans as
they were fortifying their winter line. He may be somewhere near
Rome. She told me she's going up there to look for him."

"How in the world does she expect to get to Rome?" Obie
asked. "There's a war going on between here and there."

"She said she'd find a way. It's impossible, I know, but she
sounds determined."

"How do you manage to talk to Rosa?"

"Through her cousin Beppe, mostly. I've learned a few words.
She's learning English, too."

Neither left the post again until the division's departure a few
days later.

CHAPTER TWENTY–EIGHT

April–May 1944

Segments of their regiment entered Anzio Harbor under darkness and were trucked inland to an assembly area. Conditions were crowded and hectic. Foxholes, bomb craters, and dugouts filled quickly with water. The enemy had a clear view of the beachhead, and their big guns bombarded it constantly. The movement of men and machines occurred at night or under smoke cover. Allied searchlights raked the lines to detect enemy movement. The daily radio broadcast of propagandist Axis Sally was intended to demoralize, but the troops considered her a joke.

After months of offensive action on the Volturno and Casino fronts, their defensive situation was challenging. Obie's sense of time became blurred. A positive element was a well-supplied beachhead. And mail came on time. Even with German aircraft bombardment, fleets of LSTs and Liberty Ships sailed in and out of the harbor daily. A letter came from his father that saddened Obie.

> *Slobber died last week after he came home from chasing a rabbit. He just lay down and died outside your barn room door. He was suffering a lot with joint aches and all that, so it's just as well. I buried him in the little cove in back of the barn. I guess with all you must be seeing, one old dog's passing does not mean very much.*

It did, however; he was unable to stop thinking about Slobber. There were significant markers in his life: His mother, school, the experience on Algonquin, and Cassie and Laura's often-changing faces. Slobber had been a constant, always there, always faithful. Now, he was gone. Obie left home knowing he might never see Slobber again, but the reality came hard. A chunk of his life was gone, reminding him that other pieces were also missing.

On the beachhead, men and even whole units did strange things to combat the uncertainty. Out-of-sight stills were built and used with great frequency; Stands were erected for selling food items and spoils of war collected over past months. Burke was in his element. Howard called the whole area "Shanty Town" and did his best to preserve military discipline, which wasn't easy, and at times impossible.

Finally, they moved into the line in mid-April. In a holding operation, they faced the enemy primarily over the clearly defined lines of roads, canals, and streams. Some areas had no such boundaries. Skirmishes and sniping went on constantly. American and German soldiers sometimes found themselves face to face. Those encounters were often deadly but sometimes resulted in a wave of the hand before ducking. The noise from big guns and German bombs striking Allied units on the surrounded beachhead frayed nerves.

Fresh Allied forces continued to pour into Anzio, and the long-awaited breakout began early on May 23. It was chaotic. The action was fast and the actuality of moving the enemy backward was a stimulus propelling every man as the regiment moved in and through Cisterna, Lanuvio, and several small villages. The expectation of forces from the south linking up with Anzio forces didn't materialize. There had been no breakthrough at Cassino.

America Forces under General Lucas pushed on along Cyprus-lined roads, into destroyed towns, and through vineyard rows, inching along with another objective always before them. The enemy resisted fiercely, using tanks, self-propelled guns, mortars, Panzer Faust bazookas, and skillful counterattacks.

Causalities mounted. A new man in Silverman's squad was killed on his first day of battle. Obie helped collect his few belongings for the quartermaster. From Georgia, the man had a wife and a two-year-old daughter.

Silverman's squad had its own evolving personality. Paul Aimes turned down a squad leader position. John Chadlowski overcame several minor battle-related injuries to become a seasoned soldier. Perkins, whom Obie had long thought of as "the youngster," could be counted on to do what he was told, but had little ability to make decisions independently. Copland was redeeming himself. "He's become a good soldier," Silverman said.

Even after months of close contact with Adam Silverman, Obie didn't know him well, except for a few isolated facts. His mother was dead. His grandfather had been a rabbi in Boston. His father ran a financial company in New York City and had a publishing company there, as well. His father's brother, an uncle, was a professor in California at Berkeley. Silverman had relatives in Rome and worried about them.

While at Anzio, Obie had become better acquainted with

Chaplain Forrester. Forrester sought him out after a service one Sunday to help secure the area; The chaplain's regular assistant was unreliable, so he began calling on Obie for certain chores. Obie was quite willing, just to have something constructive to do. Now, however, with him on the front line and Forrester busy serving the wounded and dying, there were few chances to talk. Their encounters entailed little more than formal greetings.

A day of relative calm finally came, a rare time of partial disengagement from the war. Obie found Forrester setting up space for a planned evening service, subject to the continued calm. When he saw that the chaplain had art supplies, he volunteered to make a sign embellished with his artwork. Obie used a crate for a table, and Forrester sat nearby, watching him work. Obie considered it an invitation to talk.

"I've always been interested in art, graphics, that sort of thing. Businesses back home used to hire me to make signs and posters . . . restaurants, stores, and the like."

"Tell me about your hometown, Obie."

Obie gave him a quick rundown of Stafford Rest's geography and history, followed by brief descriptions of families, including his own. The chaplain laughed at his word pictures about the peculiarities of several residents. Obie didn't mention the Hunt family.

It became clear that Forrester had something on his mind. After a few minutes, the chaplain said, "Forgive me if I'm wrong, Obie, but I get the impression that you're on a spiritual path of some sort. Maybe I think that because I overheard your prayer that night near Cassino. Am I right?"

"When I was younger, religion was a big part of my life."

"And now it isn't?"

"Things have happened to make me change my mind." He hoped that wouldn't invite further questions.

"Obie, it's my duty to mentor servicemen. I hope you don't mind my probing? I'm a good listener, too."

Obie spent several minutes telling Forrester about his relationship with Pastor Charles, adding, "He thinks I'm destined to do church work of some kind. I hate to disappoint him, but I'll never do that."

"If you ever want to discuss things, I'm available."

With a few final flourishes, Obie finished the poster. "Thank you, sir, but there are some things I don't want to talk about." He wanted to make it clear.

"God works in mysterious ways, Obie. If you don't mind, I'll check on you periodically to see how you're doing."

* * *

A letter came from Cassie. They had just secured a village and Obie was so busy that he carried the letter in his pocket for several hours without a chance to read it. When a break finally came, he sat under an oak tree, desperate for sleep but wanting even more to read Cassie's words.

Dear Obie,

It's early May here and so pretty with the trees putting out their leaves. Gardens are being planted, and the smell of the earth is in the air. Last night I was looking out my bedroom window at the full moon and wondered if you could see it too. That's silly, I guess, since you are so far away.

I have a request. Please send future letters in care of Joyce Brannon. You know her. She's from Stafford Rest and in my class. I've enclosed her address. You're probably curious about this, so I'll just say that this way the mail will go through secure hands.

Good news. I've been accepted at Syracuse University for the fall semester. Frances Gibbons is finishing up her first year there. I've been talking to her about it. Dad's sister lives in Syracuse, and I'll live with her. It's exciting.

I saw your father last week. He looks lonely. I don't believe he's been drinking, but it's hard to tell. He was gone a long time on some job. Now he's doing odd jobs around here. I went for a walk up on Blackberry Hill not long ago, and I see he's planting a vegetable garden, although not a large one.

I'm sorry about Slobber. He was a part of all our lives.

I forgot to tell you something in my last letter. Well, no, in reality, I didn't want to upset you. But I feel I can't wait any longer to tell you. Laura is pregnant. She and Ben are expecting in early June.

Mom told me in January, and I admit my first thought was that it might be your child. When she told me the due date, I didn't know whether to be happy or sad. I don't know how this news will sit with you. I hate to be the bearer of news that will cause you more pain, but I believe you should know. Please don't hate the messenger. I can keep you up to date, but only if you want me to.

> *Please, dear Obie, be safe and write often so I know everything is well.*
>
> *With Love, your friend, Cassie*

Obie folded the letter and put it in his jacket pocket. He lay back in the grass and closed his eyes. *Laura was having a baby?* He tried to get his mind around the fact. He fought anger. She was another man's wife; she had the right. Still, it hurt.

As he lay with the warm sun on his face, he was reminded that spring had come to Italy as it had in Stafford Rest. He sat up, surprised to see the little reminders that creation, and re-creation, were happening even in a battle zone. Vineyards were filled with green, and tree foliage had begun to cast shadows that would become shelters against ever-warming days. Birds still sang and flowers still bloomed. Babies were still being born.

They were soon on the move again. Units finally broke through German lines in the west, allowing two large Allied forces to join. The Gustave and Hitler lines farther east had not yet been breached because of the strength of the well-entrenched enemy. General Clark decided a more worthy objective lay north and directed his troops toward it. The prize was Rome itself.

* * *

After the Anzio breakout and long-awaited linkup with troops from the south, the pace toward Rome quickened. Roads were littered with remains of German tanks, trucks, personnel carriers, and command vehicles, attesting to the urgency of the enemy's retreat and the accuracy of Allied artillery and airstrikes.

Progress was not accomplished without pain, however. They were assigned to check out a village a mile off the main road that the enemy had supposedly abandoned. During their approach, several men carelessly threw their heavier weapons onto a truck used to carry various company supplies. The truck had a flat tire requiring several minutes to fix, a situation that placed it two hundred yards in the rear. Silverman, forever vigilant, had made his men keep their arms close. Copland lugged a heavy BAR. Dusk was fading into night.

A bridge high over a small stream marked the town entrance. Fifteen-foot-high restraining walls secured the banks of the fast-moving stream under the bridge for several hundred feet in both directions. The village was of typical architecture, with stone houses lining a cobblestone main street. Low hills overlooked the town on three sides.

Half of the platoon, including Obie's squad, had crossed the bridge when a barrage of mortar and rifle fire opened up from the hills. A tank appeared at the far end of the long street, halting their progress. The men, strung out up the street, leaped to shelter in doorways, behind bushes, and along a low stone wall.

As if by prearranged signal, an artillery shell whistled overhead and took out the bridge with such accuracy that it disappeared along with three infantrymen crossing it. Smoke and dust settled on rubble and broken bodies in the stream below. Other shells followed, creating instant craters along the street. Obie realized they were in a precarious position with the platoon cut in half, retreat blocked, and hiding places in short supply.

With Matt beside him, he reached the wall. He could see that the troops on the other side of the stream were taking a similar pounding but were exercising their option to retreat. Obie's half-platoon was, for the moment, at the mercy of the enemy. The artillery barrage lasted five minutes. Small arms and mortar fire continued. It was nearly dark.

Howard was close by. He seemed angrier with himself than at the enemy. He called for Silverman and another squad leader, Jones.

"Sergeant Jones is wounded, sir," someone responded.

"Can he hear me?" Howard asked.

"Yes, sir, I can," Jones replied.

Obie was close enough to hear the conversation. Howard said, "Sergeant Permine is back across the river, so I'll lead your squad against that tank. Otherwise, it's going to rip us apart. Silverman, you keep your squad in reserve."

"Taking out that tank will be hard," Silverman said. "Our anti-tank equipment is back across the creek."

"Dammit, I know that! This is my fault, and it's up to me to get us out of this mess."

"Sir," Silverman pleaded, "We have enemy on all hillsides. They can see every move we make. There may even be more tanks up there. Wouldn't it be more prudent to wait until it's dark and fall back and find a spot farther downstream where we can ford?"

"That's an uncertainty. I want that tank destroyed!"

"At least call down artillery first."

"Negative. Our troops are much too close. Sergeant Jones, send your men over here on the double. Silverman, if anything happens to me, you're in charge."

Silverman called his men together. The clatter of machinegun fire continued. Obie watched as Howard, leading Jones' squad, moved out and up the street. They ran zigzag patterns toward the tank. Mortar shells fell on them again. A scream came from beside the wall as someone was hit.

"Corpsman!" Silverman yelled. "Get that man out of there!"

Howard and his men were still fifty yards from the tank whose turret gun pointed down the street toward them. Obie watched as Jones' squad closed on it. It fired twice without inflicting damage. Howard and a soldier leaped onto the tank at the same time. The soldier lifted the turret entrance lid. Howard dropped in a grenade and shut the lid. Both men jumped from the tank, one on either side. Black smoke rolled from the vents. A figure with clothing smoking emerged halfway from the turret entrance, struggled a moment, and became still. A cheer went up from the troops still hiding from enemy fire.

At that moment, two more tanks came from a side street above the destroyed tank. Behind those tanks were German infantrymen, at least a squad in strength. The soldier who had helped Howard destroy the tank ran for cover. Howard appeared to be trying to reach the wall in the other direction. Bullets kicked up rock dust around him. Howard fell headfirst onto the cobblestones and didn't move. Obie went numb.

Silverman's voice jarred him. "Dammit! Dammit to hell!" After a moment, he ordered, "Corpsman, get up there and get the lieutenant!"

Two additional tanks materialized at the top of the street, each followed by a squad of enemy soldiers. Silverman called out again, loud enough to be heard all along the street. "Squads! Pull back! Back to the bridge!"

The retreat was anything but orderly. As tanks fired indiscriminate blasts down the street, rifle and machinegun fire caused more causalities. Medics carried the severely wounded on stretchers while walking wounded were helped by fellow soldiers. They reached the blown bridge where Silverman directed disorganized and confused men downstream toward a point where they might cross.

"Where the hell is the rest of the platoon?" worried Silverman. "Did they run all the way back to Anzio? We could use some help here."

The tanks were still advancing. A corpsman slipped into the group. Silverman asked him, "You get everyone?"

"Almost," the medic said. He seemed confused, glancing over his shoulder at the tanks and enemy troops. "We couldn't find Lieutenant Howard. He was hit, and I think he went through that wall. I looked but didn't see him."

"You should've looked harder."

The corpsman stared at the ground. "I'm sorry. I tried."

"Go on . . . get down to the stream." Silverman gave the medic a shove. "Hurry up."

Their squad members had managed to stay together. Obie said to Silverman, "We can't leave him. I'm going back."

Silverman glared at him. "Gainsworthy, I don't intend to abandon him, but my primary responsibility is to get us out of this mess. We'll send someone back as soon as things quiet down, but we have to get across that stream right now. I don't think they'll follow us."

"Sarge, I'm going to find him," Obie said. "We might not have another chance."

"You're nuts," Burke said.

Obie heard murmuring within the squad. He sensed they agreed with Burke. "I seen him go down too," Perkins said. "He didn't move."

Silverman spun around and said, "Get down there quick," indicating the direction they should go. His tone left no doubt that the issue was settled.

Obie slung his M1 over his shoulder. "Go ahead. I'll find you across the creek when I get back," he said as he turned toward a side street.

"Wait," Silverman said. Obie thought he was about to order him back. "We'll find him later, one way or another. I'll go find him myself."

"I have to go see," Obie said. "I'll go up this side road and come in behind the tanks. If he's dead, I'll catch up with you."

"There are still squads of Germans up there."

"I'll be careful."

Silverman turned to the group. "I'm not asking for volunteers, but you have my leave if anyone wants to go with Gainsworthy."

No one spoke. Matt averted his eyes when Obie looked at him. Silverman slapped Obie on the shoulder. "Good luck, soldier!" Silverman, along with the other squad members, melted into the darkness.

The realization that he was alone brought a moment of anxiety. This might well be a fool's errand; Howard was probably dead. Obie had watched him fall the same way deer fell when instant death came. He had every excuse to turn back. It required only seconds to decide; he must continue.

Obie hadn't stood still while processing those thoughts. What he'd called a side street was more a footpath. He'd taken only a few steps along the path when he discovered a feeder stream paralleling it. The creek offered more cover, so it made sense to follow it up the incline.

Firing, although diminished, still came from the roadway. It sounded like the tanks had stopped at the bank's edge where the bridge had spanned the stream. They were probably firing random shots across the stream.

His quickly devised plan was to continue up the little stream using bushes, trees, and garden walls to hide from enemy positions that might be on the hill. He would come out above the spot where Lieutenant Howard had fallen. He must get there ahead of the tanks that would be coming back up the street.

Firing across the stream ceased, as it had from the hills. Obie stopped and stood motionless. There came the distant rumble of tank treads on cobblestone. The enemy had begun retracing their route. The only other sounds were the chirping of spring peepers from nearby pools of water and the gentle gurgle of the small stream. For a moment, he imagined himself at the foot of Blackberry Hill on the path to the Morass. He quickly thrust the distracting image aside. There was work to do.

He moved on, trying to be quiet. He imagined German troops sitting up in pillboxes and bunkers waiting for him to get into range, a tactic they were known to use. There was still time to turn back.

"Es ist jetzt ruhig."

Obie froze; he felt the veins in his neck pulsating. The voice had come from above, no more than a hundred feet away.

A second voice, more guttural, spoke. *"Ja! Gott hört manchmal unsere Gebete."* There was skeptical laughter, indicating he hadn't been discovered.

He kept close to the creek bed, hoping the running water would muffle any noise he might make. He imagined he could see the rock wall to his left. From that direction he heard the snap of a twig and an exhaled breath. *He wasn't alone.* He brought his M1 up, ready.

"Dodgers." The word was hardly audible.

"Giants," Obie whispered back. The sign and countersign of the day had been exchanged.

Obie crawled in the direction from where the voice had come. "Who is it?" he asked.

"Howard."

"Lieutenant Howard, we thought . . ."

"Who is it? I can't see you."

"Gainsworthy, sir."

"By glory, I'm glad you're here, Gainsworthy."

"Are you hit bad?"

"In the chest . . . and my leg. I can't walk, but I can crawl. I came through a hole in the wall up there. I've lost blood, and I've passed out twice. I'm lightheaded right now, Gainsworthy."

"I'll get you out . . . carry you if I have to." That wouldn't be easy; Howard wasn't a small man.

"Negative, Gainsworthy. You get on back to the platoon and tell Silverman where I am. He'll send a patrol to get me when things quiet down. Did they get back across the stream?"

"Yes, sir, I believe they did. That's the direction they were headed when I left them."

"Damn, this is all my fault," Howard said. "Could you pinpoint the enemy position well enough to direct artillery over here?" His voice had become so weak that Obie feared he might be losing consciousness again.

"Sir, we're right on top of one of their positions. They're right over there. It's too dangerous for you to stay here."

"You do what I'm telling you, Gainsworthy. Tell Silverman exactly where these enemy positions are. Tell him there's at least a platoon holed up here, plus tanks."

"Sir, I can't leave you."

"You sure as hell can . . . and you will. That's an order." The last few words were accompanied by a fit of coughing severe enough that Obie looked toward the enemy positions for an indication they might have been discovered.

He heard scurrying in the closest bunker, and machinegun fire raked the area around them. Inaccuracy indicated their exact position hadn't been pinpointed. They would soon find the range.

"Sir, we have to go."

Howard didn't respond. Obie shook his arm. It flopped. Order or not, he hadn't come all that way to leave Howard behind. He lifted the officer across his shoulders and managed to gain his feet.

Flares lit the area. Excited chatter came from above them. They'd been seen.

He tried to pick up his M1 but feared that if he bent over he wouldn't be able to get up. He left it.

Until now, Obie had never wondered how fast a man could move with one-hundred-eighty pounds on his back. He'd helped his father carry deer from the woods, but it had been at his leisure, not with someone shooting at him.

He gained extra speed downhill as his legs churned and his feet splashed through the marshy streambed leading to the larger stream.

"God, make me strong. Jesus, help me!" The words were uttered aloud.

Machinegun fire came from several locations. He heard the familiar pop of a bazooka. He felt the force of an explosion several yards to his right but stayed on his feet. There was another pop; the blast was closer.

How much farther? Obie's chest was burning. It seemed a miracle when he saw the larger stream ahead in the brief lifespan of a flare. He nearly lost his balance going down a twenty-foot-high bank. Water soon covered his boots. He struggled to carry his burden up the far bank. When he could go no farther, he sprawled in the wet grass with Howard on top.

"Who's that?" The voice came from the underbrush.

"It's Lieutenant Howard," someone else said. "Get a corpsman over here pronto."

Hands tried to help Obie, but he lay on the ground, utterly spent.

"You okay, soldier?" a sergeant Obie recognized asked him.

"I'm all right, but I need to talk to Sergeant Silverman . . . or anyone who can get in touch with an artillery unit."

CHAPTER TWENTY-NINE

June 1944

The pace toward Rome was unrelenting. Obie was surprised when Silverman announced that they had been in battle zones for eight straight days. Howard's replacement was Lieutenant Burnside, one of the officers Obie and Silverman had picked up in the harbor at Naples. If Burnside recognized them, he gave no indication. The usual speculation circulated about what this "ninety-day-wonder" was made of and how long he would last. He soon showed an audacity level that transferred well to combat situations. As days went by, Burnside gained a reputation of being fearless—with a touch of recklessness. Even Burke respected him.

The enemy was on the run but fought back with relentless fury. After taking each village or hill, the platoon braced for the usual counterattack. Land mines the Germans left behind tormented their steps. Time became meaningless except for the day and night's constant and repeating division. The order of towns and villages became a confused jumble in Obie's mind, although Lanuvio was freshest in his memory; it had cost their squad. Timothy Copland and Edward Grugs were killed there. Burke was wounded. Aimes, who escorted him to the rear, said Burke's wound was minor. Grugs, with a chest wound, was taken to an aid station where he lingered several hours before dying. Copland died quickly and honorably; Silverman dared anyone to mention the one incident where Copland had surrendered to fear.

Rome was within sight, and the enemy's retreat heightened. Elements of several divisions had already sent platoons to secure bridges over the Tiber River. No one wanted to stop. Nevertheless, their halt was a general one ordered by the regiment and just long enough for a few hours rest. Their company set up makeshift headquarters within an abandoned building not far from the road. The stone structures were in good shape, better than most of the temporary sites on their northern journey. Platoons staked out their territories in various buildings.

Obie's platoon took residence in a barn across the road from the stone buildings. A house by the barn had been destroyed either by

Allied units or as a farewell gesture by the enemy. Smoke still curled up from the rubble.

Orders came down from above for men to spruce up for their entry into Rome. A stream ran nearby, and many were already washing clothes to remove weeks of mud, grease, and grim accumulation. Bushes, vines, trees, and other spaces suitable for hanging and drying were covered. Obie and Matt stripped naked and stood in the shallow stream with scores of other men. They lathered their bodies and let the flowing water wash away the suds. The cold shocked Obie's system, but being clean was exhilarating.

In the barn, they placed their bedrolls on piles of straw in the loft. Familiar barn smells of manure, animal urine, and hay reminded him of Uncle Abner's farm. There had been recent animal occupants in this barn; except for a couple of goats roaming outside, none was around. Perkins and a soldier from another platoon chased the goats. Perkins had his helmet ready as a pail for milking the female.

Mess cooks served a meal of cold K-Rations. A picnic-like atmosphere prevailed. No fires were allowed since they would invite enemy gunners who might not be out of range.

Obie prepared to rest, hoping he wouldn't be called for guard duty. He was surprised when Captain Forrester appeared at the barn entrance.

"Private Gainsworthy," the chaplain said, looking apologetic, "can I have a few minutes of your time?"

"Of course, sir." Obie stepped away from the wooden ladder.

Matt looked at Obie quizzically, "What's going on?"

Obie and Forrester went out into the night. Stars were visible, and a slight breeze was blowing. "I have some news you might like to hear," Forrester said.

"They're sending me stateside?" Obie said, laughing.

Forrester smiled. "Well, not quite, but it's good news anyway. You're going to get a medal. It's not official yet, so I shouldn't be telling you. I will anyway because you deserve to know."

It felt awkward, and he wasn't sure how to respond. "Is this because I carried Lieutenant Howard across the creek?"

"Yes, because you carried Lieutenant Howard across the creek . . . although that's most certainly an oversimplification, and for pinpointing locations our artillery was able to take out. But you saved the lieutenant's life, pure and simple. I was in the hospital tent when they brought him in. He'd lost nearly half his blood."

Obie remembered his field jacket being so blood-soaked he could have wrung it out. Supply had found him a new one. "How is he?" he asked.

"He's in Naples, and word is he'll recover. This is the second time he's been wounded, and this time it's serious enough to send him home."

"I'm glad for it."

"After they had him stabilized, I overheard a conversation between him and the company commander. I heard Lieutenant Howard say, 'Silver Star. Nothing less. He gets it, or I'll resign my commission.' That's what they're recommending you for, Obie, the Silver Star."

"I don't deserve . . ."

Forrester grabbed his hand and shook it. "Obie, you do deserve it . . . and more."

* * *

The fringes of a long tree-lined road, the terminus of the Appian Way, held thousands of people as a procession of trucks, tanks, jeeps, and various military vehicles squeaked, clanged, and lumbered through the outskirts of Rome. Division after division passed through one massive cheering and celebrating civilian review. The Fifth Army had arrived.

The previous two days had been total confusion as regiments and divisions of several countries jockeyed for the first position into the Eternal City. Some took main roads, Routes 6 and 7. Others went on side roads to escape the congestion. At the same time, rearguard bands of retreating German troops had to be dealt with. There was much speculation about whether the enemy would run or stay and fight. In the end, they fled and left the city to the Allies, much to the relief of the residents.

Burke had returned, a bandage on his left arm which had been pierced by shrapnel. In Burke fashion, he managed to obtain a truck which Silverman's squad had to themselves. Rivera drove. Aimes rode with him in the cab. The other squad members were in the open back.

Crowds formed unbroken lines along both sides of the highway. The cheering was continuous. People threw flowers. Some ran along beside vehicles offering open wine bottles in gestures of appreciation. A full bottle was pressed into Perkin's outstretched hands. He passed it around. Signs all along the streets welcomed the Allies. One in English read, "WHERE THE HELL HAVE YOU BEEN?"

"Is the war over?" Perkins asked with a slurred voice. He'd been sampling a significant number of wine offerings.

"Gawd Almighty!" Burke shouted at Perkins. "We're only half-way to the Alps!" He muttered, "Ignorant bastard." Perkins failed to show he'd heard the insulting remark.

They entered the city's heart, and Rivera pulled up to a large fountain. The men piled out. Some removed their boots and waded, surrounded by still-celebrating citizens. Others were content to toss in coins, presumably making wishes. Pigeons whirled and swooped in great numbers. Obie and Matt went to sit on the steps of a large public building. Rome had been their goal for so long that it seemed strange sitting there quietly on the cool stone steps with their M1s between their knees. An unending stream of people flowed around them.

Silverman approached with a map in his hand. "We'll be here a while, and there's someone I have to find. You two want to go with me?"

"Sure," Matt said, and Obie nodded.

Silverman drove a borrowed jeep. Obie watched windows and doorways along the streets. The masses were joyous at the German exit and the arrival of the Allies, although there would be factions and individuals feeling otherwise; there would be instances of retaliation, and there might even be enemy soldiers left behind to harass. There were hoards of people everywhere, even on side streets. The scope of the celebration was thrilling. After traveling several blocks Obie asked where they were headed, although he thought he knew.

"I have relatives here," Silverman said. "Father's brother and his wife and daughter."

"Have you been here before?" Obie asked.

"With Father seven years ago. I stayed all summer with them."

"Are they Italian?"

"No. My grandparents lived in Austria. They had three sons. Father and one uncle went to America. My other uncle and his wife came here. I'm worried about their safety."

Matt asked, "Why are you worried? Have you heard something?"

"Father told me their letters came regularly until a few months ago, and then they stopped."

"Maybe the Germans disrupted the mail."

"Undoubtedly. Some letters that Father received were delivered by friends who sneaked them out."

"Are they in the Resistance," Obie asked, "or involved in politics in any way?"

"I don't believe so, although I don't really know. They have a small bakery and shop. They're just a father, mother, and daughter trying to live a normal family life."

Matt asked, "Would the Germans have any particular reason to hurt them?"

Silverman's face took on a hard and painful expression. Obie could see that Matt's question had offended him and expected an angry response, but Silverman said calmly, "Burroughs, do you have any idea why we're fighting this war?"

"Well, I guess to stop the Germans from taking over the world."

Silverman's words were composed, but a fire lit his eyes. "That's right, although it's become a personal matter for some of us. I'll bet you joined the Army to stand up for what's right, a value your parents probably taught you."

"I guess so," Matt confessed.

Silverman smiled and continued. "And that's a good thing, Burroughs. Good people generally recognize evil when they see it and will take a stand against it. Our country and other countries have risen to the occasion, even if somewhat late, but risen nonetheless. My family and I are members of a group that this great evil isn't just trying to hurt but to exterminate. And if they win this war, they might succeed. For me, *that's* what's at stake."

"The Jews, you mean?"

"Yes . . . the Jews. You and Gainsworthy fight for an ideal, and that's certainly worthy. And I fight for that too, but I also fight because people I know . . . people Father and my uncles know, are dying for no other reason than the fact that they're Jews. Hell, these Nazis don't need reasons to do harm, Burroughs? They hate and kill Jews. They hate and kill members of *any* group that doesn't fit Hitler's Arian race criteria. They want us gone from the face of the earth."

Obie said, "Germans aren't stupid. How can they believe something like that?"

Silverman said, "Of course, not all Germans feel that way, but enough do that such ideas find fertile ground. It's a progression. Good people don't all of a sudden start hating someone enough to want them dead. It starts with death of another kind . . . a 'social death,' I suppose you could call it. I suspect it's brought about by the long-held idea that Jews are inferior and not worthy of associating with the general population, either socially or physically."

The truth of Silverman's words dawned on Obie and was painful. "And then it gradually becomes a smaller step toward 'extermination,'" he said.

"Exactly!"

"Well, that'd be a huge step for me," Matt said.

"And for most people, Silverman replied. "However, once those hate seeds are planted, they grow. And it's not only Jews who're ostracized. *Here's a question.* Where are the Negros in this war? Do you see their faces in our company? Of course not. Is that because they aren't in this fight the same as us?"

"They have their own units," Obie said.

"Exactly! And why is that?"

Matt answered. "I guess they want to be together."

"Unfortunately, that's not the real reason. We exclude them. That's the truth of it. Seeds of prejudice are allowed to grow, even in America, to the point where we limit our associations . . . even on battlefields."

Silverman's observations made Obie question his own thinking. Had he gone along with the idea that certain groups of people were separate because they wanted to be? What about the Gibbons family? Had he just assumed they'd settled in Stafford Rest because some unknown event had separated them from their group? Did he think of Jews the same way? Silverman was a Jew, and he certainly wasn't to be regarded as anyone different from himself. Obie had never considered himself prejudiced against anyone. So, how had he failed to question such blatant injustices as those Silverman was naming?

Silverman wasn't finished. "Did you know that every Jew in Rome, and there are more than eight million, has been forced to carry a document that says 'Hebrew Race?' I've heard that any Jew caught without the document is liable to be shot on the spot. That's why I worry about my relatives." Silverman clutched the jeep steering wheel tightly. His face was flushed.

They were silent until Obie asked, "Do you remember where they live?"

"It's just a few more blocks."

They entered an area by the Tiber River where buildings were closer together and more austere. There was a feeling of poverty, but poverty with pride. Most balconies and areas beside doors and windows held plants, large and small. Many were wilted. The crowds were not thinner there. If anything, the celebration was louder than the one in central Rome.

"Welcome to the Jewish Ghetto of Rome," Silverman said and added with a rye grin, "a place where Jews get together."

"It's bigger than I expected," Obie said.

"I remember going to a synagogue near the water with Uncle Yarden's family. You probably think it looks rundown here, but the real slums are across the river in Trastevere. Poor Jews live here, poorer ones over there."

Silverman pulled the jeep to a curb. A man, apparently in his late eighties, was hobbling along carrying a large pail with water sloshing over the sides. The bucket looked too heavy for him.

After they exited the jeep, Silverman spoke to the man. "Sir, how are you today?"

The man squinted through thick wire-rimmed glasses with scratched lenses. He placed the pail on the sidewalk. Replying in English with an accent, he said, "It is a good day. My rheumatism has subsided so that I can water the plants. The Allies have finally come. We have waited for so long. Look at the joy!" He gestured toward the crowds.

Silverman said, "Father, we are Americans. I didn't expect to see so many people."

"The Germans have left. That is why you see so many here. If you had been on this street as late as yesterday, you would have seen no one except a few fearless ones and me." He swept his arms out to indicate the buildings around them. "These have been empty for many months. As you can see, however, many people have now returned."

"Where have they been?"

"In hiding . . . those the Germans did not carry away."

"Were many taken?" Without waiting for an answer, Silverman said, "Do you think they'll come back, too?"

The man's expression changed as though a dark curtain had descended. *"They are gone."*

"Gone?"

"Yes, gone. They will not return."

"When? When did they go?"

"At different times. It started some months ago. September and October, I think. See . . . their plants are dead. I have managed to water and save a few pots in this block."

"Sir," Silverman said, and his voice shook. "Do you know the family of Yarden Silverman? They live here. Right over there," he said, pointing.

The old man appeared thoughtful. "Silverman . . . Silverman. There were so many people here. I don't know. Wait! A daughter, sixteen years perhaps? And a wife?"

"Yes, at the corner over by the water fountain with the horse sculpture?"

"Aw yes . . . Yarden Silverman and Shira, I believe. I knew them, but not well. They had a bakery and lived over it. I do not know the daughter's name."

"Her name is Jael. She is seventeen. Have you seen them? Are they in their apartment?"

The man hung his head. "American, I am sorry. The Germans took them away. They are gone."

"Gone?" Silverman looked incredulous.

"Those taken away do not return."

"Where were they taken?"

"To Germany, I believe. They were forced onto trains and trucks here. I was told they were herded onto a big boat, a ship. In Tiburtina alone, I was also told, more than a thousand men, women, and children were loaded onto freight cars."

"Did you see them take the Silvermans, sir?"

"I think that I did."

Silverman appeared ready to collapse. He placed his hands on the railing of an iron fence and gripped it so tightly that his knuckles turned white. Although he made no sound, Obie saw he was crying. The man limped to Silverman and put a hand on his shoulder. Obie didn't know what to say, and Matt looked perplexed, as well. The scene was not a familiar one where Silverman was involved. He was the strong one.

Silverman soon composed himself. He addressed the man. "Who did this?"

"The Germans. They did it."

"No, I mean *who?* What man? What monster? Who gave the order here in Rome?"

"Gestapo Chief Kappler, I suppose." The old man, appearing overwhelmed, sat beside Silverman on the steps. "And SS Captain Schutz. They first stole all the gold they could find before taking the people away. The Germans are no longer in Rome, so what can you do?"

"They're still in Italy, and they'll soon run out of hiding places. I hope to be there when they do."

"Hate sometimes feels good," the man said, "but it can also bite the one who hates. Be careful, American. Do not get bitten."

"Can I get into their apartment?"

"Maybe, but it will be of no use. The Germans took everything of worth, followed by other looters."

"I'll look anyway."

The man waited on the street. The bakery was bare. Obie and Matt followed Silverman up the stairs, where he pushed open the unlocked door. Rooms were stripped of all furniture. Silverman searched cupboards and closets for several minutes; nothing was left to indicate a family had ever lived there. When they returned to the street, Silverman asked the man, "Why is it that *you* were not taken?"

"The partisans hid me." He rose from the steps where he'd been resting and hobbled to Silverman. "Rabbi Zolli, Chief Rabbi of Rome, sent men to protect me. I hid in the home of a Catholic family for several months. I finally got tired of that and came back here. The Germans would not have taken me, anyway, I think. I am too old. They would have shot me as they did many elderly ones."

"Father, is there any chance I'll see my relatives again?"

"I think not. I am sorry. It is not to Babylon that they have gone."

"I understand, sir. I thank you for your kindness." Silverman turned to go. Obie and Matt followed.

The man called after them, "American, you are thinking of avenging them, are you not?"

Silverman's answer came quickly, a determined utterance. "I am, sir. I am!"

Shaking a crooked forefinger, the man said, "Do not get bitten."

Silverman didn't answer.

* * *

They moved back to their assembly area on the city outskirts that evening. Obie was pained to see the change in Silverman. An aura of self-confidence had always surrounded the sergeant. Now, a layer of grief and anger was superimposed. Perkins bore the brunt of Silverman's mood when he complained about some minor matter. The men in Silverman's circle learned quickly to avoid unnecessary contact. Even Burke fell silent. Obie quietly informed the others of what had transpired in the Ghetto.

That evening, Obie and Matt sat on the ground outside their squad tent cleaning their weapons. A company clerk came looking for Matt. "Someone wants to see you," the private said.

Matt wasn't in the best of moods, either. "Well, I'm right here. Send him over."

"Thing is, this person's not a 'he' but a 'she.' They won't let her leave company headquarters. She wandered in a few minutes ago. Had a piece of paper with the name of our outfit on it. Nobody can figure out how she got here. They were going to lock her up until she begged them to send for you. She doesn't speak much English but knows your name, and she . . ."

Matt jumped up and ran toward the company tent cluster. Obie secured their weapons and followed.

Rosa sat on a campstool with a master sergeant standing over her like a big cat over its prey. A captain stood nearby. Her dirty face was tear-stained. When she saw Matt, she started to get up. The sergeant looked ready to stop her, but the captain laid a hand on his arm. She leaped into Matt's embrace. He held her close for a long time. Beyond her filthy condition with torn and threadbare clothing, she looked exhausted.

The captain cleared his throat and spoke. "I'm Captain Andrews, and this is Sergeant Owens. We're from Regiment. Your company commander called us down." He turned to Matt and said, "Private Burroughs, how do you know this girl?"

"She's my girlfriend, sir."

"You work fast, private."

"Oh, no, sir. I didn't meet her in Rome. We met in Naples."

The sergeant spoke up. "But how did she get here?"

Matt shrugged. "I don't know, Sergeant."

"She doesn't speak much English," Captain Andrews said. "We need to get an interpreter."

"I speak some Italian," Obie said.

"And who are you, private?"

"Private Gainsworthy, sir."

"Well, Gainsworthy, see what you can find out. However, I have doubts that she's a threat to us."

The sergeant said, "You never know with these people." His tone was one of superiority.

The attitude angered Obie. "It's her country! She has a right to be here!"

Captain Andrews' tone was gentler. "Yes, I'm sure she's okay, but I need someone to explain this situation. I may have to make a report."

Matt released Rosa from his embrace but continued to hold her hand. His smile seemed frozen in place. Obie saw that he was too excited to be coherent, so he took it on himself to relate events in Naples, excluding Matt's unauthorized excursions to see Rosa. After he finished the story, he said, so there would be no doubt, "They're in love."

"Yes, I can see that," Captain Andrews replied. To the sergeant, he said, "You can go. I can handle it from here on." He turned to Obie, "Ask her how she got to Rome."

Obie said, "Rosa . . . greetings." She extended her hand, the one not holding on to Matt. She was even thinner than when they first met. Her cheekbones were prominent, and her body was emaciated. Her tattered gingham dress with rose patterns on a blue background was the same one she was wearing the first time he saw her.

"GI Obie. It is good to see you again. Nearly as good as seeing GI Matt."

"Rosa, how long have you been in Rome?"

"Several days."

"The captain wants to know how you got from Naples to Rome. I'd like to know that, too."

"I walked."

"From Naples?"

"Yes. A British Army truck gave me a ride once. I walked the rest of the way."

"*How?* It's a war zone. How did you manage? You had to come through both Allied and German lines."

"I sneaked along at night. I walked awhile, and I listened. I went where there was less noise and little activity. I have friends in Naples who told me where I should go and people I should see along the way who would help me."

"What friends?"

"Just friends." The words were so defiant that Obie knew she would never reveal names. "You call them partisans," she said, "Italian civilians who fight the Germans."

"And how did you get past our guards into this encampment?"

Rosa laughed. "Easy. I sneaked past when they were looking the other way. Remember, I have gained much experience."

"Yes, I guess you have," He was sure the respect in his voice was showing.

"GI Matt wrote down the name of your unit. I showed it to people, and they pointed where to go."

"Have you found out anything about your father?"

"Not yet. I found people who have seen him, and I know where to look next. He has been with the Germans and may still be. I will follow them."

Obie told the captain and Matt all that Rosa had said. When he finished, Captain Andrews had an orderly bring her food.

"Sir," Obie said, "She's been through a lot. Maybe a chaplain should talk to her."

"You're probably right. Who do you have in mind?"

"Captain Forrester."

"He's Protestant. This girl is probably Catholic."

"Yes, sir, I know, but Matt . . . Private Burroughs is Protestant, and he's involved too. He knows Captain Forrester."

"Very well, Private Gainsworthy. Considering her condition and the story she tells, she's obviously not a threat to us. I'm placing her in your hands. See that she's gone off this post by eleven hundred hours. Moreover, someone may be contacting you in a day or two concerning how security was breached. See if you can get some more information about it from the girl."

"Yes, sir. Her name is Rosa."

"Rosa," the officer said as he rose to leave, "I suspect you are a special young lady."

Obie believed so, too, in light of what had been revealed in the past few minutes.

CHAPTER THIRTY

June 1944

Obie was amused at Forrester's puzzled expression as he observed the strange couple standing before him. He understood the chaplain's bewilderment.

"You want to get married? *Right now?*"

"Yes, sir," Matt replied. "We do."

"I don't know, Private Burroughs. This is a situation I don't know anything about."

"I can tell you whatever you want to know, sir," Matt said. "Better yet, Obie can tell you. He tells it better than I do."

"They're *really* in love," Obie said. "There's more, but that sums it up pretty well."

"I'll take your word on that, but it wasn't exactly what I meant. I'm not familiar with Italian marriage laws. There may be licenses required. Birth certificates and the like. How old is she?"

"She's seventeen," Matt said. "Her name is Rosa . . . Rosa Rizzetti."

"I don't even know the marriageable age here. I'd have to research it."

"Sir," Matt pleaded, "they say we're pulling out in a few days, maybe even tomorrow. We have the Germans on the run and need to keep going. This might be the only chance for Rosa and me to do what's right."

Forrester ignored the urgency of Matt's plea. "Also, there's the Church issue. I could go ahead and perform a marriage that I'm sure the Catholic Church won't accept. I suppose it could be made legal later. Nevertheless, this could cause Rosa problems down the road."

"Are you saying you won't marry them?" Obie asked.

"I'm sorry. I don't see the urgency, especially with the problems it'd create. Wouldn't it make more sense to wait until the war is over?"

Obie hesitated, then asked Matt, "Should we tell him?"

"I say 'yes,' but it's Rosa's decision."

Obie held her hands in his. "Rosa, I know you want to marry Matt. He loves you and you love him. However, there are some good reasons you should wait." After relaying Forrester's protests, he said, "If we tell him what you told Matt and me, it might make a difference."

She didn't hesitate. *"Tell him!"*

"Sir," Obie said, first clearing the lump in his throat. "The meetings Private Burroughs had with Rosa in Naples have resulted in more than their falling in love. Rosa is expecting a baby. She's more than three months pregnant."

Forrester emitted an audible sigh and turned his back on the trio. Obie couldn't tell if he was thinking or praying. As he turned back, he sighed again and said, "This does make it a different situation. Suppose I contact a Catholic chaplain? He could give us some advice, maybe even perform a ceremony."

Obie relayed the information to Rosa. She shook her head. "No, I fear he would forbid it. I do not want to wait. I want to get married today. If I have to do it again later or do some penitence, it will be all right. Tell your chaplain I believe he is a man of God, and if he marries us, God will approve. I can fix it with the Church later."

"Your Church may not agree," Forrester said after Obie translated.

"I will . . . take . . . uh . . . the chance," Rosa declared with a resolute fix of her jaw. Obie was happy that she was learning English.

"Very well," Forrester said. "I'll perform a ceremony. I'm not sure it will have any legitimacy in Italy, and it may put Rosa in jeopardy with the Catholic Church. Make sure she understands this." Obie heard him mutter, "It may even get me in hot water."

Forrester sent for a nurse acquaintance on duty in one of the hospital tents. He explained the situation to Nurse Barbara, who got another nurse involved. They were excited about helping and would arrange for Rosa to bathe in a secluded location. They could do nothing about her dress except discard it. Barbara found one of her civilian dresses.

"I didn't know why I brought it with me," she told Obie as she brushed Rosa's long hair. "Now, I know. She can have it with my blessings."

Obie rounded up a few men from his squad. Silverman couldn't be located. Obie stood up for Matt and Aimes gave the bride away. The two nurses were the bride's maids. Even Burke got into the action; whether by bribery or deceit, he came through with an eight-hour pass for Matt.

Forrester gave a short talk to the couple as part of the brief and simple ceremony. "Times are hard. There's going to be a period of separation. How long, we don't know. It could be a long time. Know, Matt and Rosa, that regardless of circumstances, God is joining you together for life, however long that may be."

The men took up a collection and sent the couple off to find a private room somewhere on Rome's outskirts. Aimes checked out a jeep to drive them to their unknown destination.

Obie shook hands with Matt and kissed Rosa's cheek before they got into the jeep. He called after his friend, "You'll have to find your own way back. Just be back by reveille. Don't make me come looking for you."

"Don't worry. I now have even more reason to help get this war over with."

* * *

On June fourteenth, Obie penned a letter to Cassie:

> *We have reached Rome. Our platoon took part in the entry into the city. With the Normandy landing in all the news, you might not have heard about it. Many of our boys think that getting here means we have pretty well finished off the Germans in Italy, but wiser people know we still have a long way to go, many rivers and bridges to cross.*
>
> *We bivouacked one day on the outskirts of Rome before moving to the vicinity of Tarquinia. This whole part of Italy once belonged to the ancient Etruscans. A couple of miles east of here are the remains of one of their cities. I plan to take a look. I wish I had paid more attention in school when we studied about places like this. Who would have guessed that I would actually be here?*
>
> *We expect to be camped here awhile. We sleep on cots, eat hot meals, and are able to keep clean. I had a hot shower this morning. That may not sound newsworthy, but we've been lucky to get a shower once a month. The Army has portable showers they truck around in the battle zones. I've been able to use those only a few times. There were so many men waiting that we each had only a couple of minutes to wash off our layers of grime.*
>
> *I have big news. Matt and Rosa are married. After reaching Rome, we found that she was there ahead of us. I don't*

know how, but she managed to get to Rome all by herself. And she's going to have a baby. Captain Forrester (I told you about him) married them. She followed us out here to Tarquinia, and Matt has been getting passes so they can be together. Cassie, they're really in love. He's learning Italian, and she's learning English, so they communicate, but it's funny to hear them. Matt has written to his parents telling them all about Rosa. His father is the mayor of a small town in Virginia and appears to have some political influence. Matt hopes he can clear the way for Rosa and her child to go there soon after the war. She says she won't leave until she finds her father and knows the rest of her family is safe. She's strong in her spirit, but I worry about her because she's so frail. I bet she won't go more than seventy-five pounds. Of course, I worry about Matt too, but for different reasons.

Obie went into detail about the side trip to the Ghetto in Rome and its ill effect on Silverman.

Silverman has not been himself since then. All the squad members have noticed it. He swears at us over minor things, and he takes too many chances. He's a brave man and normally has a level head, but he's going to get himself killed if he doesn't stop it. He's very angry, and it's not the kind of anger that has relief. It just seems to go on and on. He volunteered to join a special recon mission behind enemy lines right after we got here. I hope he makes it back in one piece.

He wanted to ask about Laura. His desire to know was one minute conflicted by anger and in the next heightened by a conciliatory frame of mind; he desperately wanted to move past caring at all. He sat for ten minutes trying to decide how to ask the question in a simple form, writing and rewriting on a separate sheet of paper before committing the words to the end of the letter.

Has Laura had her baby yet? You said your mother was going to Boston to take care of them. What does she tell you? Cassie, I appreciate your letters. Please keep them coming.

Your friend, Obie

That evening as he lay on his cot, Cassie, not Laura, occupied his mind. He always called her "friend," and she didn't express anything beyond that in her letters. So why was he looking for a hint of something more? Perhaps it was because Laura had told him that Cassie was in love with him. Laura's word, however, was never to be trusted.

Cassie wasn't one to hide her feelings about anything. They'd talked about love when they were children, and there was that cold day on the ridge when Cassie wanted him to define "love" and then asked him to kiss her. He'd complied out of duty, only to find that he enjoyed it very much. He'd suppressed that, however, because his feelings for Laura had so occupied him.

The thought hit him so hard that it felt almost like a physical blow, and he said out loud, *"Laura's gone . . . and good riddance!"*

* * *

Rejuvenation of war-weary bodies required time. Obie, like others, slept, read, went to movies, and attended training sessions when ordered. He also spent time assisting Forrester. The chaplain was a whirlwind of activity and needed help keeping up with mundane chores. Obie obliged, although he still arose tired each morning. Sleep was interrupted by dreams, often war-related and nightmarish in content. Twice, he awoke with someone shaking him. He couldn't remember calling out. Sometimes he heard the cries of other men in the middle of the night.

When Aimes mentioned that he was planning to visit the nearby ancient Etruscan ruin, Obie asked to go along. After two hours of listening to Aimes' lecturing at the site, Obie insisted they follow another road south, a roundabout route that he expected would add a couple of miles to their trip.

Obie had good reason for going that way and had planned the diversion. He'd taken out his little Bible the previous evening, a habit he'd failed to break, despite trying. After reading a few verses he'd lost concentration and snapped the book shut. This time it slipped from his hands and dropped to the ground. As he picked it up, he saw that a white page in the back held his own penciled words dictated on the day his mother died. His Aunt Angie had told him about their family in Italy, and he'd recorded all the names, ages, and relationships. Now, one word stood out: Tarquinia! Beside that word he had written, "Family lives four or five miles to the southeast."

The Petitucci household had to be close—where or how far, he had no way of knowing. He'd recently received a letter from Aunt Angie, but she hadn't given him the address he'd requested. Exploring the area might give him ideas for narrowing his search. Obie's additional notes revealed that his mother's older sister, Maria, had married Donato Bertoni. Obie explained the situation to Aimes as they walked.

The region they entered contained isolated sites looking like ruins from other times. Generally, the terrain consisted of rolling hills covered with vineyards, olive orchards, and fields of grain not yet ripe. Wind gusts gyrated through the grain, setting off capricious green waves. Sunflower and poppy grew along the roadsides. Puffy white clouds with dark underbellies threatened showers, but here and there were patches of blue. Occasional shafts of brilliant sunlight fell on the landscape and buildings highlighting the scene and elevating Obie's mood.

Smaller and more modest farms and vineyards were scattered about. The war must have bypassed this particular area, although reminders of its presence were evident in another direction; overhead, they could see and hear bombers and fighters making their way to and from the north, where the Allies were still about the business of punishing the enemy.

The dirt road became narrower with sycamore trees along both sides drawing a canopy of branches over their heads. There were many side roads and splinters, some like footpaths, causing Obie to conclude that knowing the general area might not lead him to his relatives. They passed several houses with names on posts and saw people on the outside. Some buildings were run-down. He eliminated those; tidbits of conversation remembered between his mother and aunts made him believe living in a dilapidated house was not something that Maria would tolerate.

Aimes reminded him that they should not be on an unknown road after dark and advised that they find an alternate and shorter route back instead of retracing their steps. Obie agreed; he would try again on another day. They'd gone a quarter mile when they saw a path to a stone house that sat a hundred feet to the right. They might get directions there, Obie suggested.

"Go ahead," Aimes said. "You speak the language. I'll wait here."

Obie approached the house with caution. For months every

home and building had been considered an enemy refuge, a mindset hard to overcome.

He saw the woman even before he reached the door. She was bent over picking peas in the miniature vegetable garden by the house. She looked up, and her hand went to her mouth, obviously surprised by his presence. Obie, too, was startled because of her appearance. Slight of frame, about fifty years of age, she could have been a more mature version of his mother. *Could it be?*

"Excuse me," Obie said in Italian. "I didn't mean to startle you."

She smiled as she stood and brushed loose soil from her apron. "It is all right. We do not get many visitors here. We are in an isolated place. You are an American?"

"Yes, we are American soldiers," he said, extending an inclusive hand toward Aimes, who sat on a bench by the road. "We need directions to return to the vicinity of Tarquinia." He tried not to stare.

She smiled. "So, you are lost?"

"Oh, no. We just seek the shortest route."

She removed her cloth gloves and held out her hand. "Americans shake hands. Is that not true?"

Her hand was soft, and strength was in her grip despite her aristocratic bearing. "My name is Obie," he said.

She was scrutinizing his face. "And I am Maria Bertoni."

The house behind her shimmered in the sunlight. *He was standing in the presence of his mother's sister—his aunt.* Against all odds, he'd found her at the first house he approached. He must clear his head and decide what to do. *Just tell her.* He hesitated.

"Are you all right?" she asked. "You look confused." Her impish look was puzzling.

"Confusion" would not begin to describe his feelings. "I'm pleased to meet you, Señora Bertoni," he managed. *Just tell her.*

Her smile didn't fade. "Call your friend. We shall have wine together."

He'd tell her soon, but he wanted to make it special. He said, "All right. We have time." He hailed Aimes.

She hadn't stopped smiling. "And when you leave here, you will find it easy. Walk over that way." She pointed to a southwest hill, a low, wheat-covered mass. "You will find a wagon road leading to a larger road that will take you to Tarquinia if you turn right. But come, my family would like to honor two American soldiers and show our appreciation for what you have done."

After Obie introduced Aimes, they all entered the house. It was large by Italian country home standards. One huge room held a kitchen and a spacious living area. The kitchen space had a fireplace and a woodstove with a stovepipe going into a sidewall. Two closed doors in the back of the room would lead to sleeping quarters, Obie guessed. A wooden staircase disappeared into the ceiling on the right side, probably leading to more bedrooms.

The big room was dark inside. Obie counted six additional people. A man sat in a chair in a corner. A woman about thirty years old sat on a stool between a pair of cribs. She rocked both cribs with a hand on each. Obie tried to remember the names written in his Bible and to guess the identity of each. *He must tell them who he was.*

A toddler, who'd been scurrying around, focused on Aime's leg. Aimes bent and patted the little girl's head. A girl about Obie's age caught his full attention. She was dark-haired and beautiful by any standards. She made her way straight to Obie and placed a hand on his arm.

"I am Teresa," she said in perfect English. "What has kept you?"

Her eyes were open wide and were the bluest eyes he'd ever seen. She was smiling, and one eyebrow was arched as though waiting for an answer.

Obie experienced a moment of speechlessness. On recovering, he replied in English, using some of Aimes' terminology, "We've been delayed by a stubborn enemy."

Aimes picked up the little girl. "Her name is Veronica," the woman rocking the twins said. "I am her mother. My name is Sonia. These are my little ones, Gerardo and Flora. They were born two months ago." Obie translated for Aimes.

"Is he your husband?" Obie asked, indicating the man in the corner.

She laughed. "Oh, no. That is Gerardo, my brother. My husband's name is Davida. Davida Barella . . . but he is not here."

Gerardo, when his name was mentioned, rose from his chair. Obie saw that his left leg was missing, nearly to the hip. He hobbled forward using a single crutch and shook hands with Aimes and Obie.

Teresa was still smiling at Obie. She said, "You did not answer my question very well, Obadiah."

"Teresa, don't be impolite," Maria said.

"I thought I did," Obie said and gasped. Maria hadn't told Teresa his name.

Maria was watching his face. She laughed and held out her arms. "Welcome, nephew. Forgive our little pretense."

"You know who I am?" He felt his eyes filling. He hugged Maria. "How . . ."

She kissed his cheek. "Michelangela. We write." She held him at arm's length. "I see your mother in you, even with your blond hair. We have known for some time that you were with the American Army in Italy. Michelangela told me your command, the group you are with. When you arrived here, we knew about it. She said you were going to look for us. We knew you would find us. It is a matter of destiny. The picture she sent us helped, also. See, no big mystery."

Aimes had a confused expression. "What's going on?" he asked.

Obie filled in the details for Aimes as his relatives gathered around and shook their hands. Teresa hugged Obie.

When Obie finally extracted himself from their embraces, he said, "You are wrong, Aunt Maria. It is still a mystery about how I found you?"

"Michelangela must have given you directions," Teresa said.

"No, no directions except to say your farm was southeast of Tarquinia."

"Then it *is* a miracle," Maria said, crossing herself.

"Hardly," Gerardo said. His voice was deep. "If you travel southeast, it would be hard to miss this little valley once you get past the old ruins."

"But this was the first place we stopped."

"There are not that many farms," Sonia remarked.

"We are happy the Allied Army has arrived," Gerardo said. "We are out of the way here, but we have followed your progress for many months. We were overjoyed when the Germans left Rome. People there have suffered so much. When will your unit be moving out?"

"Probably not until . . ." Obie stopped. Soldiers had been warned not to give information to civilians. "We will go when we receive orders," he said, stating the obvious.

Obie saw Gerardo wasn't fooled, nor did he appear insulted. "I understand your caution. I, too, am a cautious man. Once, I was not, and see what it cost me." He patted his pinned-up pants leg.

"What happened to you?" Obie asked.

"German mine. I was carrying supplies to one of our partisan groups in the mountains south of Rome."

"He nearly bled to death, my son and your cousin," Maria said, and Obie saw great sadness in her eyes. A tear ran down her cheek.

Gerardo hobbled forward and held his mother close. "She does not cry for me. She cries for her older son, Martino. My brother was killed a year ago, executed by the Germans. He was in a resistance group in Rome. Now, she has only Sonia, Teresa, and me. And, of course, her grandchildren."

"I didn't know," Obie said. "Angie . . . Michelangela did not tell me about that. I am sorry."

Maria wiped her tears, removed a dark bottle from a shelf, and poured wine into glasses of various sizes. Obie and the others lifted their glasses to toast the Allies.

"And to the future," Maria added.

Obie soon informed them of the necessity to return to their unit before dark. "I can't tell you what this has meant to me, Aunt Maria," he said as he hugged her.

"You will come back to see us, will you not?" Maria said. "We have much more to say."

"I will, I promise. I want to hear firsthand about all the relatives my mother told me about as I was growing up."

"Violetta was such a beautiful little girl. I missed everyone so much after they left for America. I cried for a long time. I cried again when I heard the other news."

"Mom was still beautiful."

Maria repeated her directions for finding the road. Teresa followed them to the gate. "I hope you return soon. I need to practice English."

"You don't need much practice. How is it that you speak English so well?"

"I went to Rome one summer, years ago, to stay with a girlfriend. Their American guest taught me."

"In one summer? You must be an outstanding student."

"I have what some call 'a facility for language.' I pick it up easily when I hear it spoken. I speak German too."

Aimes, who'd been silent, spoke. "And how did you learn German?"

She appeared taken aback by the question. After an uneasy silence, she said, "I also had a German friend."

"Schoolmate?"

"No, a friend."

Obie wanted to divert the conversation. Something about this girl brought out his protective side. "I forgot to ask," he said. "When did your father die?"

"He died four years ago. He was only fifty. He was ill for several years."

"And where is your brother-in-law? Davida . . . is that his name?"

She hesitated before saying, "He is away for a while. He has war business . . . you know."

"He is a partisan too? Is that it?"

She nodded and looked about to say something more. He waited. She was silent but leaned and kissed his cheek.

"I'll be back soon," he said. "I promise."

That evening, Obie reviewed the day's events and pictured each relative in his mind. They were strong people, especially Maria. She was a regal lady; it was easy to imagine his mother's likeness in her face. Nevertheless, beautiful and talented Teresa had a question hanging over her head. He was determined to learn more.

CHAPTER THIRTY-ONE

June–July 1944

Army buses made scheduled runs along a protected route into Rome. Obie, Matt, and Rosa visited the city for a day. Obie went sightseeing while Rosa and Matt pursued her family matters; she had received word from a cousin that an escaped captive worker had passed along information that her father, Vincente Rizzetti, was in a group taken farther north, possibly to the Po River Valley. She was searching for the source of that information.

"If it is true, I will go to the Po Valley," Rosa declared as they neared Rome.

"You will not," Matt said, none too gently. "You'll take a train back to Naples to care for your mother, and I'll join you there as soon as the war is over."

Rosa was still struggling with English, so Obie restated the content of Matt's outburst. Matt appeared to take Rosa's silence as acquiesce; Obie wasn't sure. Matt's seventy-five-pound wife was a tiger not easily caged by words.

Obie went exploring alone. Trolleys, where operating, covered several sections of the city. He soon realized he could never see everything in a month, much less in one day. He was awed, not only at the elegance of structures and ruins but also by their ages. There was nostalgia in knowing that his mother might have walked these same streets and seen these same sights when she was a little girl. Perhaps Maria could tell him of such things. He must see Maria and her family again before being called back to the front.

He was cautious as he visited sites. Although the Germans had left the city to the Allies, there was lingering unrest. He saw it in the way people looked at one another. "Political groups all over Italy, particularly in Rome, might not remain silent," Aimes, ever the teacher, had commented. Those factions, Christian Democrats, Liberal Party, Labor Party, Socialist, Communist, and others, had banded together against Fascists and Germans, their common enemies. With the Germans gone, there would be jockeying for leadership in whatever government was established. Those groups had practiced violence in the past months; the general opinion was that they wouldn't hesitate to use it against one another.

He had wanted to see the Vatican. Captain Forrester had whetted his interest; what mysteries might be inside, what ancient dust-covered texts lay locked in vaults awaiting discovery? But, as it grew late, he knew there wouldn't be time.

Not everyone was intrigued by the Roman Catholic headquarters and home of the Pope. Obie had overheard Silverman speaking angrily to Burnside about the Vatican. He called Pope Pius XII "cowardly" for not doing more to protect Roman Jews. Burnside had argued that the Pope had more to worry about than his safety, that the Germans could have taken over the Vatican whenever they wished and wreaked destruction. Silverman had stalked away, not wanting to hear it.

Obie met Matt and Rosa for the return trip. Rosa was quiet on the bus ride, obviously disappointed that she'd learned nothing new of her father's whereabouts.

The day after the jaunt to Rome, Silverman returned from the north. His already thin fame appeared emaciated. He slept for two days. It was early morning of the third day when he finally emerged.

Obie found him in their makeshift company chow hall. The sergeant's aggressive manner had subsided and Obie hoped he'd finally finished his vendetta.

They sat at a table with a tablecloth stained by spilled coffee. Obie told him about finding his relatives.

"That must have been a happy reunion," Silverman said.

"Not a reunion, really. I'd never met any of them until two days ago. I'm going to write my Aunt Angie about all this, so I need to learn more. I'd like to go back today. Aimes isn't interested in going again, and Matt spends all his spare time with Rosa. Would you like to go with me?"

"Okay," Silverman said quickly. Obie had hoped for such a response, but expected it to need persuasion. "Family connections hold the strongest ties," Silverman said.

Obie guessed the direction of Silverman's thinking. "No news yet about your Uncle Yarden's family?"

"Nothing." Silverman's eyes narrowed. "It doesn't look good."

Obie asked, even at the risk of angering Silverman, "Is that why you're sticking your neck out to kill Germans?"

Fuming words tumbled from the sergeant's mouth. "I fight for the survival of my people, who are being systematically murdered. I fight for the survival of my religion, which they want to destroy. Most

of all, Gainsworthy, I fight for my uncle, aunt, and young cousin."
Silverman stopped, out of breath.

"Okay," was all Obie could think to say.

After a moment, Silverman said, "Let's get going. I want to meet
these relatives of yours." It was encouraging that Silverman was finally talking, if only emotionally.

* * *

Silverman acquired a jeep. "I'm damned tired of walking," he
said.

The final half-mile road to the stone farmhouse was tight quarters, even for a jeep. Once, they had to stop for two cows and a heifer
leisurely crossing, presumably to chomp grass alongside a ditch.
Their big eyes stared accusingly at them as Silverman edged past. It
was another bright and sunny morning, typical of the weather since
encamping at Tarquinia. The scent of cypress and cedar mingled
with familiar farm smells.

Silverman parked the jeep by the gate. Maria was in her garden
again. She stood, smiling as they approached. He noticed again how
much her face was like his mother's, both in her searching expression
and the gentleness of her mouth.

"We are honored to have you visit us again, Obadiah," she said
in broken English. She'd spoken only a few words of English the last
time; Maria was full of surprises. "You have brought another
friend?"

"Yes, Aunt Maria, this is Sergeant Silverman. He's one of those
brave Americans of whom you spoke. He has earned many medals
for his bravery."

"I am pleased to meet you, Sergeant Silverman."

Silverman was meek and gracious, bowing slightly. "Señora,
Private Gainsworthy . . . Obadiah, was too lavish with his introduction. I'm simply a soldier doing his duty."

"I am sure you are much more. But, let us go inside. The others
will be delighted. We will celebrate."

Obie put an arm around Maria as they walked toward the side
door. It seemed so natural, his warm feelings for her. There was
much to tell Angie.

The sound of a slamming door came from a small barn behind
the house. Obie stiffened. Months of living on the edge of terror sur-
faced, and he whirled, putting himself between Maria and the barn.

At the same time, he placed his hand on the handle of the thirty-eight in its holster. Silverman had been even quicker; he was kneeling with his sidearm leveled at the building.

Maria screamed. "No! Please! There is nothing to be frightened of. There is no enemy here."

Silverman paid no heed. "Gainsworthy! Check it out." He turned to Maria. "Get down, Señora!"

Maria remained standing. "Sergeant Silverman, please . . ."

Obie hesitated.

"Get going, Gainsworthy," Silverman said.

Obie ran toward the barn. He was ready to kick in the low wooden door when it opened and a man stepped out with his hands on top of his head. He was wearing a worn and faded German uniform. His face was white with fear.

"Do not shoot me . . . please!" he said in English.

Silverman arrived to grab the German and throw him to the ground. Gesturing toward the barn, he said, "Check it out. There may be more."

The barn was empty, and Obie returned to find Silverman kneeling on the German soldier's back, his pistol against the man's temple. Maria was crying and tugging on Silverman's arm. Family members swarmed out the back door of the house. Teresa threw herself at Silverman, shoving him so violently that he almost fell backward.

Silverman regained his balance and pushed Teresa aside. "This man is my prisoner. If you don't all step back, I'll shoot him right now."

The threat brought results. Veronica clung to her mother. The babies were crying. Gerardo hobbled up to the group with an expression of concern.

"Please, do not hurt him," Teresa said.

Silverman responded, "This man is a German soldier. He's the enemy! If you've been harboring him, it makes you the enemy too."

The disturbing events, coming so swiftly, had Obie reeling. He'd come expecting a family gathering, not chaos. "Silverman, these are my relatives . . . *my family*. You have to listen to them."

Silverman's words were like ice. "You're an American soldier. Don't forget it."

"I'm not forgetting it," Obie said, responding in the same vein, "but we're going to listen to what they have to say." He slapped a hand on Silverman's shoulder.

"Watch it!" Silverman's warning further chilled the air with meaning.

"The hell I will!" Obie roared. "I'm not going to let you do something stupid just because you're determined to kill every German you meet. This man has surrendered."

Silverman rose. Obie held his breath. The sergeant jerked the man to his feet but kept his weapon against his head.

Gerardo came toward them on his crutches. One empty pant leg was pinned to his back pocket. His confusion had changed to anger. He leaned on one crutch and put the tip of the other under Silverman's nose. "Put the damned gun down, American," he said in Italian. "This man can do you no harm."

Obie translated, softening the intent. Gerardo moved the cane tip down and suspended it two inches from Silverman's chest. Obie hoped it wouldn't touch.

"He has been with us since last October," Gerardo said. "He surrendered first to us and has since become a valuable source of information to the resistance."

"How do you know he's not a spy?" Silverman asked.

Maria spoke up. "Anton has given us information leading to the destruction of German supplies and equipment. I will vouch for him with my life."

Silverman slowly lowered the pistol. As he did so, Gerardo retracted the cane. Obie breathed easier.

Silverman said to Obie, "I want to be sure this is not a trap. Check the house. There might be hostages inside that these people would say anything to protect."

"These people? Sarge, these are my relatives . . . and this is the whole family."

"Check the house! Dammit! Now!"

"Yes, sir," Obie replied without attempting to blunt his sarcasm.

He went inside and did a complete circuit of the kitchen and living area before searching upstairs rooms. When he returned to the group by the barn, the German stood away from Silverman, and Teresa held his hand. *So that was it, what she'd wanted to say.*

"What are you going to do?" Obie asked Silverman.

"I'm not sure. Headquarters will want to interrogate this prisoner. We're obliged to take him in."

At least Silverman was acting rationally again. "Let's talk to the family first," Obie said. "They can tell us more."

Obie explained to Maria that Silverman wanted to know

everything they knew about the German soldier. They went to sit on benches situated around the main door entrance.

Anton Hazen was his name. He'd been a translator attached to the command of SS Colonel Dollmann. Because of his work, he was privy to secret information. While being loaned for several days to the command of SS General Wolff, he'd learned of a rumored German plan to kidnap the pope and take him north. He tried slipping the information to the Vatican. The clandestine act was discovered by one of Wolff's men. Sure that he'd be executed for treason, he ran away. He'd been helped, he believed, either by Colonel Dollmann himself or by one of his staff.

"He was making his way through here when we found him," Gerardo said and waited for Obie to translate.

"Why would Dollmann help you?" Silverman asked.

"He liked me. And he was sympathetic to the Vatican."

"And just why would *you* try to warn the Vatican?" Obie asked.

Anton looked at Obie as though it were apparent. "I am Catholic," he said.

"Was there really a plan to kidnap the pope?"

"I do not know. I attempted to report what I heard. If there was a plan, it was thwarted."

It took Gerardo several minutes to relate details of the ways Anton had helped. Finally, Silverman asked him, "With the Germans out of Rome, what are your plans? This man will no longer be of help."

With Obie translating, Gerardo explained. "If you had come two days later, neither Anton nor I would have been here. Davida, who has been in the north, is coming to take us behind German lines. Anton will be invaluable. He knows much, not only about the German high command but also about how troops and supplies are moved. If you give him to the Allies, they'll question him and put him in a prisoner camp where he'll be lost to our cause."

Silverman continued to press. "German spies are efficient and tricky. How do you know he's not been gathering information which, once behind enemy lines, he'll use to expose your whole organization?"

"I can answer that," Teresa said. "Anton is coming back for me. We'll be married." Her blue eyes bored into Silverman's. "We love each other."

"Yes," Anton said.

"And what if that is part of a spy's scheme? What if he has no plans of ever coming back?"

A flicker of doubt crossed Teresa's countenance, but only for a second. She stepped to Anton's side and said, "He will return. I am carrying his child."

Later, after damaged feelings were soothed and Obie had promised to come again, they rode back toward the encampment. Obie was angry and felt no inclination to soften his words. After flinging a vulgarity at Silverman that cast doubts on the sergeant's honor, he stated, "You treated my family with disrespect."

Silverman looked contrite. "Maybe I did lose my head a little."

"We're going to win this war, Sarge. The rest of us will help you win it. You don't have to do it all by yourself."

"I'm sorry about the family reunion. I messed things up. I'll make it up to you."

Obie didn't respond at once. He could stay angry, but what would it accomplish? Finally, he said, "You've already made it up to me, Silverman. You've saved my neck more than once. Let's just forget it."

"No, I meant it. I'll make it up to you. I'm not yet sure how. Somewhere down the road, though, I'll do something to make a difference in your life." He laughed. "And you can be sure I'll let you know when I do."

The mood had lightened. "I'll believe it when I see it."

After turning in his paperwork at the motor pool, Silverman said, "You've found your Italian relatives, Gainsworthy, and they're all safe for the present. But, do you think I'll ever see mine again?"

"I don't know, Silverman. I really don't know."

In truth, he doubted it.

* * *

The rest period ended before Obie had another chance to visit his Aunt and cousins. The division went north and soon engaged the enemy at Piombino, San Vincenzo, and Cecina. With shorter routes from captured coastal cities, supply lines should have brought improved living conditions. Instead, the increased speed with which divisions moved made it difficult for supply units to keep up. Front line troops were left wanting clean clothing and better meals. Nevertheless, a renewed sense of optimism was evident; at this rate, the Italian campaign might be over by fall.

A letter from Cassie arrived. Obie guessed the news it contained even before he tore it open.

> *Dear Obie,*   *June 30, 1944*
> *I'm sorry about the gap in my writing. First, there were my exams, and then I went to Syracuse. I just got back. The big news is that Laura delivered a seven-pound, three-ounce baby boy nearly a month ago. I thought you would want to know. She and the baby are both doing fine. My little nephew is named Daniel Pinkerton Williamson. How's that for a serious name? Mom says they are already calling him Danny.*

The remainder of the letter was news of Stafford Rest, except for some personal information that Cassie included at the end:

> *I'll be going to Syracuse University in the fall. I was there, getting things ready to live with my Aunt Lorena. She's my father's sister and has never been married. She's a teacher, which is what I'll be. Except for visits, I doubt I'll ever return to Stafford Rest. It's not that I don't love it here, because I do, but I feel like my life is being controlled.*

He read the letter through twice more before stuffing it into his knapsack. *Laura had her son.* It was now a fact. Anger caused him to clench his teeth; their shared dream had been a son. *What happened?* Obie wiped his eyes with a sleeve and hoped no one was watching. By the time he reached his squad's bivouac space, he had calmed. He would evict Laura and her son from his life—every thought of them—forever.

The following day Obie was called to a company headquarters tent. Lieutenant Burnside and Captain Forrester were seated on campstools behind a makeshift desk, a damaged door suspended between two upright oil drums. *What had he done to land himself in trouble?*

Burnside was first to speak. "Tomorrow, the division is having a parade, and medals will be awarded. You'll be awarded the Silver Star, but I'm sure you already knew that." Burnside glanced at Forrester. Obie had, in fact, already seen the posted order.

"I'm honored, sir."

He was ready to make a statement about his unworthiness for the award when Burnside's upraised hand stopped him. "Captain Forrester told me you might display modesty. I want you to know that we're proud to have our men recognized for gallantry in action.

This award was issued under President Franklin D. Roosevelt's direction and the provisions of the Congress of the United States of America. It's a great honor, not only for you but also for our division. You'll be accepting it for all the men you serve with. I want you to stand tall tomorrow with your chest stuck out."

Burnside's unexpected speech humbled Obie. "Yes, sir, I will."

"But that's not the main reason I called you here."

"Yes, Sir." Maybe he was in trouble after all.

"Captain Forrester can better explain it."

Forrester said, "My assistant, Corporal McDonald, was wounded last week and is in the hospital in Naples. He's probably going home. I need an assistant. Private Gainsworthy, you've helped me many times during the past months, all on your own time. I'd like you to be my assistant, full time."

Obie had trouble taking in the full meaning of the offer—or maybe it was an order. Being a chaplain's assistant was a significant change from what he was doing. "I'm not qualified for the job," he said.

"Captain Forrester thinks you are," Burnside said.

"You've already been doing much of what's required," Forrester said. "The rest can be learned on the job. I'll teach you."

Helping as he had in the past entailed such chores as passing out flyers, cleaning the area, or finding musical instruments. This might mean the "God stuff." Could he deal with that?

"Would it mean leaving my unit . . . my platoon?

Forrester glanced at Burnside, who said, "You'll be assigned to Captain Forrester, but it's considered a loan. You'll still be attached to your old unit and will quarter with them when they're in reserve or off the battle line. In addition, you can still be called back to take up slack anytime you're needed. Is that clear?"

"Yes, sir. I understand. Sir, do I have a choice about this?"

The answer came quickly. "No, private. Your new assignment is with Captain Forrester. We can reevaluate it later if he thinks it necessary."

CHAPTER THIRTY-TWO

July–December 1944

Obie was relieved from all other duties and started working at once with Forrester. A lull in troop movement allowed them to move into an undamaged dance hall on the camp's edge. Obie followed him to the back where there was a desk, table, and a couple of wooden chairs. Forrester invited him to sit.

"A good place for a service," Obie said, indicating the ample open space.

"Indeed. It's not often I find something like this. My services are usually in the open with a barrel for a table, or anything else handy. We'll have a good crowd if we're still here Sunday."

Obie needed some answers. "Sir, why did you choose me for this job? You could have found someone with more experience."

Forrester smiled. "You and I had a brief little conversation back at Casino, if you recall, and we've had others since. Back there, I happened on you when you were at prayer. Forgive me again, but I listened and was impressed by your sincerity. I asked around. You have good references. Lieutenant Burnside and Staff Sergeant Silverman both recommend you highly."

"Silverman's a Jew. How can he judge Christian qualities?"

"He can judge your moral qualities. Obie, we all serve the same God. Out here, lines between faiths are blurred. Ironically, it takes the horrors of war to do that."

"Do other chaplains think like that?"

"I think most do, or eventually come to adopt such a view. I feel as though I'm serving not only people of my denominations and faith but also others. That doesn't mean we don't retain our doctrines and beliefs. We do. But we also reach out. Doctrine takes a backseat." It sounded like something Jacob would say. "So, will you be content to trade in your rifle . . . for this?"

"I can't help feeling I'm letting my squad down."

"You're not, I assure you. You're simply trading one way of serving for another."

"Sir, there's something you should know that might make you change your mind about me. What you saw and heard at Cassino was me simply fulfilling an obligation to my minister back home. I wanted to be able to tell him that I'd prayed."

"And you *did* pray. I saw you and heard you."

"It didn't mean anything. I've come to believe that God doesn't listen to prayers . . . if there's even a God."

Forrester looked as if he were clenching his teeth. "So, what I'm doing here is all nonsense? Is that what you believe?"

"No, Sir. Of course not. I see how the men need you. I see how your words comfort wounded men. You make things easier for them, especially when they're . . ."

"Dying?"

"Yes."

"Obie, what happened to you?"

He answered without thought. "I've lost the faith that I had while growing up."

Forrester studied his face for an uncomfortable period before saying, "From what you've told me of your background, I think it would take a rather traumatic event to cause such a turnaround. So, I ask again . . . what happened to you?"

Obie felt he'd been led into a trap. Only Matt and Silverman had been given details about Laura, and those were sketchy. Telling the chaplain would be different; the man might try to provide him with solutions. Obie would make his own decisions; he didn't need a solution.

Nevertheless, if he told Forrester about Laura and his feelings about the whole matter, perhaps the chaplain would see that he needed someone more qualified to assist him.

"I had faith in prayer, faith in God," Obie said. "I promised to serve God in whatever way he wanted. I didn't break that promise. He deserted me."

Forrester's question was unexpected. "Was it a girl, Obie?"

"Yes"

"Do you want to talk about it?"

"No."

"Is it something you can't forgive?"

"I have hate in my heart for her . . . and for her mother. Yes, it's something I can't forgive."

"Obie, I can help you if you let me. Being unable to forgive can place a stone wall between God and us. The stones of the wall may be hefty, but they can be removed, even if only one at a time. A wall between God and us *can* be torn down."

"The stones of my wall are too heavy, I think. I can't forgive them. I don't even want to try."

The chaplain's expression showed distress. He said, "It's something we can work on, and maybe later you can give me more details."

"Do you still want me here?"

"Of course, I want you. And I'm sure you'll do stellar work. I believe you understand that it's an important job."

So much for going back to the squad. "What will my duties be?"

"Pretty much what I determine. There are some official guidelines we have to follow. There's no MOS for a chaplain's assistant, so you'll remain a member of your battalion, but on special assignment."

"Chaplains don't fight. Will I be under that rule too?"

"No, and actually, there are no definitive rules prohibiting chaplains from fighting, though there are consequences if it happens. Were I to take up a weapon or give away a troop position, either enemy or allies, I'd lose the protection the Geneva Convention gives me. I expect you to follow my example when you're with me on the battlefront. You'll remain an infantry soldier when not with me, and you could even be called back to your unit at their discretion. Mostly, your job will be to follow me around and help me with what I do. I visit sick and wounded and comfort men who are dying. Often, it's simply a matter of visiting with the men, whether they're on the line or not. I also counsel men with long-distance marital problems and some who are simply afraid and need courage."

"I can certainly understand that kind of fear, sir."

"Yes, I'm sure you can. I preach and teach too, so scheduling, arranging time and place, preparing the site, and supplying materials such as hymnals and Bibles will all be your duties. My pulpits are mostly rocks, stumps, and jeep hoods, so there's not much preparation there. Sometimes, we can have more formal services when we can confiscate a building like this one. There's also the matter of working around Catholic services. We don't want to schedule the same space simultaneously, so you'll talk to them before our more formal gatherings."

Forrester rubbed his chin, apparently thinking. "One thing you must understand, Obie. I'm the chaplain. I look to spiritual needs, and I do my counseling one-on-one. You won't be involved there, but working so closely with me, you might become privy to private information about people. I'll expect that whatever you hear will go no further. It's not just part of our guidelines. It's a moral duty."

"I understand, sir."

"Can you type?"

"Yes, I can. I was a reporter on my high school newspaper."

"Good. I'm behind on some paperwork, so you can start right there.

* * *

Two days later, the regiment went up near Riparbella to relieve another infantry unit, so they never had a chance to use the dance hall for a service. From Riparbella, they moved north, rooting out rearguard pockets of the enemy.

Obie was no longer an active member of Silverman's squad, but he saw the men often and quartered with them when he could. He soon acquired the good-natured nickname "Preacher Man." He didn't like the epithet but put up with it.

Forrester kept himself and his new assistant busy on and near the front lines. The chaplain made his presence known in the field hospitals and aide-station areas when not busy helping medics pick up wounded men. Forrester was a brave man and, at times, foolhardy.

Obie didn't pry, but details of the Presbyterian chaplain's life emerged through casual conversation. He was married with four children. The oldest was in the Pacific, a marine. Obie expressed surprise that he had a son that old.

"I'm forty-one."

"So, you didn't have to come here? Why did you?"

"I'm God's servant, Obie. He sent me. It was tough leaving my family and children. I had a wonderful pastorate, a large church in Indianapolis, and I'd been offered teaching positions in two universities. Right now, this is where I can do the most good. I've been with the division throughout Africa, Sicily, and here. I'll stay a chaplain until the war is won." He hesitated. "Or until I can't go on anymore."

Forrester went, wherever necessary, to administer spiritual and physical assistance to the wounded and dying. It sometimes occurred under a ceasefire, but more often was a matter of crawling long distances while dodging bullets. At first, Forrester didn't allow Obie to accompany him on the most dangerous excursions. Obie argued the point, saying it could be no more difficult than what he'd been doing since arriving in Italy. Even while pushing the limits of his role, Obie tried to exercise sound judgment. Thankfully, Forrester said no more on the subject. They got along well, with Forrester encouraging a formal familiarity.

Obie continued to worry about Matt and Silverman—more about Matt. He checked on him daily. Indeed, Matt was healthier than ever, a seasoned warrior. He was anxious, however, to get back to his wife. Their baby was due in December. Undoubtedly, the Allies' task would be completed by then.

* * *

As a frontline infantry soldier, Obie had already experienced the horrors of war. He'd seen men with their bodies blown apart and boys still in their teens blinded. Experienced combat soldiers had looked past him with vacant stares, and he had observed young officers frightened beyond caring. Cries of the dying still disturbed his dreams. The sudden and permanent silence of a man recently full of life was an awful and shocking surprise. Nevertheless, the personal business of fighting and surviving had acted as a barrier that kept him from internalizing all the horror.

Under Captain Forrester, Obie gained a new perspective on the war. He was unable to look the other way. He must stare at the maimed and dying as he assisted the chaplain. He must listen to their dying words, write them down, and help prepare a letter to their next-of-kin. As letters were readied, he imagined them received into the trembling hands of anxious mothers or wives. How had Forrester kept at it for so long?

There were skirmishes, and there were brief pauses in the Italian campaign. The overall result, however, was that the Allies continued their relentless march north. In late July, they reached the Arno River, one hundred fifty miles north of Rome. A slowdown occurred and the regiment rested for several weeks near Florence.

The High Apennines loomed ahead, reaching farther into the sky than any Italian mountains the Fifth Army had yet encountered. There, in conjunction with an inhospitable terrain, stretched a German-built fortification they called the "Gothic Line." It barred the way to the Po River Valley beyond. Serious talk in the regiment circulated, designating the Po Valley as where the German army would finally be trapped. So close, yet so far, Obie mused.

In mid-September they camped at Legri, near the Gothic Line, in preparation for attacking it. The enemy had ample time to fortify, and breaking through would be difficult.

Everyone was edgy, including men of Silverman's squad. Silverman himself was affected. He lacked the patience toward new men he'd shown to Obie and Matt. Never the casual socializing type, he kept to himself more than ever. Obie engaged him in conversation whenever he could. One such opportunity came when he saw promotions listed on the company board. Silverman had been promoted from staff sergeant to technical sergeant, and Obie found him in the squad tent sewing on new stripes.

"Congratulations, Sarge. Are they giving you a new job?"

"I've requested they let me stay here."

Obie was unable to resist the opportunity. "You've done your share . . . more than. Maybe you should let them reassign you, maybe something behind the lines."

"Gainsworthy, can you imagine me a supply sergeant in a rest area?"

Obie laughed and changed the subject. "We have some new men, I see."

"We do. Cavendish, Bendeski, and Thompson. They arrived a week ago, right out of boot camp. Kilbarth and Lambert, whom you know, have been with us since Tarquinia. They've proven themselves. But, these newbies . . . I've been trying to whip them into shape for the coming offensive. They think they know it all."

"They'll learn. We did."

"If they stay alive that long." Silverman sounded melancholy.

The sergeant was still troubled, and Obie knew what was bothering him. "Have you heard from your father?" he asked.

"I had a letter not long ago. He has contacts in many places but hasn't found anything about my uncle and his family. Frankly, I don't believe he will. I think the Krauts took them to Germany, or someplace where they're either in a consecration camp . . . or dead."

"You could be wrong about it," Obie said, hoping he wasn't further alienating Silverman.

"Some things are too horrible for people to accept. The world's eventually going to learn the extent of all this. In the meantime, I'll continue to kill Germans because it's the way to rid the earth of this scourge."

Silverman had continued to sew as he talked. Now, he glanced up. "My friend, I know what you're trying to do, and I appreciate it. I know I've been acting strangely by your standards. I'll probably continue to act this way because I don't know if Uncle Yarden, Aunt Shira, and Jael are alive or dead. If they're dead, what I do is revenge. If they're alive and starving in some prison, I must do everything possible to speed up the Nazi's defeat."

"Even if you die in the process?"

Silverman had a way of going silent when Obie most wanted an answer. He didn't pursue the subject further.

Letters came. The one from his father had little more detail than usual. Charles Lansing, in his second letter since Obie's arrival in Italy, told of finishing the church's new education wing and, as a result, attracting new members. Cassie wrote at least once a week; she'd talked to his father; Laura had been home for a visit; Danny was a beautiful baby, growing and doing well. Cassie included an observation about her sister:

> *I don't know what Laura's problem is. I feel sorry for her. She often looks like she has been crying. When we talk, she seems to look right through me. She does love Danny, though. They look so peaceful together, especially when Laura is nursing him.*
>
> *Obie, she didn't ask about you, but I could see she wanted to know, so I told her all the things you have been doing. I didn't show her any of your letters, though, since I didn't think you would like that.*

Cassie's words brought up pictures that had persisted, images he wanted to purge. That night, he dreamed of Laura. She sat in a high-backed chair with a towel over her shoulder and Danny in her arms. Obie approached and sat beside her. He bent toward her, and she pushed him away. He fell to the floor. Cassie helped him up and placed her head on his chest. Sighing, she said, "It is from your rib that I was made, Obie. Don't you know that?" He awoke, sweating. The dream's realism stayed with him for days.

* * *

Laura Williamson sat in an alcove off a spacious dining room, breastfeeding Danny. The nook had become her little space of retreat from an exceedingly busy life. Danny required most of her time. Ben was loving in many ways, but there were certain things about which he was adamant; she must run the household on his strict timetable and assure that his preferred diet was adhered to. He insisted that she purchase and prepare all the food. Everything must be on time and in proper quantities. Once, when she asked him why they didn't hire a cook and housekeeper, he was annoyed. "We can't afford it . . . not yet. The house takes too much of my income."

"We didn't need a house this big. We should have bought a smaller place until your practice is better established."

"You don't understand, Laura. Social contacts are building my practice. Appearance counts. We can soon hire help, but not yet. For now, I'd appreciate it if you could just make the household work so I can concentrate on my profession."

Despite Ben's insistence on diet, and his annoying emphasis on domestic orderliness, planning and executing social engagements in their home was left to her, a chore she liked. Ben was being accepted by the well-to-do as they discovered the extent of his skills as a physician and surgeon. She guessed that, in the minds of those patients, his expertise overrode his lack of social graciousness. She had to admit that his competence, paired with what he often called her "beauty and charm," made an excellent combination.

She never doubted his love for her but was unsure how attached he was to Danny. He held the baby as though he were afraid of breaking him. How could a man with such delicate hands for exploring and repairing human flesh fear holding a small child?

Ben had one great dread: The draft. The services needed Doctors, and he was still young enough to qualify. He was classified 4-F because of flat feet, and she was sure that would keep him home, but he still worried that he'd be called to take another physical. Laura could not imagine her husband in a military uniform.

She finished nursing Danny and held him across her shoulder to burp, tapping him lightly on his back to stimulate the process. Her three-day trip to Stafford Rest two weeks previously was still fresh on her mind. Ben had tried to persuade her against going. Her excuse, a true one, had been that her father would never see Danny unless she took him there; Pinky seldom traveled farther than Albany or Plattsburgh and vowed he would never again go to New York City or Boston. Seeing Cassie after so many months was pleasant, but Laura was saddened when she sensed that a barrier had grown up between them, a wall neither sister wanted to scale.

The problem was obvious. She'd wanted to ask Cassie about Obie, to see her reaction. Although Cassie seemed eager to tell her about Obie's difficult life in Italy, she'd revealed nothing personal. Laura hoped she might share a letter so she could gauge his situation for herself, but she hadn't. She lucked out when she saw Cassie had left Obie's latest letter on her nightstand. With only a momentary sense of guilt, Laura read it. The letter confirmed what she suspected. Obie was Cassie's friend, nothing more. It was none of Laura's business since Obie would never be a part of her life again. She did pity Cassie, however. Her sister was in love, a doomed, one-sided love. She'd wanted to tell Cassie that, wished she had.

Laura had tried to forget Obie, but with limited success. The swift succession of the past year's events, the whirlwind marriage, the move to Boston, and getting used to living with a taciturn perfectionist had all happened so swiftly that her life had, for a time, seemed unreal. She'd complained once to her mother, only to be met with a lecture about how lucky she was.

She knew now that it had been the right decision to marry Ben. She still thought of Obie sometimes but was determined to get him out of her head forever. He was a ghost to be exorcised. Hating him would help her do that. *She must hold on to the hate.* She loved her life in Boston, loved the socializing, and enjoyed the promise of rearing her child with advantages he could never have in the Adirondacks. Even with some difficulties, she would make it all work.

* * *

The regiment was soon on the move again. Resistance was light at first but gradually increased. The Germans left numerous minefields in mountainous regions through which they passed. There were several minor skirmishes. The capture of Montepiano was especially hard because travel was so difficult and supplies were hand-carried, sapping energy. The Allies broke through the Gothic Line in several locations. The rainy season arrived, and roads and trails became quagmires. They pulled back for a rest at the end of September.

October brought more of the familiar fight, pull back, and fight again routine. Obie followed Forrester like a pet dog and performed his duties without disobeying. Being a dutiful follower, however, was becoming more complex. Sometimes bullets whizzed close, and Obie wanted to grab a weapon. The new man, Kilbarth, was killed on Mt. Venere—or was it Mt. Belmonte? Events, and their sequence, became blurred in his mind.

The regiment pulled back yet again. The enemy had managed to bring up more troops and strengthen defenses in other ways. The consensus was that the Allies would simply be holding ground until spring. It was near year's end when they stopped in an assembly area near Piancaldoli.

The squad found an unoccupied barn. Matt was angry. "Damn it!" he said to Obie, who was unfolding a bedroll. "I thought by this time we'd have the Krauts whipped. Thought I'd be back down to Naples. Rosa's expecting this month. Maybe she's already had the baby. I won't get to see them for months."

"I'm sorry, Matt. I really am. I believe, though, that we'll finish this in early spring. We'll bomb them all winter. They'll be softened up, and we'll push right through. We're not far from the Alps."

"Far enough."

Burke appeared. "Hey, Preacher man! I have a proposition for you."

"Not interested, Burke."

"Let me tell you something." He moved in so close that Obie smelled liquor on his breath. "We deserve something out of all this besides a few bucks a month and an honorable discharge." He laughed. "Even that's in doubt, in my case."

"What is it you want to say?" The man tried his patience.

"I already have a bankroll that'll put me in a good business after this is over. Nobody should be ashamed of getting what they can from this war."

"What does that have to do with me, Burke?"

"Some of these GIs will pay big money for souvenirs. Officers, especially?"

Obie knew where the conversation was going. "Listen, Burke . . ."

"Hear me out, Preacher man. You're in a real good position, close to German troops . . . their bodies, I mean. It'd be easy to get weapons, helmets, even wallets. I can make it worth your time."

"That's disgusting," Matt said.

"Shut up, cockroach," Burke said. "I'm talking to the Preacher Man here."

"Burke," Obie said, "if you say anything else, I'll report you to headquarters."

Burke became angry, but his voice held steady. "Don't you know headquarters is where I do most of my business?"

"Tell them anyway," Matt said.

Burke whirled toward Matt. "And you, you don't even deserve to be called a "cockroach." You're a bedbug. I can squash you with

314

my thumb."

Matt laughed, much into the banter. He could hold his own at exchanging insults. Burke changed the complexion of the situation when he said, "What do you know anyway, bedbug? All you know how to do is knock up some pitiful little Italian girl who's gonna take her bambino and hide from you. I bet she'll be with some other GI as soon as she gets out of bed."

From his sitting position on the floor, Matt leaped to his feet in one beautifully executed movement combining the forward motion of his body with the swinging of his right arm. It happened so quickly that Matt's fist smashed into Burke's broad nose before Obie had time to blink. Blood spurted, and Burke fell like a chopped-down tree.

Obie could hardly believe what he'd seen. Some others had the same reaction; they came running and crowded around Burke, who wasn't moving.

"Is he dead?" someone asked.

Perkins stood over Burke, grinning. "Nope. Knocked out . . . just like Joe Lewis hit him."

Matt was nursing his right hand and mumbling to himself. "Damned fool! He should of known not to say that about my Rosa. No sir! No way!"

CHAPTER THIRTY–THREE

March–April 1945

The morning evolved like the previous one, with heavy winds bringing snow squalls from the Great Lakes. Cassie knew it would probably be shirtsleeve weather before the day was over. Her Aunt Lorena had said that morning, "Typical spring weather for Syracuse."

It was early afternoon when she arrived home. Her aunt's modest residence sat on a quiet tree-lined street, a fifteen-minute walk from the university. Her heart raced when she took the familiar V-Mail envelope from the front porch letterbox. The postmark was March 21, a week earlier. She couldn't wait; she sat on the porch steps and tore open the letter.

Dear Cassie,

Here it is spring again, and I'm still in the same place. It's been an interesting winter. We had a system of rotation where we spent some time in the mountains, at the front, and then some time off. Winter here is no fun, but overall, it was better than last winter. Except for occasionally taking potshots at one another, our platoon has had no major contact with the enemy. Some platoons have had brief fights. Many of the guys slept in foxholes in the snow and mud. For the most part, I've avoided that. Being a chaplain's assistant has a few advantages.

Our platoon leader, Lt. Burnside, has hinted he may call me back into active combat once we start the big push through the mountains. We're already seeing increased action from the Germans, and I'm sure we'll move out soon. From what is happening all over Europe, and here, I believe this war will soon be over. I surely hope so.

Sgt. Silverman is still restless and itching to get going. Matt hasn't found out anything about Rosa or her baby. I keep hoping he'll not go AWOL. I told you about him hitting Burke and breaking his nose. I thought Burke would try to get even, but he hasn't. In fact, he's been friendlier with Matt. He seems to respect him more.

Do you still love college? I think I would like it, too. I don't know if it can ever happen for me. There are too many things against it. I've saved almost all my pay, but that wouldn't go very far in

316

financing college. I'm not so sure I'm college material, anyway. Sure, I know what you would say about it, but there's a big difference between excelling in a little Adirondack high school and out in the big world. In spite of having some newspaper writing experience, I sometimes feel like a dummy. There's so much to learn. Talking to people like Aimes and Silverman makes me aware of how little I know. Big words flow out of Silverman's mouth like water out of Cedar Creek in the spring, and I know only about half of them, although I pretend I do.

Working with Capt. Forrester is more demanding than fighting in some ways. I come face to face with men who are badly wounded and dying. It makes me much more aware of how precious life is. I've lost several friends, and I worry about the others, especially Matt and Silverman.

I'll try to write more often.

Your friend, Obie

Cassie reread the letter several times that afternoon while trying to work on an assignment due the next day. She wasted several sheets of paper with false starts and another when her ink pen leaked. She was unable to concentrate. The end of the letter, the part about his concern for his friends, reminded her of her own fears—which had escalated.

The previous fall, the day before leaving for Syracuse, she had gone to see Ken Gainsworthy. As she approached the house on the familiar road up Blackberry Hill, she worried about whether or not Ken would be sober. She was leaving early the following morning, so it would be her only chance to talk to him. What she wanted to ask him was important. When he quickly answered her knock, she was relieved.

"Cassie, it's good to see you," he said casually, as though her presence was the most natural thing in the world.

"I can't stay long. I'm going away to school tomorrow, and I haven't finished packing."

"Syracuse, isn't it?"

"Yes, and I'm really excited."

"Education's a good thing, I guess, especially for girls. We need teachers, and nurses, and the like."

Although Cassie had wanted to empathize her opinion that boys also need education, she remembered the purpose of her visit. Debating with Ken wouldn't accomplish it.

"Mr. Gainsworthy . . ."

"Call me 'Ken.'" He had said it before.

"Okay, Ken," she said. "You know, don't you, that Obie and I write?"

"Yes, I know."

"I get a letter from him about once a month, sometimes more often. If it goes any longer, I start to worry." She had chosen her words with care. "Without a letter, I might think something had . . ."

Ken said, without hesitation, "You might think he'd been killed. Isn't that it?"

"Yes. that's it." There was no use mincing words with Obie's father, who was himself no mincer of words.

"He lives with great danger."

"I worry so much about him."

"Cassie, do you want me to tell you if Obie was killed or wounded? Is that it?"

"Yes."

"As next-of-kin, I'd be the one to get the message."

"I'd know in time, but I'd rather hear any bad news from you. Would you let me know?"

"Yes, I will."

"Can I count on it?"

"You have my word on it. Anyway, I believe he'll be okay."

She'd struggled for the right words, but Ken had understood at once and cut right to the heart of the matter. "Thank you," she said.

"Give me your address. I'm not going to have any conversations with your mother."

Cassie smiled at the memory of that visit to Blackberry Hill. There were two opposing emotions every time she lifted the lid of Aunt Lorena's letterbox. There was the anticipation of finding a letter from Obie against the fear of receiving one from Ken Gainsworthy.

Her doubts about whether or not God heard her prayers didn't keep her from whispering one every night and often during the day. She pushed her book and papers aside. "God, please keep Obie safe and bring him back to me."

* * *

The Allies used the winter season to build supplies in areas around Florence. Early in April, they attacked north, where they tested and broke through enemy lines at various locations. The main thrust began in mid-month. Progress was swift, with the 10th Mountain Division advancing through the mountains into the Po Valley to try and cut the enemy forces in half.

Several divisions, Obie's included, advanced toward the city of Bologna. The Germans had time to shore up defenses in the area, and resistance was heavy. However, in a week, Obie's regiment assembled east of Highway 65 and was in the main force that smashed its way into Bologna. The Germans were reeling.

Two days later, the regiment moved up Route 9 and secured Modena, and a day later was ready to enter the small village of Reggio. There, they met heavier resistance. Obie's battalion was east of town and under machinegun and mortar fire from two positions. Enemy bunkers were fifty yards apart, and the platoon pounded the positions with bazooka rounds for several minutes. Obie and Forrester were in a protected area and close enough to hear strategy conversations. Obie stuck his head out often to assess the situation.

A shallow drainage ditch lay fifty feet from the larger left-side bunker. The rest of the way to the enemy entrenchment was over exposed ground. Distance from the ditch to the right-hand bunker was farther, broken up by a mound of earth and a few scattered bushes that might offer protection. A rise of ground lay between the two enemy positions. Burnside put a patrol in place to attack the bunker on the right while a larger force was prepared to assault the other. The patrol reached the bushes in less than a minute but was pinned down by fire from both bunkers. Burnside called for Silverman and Burke, who crawled to the officer. Obie strained to hear.

"What's your take on this situation?" Burnside asked Silverman, who had once told Obie that he admired the young officer's habit of asking opinions of his experienced combat men.

Burke, standing nearby, said, "All-out assault."

Sergeant Permine, who had joined them, asked, "Lieutenant Burnside, couldn't we call down artillery?"

"No. They're out of range. Anyway, a few yards short and it'd be us taken out!"

Silverman said, "Reluctantly, I agree with Burke. If we try moving our men back out of this situation, we'll lose some, with nothing to show for it. Let's get it over with quickly."

"Wouldn't it be better to wait until dark?"

"Let's get the job done," Burke said.

Burnside made the decision. "Sergeant Permine, Pass the word to the other squads. Tell them to go on my signal."

At that moment, a voice came from across the ditch. "Lieutenant . . . Kirkland's been hit!"

"How bad?"

"Bad. Really bad. He needs a corpsman."

"Do the best you can for him. We'll get to him as soon as we can. Lay low there."

"Lieutenant, he's asking for a chaplain. I think he's dying!"

Forrester rose at those words and began a crouching run toward Burnside. Obie followed.

Forrester spoke above the noise of battle. "I'm going over there."

"The hell you are!" Burnside replied.

"They'll respect me," Forrester said. "They'll hold their fire."

"No. I won't allow it."

Forrester assumed a tone Obie hadn't previously heard from him. "May I remind you, lieutenant, a captain outranks a lieutenant." Not waiting for an answer, he grabbed a stretcher and sprinted toward the ditch.

Burnside called after him, "And may I remind you that I'm platoon leader, and I direct battlefield operations." His voice trailed off as though knowing his words were hollow. He turned back to the men whose advice he'd sought. "Cover him!"

The verbal exchange had happened so quickly that Obie had little time to react. He wanted to follow Forrester but waited. He watched as the chaplain ran along the ditch and jumped onto higher ground, exposed to enemy fire. It was a familiar routine with Forrester letting the Germans know who he was and slowing his actions until he had their signal to proceed. At times, both sides allowed medics to pick up wounded and dead. Forrester had told Obie of an occurrence where officers and men came out and talked and smoked together before going back to killing one another. However, this wasn't a "time-out" situation; they were dealing with a desperate enemy.

Forrester held the stretcher over his head to indicate his intentions. He walked resolutely toward the group of men clustered behind the mound of earth.

A single shot rang out, and the chaplain dropped the stretcher and went to his knees. Another shot followed, and he sprawled full length on the ground.

"Dear God!" Obie said.

"Damn! The bastards shot the chaplain!" someone shouted.

Obie hardly realized he was in the ditch until he heard water splash over his boots as he ran. He heard Silverman's voice behind him. "Gainsworthy, get back here!"

Obie jumped from the ditch and ran toward the men. He heard the machinegun and knew tufts of grass were exploding around him. Someone from the group of besieged men had dragged Forrester forward. Obie made a desperate dive toward them and landed beside the chaplain.

The "safe" space they occupied was smaller than Obie had expected. Raising the head or hips, even a little, would mean exposure to enemy fire. Johnson, a squad leader, rolled beside him and said, "Kirkland's gone. The chaplain's in a bad way, too."

"I'll be all right," Forrester said.

Obie was relieved to hear his voice. "Where are you hit, sir?"

"Left shoulder. Somewhere there. Maybe stomach too."

Obie scrunched into position to examine the wound. A hole was visible on the front of the chaplain's jacket a few inches above the left pocket. Blood was spreading into the fabric. Moving him slightly, he saw another blood-soaked area at belt level.

"Why did you come?" Forrester asked. "You didn't have to." Before Obie had time to answer, Forrester moaned. "Lord, it hurts."

Obie tried to stay calm. "We'll get you back to an aid station."

"No, you take Kirkland."

"Sir, Kirkland's dead."

There was a moment of hesitation. "Where is he?"

"He's over here," Johnson answered.

"Take me to him."

"He's right here," Johnson said. "If you can roll over once, you'll be right beside him."

"Help me, Obie."

Forrester groaned again as Obie helped him scoot and roll until he was beside Kirkland. Obie risked exposure as he hopped over the two men. Forrester fumbled with the flap on his fatigue jacket. "Bible," he said, his voice weak.

Obie dug a leather-bound Bible out of Forrester's pocket and placed it in the chaplain's hands. Firing from both sides began with such tumult that Obie found it impossible to hear. The yelling of men and guns firing merged into one confusing din as the platoon closed on the two bunkers. Men around Obie leaped to their feet and joined those surging across the ditch toward the enemy. Obie lay flat with an arm over Forrester to prevent him from rising.

It seemed an eternity before the firing stopped; Obie knew only two or three minutes had passed. He raised his head and saw several GIs standing around the bunkers. Their relaxed stances told him the objectives had been taken.

Forrester sat up, with Obie helping him. The chaplain opened his Bible and read the Twenty-third Psalm in a trembling voice. Obie closed his eyes as Forrester prayed softly, sending Kirkland off to "a more glorious life with our God." When the last words were spoken, Forrester passed out.

Medics soon arrived and loaded the chaplain onto a stretcher. Obie was ready to follow when Matt approached at a trot. "Is he okay," he asked of Forrester.

"Don't know. Hope so. What's happening?"

"Burnside's calling for you."

"Guess I'm in trouble?"

"No, it's not that. Someone's hurt. Bad. We had three causalities besides Forrester and Kirkland. Two aren't serious. One is, and you'll be surprised who it is."

"Who? Is it Matt?"

"No."

"Silverman?"

"It's Burke."

The tightness in Obie's throat relaxed. "What happened?"

"We were storming the bunkers. Perkins was right next to Burke. You know how Perkins is. He jumped into a bunker without looking. A machinegun was pointing right at him. Burke knocked Perkins down and took several rounds in his chest. I think he saved Perkin's life."

"What does Burnside want with me?"

"Don't know. He's with Burke and the medics. Said for you to hurry."

Burnside stepped back from the bloody stretcher as Obie approached. He whispered, "Gainsworthy, Burke's in a pretty bad way. He asked for you. Actually, he asked for Captain Forrester, then for you when we told him Captain Forrester was wounded and that there are no other chaplains in the vicinity."

"Why me, sir? What does Burke want?"

"I don't know. Ask him. Better be quick, though."

Obie knelt beside Burke. The man's eyes revealed his pain. He reached up and placed a hand on one of Obie's. "Gainsworthy . . ." His voice was weak and raspy. "Preacher Man . . . Gainsworthy, I want you to pray for me."

Obie was shaken. Of all the words that might have come from Burke's mouth, none was more unexpected. He recovered his composure. "Burke, I don't know. I'm not what you think I am."

"You *do* pray, don't you?"

He lied. "Sometimes."

"Pray for me, then."

Obie felt the weight of the impossible situation. He'd spent nearly two years denying God's existence, and now he was supposed to play the hypocrite and pray in the presence of the men in his platoon.

"Give me a moment, he said to Burnside."

He turned away. What was he to do? Was God testing him— the God he didn't believe in? Did he *really* not believe? In some battles, he'd cried to God for help but had later dismissed it as surrendering to extreme fear. *Was God still there despite Obie's dismissal?* He couldn't know for sure, but he did know that these men believed— and expected him to say comforting words to a dying man.

He turned back to the group. "All right, Burke, I'll pray for you." He felt for the little Bible in his jacket pocket.

"Gainsworthy, I'm sorry for what I asked you to do." Burk said, "You know what I mean."

What would Forrester say? "It's okay, Burke. I forgive you. God forgives you," Obie said.

"You really think so?"

"I do." He wished he could be sure.

"I've done bad things . . . things I'm sorry for."

"We all have. You've done good things too, Burke. Burroughs told me you saved Perkins."

A smile appeared on Burke's broad face. Following Forrester's lead, Obie read the Twenty-third Psalm. Then he prayed aloud as best as he could, his voice often breaking as he put together words he thought appropriate. "Lord God, this good soldier, Maxwell Burke, has asked forgiveness for his sins. I know you heard him, and I know you will forgive him." He let other words come as they would, not trying to filter his feelings of inadequacy. He ended the prayer with, "Bless us now on this battlefield and forgive us all for the terrible things we have to do."

He didn't realize how many had gathered around the stretcher until he opened his eyes. Matt stood beside him; Silverman and Burnside were across from him, and several other men, some not in their squad, stood nearby. Matt had tears in his eyes. He said, "That was a good prayer, Obie. I never thought I'd cry over Burke."

Burke's voice was weak. "Tell Burroughs I'm sorry for the things I said. Tell him he ain't no bedbug. He's a man . . . a big man."

"I'm here, Burke," Matt said, bending down. "And I'm sorry I hit you."

Burke smiled and went, as Obie later that evening wrote in a letter to Cassie, "somewhere beyond the terrible world he's endured for three years."

*   *   *

Pinky Hunt hoped he might have misunderstood Abigail's words. He tapped the contents of his pipe into one hand and dumped still smoldering ashes into an ashtray on the kitchen table. He stared at her for a few moments before saying, "How's that again?"

"I said this war might be the best thing that's ever happened to us."

"Abigail, why on earth would you say such a thing? This war is a tragedy for the country and the world."

"Well, I didn't mean it like that. It *is* a terrible thing. I meant that it's also provided us with profit opportunities we wouldn't have had otherwise."

"What do you mean? It certainly hasn't helped my furniture business."

"Real estate. That's the big opportunity."

"Well, your little agency has grown, but I fail to see how the war has influenced it."

"I'm still planning to open an office in Evergreen. My real profit won't be just bringing sellers and buyers together, although that aspect has been growing. My real profit will be in selling property that I own . . . property I'm buying up cheap."

"There's only so much good land here."

"No, there's still prime land. The two big farms by the lake are what I really want. I already have a couple of the small farms farther up the shore. I'll eventually get them all. I'm right now negotiating for the Eps farm."

"What could you possibly do with the Eps farm?"

"I'll sell off lots along the waterfront to the young families who'll eventually be coming here."

"You'll never get Abner's farm. He won't sell."

"Yes, he will. They're getting old, and he has no children to leave it to. His father is in a bad way, I hear. I figure when he passes, Abner will give it all up."

"I doubt it. You can't have everything you want, Abigail. You weren't able to get the Boswell land." He took secret pleasure in the angry expression his words brought.

"I'll get that too. You mark my words. I'll also get Blackberry Hill."

"Ken Gainsworthy would never sell to you. Even if you get the rest, you'll never get *his* land."

"I can outsmart that drunk any day of the week, Pinky. Anyway, it's not even his land. It belongs to his father."

"What makes you think Jacob won't leave it to Ken?"

"He's too smart for that. He knows Ken would let it run down. He'll leave it to Abner, and I'll get it from Abner when he sells the farm to me."

Pinky studied her face. Where was the woman to whom he'd been married for twenty-two years? At forty-five, she retained much of the beauty and grace first attracting him, but she'd changed. He'd always recognized and accepted her aggressive nature and bent toward independence. But, in recent years, those qualities had magnified and changed from forgivable quirks to obsessions. Missing, as well, was compassion, although she'd never possessed much of that.

That knowledge brought sadness that threatened to blow a big hole in his life—a hole through which love might escape. An image of Vi Gainsworthy came. Even five years after her death, her memory persisted. He should have told Vi how much he appreciated her devotion to his family. Why could Abigail not be more like Vi?

"I believe, Abigail, that you'll regret all this," he said.

"Buying property, you mean?"

"That too." Confrontation with Abigail was an exercise he preferred to avoid. "Let's talk about something else."

She wasn't ready to let the subject go. "I'm the one who makes this family prosper, you know. We'd have much less if it were left to you and your wishy-washy ways."

He was silent, and she continued. "I'm the one who taught the girls to make a proper place in life. One is married to a successful doctor, and the other is in college and will eventually make her own mark . . . and at more than just being a teacher."

"That reminds me," Pinky said, "That reporter in Elizabeth-town dropped in at the factory the other day. He says the Army gave Obie Gainsworthy a medal. Some real high award for bravery. He says it happened some time ago. He's investigating it."

"Well, that must be a mistake. Obie Gainsworthy will not do anything to get a medal for bravery."

"There's already talk of doing something for him when he comes home. A parade, most likely."

"He doesn't deserve any recognition."

"How can you know that? Just because you don't like him has nothing to do with his bravery. I like Obie. I've always liked him. If Cassie's in love with him, as you say, I don't see the harm."

"*Never!* I don't want him near either of my girls."

Pinky let the subject rest. Why risk the stress?

* * *

Forrester's shoulder wound was severe but not life-threatening. The one in his abdomen was more serious. He was stabilized, the surgeon told Obie, but not out of danger. Obie walked beside the chaplain's stretcher to the ambulance that was taking him to Florence, a stopover before a flight to Naples.

Forrester laid a hand on Obie's arm. "Have you forgiven her?" he asked.

Obie, surprised, couldn't find words. "Well . . ."

"You must forgive, Obie. Forgive them both. That's an order." He smiled.

"Yes, sir. I'll try."

"Don't be surprised if God leads you into unexpected places. And, if you ever get to Indianapolis, look me up."

"I will, sir," Obie said as he stepped back and saluted. The door closed, and the ambulance sped away.

Obie picked up an M1 at company and went to join his squad. He didn't even consider following the proper protocol of reporting to Burnside for his okay. They could hunt him up if they wanted him to assist Forrester's replacement. No one seemed surprised by his return except Matt, who joyfully clapped him on the back.

Aimes had left the squad. Caught with his helmet off, a bullet had glanced off the stock of his M1 and tore a gash up the side of his head, barely missing his ear. He was patched up at an aid station and told to go back to his company. He refused, saying he believed his luck had run out. He was arrested for insubordination, and an official investigation threatened to bring a dishonorable discharge. Furious at the suggestion, Silverman had stormed into Burnside's tent and demanded that he do something. Obie, listening outside, feared Silverman had gone too far and expected he too would be disciplined. Incredibly, Burnside was sympathetic. He knew the full bird colonel from the regiment presiding over the inquiry. Aimes was quietly moved to a supply company job.

Silverman later told Obie he had overheard the colonel say to another officer a few minutes after the inquiry, "Why do we keep these men on the lines so long? Some have been there for years. I'd have found a job for Sergeant Aimes anywhere before letting him go to the damn brig!"

Silverman bought Burnside a bottle of Scotch.

CHAPTER THIRTY–FOUR

April 1945

Pinky Hunt mailed a package at the post office on Main Street and was about to leave when Lloyd Baumgartner entered. The mayor was excited. "Pinky!" he said loud enough that Mrs. Andrews, who had just stepped up to the window for stamps, was startled. "You remember what we talked about the other day . . . about Obie Gainsworthy getting a medal? Well, that reporter was right. Ken got a letter from the war department yesterday. Showed it to me this morning. He's real proud."

"What is it, the medal?"

"Silver Star." Lloyd stretched the words, emphasizing each.

"It's a high award, isn't it?"

"Indeed, it is. Some of the other area boys have earned medals, too. It seems that Obie rescued a fellow soldier who was wounded . . . carried him on his back with Germans shooting at them all the while. After that, he told the other soldiers where to shoot to kill a whole caboodle of them. It's all in the letter. I copied it down. It'll all be in the next County Gazette Weekly. Might even make other regional newspapers."

"You don't say!" Pinky relished the news. It would upset Abigail's day. "I'm not surprised, though," he said.

"He's a fine young man. Wasn't he sweet on your Laura once?"

Pinky was aware that most of Stafford Rest knew about Obie's feelings for Laura. When she married Ben Williamson, they were surprised. He suspected Abigail knew more about the situation than she was telling him.

"Yeah, Lloyd, he was. But you know how these young people are. They change their minds."

"Well, it's a shame for sure. They'd of made a good match. Not that she didn't do all right, anyway."

Mrs. Andrews, with stamps in hand, turned and said, "Now, listen here you two . . . I like Obie a lot. He did a better job than anybody on my lawn. But Laura's made an excellent catch. Marrying a doctor is something most girls can only dream about." She marched past them before either recovered enough to respond.

"Well, I guess we've been told," Lloyd said, grinning.

"We have. Somebody mentioned a parade the other day when this medal thing was only a rumor. Is a parade really in the works?"

"It will be. You can count on it . . . as soon as Obie gets home. And that could be soon the way things are going in Europe. Some other area boys have earned medals, too, so we'll honor them all."

"Let's keep it all in our prayers, Lloyd, that this war will soon be over in Europe, and the Pacific, too."

Their expressions of hope bolstered Pinky's spirits. Nevertheless, his thoughts returned to Mrs. Andrews' words that still in his ears. "Laura's made an excellent catch." *Had she really?* He loved his little grandson, but something had changed Laura's demeanor, evident during her last visit. His elder daughter was not as happy as he would have liked, and he had no idea what he could do about it.

* * *

The German army in Italy had been cut in half, and their defenses were in shambles. The Allies had a bridge over the Po and were quickly cutting off escape routes to the Alps. In Germany, the war had been taken right to Hitler's doorstep. Rumors of an imminent surrender of the entire German army circulated. Morale was high. Patience was not.

After an easy advance north through Parma and around Fidenza, forward patrols in Obie's battalion discovered that Busseto was heavily fortified. "I hope we bypass it," Burnside said. "We're essentially mopping up, anyway."

Division commanders had other ideas. The enemy was surrendering in large numbers. Captured German soldiers were tired and dispirited. Nevertheless, the compulsion was to leave no enemy pockets behind. They would "tidy up" as they went.

They stopped early one morning, barely out of range of German guns. Obie paced back and forth, nervous and wanting the job to start—so it could be finished. This would be his first time on the line in months.

Another dream had come during the night. Rosa held out a naked baby boy. As both Obie and Matt reached for the child, a burst of light enveloped them. Obie had no sense of waking, only an awareness of being conscious. His sleeping bag was damp with perspiration. There was nothing sinister about the dream; it gnawed at him, nonetheless.

During the past few weeks, Obie had felt a change in himself. The catalyst had been his prayer for the dying Maxwell Burke. That prayer had words borrowed from prayers he'd heard from Forrester and Paster Charles, but the satisfying sense came later that he'd spoken words of truth.

On this day of battle, he wondered if he'd been hasty in dismissing God. What if he'd let his rage at Laura and her mother translate as hatred toward God? His anger toward Laura had subsided; he had Cassie to thank for that. So why would he still be angry at God?

On impulse, he took out the bible from his jacket pocket. With nowhere to go for a quiet retreat, he sat on the ground and leaned back against the big rear tire of a supply truck. He leafed through the Bible, letting the pages fall open wherever they would, then quickly punched his forefinger at a paragraph. It rested on a place near the end of Psalm 121. He read slowly, hoping to find something calming.

> *The Lord is thy keeper: the Lord is thy shade upon thy right hand. The sun shall not smite thee by day, nor the moon by night. The Lord shall preserve thee from all evil: he shall preserve thy soul. The Lord shall preserve thy going out and thy coming in from this time forth, and even for evermore.*

Obie took a nub of a pencil from his pocket, underlined the words, closed the Bible, and put it back in his pocket. He sat still, oblivious to the preparation for battle around him.

He became aware that someone had come to sit beside him. It was several seconds before he realized it was Matt. His friend said, "Obie, you sleeping?"

"No . . . just thinking."

"What about?"

"Life and other serious stuff."

"You scared? You've been acting funny."

"Yeah, a little bit scared."

"Me, too. We're close to the end of all this. It'd be a shame to . . . well, you know."

"Matt, we'll get through it. Keep thinking of Rosa."

"Yeah, and the baby too. Do you realize that I have a son or a daughter somewhere in Italy who's five months old?"

"It's a son . . . and I'm sorry you haven't heard anything."

"I hope Rosa went home like I told her to. Papa's still working on getting them to the States. That's not easy because of the war." He hesitated before asking, "What did you mean when you said, 'It's a son?' How do you know I have a son?"

"I saw him in a dream."

"You believe in that kind of thing?"

"I don't know. Maybe."

"If you believe it, then I believe it too. *I have a son.*" Matt seemed thoughtful as he picked at pebbles on the road between them. "There's something else I'd like to talk about," he said.

"Okay."

"I asked you once to pray for Rosa and me. Did you?"

Obie tried hard not to look Matt in the eyes. "Not much, but I did when I could." There had been a couple of occasions in the heat of battle.

"Well, if you prayed, it's worked so far. Now, there's the little one . . . our son. Maybe you can pray a little harder?"

"Matt, why don't you talk to the new chaplain?"

"I don't know him like I know you."

"The thing is, I'm not worthy to pray for anybody, including myself."

"I heard you pray for Burke when he was dying."

"Burnside made me do it."

"You did a good job."

"Don't you ever pray, Matt?"

"No, not really. Not much. Well, I have some, lately. I never learned how when I was growing up. Never believed much in it."

"It seems you believe now, though?"

"I guess I do."

"Did the war do that?"

"Maybe . . . some. Mostly, it's been knowing you. You talk about being unworthy, but you worked for Forrester and helped him care for the men. It seems like you have a lot of faith even though we've been through some pretty rough stuff."

Obie could find no further words on the subject. He hoped Matt would not guess the extent of his doubts.

Silverman came by to inform them that they were moving out. As they got to their feet, Obie said, "Matt, I'll pray for you and Rosa and the baby." He was determined to keep that promise.

* * *

As the battalion moved toward Busseto, enemy fire came from a farmhouse two hundred yards away. Burnside's platoon was assigned to break off and silence the bunker. The enemy force was small but well-entrenched. Firing back and forth continued for several minutes. Obie hoped they might merely sit and trade potshots until the Germans surrendered.

Burnside was out of patience. He called his squad leaders together. Silverman's squad was to approach from the right side in a diversionary movement while three other squads would attack in force on the left side. The land around the farmhouse was flat and covered with cultivated fields and vineyards. Hedgerows offered minimal cover. Silverman led as they crawled through grape arbors that supported vines with new leaves. They stopped every few yards and waited for the signal to move again. The plan was to get close before charging the bunker. They covered half the distance, and the absence of enemy fire gave hope that they hadn't been discovered.

Matt was lying beside Obie. They pressed themselves close to the ground. Following a volley of rifle shots, someone down the line screamed in pain.

"They've spotted us," Matt said.

Increased volume of firing in their direction confirmed Matt's words. A hail of bullets and mortar found random victims. "Corpsman! Corpsman!" came cries from two different directions.

"Rivera's been hit!" Perkins shouted, sounding near hysteria.

Minutes later, Obie heard Silverman telling Burnside that Rivera was dead. All this time—with the war nearly over. Why? Rivera had just the previous day talked about his plans for going to medical school. Obie pressed his face against the smooth stock of his rifle. Would it never end?

"Fall back! Fall back!" Burnside yelled.

Silverman, a few feet away, repeated the order. Obie was halfway up, not knowing if he should run or crawl. "Come on, Matt. Come on. Fall back!" he yelled.

Matt didn't move. Obie dove down beside him. "Come on, Buddy. Don't freeze on me now."

Obie shook him hard, causing his head to turn. A round hole on Matt's forehead had a barely discernible trace of red around it. His eyes were open, but there was no light in them. Matthew Burroughs, his friend, was gone.

* * *

Silverman flattened himself on the ground beside Obie and Matt's body.

"It's over, Silverman! He's dead!" Obie said, nearly choking on the words.

"Leave him. We have to fall back, or we'll be dead too."

"I won't leave him."

"Yes, you will! We'll come back for him later. Grab your weapon and move."

Obie felt rage boiling up inside. His chest hurt. It was as though his soul had been scalded. *"They killed him!* The damn Krauts killed Matt!"

"He's dead. We can't help him."

Obie had a vague awareness of his anger taking him beyond rational behavior. He could no more control his emotion than he could stem his flow of tears. Nor did he want to.

"They've killed so many of our friends. They killed Rivera. Now they've killed Matt. They killed your relatives, too, didn't they, Sarge?"

"Yes, by God . . . they did!"

"Cavendish had a Thompson. Where is it?"

"Over there," Silverman said, gesturing. "I have one too." Silverman's eyes were on fire.

"Let's go get the bastards!"

"Sure as hell!"

Obie bolted to where Cavendish's body lay. He picked up the machinegun and broke into a run toward the farmhouse. Silverman stayed with him, step for step. They hardly swerved or ducked as they ran forward.

Sandbags, stacked four feet high, shielded the front of the house. Obie pulled the pin of a grenade as he ran. Not expecting such a frontal attack from a retreating force, the Germans were taken by surprise. Several men were inside the bunker. Obie tossed the grenade and opened fire as he leaped onto the sandbags. Silverman threw a grenade and sprayed the interior with machinegun fire. Both grenades exploded simultaneously, and the blast rocked Obie backward for a moment. Amid smoke and confusion, he regained his balance and fired the Thompson until the weapon had no more ammunition. He picked up a German rifle and continued firing. Screams came from the fallen Germans. Neither he nor Silverman stopped until none was moving.

"Bastards!" Silverman's voice was loud and high with exhilaration, as though he were drunk with joy. Obie realized that he, too, was screaming.

Other men reversed direction and swarmed over the bunker and into the farmhouse. With no more enemies standing, Obie was spent. He sat and put his head in his hands. "Matt, damn it. Matt. I'm sorry. I should have looked after you better."

He stayed in that position a long time, even knowing he had to return to where his friend lay. If Matt's body hadn't been picked up, he would stay there and wait. There was Rivera, too; he would need looking after.

Obie was so tired he wasn't sure his legs would hold him erect. He was surprised to see Silverman sitting on the stacked sandbags several yards away. He looked exhausted, as well. He'd accused Silverman of being obsessed with killing Germans; it appeared he had become Silverman. They gazed at each other, expressionless.

Lieutenant Burnside approached Obie. "Gainsworthy, that was foolhardy. I've learned to expect better of you and Sergeant Silverman, especially him. But you undoubtedly saved lives by leading this charge. I'm going to recommend you both for a medal."

"No. Don't do that, Lieutenant. Do it for Sarge if you want to, but I don't want it. I won't take it!"

"You'll change your mind when you've had time to think about it. You have a Silver Star. You could have another. Such an honor could help build you a career in the Army."

"What I'd like is to have my friends back. Will another medal give me that?"

"Gainsworthy, I'm sorry about Burroughs and Rivera, but you've got your whole life ahead of you. Think about it. I'll talk to you about it again in a couple of days. I'm sure Sergeant Silverman will accept the honor."

"Lieutenant, you're wrong about that . . . sir."

Burnside turned, apparently unaware Silverman was standing behind him and had overheard the conversation. "Sergeant, I'm proud of this platoon, and when my men do something above and beyond the call of duty, they should be rewarded for it. It gives honor not only to those men but also to the whole platoon . . . and the regiment."

"Forget it," Silverman said before stomping away.

Annoyance swept across Burnside's face for an instant before he composed himself. Obie believed he would call Silverman back, but his stance relaxed. "You two are tough nuts," he said as he walked away. Then, he turned and said, "I wish we had more tough nuts like you."

Obie's fury had cooled, but was far from dissipated. He seemed capable of only two emotions, anger and grief, and he was fighting off grief as long as possible. He took in the immediate scene with perverted pleasure, fixing in his mind the bloody picture of German bodies scattered within a fifty-foot circumference. Some were draped over machineguns and sandbags. Some lay face down. One was on his back, open eyes staring at nothing. One thing they all had in common was that none moved. They would never move again of their own power, the price extracted for the lives of Obie's friends.

An officer in the back was in a sitting position, an expression of disbelief frozen on his dead face. Perkins was going through his pockets. He took the belt and holster from around the man's waist and brought them to Obie.

"What Burke and Deboise used to call 'the spoils of war,'" Perkins said. "Here, you take it. You earned it."

On any previous occasion, he would not have considered accepting such an offering from Perkins or anyone, as well-meaning as they might be. Now, he took it with no hesitation. He removed the Luger from its holster and felt how its shape conformed to his hand. Such a pistol was a prize, a much sought-after German weapon. It would remind him of what had happened here, of the toll he had extracted from the enemy. He folded the belt around the holster and stuck it under his arm as he started back toward the place he'd left Matt.

There had been nine Germans in the house. They were herded out and forced to sit along a rock wall several yards away and close to the path Obie would take. Two GIs were guarding them. Obie looked away. They were alive. Matt was dead. It was not a time he wanted to see live Germans.

The prisoner at the end closest to the path drew his attention. He was young, no more than seventeen or eighteen. He smiled at Obie from a grimy face. There was not the hate there that Obie had seen on many prisoners' faces. He appeared to have surrendered to a fate over which he had no control.

The boy put a hand in his jacket pocket and started to pull something out, standing at the same time. The GI guard who was closest yelled, "Watch out, corporal! He's got a weapon!"

Obie acted from instinct. He pulled the Luger from the holster under his arm and pointed it straight at the German's head. For an instant, the boy hesitated, and Obie held his fire. The hand came out with a dark object showing. Obie fired the Luger.

An expression of surprise formed on the German's face. He uttered a single word, "Mutter!" His legs buckled, and he fell in a heap in the dirt and was still. Blood was flowing from somewhere on his face. Obie imagined he heard a cry of anguish from within the group of enemy soldiers.

The guard came and prodded the boy with his rifle. "He's dead," he announced. "Good shot, corporal." He turned away as casually as a farmer might turn from a slaughtered hog.

Obie stood still for several seconds. Firing at vague figures who were firing at you was one thing. Shooting a human being in the face from ten feet away was something else. Had he seen a weapon in the German's hand? It had happened so fast that Obie was unsure. He knelt and felt under the boy for the pistol that must be there.

What he found surprised him. The dark object was a Bible, not much different in size and color from his own. He searched thoroughly but found no weapon. There came the realization that he'd killed an unarmed prisoner. He was desperate to feel something, remorse, pity, or regret. There was only the onslaught of grief over Matt. He put the Luger back into its holster and the German Bible into his pocket. "Damn them all to hell!" he growled.

CHAPTER THIRTY-FIVE

April–October 1945

The war in Europe was not yet over. Drained of emotion, Obie struggled across a personal desert of uncertainty. Anger had finally dissipated, and he barricaded himself against grief. Robot-like, he performed his duties divorced from feeling. Even a letter from Cassie telling him that Laura was pregnant again had little effect. *So what?*

The regiment reached the Po River and took nearly five hundred prisoners before returning to Fidenza. From there, they were trucked almost two hundred miles to Bergamo and then to Milan. An acceleration of significant events began: On May 2, near Arborio, they learned that the German Army in Italy had surrendered. The report of Hitler's death soon followed. A week later, Germany surrendered all its forces, ending the war in Europe.

Celebration spread quickly, and great joy erupted throughout the civilian population. Obie was bolstered by the realization that the fighting had finally stopped. Although Matt's presence would have made it a far brighter season, he was happy for those who had survived the war.

There were still duties to perform. He was assigned to help pick up prisoners and participate in other mop-up activities. The regiment moved several times in the weeks following the surrender. They spent time near the French border and participated in a parade at Susa. In mid-July, they settled in for "training, recreation, and education" in northwest Italy.

Service members had started returning to the States. The order of return was subject to time in battle zones, marital status, and the number of dependents. Silverman had accumulated more than enough service points for discharge; he believed he'd be home in August. Obie, with fewer points, knew that unless the Pacific war was over, he might be sent there. Even if complete peace came, he'd be leaving Italy no earlier than September.

Silverman secured a pass to Rome but was unsuccessful in learning anything new about Yarden Silverman and his family. In the meantime, his father was arranging a trip to Germany. Silverman declared that they would never give up until they discovered the truth.

Silverman and Obie were now on a first-name basis. Obie soon learned that "Adam," the prospective civilian was far different from "Silverman," the wartime leader; he appeared to be letting go of the hate that had held him captive. Relapses did come; he blanched and swore when he heard or read about the atrocities uncovered around Europe, but he was no longer bent on revenge at any cost. Aimes, who had recently returned to them, declared him "mellowed."

Obie and Adam went to San Remo on a three-day pass, slept in real beds with scented sheets and fluffy pillows, and ate in restaurants serving food with flavors surpassing any Obie had enjoyed since sitting at Angie's table. They drank more kinds of wine than he knew existed. Women were everywhere.

They sat on the sun-filled patio of one of the city's finest eateries, a restaurant near the water. Adam gestured toward a nearby table where two young women sat. "They need company, don't you think?"

"They're pretty, all right, but I don't know if I'm ready for that," Obie said while pouring himself another glass of wine.

Adam looked exasperated. "Will you ever be ready?" When Obie gave him no response, he continued. "You know, Obie, if anyone has earned a right to enjoy some female company, it's us. Look around you at all these GIs. The world's still celebrating, and they're going crazy here. It won't let up for a while. What's the harm? We're not married. Is it your religion . . . or is it still Laura?"

"It's certainly not my religion. And no, it's not about Laura." He stopped, unsure he should give voice to something that had been growing in his mind. "Adam, I've been thinking a lot about Cassie. There's no one I admire more. We . . ."

"You mean Cassie, the one you write to?"

Obie was surprised that Adam remembered. "Yes, Laura's sister. She's a good friend . . . the best."

"Maybe it's really her you're in love with." Adam laughed. "Maybe you've been fooling yourself all this time. Obie, that'd be a good thing. I think Cassie may be just what you need."

In love with Cassie? Could that be? True, his thoughts had been focused on her lately; he'd been asking himself what their relationship was. But, shouldn't love be something you simply know—and not something you have to figure out?

"We're the best of friends, that's all."

"Well, it's something you'll have to sort out. Now, about these girls over there."

"I don't know, Adam."

"Well, my friend, you'd better make up your mind pretty quick because, in about a minute, I'm going over there and introduce myself to that pretty lady in the blue dress before someone else does. And, in case you haven't noticed, her friend's just as pretty."

The wine was working. "They don't look as if they want anything serious."

Adam laughed so hard he almost choked. *"Serious?* There's nothing serious about all this. All these men will be going home in a few weeks, and the women know it. Everyone knows it. People are celebrating by taking pleasure in the things humans take pleasure in. As for me, I'm going to concentrate on walking a straight line to meet that beautiful woman. If you change your mind, come on over. I'm sure your language skills would be a great asset." He rose, smiled, bowed toward Obie, and made his way to the table where the two girls sat.

Obie drained his wine glass. He watched as Adam introduced himself, laughed with the two young women, and sat beside the one in the blue dress. The other girl, no older than Obie, looked toward him in obvious invitation. He wanted to join them but still looked for excuses. Finding none, he picked up the nearly empty wine bottle and walked a wavy path toward Adam and the two women.

* * *

In the days following the San Remo interlude, Obie and Adam took other recreational jaunts that helped revive Obie's troubled spirits. Eventually, the time for parting came. Due to leave the next day, Adam kept his fingers crossed about returning to college. He'd applied to Berkeley shortly after the fighting stopped, hoping to get there in time for the fall semester. It was a leap of faith. On the eve of departure, Adam returned from a mail call holding up a letter.

"I'm going to Berkeley, and they accepted all my credits from Boston College."

"I'm happy for you."

"I'll make the fall semester, too, providing I can muster out as soon as I get to the States."

"Good luck."

"Obie, I did something I haven't told you about." He held out a folded sheaf of papers. "I ordered application forms for you, too.

You should go to college, and Berkeley's an excellent school. You told me you had good grades. You should go ahead and fill out the application. There's little chance of your getting in before the second semester, but better late than never. Don't wait too long, though, because colleges will be flooded with applications from returning servicemen."

Obie didn't want to hurt his friend's feelings, but he did want to be honest. "I may not get there," he said. "Don't forget. The war in the Pacific isn't over."

Adam proceeded as though he hadn't heard. "I did something else. I told Uncle Hershel about you. He wants to help. Said he'd open some doors if you do your part. You will apply, won't you?"

"I'll give it some thought."

As much as Obie delighted in the war's end, he feared the uncertainty it brought. Two years ago, he was open to believing that God gave people special missions in life. If he had clung to any fragment of that belief throughout the war, Matt's death and his own bloody rampage had destroyed it within minutes. His life was taking a far different path.

Prayer hadn't kept Matt safe, so what good was prayer—and faith? He must find a new direction. Where would he go? He'd need to look for work, or prepare for an occupation. Adam's encouragement brought a sliver of hope concerning the future. A college education would make many things possible. Remembering his grandfather's words encouraged him: *Perhaps it was time to make wine.*

He'd heard of Berkeley. There was no harm in considering it. He'd ration hope, however. Of one thing he was sure: He would not return to Stafford Rest. Too many bad memories. That part of his life was finished. California was about as far away as possible, suiting him just fine.

Obie saw that Adam was looking for a more definitive answer. "What would I have to do?" he asked.

"That's the spirit. The first thing is to fill out the application and write to your high school for a transcript of your grades. Have them send it right to Berkeley. Then, send these papers to Uncle Hershel. I've written down his address for you. And write a letter telling him all about yourself. Now, Obie, this is important. Do a good job with the writing. Uncle Hershel is my relative, but he's still a scholar and expects scholarly work."

"Has he been at Berkeley long?"

"A long time. He's young at heart, despite his age. My Aunt

Gerdie died a few years ago, and he remarried last year. I haven't met her. Father says he's robbed the cradle. Virginia is half his age."

Obie appreciated Adam's help, even if nothing ever came of it. The eve of their parting was emotional. "We've been through a lot together," Adam said, "and I'm sure I'll see you again soon. You'll like my uncle."

"I hope to get the chance. Anyway, I'll come and see you sometime, regardless."

They talked well into the night. Adam told him more about his family. His mother died when he was ten. They moved from Boston to New York a year later. He had a sister, Naomi, who was twenty. His father, already wealthy, had started two businesses in New York City, a financial firm to "make his fortune" and a publishing house as a "benefit to humanity." He expected that Adam would eventually take his place in Silverman Financial.

"Is your father really going to Germany?" Obie asked.

"He is. And, as always, he's in a hurry. My guess is he's greasing some palms."

"Must be expensive?"

"Money helps, sometimes . . . and Father has plenty of that." Obie detected a bit of sarcasm.

A period of depression followed Adam's departure. In addition to saying goodbye to his friend, a letter came from his father bearing news that hurt, although it didn't surprise him. Jacob Gainsworthy, one-hundred-two years old, had "died in his sleep with a cool Adirondack breeze blowing through his open window."

Events took place that raised his spirits. "Atomic bombs," secret weapons taking them all by surprise, were dropped on cities in Japan, bringing about surrender in a few days. Obie now believed he'd be discharged from the Army when he returned to the states.

Cassie, who was home for the summer, wrote often. She said, "They want to give all you service boys a parade when you get back," she told him, "Especially you and a couple of others because of your important medals." She told him about Jacob's military burial; she had attended and was touched. At the end of her letter, she asked him to reconsider his stance about not returning to Stafford Rest.

Obie, you can go off somewhere to school after that, but you should come back here first. I think you should face a few things still bothering you. Above all, you and Laura need to talk. She comes home often, and I can arrange for it to happen. I know she's married, and that won't change, but you two have to talk, at least to discuss what happened between you. You and she are the most important people in my life, and I hate to see you alienated. Please!

Obie swore as he crumpled the pages, then smoothed them out. There was no need for anger toward Cassie. She meant well.

Would it be this way forever? Could he never fully forgive—or even seriously want to? He'd tried several times after talking to Forrester, but a dark moment always came, reminding him of the two women who had caused him so much pain. Even when he and Adam were with the girls in San Remo, a time of letting go, what should have been a delightful experience was soured.

Obie had never wanted intimacy with anyone except Laura. The Italian girl's name was Mirabella. He realized later that his attitude toward her had been one of dismissal, and he felt ashamed.

A disturbing thought came. Would Cassie care that he'd been with Mirabella? Should he tell her? Knowing her so well, he concluded that she'd probably laugh at his naïveté, as Silverman had.

He speculated about why Cassie had been on his mind so much: Loving Laura had probably been tied to sexual desires, whereas Cassie was the sister to whom he'd always turned for companionship; he'd craved her warmth, even though that was tempered by her assertiveness.

Despite all Laura's lies, was it possible that her claim about Cassie being in love with him was valid? Would that be a good thing? The smart course would be to spend time with her after he returned home to sort it all out. But, maybe that was impractical; too many things had happened to him in the more than two years since seeing her. Grudgingly, he concluded he might be unable to have a serious relationship with Cassie—or with any woman.

With Adam gone, he concentrated on the two things he must accomplish before leaving Italy. First, he would return to Tarquinia on a three-day pass to see his relatives. Many men wanted passes; his was scheduled three weeks ahead.

He would also search for Rosa; he owed it to Matt. She must have been notified of his death if she were home in Naples. He knew Matt had taken care of all the paperwork needed to provide her with insurance and other benefits. She could be anywhere if she'd continued looking for her father, as she'd vowed to do.

He prepared himself for the possibility that he might never see Rosa again. Would she care? That question bothered him.

342

Everything had happened so quickly. Matt, who often acted with compulsion, had fallen in love with the same abandon. Rosa, trying to survive, might have seized an opportunity. Even if she hadn't truly loved him, she'd borne his child, and Obie wanted to tell her how Matt had died so the child would know something of its father.

Obie was sure he'd be sent to Naples to board a ship for home; that's where Adam had gone. Finding Rosa should be easy if she were there.

His three-day pass came sooner than expected, and Obie took a train south and a bus east to Tarquinia. Maria greeted him with open arms. Gerardo was home. Obie wasn't surprised. Any man who could sneak behind enemy lines on one leg could find his way home after the war. Teresa, with the beautiful blue eyes, proudly thrust out her little one for Obie to hold.

"Where is Anton?" Obie asked dubiously, realizing more variables existed in that relationship than in other family ties.

"He is not yet with us," Teresa said. Sadness touched her face, but gently.

Gerardo explained. "He will come as soon as he can. The Americans are holding him. They seem not to know what to do with him. Several of us testified about his work in Italy, valuable work that led to much disarray in the enemy forces. He writes almost every day. He will join us soon, I am sure."

The time with them was too short. Maria told him as he prepared to leave, "Obadiah, you are my sister's son, and we love you. Do not forget us."

"How could I? I'll return someday."

"Yes, you will. We will look forward to it," Maria said.

The hour was late when he returned to his unit. He was surprised to find everyone packed in preparation for leaving for Naples the following day. It was nearly daylight when he finally fell asleep. He was still tired as they boarded a train starting for Naples.

How different the landscape, or maybe his perception of it. Mountains, hills, villages, and vineyards were no longer bastions of terror where death awaited. He was changed too, marked forever by this strange, yet now-familiar world. A part of him would retain an element of the struggle known and endured here. He was going home. Many would not.

As they neared their destination, the train's movement and the deepening twilight caused flashing and shadowy forms on the windows. Obie imagined he could see the faces of men he'd known.

Dead men. There was Copland, blowhard and cowardly, who came back to die bravely; Meinard, who wanted to prove that not all Germans were bad; Rivera, who would have gone home to become a doctor but would instead sleep in the soil of Italy; Burke, bigger than life and meaner than a cornered wolverine dying with a prayer on his lips; there was friendly Grugs, whom he wished he'd known better. Moreover, Matt's face was everywhere he looked.

He would never forget the others, either, the ones who had made great sacrifices: Deboise, who went home to Arkansas minus a leg; Aimes, whose demons caught up with him; Captain Forrester, brave beyond explanation, and Howard and Burnside, lieutenants who beat all the odds and were able to go home.

By the time they reached the outskirts of Naples darkness had descended, and shadows had diminished, unlike his reflective mood. Some men were just plain lucky. Obie, Perkins, Aimes, and Silverman were the only original patrol members making it to the war's end. Perkins, who came to Italy as a boy and was going home a man, was sitting in the seat in front of him.

Was it luck after all, or was it all part of a plan? He had great uncertainty. What was in store for him? He was barely nineteen years old but felt like an old man. He'd come through the war without a scratch. He had scars, nonetheless. Although he'd come to terms with the destroyed dream of serving God, a part of him mourned the fact.

The word "unworthy" kept pecking at his mind. As much as he'd wanted in the beginning to avoid killing people, he had. His dialogue with Charles Lansing had modified that quandary, and despite his angry declarations, he'd never really doubted God's existence. So, if God was still there, there had to be some accounting for his having killed out of anger and revenge. He'd even committed a war crime by murdering a soldier who had surrendered.

He'd previously believed that God was eager to forgive. But Obie's actions were such that he could probably never find forgiveness. Even if he could, how could he forgive himself? How could he ever again call himself "Christian?"

He heard Perkins address a soldier sitting beside him, "I think we're about there."

Obie was drawn back to reality. He closed his eyes and listened to the slow clacking of wheels on rails as they pulled into one of Naples's train stations.

* * *

Obie was assigned guard duty for three straight days, a detail that irritated him because he was desperate to get into Naples. When he was finally free from that boring routine, he formed plans to find Rosa. They would be boarding a ship in two days, so time had become a factor.

He caught a ride on a supply truck headed for the wharves. It dropped him off as close as he could remember to the street where he and Matt had first found Rosa, for he knew that she lived nearby.

The neighborhood had changed; reconstruction had already started, and litter was not as evident. The little cafe, *Ristorante di Giuseppe*, where they'd eaten nearly two years before, was still there. It was much the same, except tables filled the sidewalk outside. The rainy season had begun, but the day was dry, and most tables were occupied. The streets were filled with people. Waves of nostalgia swept over Obie as he remembered the time with Matt, a time of innocence before they were ever in battle. He needed to move past that way of thinking and put those memories behind. Matt was dead. He'd probably say, "Get on with it!"

He was unsure how to proceed in his search for Rosa. He'd lost the address Matt had given him; Rosa's address was not something he'd thought he'd ever need.

Her family lived close by, but there were many apartments in the two and three-story buildings. He could knock on doors, but thoughts of such a time-intensive activity overwhelmed him; that would be a last resort.

Thinking it best to stay in one spot, he took a table and ordered coffee. He could see both sides of the street. Maybe he would recognize someone; he laughed to himself, realizing how few people he knew here. But, if he sat there long enough, Rosa would come by. Or maybe she wouldn't; she might still be in northern Italy searching for her father.

He nearly dropped his coffee cup when he saw someone he knew coming up the sidewalk. He jumped up and grabbed the young man by his arm. "Beppe!" he said to Rosa's cousin, the one who'd shown up briefly the night they met Rosa.

Beppe took a couple of steps backward, looking frightened. Obie continued holding onto his arm. "Please," Beppe said, "I did not do it."

"Beppe, you are Rosa's cousin, are you not?"

Beppe was confused, as well as frightened. Obie needed to convince him that his interest was only in finding Rosa.

"Listen, Beppe, do you remember that I was there the day Rosa met Matt? Matt Burroughs? Do you remember?"

"Matt Burroughs?"

"Yes, and I am Obie. I wish to find Rosa, your cousin. Is she here?"

Beppe relaxed and smiled. "Ah, yes, I remember. I helped them talk."

"I have to see Rosa. Is she here?"

"Aw, poor Rosa. She is so sad."

"Then she *is* here?"

"Yes, yes. She lives with her mother and sisters, and her bambino."

"Did her brothers return safely?"

"Yes, but they live apart."

"Beppe, would you tell her that Obie is here to speak with her?" He was trying to be patient.

"Yes, I will go get her. She is two streets away." He turned to leave.

"Wait, Beppe! Tell me, does she know that Matt was killed?"

Beppe stared forlornly at the ground and sighed. "Yes, Senior Obie, she knows. She has known for three months. She is very sad, but I am sure she will be glad to see you."

"You called her child a bambino. It is a boy, then?"

"Matthew is his name."

"Beppe, tell her to bring Matthew with her."

* * *

Rosa leaped into his arms at the cafe. She clung to him with a fierceness that surprised him, considering her thin body. She had arrived in just a few minutes, running as fast as she could while pushing a baby carriage.

"Oh, GI Obie. It is so wonderful to see you. So wonderful . . . and also so sad."

They went to sit beside a fountain in a little park that had been returned to life by a loving infusion of new plants and flowers. Obie played gently with Matthew, who grabbed one of his fingers and wouldn't let go. Obie told her about the battle in which Matt died and of things he had said that day. She cried, and Obie was ashamed he'd ever doubted her love for Matt.

"Matt was my best friend," he said, holding her hand. "You have your life ahead of you, Rosa, and you should go ahead and live it to the fullest. Matt would want that. Be sure to tell Matthew all about his father."

"Oh, yes. I will never forget Matt. I will always honor him."

They talked about many things. There had been no trace of her father. She would not give up, however. She had stayed in Rome awhile, delaying Matt's request to return to Naples. Matt's parents were coming to see them as soon, she said.

"Rosa, are you going to stay in Italy? Matt told me his father tried arranging for you to go to the United States. What will you do?"

"I will stay here. This is my home. I must still search for my father. I have told Matt's parents in my letters, and they understand. They have offered to help. I have declined. They are wealthy, but I prefer to make my own way."

Obie admired this girl whose pride was so out of proportion to her size. They were together for more than an hour. He held her close and kissed her cheek when the time came for parting. "Goodby, Rosa. I'll not forget you."

She called after him, "We will see each other again someday, somewhere."

* * *

The evening before he was to board the ship, Obie packed and discarded items that wouldn't fit into his duffle bag. Although he had few souvenirs, he kept the Luger. Soldiers were not supposed to take weapons home, but nearly everyone did by hiding them deep within their duffle bags.

While discarding his frayed fatigue jacket, a pocket revealed the Bible he'd taken from the young German soldier's body. He was undecided about whether or not to keep the Bible until he saw bloodstains on the back. He didn't need a reminder about his hasty actions that had destroyed a life without cause. It didn't help that he'd reported the incident to his commanders and had them declare him innocent of any wrongdoing.

He was ready to follow his impulse and toss the Bible into a trash retainer along with the jacket when he noticed the ribbon bookmark. Curious, he opened the Bible to see that the soldier had underlined a passage.

How strange. He'd once looked to his own Bible for guidance. Now, he held the Bible of a man he'd not known—would never know. He must have looked to this Bible for guidance and prayed in quiet times. Not only had the man's prayers gone unanswered, one impetuous squeeze of a trigger had assured that they never would be answered.

Obie dug into his bag on impulse until he found his own Bible and placed it beside the German one. They were alike, with similar black bindings, and were about the same thickness. He leafed through the German Bible. Although unable to read it, he could identify books and familiar passages. He looked at the underlined portion and the heading. It was Psalm 121. He grabbed his own Bible and read the passage he had underlined before their last battle— Psalm 121. The passages underlined were nearly identical, as well as he could determine.

Events of the past two years came crashing in on Obie: Death and destruction; Rosa with her bright eyes and starved body; friends gone, and Matt's death. All that was enough to deal with, but now this, a bloody knot that would tie him to a young German soldier who had died at his hands. Obie sought out a dark corner where he might vent his grief.

Part Three

1945–1948

Wine

CHAPTER THIRTY–SIX

November 1945–September 1946

"Come home with us, son," Ken Gainsworthy said. "Lots of folks there are wanting to see you."

"Dad, I have other things to do."

Obie remained firm in his decision; he would not return to Stafford Rest, and Abigail Hunt wasn't a factor in that decision. After two years in the Italian campaign, her threats were as fluff on the wind. He was going to California, to Berkeley. His acceptance letter to the university, which Ken had forwarded, reached him in late October while he was still mustering out.

Nevertheless, he went to New York City to spend three whirlwind days with Ken, Abner, Claire, Angie, and Izzie. The city was bursting at the seams with returning service members. His family had traveled there at Ken's insistence for a time of dining and reconnecting. Angie took Obie to several stores for a supply of new civilian clothing.

Even while knowing that Obie was determined to forsake Stafford Rest, Ken had a persuasion strategy. "There's a heap of respect for you there, now," he said. "You don't have to go to a school so far away. You talked about forestry once. You could go to Paul Smith's College. It's close to home."

"Dad, I'm going to Berkeley. It's a good school. I never thought I'd have such a chance, but doors have opened for me."

"I've missed you, son. I wish you'd come home."

Such an admission from his father was rare. Obie was tempted to relent and make a brief visit to Stafford Rest but then resisted the notion. When he saw them off at Grand Central Station, he said to his father, "I'll write."

Obie stood on the station platform and watched them through their coach windows. Ken took a seat by Angie; that had occurred with regularity during their reunion. Could there be amorous feelings between his father and his amiable and pretty aunt? Probably not. Their closeness was undoubtedly a family thing.

Obie's next stop was in Virginia. He'd feared Matt's family

might harbor resentment because he'd survived the war and Matt had not. The worry was unfounded; Mervin Burroughs couldn't hear enough about his son's part in their battlefield encounters. Carla left the room when those conversations started. Tina, their daughter, often sat on the perimeter listening. However, the whole family participated in a discussion where Obie told them of Rosa and her son.

"We're making plans to go see them as soon as we can," Carla said. "What's he like . . . little Matthew?"

"Reddish hair, fair skin, blue eyes. A lot like Matt."

"What about Rosa?" Tina asked. "Tell us about her."

"We know quite a bit already," Mervin said. "We've corresponded. You can judge a person pretty well by their writing, even through a third party. She's learning English, but the writing part seems hard for her."

"We like her," Carla said.

Tina was wistful. "Maybe she'll eventually come here with Matthew. I know she'd be like a sister. She's only three years older." She turned to Obie. "I'm sixteen now, you know."

Mervin asked, "You're how old, Obie? About twenty-one?"

"Nineteen."

"You look older," Carla said, placing a hand on his cheek. After a moment, she continued. "We've tried hard to persuade Rosa to come here. We had it all arranged once, but she refused. She told us why she feels that way, but I'd like your opinion."

"You have to understand Rosa's situation," Obie said. "She's devoted to her family. They all suffered terribly through the war. Her mother was sick and malnourished, as were Rosa and her sisters. Her two brothers were away with the Resistance, and her father was taken to northern Italy by the Nazis as a slave laborer. He's still missing. I don't think they'll find him alive, but she refuses to give up hope. That's probably the reason she wants to stay in Italy."

"What terrible things to endure," Carla said.

Obie wanted them to understand the extent of their daughter-in-law's bravery. "I'm sure you heard this from Matt, but I'll tell you again. She walked from Naples to Rome by herself, looking for her father. She went through brutal mountainous terrain and Allied and enemy lines, and she was pregnant with Matthew at the time. She was skin and bones when she found us."

"That was when they married, wasn't it . . . after she reached Rome?" Carla rubbed tears from her eyes.

"Yes, it was."

Obie told them about the ceremony, the borrowed dress, the reluctant chaplain, and the sendoff to Rome for a short honeymoon. He was pleased to tell them about the peaceful days the couple had enjoyed at Tarquinia.

"We're still hopeful we can bring her and Matthew here," Mervin said. Obie didn't voice his opinion that it was unlikely.

Obie stayed a week with the Burroughs family before heading south. At the train station, he promised to write. Tina kissed him on his mouth before he could turn his head away. "Write to me, too," she whispered.

He made no promise; Tina was pleasant and obviously wanted more than friendship. Obie had no desire for that; it would dishonor Matt's sister to pretend he did.

Later, on the train, he wondered about himself. Was he normal, or had something been broken? He'd considered Laura exorcised from his head, but sometimes it seemed she was still there, lurking in a dark corner.

And what of Cassie? What was she thinking? *Was she really in love with him? Maybe she was.* He wanted to love her that way—if he could only straighten himself out. He'd have arranged a meeting with her if she hadn't been away at school. Maybe he could make that happen soon so they could have a real discussion.

He took his time traveling. Most of his Army pay had been saved, and after mustering out, he possessed what seemed a sizable amount of money. In Key West, he stayed in a boarding house by the water, sleeping late, walking on sandy beaches, and eating like a starved lumberjack. He lounged in luxury through Thanksgiving and Christmas before going to Tampa. After a few days there, he took a bus up the west coast of Florida, followed by a leisurely train trip through the southern states and across Texas, New Mexico, and Arizona.

He bought tickets to cities he'd marked on a map, places he'd read about or heard mentioned by other soldiers. He stayed a day or two at some locations, bought another ticket, and rode on to the next destination. It was more expensive traveling in that fashion, but he enjoyed soaking up the essence of interesting cities.

He reached San Diego the middle of January, poorer, but rested in mind and body. It was a city he liked, and he would have stayed longer had not arriving in Berkeley on time been a factor.

* * *

Adam met his train in Oakland a few days before the start of the second semester. He insisted Obie move in with him in his small house near campus. Obie had intended to live in a dorm, but Adam convinced him otherwise. "I'm pulling rank," he declared. "Half rent here isn't much more than you'd pay the school. Besides, I don't like living alone, and I'm betting you wouldn't like living with a bunch of rowdy students."

"The university might make me live on campus."

"You're a veteran. You have privileges. Anyway, my uncle can fix that."

It took only a day or two for Obie to fall in love with the University of California at Berkeley. The buildings, the grounds, the sounds, and even the soil seemed special. The scent of eucalyptus trees permeated the air. Even so, he was appalled at what appeared to be chaos in the students' everyday activities on campus.

"I accept that everyone here has their own ideas about anything and everything," he said to Adam, "but I don't understand why they feel compelled to tell everybody, and loudly, at that."

Adam laughed. "Adjust, Obie. You're no longer in the military or the Adirondacks. This is an open culture. Ideas here matter more than the chain of command . . . or lumber."

Obie was defensive for a moment and nearly responded with, "Ideas are not scarce in my mountains." With a touch of sadness, he realized his own choices made him ineligible to claim the Adirondacks as *his* mountains.

"It seems to fit you well here, Adam. You look content."

Obie had noticed a significant change in his friend. Having been in school an entire semester, Adam appeared relaxed and exhibited little of the bellicose behavior so evident during the last months of the war. His mood grew dark only when speaking of his father's unsuccessful attempts to discover the fate of his relatives.

For the most part, Adam appeared to be a new person. "I've found a place here," he said. "I'm able to continue my education in an atmosphere of peace and acceptance. I'm not 'that crazy Jew' anymore."

Obie's first encounter with Hershel Silverman occurred soon after he completed registration. It was memorable. Adam escorted him to his uncle's office on the second floor of a building near "The Tower."

The man behind the big oak desk was diminutive, his slender face dwarfed by masses of unruly beard and hair. How could Adam possibly be related?

Adam introduced them and started to sit down, but Dr. Silverman waved him toward the door. When they were alone, Dr. Silverman said, "Obadiah, my nephew gives you high marks."

"I'm hopeful that I can live up to his expectations. And, I want to thank you for the help you've given me."

"It's nothing, young man, compared to what men like you have been through. It was my pleasure to expedite matters related to your enrollment at Berkeley, but I can't take much credit for that. Your high school records were in order, and I'm sure you would have been accepted even without my help. But, tell me about yourself."

After Obie had given him a brief history of his family and his early mountain environment, the professor asked, "And what are you studying? What will be your major?"

"Journalism. And I expect to have a minor in art."

"A rich combination, and I hope you'll take some courses in my field of psychology, as well."

"Thank you for that suggestion. I certainly will."

"A word of advice, Obadiah. Your letter to me shows that you'll need work on structure, grammar . . . that sort of thing."

Obie felt apprehension at the professor's words, having been sure he'd written a masterpiece.

Dr. Silverman seemed to see his discomfort. "Oh, no, Obadiah. I didn't mean to criticize so heartlessly. Those things you will learn easily. I was going to say that I admire how you write from the heart. That's not something learned. You either have it or not. I venture to say you'll be a success in your chosen field. I have an extensive private library and can point out a few books that will be valuable for you to read, to form a good foundation, so to speak . . . and to inspire you."

He stood and went to a bookcase by a window, took a volume and handed it to Obie. "Have you read Sandburg?"

"Carl Sandburg? Yes, some." He hoped that wouldn't be tested.

"Do you remember what he said in a poem, 'Nothing happens unless first we dream?' There are other dream sayings of his in this volume. Take it with you."

"That's very kind of you, sir."

"You will pursue your dream wholeheartedly, will you not?"

"Yes, sir, I will." The professor's mention of pursuing dreams brought something to mind. "My grandfather had a saying about looking to the future. He called it 'making wine.'"

"Ah, yes. I see. Patience for waiting for the good thing to come. Your grandfather is a wise man."

"He died last year. I'll miss his wisdom."

Dr. Silverman was studying his face. "I mentioned 'success' earlier. What does success mean for you, Obadiah? Is it money?"

Obie had struggled for survival in Stafford Rest, so his thoughts about wealth had taken on some significance. Nevertheless, he suspected Dr. Silverman wanted to downplay its importance, and pleasing Dr. Silverman seemed important. How would Jacob, who had little use for money, answer the professor's question?

Obie chose his words carefully. "Success is having the happiness of knowing you're helping someone. Money's less important."

Dr. Silverman nodded, appearing pleased with the answer, but said, "My brother, Adam's father, runs a successful financial firm in New York City. As for me, I draw a decent salary as a professor at an acclaimed university. I provide sufficiently for my young wife. I'm far from rich, however. I spend little except to supply us with basic needs such as food, housing, and books. Please excuse my lack of modesty, Obadiah, but my teaching and council do have far-reaching effects. Now, who do you think helps humanity more, my brother or me?"

Obie answered confidently, "You, sir."

Dr. Silverman smiled and said, "Simple answers are not necessarily truth. My brother is rich and uses those riches to aid hospitals, schools, and municipalities. During the war, he made countless trips abroad to aid Jews and other persecuted groups, often at great risk to himself. In addition, he provides scores of scholarships to colleges and universities. He doesn't have to do that. He does it out of a sense of responsibility. He touches far more lives than I ever could. My point is, Obadiah, in following your dream . . . or making your wine, you should not be overly prejudiced against personal wealth. How you use it is what counts. It's also well to know that arriving at answers is not always simple. Truth can be slippery."

They talked of many other things, and when Obie left Silverman's office, he felt his brain had been sucked dry. Was that how it would be, professors reaching into his depths to find out what was there?

Once the semester was underway, they found time to take out-ings. The Bay and cities along its eastern shore captivated Obie. They took a ferry once to San Francisco, where he was overwhelmed by the number of people, much the same feeling he'd had in New York City.

Adam had purchased a used Cadillac soon after his arrival. He took Obie to Walnut Creek across the eastern hills and Santa Rosa farther north. They ventured into the Napa Valley wine country, often stopping to sample the many varieties.

In time, he absorbed the knowledge that he had complete free-dom to study, learn, and think for himself. He sensed the beginning of an era where he could pursue what he'd long believed beyond his reach, a chance to become, as Jacob had stated, "whatever you want to be."

But frequent nightmares tainted his complete happiness with vague figures of men in battle flashing before him. Particularly dis-turbing was the recurring face of the young German soldier at the wall.

Their little cottage was on a side street, tucked between two larger residences. Separate bedrooms and a common area adjoining a tiny kitchen gave privacy and, at the same time a sense of togeth-erness. Outside walls were stucco, and the roof was covered with red tile. Sloping up from the sidewalk, the miniature front yard held a cornucopia of flowers and plants, many of a variety Obie had not seen before. Some appeared dormant because of the time of year. A small covered back porch with two wicker chairs invited disengage-ment from serious activity. A lemon tree grew within reach from a porch railing. Birds flitted back and forth with regularity and stun-ning variety. And this was winter, Obie marveled.

He worried at first that his GI Bill money, supplemented by part-time work in a campus library, would not suffice. That worry was mitigated by a letter from Pinky Hunt. The letter did more than promise to relieve financial difficulty; it cleared up a mystery and gave him new insight into Grandfather Jacob's character.

Dear Obie,   *February 27, 1946*
When Ken told me you were enrolled at Berkeley University, I could hardly keep from whooping for joy. He called it good fortune, but I quickly corrected him on that. What the government is giving you is a little payback for your sacrifices for your country. It's not a debt fully paid because no amount of money can repay what we owe

you boys who went so far away and fought for a cause so worthy. We're all genuinely proud of you, Obie.

A check is enclosed. You will receive that amount each month as long as you are in school, in both undergraduate and graduate work, should you go on to that. You might be confused about where this money comes from. Abner and Ken have said you know nothing about it.

After your mother died, you and Ken needed a little extra help. Stafford Rest has good people. They step up to help. Churches step up, too. And there is also this fund from which your present check is drawn. You and I once talked about the Love Fund. You received a small amount from it while in high school, as several others did.

What you have not known, Obie, is that your grandfather, Jacob Gainsworthy, is responsible for the fund's existence. You undoubtedly think of him as a good and humble man who loved his family more than his life. He was that, but he was also responsible for bringing hope to the lives of numerous people.

I once told you about his saving the life of a man named Bernard Templeton. Templeton owned a factory in New England and was wealthy. When he died, he left a part of his fortune to Jacob. Jacob never felt he earned the money, and after talking it over with Prissy, your grandmother, they decided to give it away. The Love Fund is the result. They set it up with my help soon after settling in Stafford Rest. Jacob asked me to administer the fund as long as I wished to do so. Once I die or give it up, Abner has the power to appoint another administrator or administer it himself. Your father comes after him, and you will be in line after that for as long as money is left in the fund. There is still enough to last for many years.

As administrator of the Love Fund, I have determined that your educational endeavors qualify you to receive this stipend. Accept it with gratitude, Obie, for it's intended for just such a situation as yours. Do not think you are receiving it because you are related to the benefactor, for Jacob instructed me that I was not to extend favoritism to anyone, including his family. He also instructed me that his identity as the benefactor is not to be revealed in his lifetime except to family members. I and some bank officials are the only persons outside your family who know of it. Since Jacob's death, your family has been free to do as they like concerning the secrecy. Abner and Ken have indicated they wish to continue it. You, too, will have to decide at some future date.

Sometime, you may be in a position to help others. Remember

Jacob and Prissy and the example they set.
    Obie, I wish you the best in your new endeavor. I've always known you as an exceptional young man, and I'm sure that hasn't changed. Come and see me when you return to Stafford Rest.

                    Your servant and friend, Pinkerton Hunt

The enclosed check nearly equaled the amount of his monthly GI Bill check. He would be able to concentrate on his studies without undue worry about expenses. More important was the knowledge about what his grandparents had done. They'd scorned wealth to help others in need. Would he do the same if he had that choice? To be honest, he wasn't sure.

                    *   *   *

The Silvermans invited Adam and Obie to dinner about once a month. As Adam had said, Virginia Silverman was a beautiful and dynamic woman who appeared half his uncle's age. Obie's impression on first meeting her was that the marriage was a huge mismatch, but when he saw how they interacted and anticipated each other's needs, he changed his mind. The meals she served were simple but elegant.

At home, Obie and Adam took turns cooking. The assortment of available fruits and vegetables was staggering. In his early teen years, Obie learned to cook to survive. Food choices had been limited to Adirondack produced vegetables and fruits, fresh, dried, and canned, along with eggs, fish, chicken, venison, and occasionally beef or pork. He had a few recipes made up of simple combinations of those foods. Obie was at a loss about what to do with many things his roommate brought home. Adam, disgusted, bought a cookbook. "Use this," he said, thrusting the thick volume at Obie. "I'm a little tired of your vegetable soup."

The meals improved. Only once did Obie draw Adam's ire. Avocado-stuffed pork chops were not well received.

"Jews don't eat pork," Adam said, pushing his plate back as he reached for an orange from the fruit bowl.

Obie was irritated. "Since when have you started practicing your religion?" "If you have, shouldn't you be going to synagogue?"

"You're still a Christian, aren't you?"

"I'm not sure."

"And I never see you going to church."

"Your point's well taken, but I'm sure your rules prohibit you from eating other things. I wouldn't even know you're a Jew if I weren't already aware of it."

Adam paused. "You're right. I'm being hypocritical. It shows how difficult it is to be a purist at anything, and I'm certainly not trying to do that. Any attempt on my part to keep kosher went out the window the day I enlisted in the military. I have relatives who follow the traditional Law and think I live in sin. I don't believe I live in sin, but I *do* draw the line at some things."

"No more pork," Obie said as he raked the chop from Adam's plate onto his own. "I'll heat up some left-over vegetable soup."

"God help us," Adam said, but with a smile.

The weeks flew by. Obie was so engrossed in his studies that images of war, Stafford Rest, and Laura became muted. A letter from Cassie served briefly to lift his head above academic waters.

Dear Obie,   *May 3, 1946*

I'm so angry with you! Really angry! I've not heard from you since the letter you wrote from Virginia. If you had told me you would be in New York City last October, I would have skipped school and gone to see you. As it was, I didn't get your California address until I was home recently. Your dad gave it to me.

You may not know this. Laura's baby was born in September last year and died in December. Benjamin Williamson was never well. They are both devastated. Mom, as usual, went there to help. You were already discharged from the Army by then, and I didn't know how to get in touch with you. Your father said you took a long trip through the south before starting school.

I'm so happy for you about Berkeley. It's an outstanding school. Please write and tell me all about it. I'm finishing my second year at Syracuse. I love it here. Aunt Lorena takes good care of me. I see Frances Gibbons occasionally. She still walks with a cane but manages to get around as well as anyone. We had one class together. She's really intelligent. I wish I had known her better...and sooner. That's Mom's fault. She never let us invite her to our parties, although I guess that doesn't surprise you.

Do you realize we've not seen each other for nearly three years? Ken showed me a picture they took of you in New York. You're so handsome. You've also changed, I noticed. There's a more serious look. But I know you're still Obie. I've enclosed a recent picture of

me. I hope it doesn't mess up the mail too much. Ha, ha.
I'm not really angry with you. Just annoyed. I can't wait to
hear from you.

Love, Cassie

The picture was small, a headshot, the kind taken in a photo booth. It struck him as he looked at the photograph that Cassie was beautiful. Her corkscrew hair was cut short, still curly, and with ringlets that looked manageable. Her face was full, her eyes wide apart. Her lips retained her pouty aspect, suggesting an independent spirit. He remembered how she looked when challenged, the way her facial expression reacted to whatever didn't please her. He was surprised by the strength of his sudden desire to see her. She would probably go home for the summer. Maybe he should relent and go to Stafford Rest—simply to see Cassie.

That idea didn't materialize; Adam went to New York to work for his father, a chore he called "dues to be paid." He handed Obie his car keys the night before his departure.

"I don't drive. I've never driven an automobile in my life."

"Well, you're a driver now. How else will you take me to the airport and bring the car back? I'll give you a lesson in the morning on the way."

"Don't I need a driver's license?"

"Not unless you get caught without one. I guess I can leave you mine, though."

"Adam, I'll wreck it for sure."

"Then we'll get another one. He laughed. "Maybe, though, it'd be good to get a license. Might be handy someday."

Obie had his license within two weeks of Adam's departure and, taking his friend's word about using the vehicle, spent part of the summer exploring places he might never have otherwise.

He had two dates with Wanda, a junior mathematics major. After their second date, consisting of a movie and a stop at a soda fountain, he realized he couldn't even remember her last name; he didn't ask her out again.

He took a week alone, visiting the Sacramento area and Lake Tahoe. From there, he drove down Route 49 through the mountains, river valleys, and little towns to San Jose before turning north again. Another time, he went up the coast to the Oregon state line. When Adam returned in early September, Obie was eager to return to classes and continue his most excellent adventure.

* * *

Cassie passed up a job opportunity in Syracuse to go home for the summer, hoping that Obie would return to Stafford Rest. It soon became apparent that he had things on his mind besides his hometown and the people there. He evidently meant what he'd said about not going back.

Laura, Ben, and Danny came home for three days in August. Laura looked gaunt and seldom smiled. Ben spent most of his time with his father, with whom he'd mended relations.

Cassie wanted to talk to Laura about Obie. They were on the patio the evening before the Williamsons were to leave for home. Cassie had long been curious about why Laura had married Ben. However, her most urgent desire was to know that Laura was not still an obstacle between Obie and herself. She wanted to take a direct approach with her sister but decided a circuitous one was better.

"Do you have a good life in Boston, Laura?"

"If you mean aside from losing a child . . . yes, I guess it's a good life."

"Ben's a good doctor, isn't he?"

"Yes, he is. He's making a name for himself. The only trouble is that he's not home much. I get lonely."

"You have Danny. I'm sure your little boy makes life interesting?" Cassie enjoyed the two-year-old who was into everything, keeping her mother on edge about all the vases and knick-knacks in the house.

"He does. I've never seen such an inquisitive child. He started talking six months ago and hasn't stopped since." She smiled, a rare occurrence, it seemed to Cassie.

"Mom said your house is huge."

"Much more than we need. I was against buying it. Ben wanted to entertain guests, part of his plan to expand the practice by courting the well-to-do."

"It seems to have worked."

"Cassie, you must come to visit sometime."

"I've never been to Boston except when we were little, and I don't remember it."

"Why don't you stop in before going back to school? You could stay several days."

Cassie giggled. "Your geography is bad, sister. Syracuse is in the other direction."

Her sister laughed, for a moment resembling the Laura of old. "You know what I mean. You probably need to get away from Mom about this time."

"I had a letter from Obie a month ago," Cassie said, trying to sound casual.

Laura quickly sat upright. "Oh, and what's he up to?"

"He's in California. He's going to Berkeley and has already completed a semester. He bragged to me that he received straight A marks."

"Did he come home . . . back here?"

"His family met him in New York when he returned from Europe. Ken says he refused to come home, and Obie told me he'll never come back."

Laura turned her head away. "He never thought he could go to college. Now he has the chance, and I'm sure he'll do well."

Cassie could wait no longer. "Laura, what happened between you and Obie? You were so much in love . . . or you said you were. Why did you marry Ben?"

Laura stared at Cassie, her eyes narrowing. "People change. But I'd rather not talk about it."

"I'm your sister, Laura. We've always talked."

"Cassie, I love you. You know that. Maybe someday I'll share it with you, but not yet. Ben was there for me. There was a time at first when I regretted marrying him . . . but we've moved past that. I'm as content as I can be, I guess."

"You're not sorry about giving Obie up?"

"That's the past, Cassie. I can't live in the past."

"Obie and I are friends, as always, but I want more than that, as you may have guessed."

"You've told me often enough." Laura appeared pensive as she added, "Don't pin all your hopes on something that may never happen. You can do better than Obie Gainsworthy."

Cassie wanted to say, "As you decided to do?" She said, instead, "You sound just like Mom."

"Is that so bad? She's sometimes abrasive, but she's been supportive in more ways than I can count."

Cassie was misty-eyed the following morning as she watched Ben back their car from the driveway. It was apparent, despite brave words, that Laura was unhappy. On the bright side, she had clearly abandoned her feelings for Obie. Obie was free to love whomever he wished. With all her heart, Cassie wanted it to be herself. She would be patient—for a while.

CHAPTER THIRTY–SEVEN

May 1947–September 1948

Another school year passed; it was Adam's graduation day. After the ceremony, Obie and Adam walked back to the house. Adam was leaving for New York the following morning. They talked past midnight, emptying two bottles of wine.

Adam was an economics major with an enviable school record. Obie knew his plans but felt compelled to ask, "What do you do now?" The question was fueled by his opinion that Adam was not pleased with the prospects of joining his father's financial firm.

"What, indeed? I do as Father wishes."

"But, is it what you want to do?"

"You have to understand . . . when Father calls, you answer."

It sounded little like Adam, the soldier who marched to a drumbeat not heard by others—nor Adam, the squad leader Obie credited with bringing him through the war. "Is your father excited about having you join the business?" Obie asked.

"Father doesn't get excited over such things. Anyway, I apprenticed there two summers before joining the Army and again last summer, so he's accustomed to my presence. He expects me to be there."

"Surely, he'd understand if you wanted to do something else."

"When Father sets his mind on something, there's no changing it. That's been a blessing for accumulating wealth, but it's tough on the people around him."

"What about your sister?" Obie knew she'd graduated from Columbia two years earlier.

"Naomi could probably handle it. She's a woman, though. I'm heir to Father's financial enterprise, at least in his eyes. Anyway, Naomi's interest is in our publishing business. She has a foot in the door there."

"Adam, what is it you'd really like to do?" Obie knew he might be pushing it.

Adam shrugged. "I'm not sure. But I believe there's something out there for me. I feel it, but I can't put my finger on it. I do wish I had more time to look. This work that Father wants me to do is quite lucrative. It's hard to turn down."

"You'd survive without much money. I do."

"You've learned how. I haven't. Sorry, that sounded arrogant. I didn't mean anything by it."

"It's okay. I sometimes take too much pride in being poor." They laughed, but Obie questioned again how Adam had become so subservient to his father. He stopped short of saying so.

"What about you, Obie? Are you going to do what you want to do?"

"Journalism. It's my career. Newspaper work, most likely, and I hope to have time to freelance."

"Maybe it'll be your profession, but I think you still have things to sort out. Your preacher friend . . . Lansing, isn't it? He once convinced you that you were destined for some kind of do-gooder work, maybe in the religious field?"

"You have an excellent memory, Adam. I haven't mentioned him for years. No, I've put that idea behind me. You know all the doubts I have about religion."

Adam raised an eyebrow. "We'll see, but we've become too serious." He raised his glass. "To the future . . . in whatever form it presents itself."

"To the future," Obie echoed.

The following day, as he helped Adam load his belongings into the car, Obie said, "When you left Italy, I believed I'd see you again. This time, I feel more uncertainty about it."

"I'll come back to visit."

"You must. We have a history."

"I'll write, too. You're my good friend, Gainsworthy. The distance between here and New York won't make that much difference."

Nevertheless, as he watched the Caddy pull out, heading toward the Sierra Nevada Mountains, Obie felt that an essential chapter of his life had ended.

* * *

During the summer of the year Adam left, Obie worked in a warehouse in Oakland. He needed both physical activity and money. The house's full rent payment would be a financial drain, so he advertised for a new housemate, but it was fall before a morose and taciturn senior moved in. Obie was counting the days until spring when the man would leave—and he wasn't going to advertise for a new housemate. He would manage it himself.

His time at Berkeley was passing quickly. By the end of that school year, he had crammed as many credit hours as allowed into each semester and was looking forward to entering the fall term as a senior. Working so hard had allowed little time for a social life.

There were many interesting women on campus, and he dated some without any intention of having a serious relationship. Clara Pemberton, also a journalism major, came closest to winning his genuine interest. She wanted intimacy, and he was unable to commit to that. After he ended it, they remained cordial in their daily contact, although he detected a coolness when they happened to be alone.

Adam came back in April. He was in San Francisco for two days on company business and managed to free up a couple of hours. Their reunion was pleasant, for the most part.

They met for lunch near campus. Adam in a suit and tie seemed peculiar. He said he was content in his work, but Obie noted his restlessness. He handled his water glass like a live hand grenade, nervously shifting it from hand to hand. "I'm learning the finer aspects of the business," he said. "My old man's a taskmaster. This is the first time he's trusted me on my own."

"What is it you do?" Obie asked.

They ordered wine, and Adam went into detail about the financial firm's inner workings and his part in it. "There's a lot to know. I'd have been better off starting at a lower level. Father had other ideas. I'm part of a team that analyzes prospective investments and determines their worth. I'm out here to interview two separate companies' leadership and visit their plants."

Adam yawned as he set his wine glass on the table. He seemed to have lost interest in the subject. "Are you in correspondence with Cassie?" he asked.

"We write to each other about once a month."

"No phone calls?"

"I don't have a phone, although I'll have one this fall. She doesn't have ready access to a phone at school, and I hesitate to call her parents' residence when she's in Stafford Rest. She said she'd tried calling me here at the journalism department but didn't get through. It just seems easier to write letters."

"Just friendly letters, I suppose."

"I guess so."

Adam wasted no words in his condemnation of Obie's inaction.

369

"I don't know her except for the things you've told me and the snippets from her letters you read to me in Italy, but you're a fool for ignoring the love of a good woman. If I ever find someone like that, I'll grab her in a minute."

"I don't know if Cassie feels that way about me."

"Don't be dense, Obie. She's in love with you."

"I believed, and hoped for a while, that she might be, but there's nothing in her letters to indicate it. Anyway, how would *you* know? You hardly ever dated while you were here. I don't think you know much about women, Adam." Obie hesitated, feeling as though he might be talking nonsense. He said, "Do you really think she loves me?"

"Yes, you fool. The question is, what are you going to do about it?"

"I'm not sure."

"It's time you show some aggression in the matter, Obie. I know you're capable of anything. I saw it in Italy, and I see it in the way you attack your studies here at Berkeley. It's the same thing. It's called courage."

"I fear courage is a fickle component in this case."

"That may be, but it wasn't absent that night when you decided to stand up against all odds and go look for Lieutenant Howard . . . or when you dragged me along to storm the farmhouse in that last battle."

For a moment, Obie experienced a surge of anger, much like that experienced while attempting to avenge Matt's death. "That was something entirely different . . . and I didn't drag you. You were with me every single step." It was the first time either had mentioned the incident; they had talked little about the war.

Adam hadn't lost sight of his original topic. "If you wait too long, you'll lose her."

Was it possible that Cassie did love him? He'd tried, unsuccessfully, to gauge her thinking based on what she wrote in her letters. He'd put off a discussion with her about their relationship, thinking it might endanger their friendship. But maybe he should initiate a conversation. *Yes, he would, soon.*

He wasn't comfortable discussing the issue with Adam, so he changed the subject. "Your Uncle Hershel told me the sad news about Yarden and his family. I'm sorry."

"All the Germans we killed didn't save them, did it?" Adam said, frowning. "I still struggle with how whole nations of people can let such things happen. It's hard to shed my anger over it."

"The war's over, Adam. Maybe humankind has learned a lesson."

"I doubt it. Injustice marches on. America's not without guilt, either. Look at the way we've treated Negroes . . . and still do. And the same with the Indians. You're in journalism, which gives you the opportunity to stand up against such things."

"I think about that, too."

"Maybe that's what your preacher friend was telling you, write about injustice . . . make a difference."

"I don't know yet what I'm going to write about. I'm still honing my skills."

"And 'forging your future,' as Uncle Hershel often says?"

It seemed a good time to revisit a touchy subject. "Have you truly found your future, Adam?"

Adam appeared pensive. "I'm not sure. Sometimes, I feel like what I'm doing isn't relative to the real needs in the world."

"You can't do everything. You're making money for your firm, aren't you? From what your uncle says, your father is quite charitable. Indirectly, you're helping many people."

"I have trouble with 'indirectly.' I need to be involved. And that reminds me. I have something to tell you, something that could affect your future."

"You're giving me the Caddy?"

Adam laughed. "The old car's long gone. It didn't fit the dignity of my position." He set his wine glass down; he seemed to have waited for the right moment. "Obie, I know you're well aware that I've talked you up to my family, first to Uncle Hershel and then to Father." He cleared his throat. "Father asked me to extend an invitation to visit us as soon as you graduate."

"I'd like that."

"There's more to it than a social visit, although I'm not supposed to tell you. He'll be looking you over, and if he likes what he sees, and I'm sure he will, you'll be offered an editorial position at Silverman Publishing."

"That's more than a year away. However, I am flattered."

"Flattery doesn't have anything to do with it. He needs good people. This will be a serious offer, and being in the business of finding good literature could be your contribution to making a difference in the world."

"Is this your way of making it up to me?"

"I don't know what you mean."

"Don't you remember what you said after the debacle with my relatives in Italy? You said you'd make it up to me for how you treated them. Is that what you're doing?"

Adam smiled. "I believe I did that already. I got you into Berkeley, didn't I?"

"Yes, I guess you did. And I thank you for it."

Adam chuckled. "That wasn't it, though. Telling Father about your superior qualities isn't it either. I have something else in mind."

"What?"

"You'll know when it's time for you to know. I'll remind you. You can count on it."

After Adam left, Obie considered his realistic career choices. A job in a company such as Silverman Publishing would give him a position of relative security or be a huge stepping stone. On the other hand, journalism had captured his imagination. To be a reporter for a prominent newspaper would suit him perfectly. Even more appealing was freelance work, allowing him the freedom to explore areas of his choosing. He was glad he still had a year to figure it out.

His twice-a-year correspondence with Charles Lansing continued. Charles had been appointed pastor of a church in western Vermont. He knew about Obie's "spiritual uncertainty" and was sympathetic in his counsel. Obie shared his wartime experiences with the pastor—all but one. He'd spoken to no one in his circle of friends about the young German soldier at the wall. Even Silverman didn't know what happened there.

In one letter, Charles wrote:

> *You say one reason for your estrangement from God is because such bad things happened in the war. Yes, your dear friend died even after you prayed for him to live. Yes, you saw others die horrible deaths. Why could God not have stopped it from happening, you say? I don't have answers to those questions any more than you do. We may never know this side of the vale. I do believe that when we place ourselves in God's hands, He looks out for us even when circumstances make us believe otherwise. Despite what you have said and what you may think, <u>He does answer prayer.</u> Like a good parent, we sometimes forget that His answer might be "wait." Or even "no."*
>
> *Obadiah, I believe you really do feel the way you say you do. You've said it many times in the past few years. I would like you to*

do something for me (and for yourself.) I would like you to go into
the wilderness. Do you remember that Jesus went into the wilderness
before beginning his ministry? I would like you to do likewise. I don't
mean to go for forty days and forty nights. Maybe three would do.
You don't even have to fast if you don't want to. Go somewhere
private and pray. Pray hard even though you don't feel like your
prayers are going anywhere. Maybe you won't even believe there is
anyone there to answer. I'll be interested in hearing the results."

Charles' suggestion had little appeal; the preacher was a dreamer. Nevertheless, he was a dear friend who'd helped through difficult times, and doubting his word seemed disrespectful. In truth, Obie had severed nearly all religious ties since the war. He'd only once attended a church service, stopping at a little Methodist church off San Pueblo. He'd not planned to enter the church but was merely walking by when his feet seemed directed toward the church steps. Nevertheless, while there, he experienced little affinity; it was as though the voices of Charles and Forrester had been silenced.

He had an interesting experience on Mt. Diablo that spring. He hitchhiked there to climb the peak alone, an outing he'd planned for some time. As he lay gazing at the night sky, a moment came not unlike the one years before in the snowstorm on Algonquin, a time when he still believed prayers were answered. His accepting that snow-blown event as significant was, of course, an illusion, the harbinger of a broken heart. Nor had prayer saved Matt. Therefore, the peace he felt while lying under the stars on Mt. Diablo was unexpected and somewhat unsettling. With the naked universe stretched out above him, words finally formed in his mind; he said aloud, "I don't know what you want of me, Lord."

That event was hard to forget. Gradually, however, he shoved thoughts of it aside. What Charles wanted for him no longer held allure. *He would determine his own future.* He had a "real world" decision to make; he would soon decide whether to pursue a journalism career or work for Silverman Publishing.

Nevertheless, a hint of expectation hovered around him, subtle, like a whispered promise. And thoughts of Cassie came often.

* * *

During the summer before the beginning of his senior year, Obie took a job at a vineyard in the Russian River Valley. The work paid less than the previous summer's warehouse job, but it was more pleasant. The vineyard rolled across three hills, an oasis of green against the brown hills of adjacent cattle ranches. When Moses Alfonso, the manager, presented him with several possibilities for places he might bunk, including a former processing shed with other workers, he chose a shack on the summit of a hill instead. The little building had been a tool shed and was barely large enough for a bunk, a chair, and a small table. He went for meals in the basement of the "big house."

Near the end of summer, Obie told Moses, "I'd like to stay on three extra days, and I want to stay where I've been bunking if you don't mind."

Moses rubbed his chin as if he suspected a catch. "You'd want meals, I suppose?"

"Not even that. I just want to stay there awhile . . . three days."

Moses laughed. "Can't say I've ever had anyone make such a request. But sure, why not."

"One thing. I don't want to be disturbed. No one is to bother me."

"Oh, I get it. You're going to take someone up there for a little private time. Bet I know who it is. Is it that little doll from Santa Rosa, the one with pigtails? I'll bet that's who it is."

"No, Moses. I really do want to be alone. I need a quiet place to think." Moses shrugged his shoulders.

His explanation to Moses was partially true. Out of respect for Charles, Obie would take his advice about "going into the wilderness." Not that a vineyard near a major highway along the Russian River was much of a wilderness, but it *was* a serene and beautiful location.

His predominant hope was to sort out career decisions—journalism or publishing. He had his Bible with him—because Charles would ask about it. He would also fast for three days. He wanted Charles to be happy that he'd sought spiritual guidance, although he believed the preacher would suffer disappointment. He intended to give his friend a truthful account, whatever it might be.

Obie gave it his best effort for two days. He read scripture from various parts of his Bible, sometimes aloud. He struggled for answers to fill a void he couldn't identify. Nor did he decide on his career choice. There was a feeling of depression on the eve of the day he was to take a bus back to Berkeley.

A kerosene lamp cast a yellow glow around the shack's interior as Obie lay on the bunk. He was tired of reading and courting hope where clear answers were not present. He drank water from a glass jug he'd carried up from the pump by the big house; it would have to keep his stomach satisfied until morning when he would break his fast at a cafe up the road. He meant to stay awake awhile before going out to look at the stars and listen to whippoorwills, but he soon grew sleepy.

His mother was nudging him awake, a familiar occurrence. The lamp had gone out; the fuel bowl was empty. He should have filled it earlier. Nevertheless, there was still enough natural light by which to see. A radiance, casting a glow, surrounded Vi's face.

"My boy," she said, sitting beside him on the bunk and stroking his hair, "have you forgotten me?"

"Mom, I could never forget you. Where have you been? It seems ages since I've seen you."

"Not far. I have not been far away. Come. Come with me," she said as she took his hand and urged him to his feet. Her hand was warm.

They left the shack, and he was surprised that it was daylight. They walked down between rows of vines onto the road leading into Stafford Rest. More quickly than they could have walked, they stood at the steps of Stafford Rest Methodist Church. Familiar faces peered up from a group of people sitting on the stone steps. Grandmother and Grandfather Gainsworthy were there, sitting with Grandmother Petitucci and several older people he remembered.

Jacob stood. "Grandson, you've been right, and you've been wrong," he said.

"How could I have been both right and wrong, Grandpa?"

"You've been right in questioning God. We grow by forming our questions, even when we know we may not get answers. You've been wrong to question God's presence in your life. He's always there above all the rules we've throwed up to hide him. I found him in the mountains, streams, woods, and . . ."

"In love, Grandpa?"

"Yes, in love. Grandson. Love counts above all. Love and hate can't exist side by side. One will drive out the other. You can't expect to find God until the hate's all gone."

"My hate, you mean?"

"Yes, grandson . . . your hate."

"How can I get rid of my hate?"

"Forgiveness. You must forgive. Forgiveness and love save us.

Please give me water, Grandson."

Obie looked down to see a pail so full that water was sloshing over the rim. Vi handed him a long-handled dipper. He filled the dipper and raised it to give it to Jacob.

No. Pour it over me. Drench me."

Obie complied, splashing several dipperfuls on Jacob's head and shoulders. Both his grandmothers rose and stepped forward, followed by others asking for water. He kept throwing water into the air, dousing those who stepped close enough.

"I'm running out of water."

"No, you are not," Vi replied. "Look in the pail."

Water was still splashing over the rim. "How could it be?" he asked.

"The Master always has enough," Vi replied. "Remember how he fed five thousand?"

The crowd on the lower steps thinned. Other figures on the top steps arose and came forward. Matt stood in front of him, a smile on his face.

"Matt, you made it."

"Yes, we all made it." With a flick of his hand, Matt indicated the group of men surrounding him. There were familiar faces. He recognized Grugs, Copland, Rivera, and Burke. Obie poured water on them, one by one. Burke was last.

"Are you surprised to see me here?" Burke asked.

"Yes, Burke, I am."

"His love is extended even to me."

"I remember now, Burke. *You died.*"

Matt said, "Death is an event. It doesn't wipe out everything gone before or what comes after. Lives set off ripples that go on forever."

Three other people, a man, a woman, and a younger woman, came forward. Obie raised the dipper, but the man held up a hand. "We have already received the Spirit from another."

"A different Spirit from this?" Obie asked.

"No, there is only one Spirit. As you are a dispenser of the Spirit here, there are other dispensers as well."

"I'm not a dispenser of anything," Obie protested. "I'm just doing what I was told to do."

"And you must keep on doing what you are told."

"What is your name," Obie asked.

"I am Yarden." He motioned toward two people with him.

"And this is Shira and Jael."

"I know who you are. How could it be? You were . . ."

"Your friend says it well. It is just an event."

A voice came from high up the church steps. The words were spoken in what sounded German, and Obie marveled at how he could understand. "Yes, death is an event, but an unjust death creates a debt . . . and debts must be paid."

Obie felt a crushing sensation in his chest. He shouted, "I know who you are. I killed you." He waited. "I'm sorry."

"I forgive you for that, *but the debt remains.*"

"Pastor Charles said that Christ paid the debt for all of us."

"Of course he did, but do you not feel some personal responsibility?"

Obie tried to get a better view. The man remained indistinct against the church's dark brick and stone wall. "What do I have to do? How do I pay the debt that I owe you?"

"You will know."

In an instant, everyone faded from his sight except his mother. They stood at the foot of the steps. Vi handed him a leash. Obie looked down at Slobber. The dog wasn't old and crippled but young and full of energy, wagging his tail. Obie knelt and ruffled his fur. Slobber licked Obie's face and rolled onto his back with his legs in the air.

"Dogs do that, turn their bellies up and make themselves vulnerable to their masters," Vi said.

"Mom, is all this real?" He was becoming panicky. A yellow light flickered. *"Am I dreaming?"*

"Dreams are often shadows of truth, Obie. They can also be glimpses of things to be."

"What is to be, Mom?"

"What are your dreams, Obie?" The yellow light flickered again, impatient.

"Finding the right path for my life."

"It is laid out for you. But you must find it."

"How?"

"Let your eyes see beyond this moment . . . this time."

"Mom, my eyes have become dim, I think."

"Your soul has eyes, too, Obie. Use the eyes of your soul."

"I have another dream too, Mom. It's about Cassie. I want to know if Cassie loves me, as Adam says."

Vi had a familiar knowing look. "Some things can be learned

by merely asking," she said.

"What about that German soldier? He's angry at me."

"He is not angry at you, Obie. He wants the best for you. He wants you to do what he cannot."

"Which is?"

"Follow your dream."

"It's hard."

"Obie, you must turn your belly up to God."

The yellow light was intense. He became aware of being on his cot. The lamp, flickering because of a breeze blowing through cracks in the wall, cast a glow on the surroundings. He sat up quickly. The vividness of his dream dominated all his senses. His mother's presence had been so real that he still felt the warmth of her hand and heard the inflection in her voice. He had an overpowering urge to pray. Vi's last words resonated in his ears as he knelt beside his bunk: "You must turn your belly up to God."

It seemed a great mystery. How do you surrender yourself fully while continuing to search for a footpath God has designed for you but which he insists you find for yourself?

The remainder of the night hosted a wrestling match pitting him against his ambitions. His previous questions about career options gradually took fall after fall until early morning when an alternate plan emerged the winner. As he walked through the rows of grapevines, hungry but energized, he welcomed the symbolism; this vineyard was to be the starting place toward his finished wine.

CHAPTER THIRTY–EIGHT

August 1948

Cassie scrutinized the long-faced man sitting on the other side of the booth in Beth's Cafe. His early morning telephone call had come from Tupper Lake, where he said he'd spent the night. She suggested they have breakfast in the village instead of on Garnet Point.

"It was easy getting your phone number since there's no other Hunt family in Stafford Rest," he said.

"It's a pleasure to meet you, Adam," she said again after Beth had taken their order. "Obie mentioned you often in his letters."

"Obie and I have quite a history, even though it spans only a few years." He was looking at her with genuine interest. "Cassie, you are as beautiful as Obie has described."

She thought she might be blushing. "He wouldn't say something like that."

"Well, not in so many words, but I'm sure it's how he sees you."

"Adam, why are you here? Stafford Rest's not exactly a tourist attraction."

"Why, it's a charming little town, just as Obie described it. I was in Albany on business and thought I'd take an extra day or two. I want to meet Obie's father, but he has no phone, so I thought you might help me."

"Ken lives on Blackberry Hill. Go on down Main, cross the bridge, turn right on Cedar Creek Road and follow it up to the end. Actually, I can take you there."

"That's not necessary, Cassie. I'm in no hurry. I'll find it."

"You'll like Ken if you admire someone who says pretty much what he thinks."

"Yes, I've gotten that impression from Obie."

"You should know that underneath that spontaneous exterior is a sensitive and kindhearted man."

"Obie told me you'll be teaching here in the elementary school."

"Yes, first grade. I'm starting next week."

Cassie suspected Adam had something else on his mind. He cleared his throat.

"I'm here to pay a debt, Cassie. I did a bad thing to Obie in

Italy. I won't go into detail, but it involved his relatives there. I was disrespectful and told him I'd make it up to him someday. I don't think he took me seriously. I'm hopeful that today I can keep my word."

She put her elbows on the table and leaned closer. "You certainly have my attention."

"I hope I'm not being too personal, but I need to ask you a question."

"All right."

"You *do* love Obie, don't you?"

"That's personal, all right. But, yes, I do love him. More than my own life."

"He loves you too, Cassie."

Her eyes threatened to overflow. "He hasn't told me so."

"Have you told him?"

"No."

"He's unsure about how you feel."

"He could *ask* me how I feel! Why hasn't he?" A wave of anger made her words harsher than she meant. She continued, "Did Obie send you to ask me if I love him? That would be insulting, in my opinion . . . and cowardly."

"Oh, no, he knows nothing of my being here."

Adam's sincerity inspired trust. "We practically grew up together," she said, "and we've corresponded for years. Surely, he's guessed how I feel."

"Cassie, let me tell you something about Obie that you may be too close to see. He's most certainly not cowardly. He's a brave man who'd risk his own life to help another person. He's done that on several occasions, but he suffers internally because of things he's been forced to do against his nature and moral code."

"I haven't seen him for a long time. I'd need to look into his eyes to see what he's been through. What about you, Adam? You were in battle even longer than Obie. Aren't you affected as well?"

"Nobody comes out of a war without scars, Cassie. Some of us can shrug it off better than others. I'm one of the lucky ones, I guess. However, we were talking about Obie's hesitancy in revealing his feelings. Part of it *is* the war. I'm sure of that, but there's also the uncertainty that makes him hold back in affairs of the heart. Maybe he's always been that way."

"Somewhat, but from what you're saying, it seems to have intensified."

"Could it have something to do with what happened between him and your sister?" She saw him hesitate. "I hope I'm not going into forbidden territory here."

"No, it's all right. I'm well aware of the pain Laura caused Obie."

"He's stubborn too, which serves him well in some circumstances. But not in this case. Cassie, I believe you may have the same malady."

"Me, stubborn?" Despite her words of denial, she knew he was right.

Adam smiled. "There's gridlock, and I believe it's up to you to break it."

Maybe it was possible. "How, Adam? What can I do?"

"Simple. Tell him the truth. Forget consequences. Stop worrying about what his reaction will be. Tell him that you love him."

"What if he doesn't love me? What if saying it damages our friendship?"

"Would the situation be any more painful than it is?"

"I guess not."

"Anyway, he does love you. I guarantee it."

"I talked to Ken yesterday. He told me that Obie had decided to go to seminary. That surprises me, considering his religious doubts."

"I hadn't heard that. It must have been something drastic to bring him to that decision."

Their food came. Cassie wasn't sure she could eat. Excitement had welled up the way it had on the ridge when she was sixteen—when Obie kissed her. She managed to force her food down. Their conversation was subdued for the duration of the meal.

After the dirty dishes were cleared away, she said, "What about you, Adam? Obie thinks you're unhappy with your work. Maybe you should forget consequences and find work that pleases you."

"You're right, Cassie. I've come to the same conclusion."

"Good." She shook his hand as they rose to leave. "Thank you, Adam. I see why Obie thinks so much of you. I hope we meet again."

"I'm sure we will, Cassie. Are you going to take my advice?"

"I'll call him tonight."

* * *

It was over a week after Obie's return from the Russian River Valley; the fall term had not yet begun. He'd recently been appointed to a senior staff position for one of the University newspapers, so he had a telephone installed to stay within easy reach of other staff members. He sat beside the stand that held the black instrument, staring at it.

He'd been making momentous decisions lately, and he'd made one concerning Cassie. *He was going to tell her that he loved her.* It was time to put an end to the uncertainty. If she loved him, it'd be wonderful. If not, it would hurt terribly, but they could still be friends.

His hesitation in initiating the call was because Abigail might answer; that was more than a fifty percent possibility. *So what?* He picked up the receiver and dialed the Hunt number. There was a busy signal. He'd try again in a minute or so. He'd no sooner put the receiver down than the phone rang, the sound startling him because it was the first time it had rung since being installed.

The voice was female. It took him only a moment to recognize her voice. "Hello, Cassie," he said.

"I bet you're surprised?"

"Indeed. Where are you?"

"In Stafford Rest. Your dad gave me your number." Her voice still had the same confident resonance.

"I just tried to call you."

"You didn't?"

"I did. I got a busy signal."

"I'd just picked it up the receiver."

"How odd that is, calling each other simultaneously, and after so long. But I've given up trying to figure out how those things happen. His heart was racing. "How are you, Cassie?"

"I'm excited about school opening next week."

"First grade, isn't it?"

"Yes, and I can hardly wait."

"So, you're a teacher? It's what you've always wanted, isn't it?"

"It's *one* thing I want." He felt her hesitation and waited. "Obie, it seems strange talking to you like this. I haven't heard your voice for so many years. You sound older."

"I am older, Cassie."

"Have you started fall classes?"

"Next week. I'm taking a few days off."

"Ken said he'd received a letter from you saying that you'll be going to seminary after this year . . . after you graduate."

"That's right. I don't know where yet. It's a big change of direction for me." He wanted to tell her about his strange experience in the vineyard but stopped short. He'd find a way later to explain it to her.

"So, you'll be a minister?" He detected wonderment in the question.

"Oh, no. More likely in the writing field. Journalism's my major, and it's in my blood now, so I'm sure I'll be writing in some capacity. But I'll serve wherever the Spirit leads me."

"You'll have another year at Berkeley and then . . . what is it, several years in seminary?"

"Three years."

"Where will you go after you finish? Will you return to Stafford Rest?"

"I don't know, Cassie. I love the West Coast, although I'm open to going wherever God wants me."

"Obie, it seems strange hearing you talk about serving God. What's changed you so drastically?"

How could he explain the momentous dream experience in the vineyard that had changed his mindset and launched the one-hundred-dred-eighty-degree turn in his life? He needed someone to untangle it for him before he could explain it adequately to anyone else.

Honesty was best. He said, "Cassie, I'd explain it if I could, but I'm still processing it. All I can say is that God gave me a sign. At least, I think that's what it was. I'll try to explain it better later."

"Okay, but I'm going to hold you to that."

"I *do* want you to understand. It's not an insignificant thing that's happened to me."

It seemed a long time that she was silent. He heard her clear her throat. "Obie, is there anyone in your life now? You know what I mean."

"No, there's no one." *He had to tell her.* "Cassie, there's something I want to say."

"Me too."

"I . . ."

"Obie, are you happy?"

"Reasonably so. I have much for which to be thankful: I survived the war; I'll graduate from college in less than a year, something I once believed was beyond me; I have a career path . . . and a spiritual path to follow. Why wouldn't I be happy?" The only gap in his life was the one only she could fill—and it was time to tell her.

"Obie, I'm going to San Francisco for three days to see a class-mate who lives there. Can I see you too?"

Cassie is coming to Berkeley: It was a revelation so wonderful he had trouble suppressing his joy. He could tell her of his love face to face, far better than over the phone.

"I'd be angry at you if you didn't," he said, adding, "Anyway, there's something I have to tell you." He hoped she wouldn't want an explanation. "When are you coming?"

"Tomorrow."

"Really? That soon?"

"I'll fly out in the morning. Dad's driving me to Albany at an ungodly hour. I'll grab a taxi to your house from Oakland. It's easier to see you first before I go to San Francisco. Obie, what did you mean when you said . . . "

He cut her off, "I'll see you tomorrow, Cassie."

As he cradled the receiver, a thought thrilled him. He put it into words. "I love Cassie. I always have. She's the missing link in my life." He repeated it louder. He didn't care if anyone passing his open window might hear. He believed that she loved him, too. He prayed it might be true. Tomorrow he would know for sure.

* * *

Obie slept little that night. Cassie had given him no definite time of arrival. He guessed it would take seven or eight hours across the country and another hour from the airport. He busied himself around the house all morning until he ran out of things to do. After lunch, he walked surrounding neighborhoods to relieve tension, picking up items at little shops and fruit and vegetable stands along a haphazard route. It was mid-afternoon when he returned home, sweaty and wanting a shower. Thinking he would have a couple of hours to wait, he was surprised to find Cassie sitting on his back porch with a carpetbag valise on the floor beside her.

She rose, not speaking. They fell into each other's arms and held on for nearly a full minute. She finally pushed him back. "You smell worse than a skunk. Where've you been? I've been waiting here for nearly an hour."

He ignored the rebuke. "I've been walking. I thought you'd be later."

"You forgot the time difference, didn't you? I bet I was well on my way before you were even up."

"No, I remembered. I just thought it would take you longer." He held both her hands in his. "Cassie, we have a lot to talk about."

"We do, but first, you go and shower." She gave him a playful shove.

He made small talk loud enough for her to hear while gathering clean clothing from the chest in his bedroom. "Don't go away," he said from the bathroom door.

"Not likely."

Twenty minutes later, they sat on the porch, wine glasses in hand. Cassie told him about her classmate, Judy Ramos, who lived in San Francisco. Judy had been asking her to visit for four years, she said.

Obie stole glances at Cassie, trying not to be obvious. Her blonde hair was a shade darker and shorter. She was more buxom, and her long legs were shapely, as he remembered. Her light blue eyes were seductive with disarming innocence. He'd been able to read Cassie's moods and emotions all his life. So why was he unsure how to proceed with the beautiful and sophisticated young woman sitting beside him?

There was something else, too. A mild discomfort lay unspoken between them as if they were struggling to rediscover each other after an absence of more than five years. Maybe the setting contributed to it; they were in a new place, physically and figuratively.

"I couldn't pass up an opportunity since you're just across the Bay." She glanced away and said, "I'll take the ferry across to meet Judy in the morning. She's expecting me."

"Where are you staying tonight?"

She looked away again. "I'll find a hotel somewhere."

"You can stay here, of course. The extra bedroom is empty . . . unless you think it wouldn't look right."

"Obie, that will be fine if I'm not imposing?"

"You're not, Cassie. Believe me."

"All right." She appeared relieved. "It's so beautiful here. There's a fairyland feel."

"It's too bad you have to go tomorrow. I could show you the campus and several other sights." He'd find a way to make her stay longer.

"Judy's been looking forward to my coming. I don't want to disappoint her."

He heard her sigh. She was avoiding his eyes. He was sure she hadn't come to California to see Judy; she'd come to see him. That fact delighted him. Unlike the Cassie he'd known, she was embarrassed—and aware that he recognized the deception. He wished to ease her discomfort. "How's your father?"

"He's fine. The factory is busy, and he spends most of his time there. Did Ken tell you he's working there? Dad says he's an excellent worker."

"He told me he was going to ask Pinky for a job. I'm happy he's settling in on something. Dad needs steady work. Being busy keeps him out of trouble." A more accurate way to say it would have been, "Away from drink."

"He's going to marry your aunt, isn't he?"

"What makes you say that?" Could it be true? He'd had suspicions about that relationship during their time together in New York City. If there had been serious intent, why had they waited so long?

"Angie comes to Stafford Rest twice a month and stays with Ken. I think he goes to Albany too."

Obie laughed. "Living in Stafford Rest is like living in a glass house, isn't it? The truth is, I don't know what they are to each other. Dad hasn't said anything. He may be forceful in giving his opinions, but he's also close-mouthed about many things."

Obie refilled their glasses. He longed to move the conversation in a more personal direction but said, "And how's your mother?" He was ashamed of the negative images that filled his head.

"Oh, Mom is Mom. You know how she is. She's busy all the time, scheming over some project. She's tried for years to get Dad involved in politics. That's like convincing Rumbles, our cat, to jump into Garnet Creek. She tried to talk me out of coming out here."

"Does she know you planned to see me?"

"I was going to tell her to strengthen my independence, but then I decided I didn't need the hassle. You're well aware of how she might feel about it."

Cassie would be surprised to know how deeply Abigail's disapproval went. He wished the distance between himself and Cassie's mother might be closed and the hurt healed. Lately, he'd forced himself to forgive her, although that was still a job unfinished. If only in a dream, Jacob had told him that he must forgive. "Yes, I know," was his guarded reply to Cassie.

They took a taxi to a restaurant on University Avenue. During dinner, he told her, as well as he could, about the Russian River vineyard experience; it had, he said, "renewed his faith and set him on a new course." He hoped she wouldn't laugh.

She didn't. "Obie, that's marvelous. And the way you tell it . . . I can almost hear Vi saying those things."

"At first, I had to keep telling myself that it was just a dream. And it *was* a dream. I can't imagine that I was actually talking to my mother and all those other people, but I do believe God was showing me something, putting me back on a pathway that's right for me."

"Well, I'm so happy that you're normal again."

He laughed. "That may be pushing it."

"During the war, I worried about your frame of mind."

"What about you, Cassie? You've had your spiritual doubts. Do you still?"

"Not as much. Praying for you all through the war helped, I think. But I admire your ability to push aside doubts and be certain in your faith."

"It involves tossing out the junk."

Cassie leaned forward, intensive. "There's something we never really talked about in our letters. I've worried that you hate my sister for deserting you. Do you? Have you?"

It was like watching a dentist's drill approach; he must put it into actual words. "For years, I had a bad time with it. But I've forgiven. It's part of the junk I've tossed. Hate and love can't exist together. I've booted the hate, and I've forgiven."

"I'm so glad, Obie. I don't understand Laura sometimes, but I love her."

They walked home. He took her hand; *it was finally time.* "What are you thinking about?" he asked.

"Obie, my greatest fear has been that you and I will drift apart, that we let our friendship fade away."

He squeezed her hand. "That won't ever happen. You got me through the war, you know. You don't know what your letters meant to me. We'll always be friends." They stopped on a corner under a palm tree. He turned to face her. "Cassie, I think we may be more than friends. For a long time now, I've wanted to . . . I must tell you that . . ."

She grabbed his hands. "Obie, shut your foolish mouth!"

He was speechless at first, then relieved. This was the familiar Cassie. "What? What is it? What have I done now?"

"I love you, you stupid man!"

"I love you, too, Cassie."

She put her face close to his. "There, I've finally told you. I want to be clear, Obie, when I say that I love you. I'm not talking just about friendship."

"I know."

"You don't know how long I've held it in my heart, hoping that you'd know . . . hoping you'd love me the same way."

"Cassie, it's exactly . . . "

"Be quiet, Obie! I'm not finished!" Her words tumbled out. "I've loved you since we were in first grade . . . even before. I worried on the way here. I knew once I told you this, it would change everything. There would be no more wishing and dreaming. We'd either be together, or our friendship would be something different . . . strained, perhaps."

"Cassie!" He placed his hands on her shoulders. "You're right. I'm stupid. I've failed to see things as they are, but I want you to know this. A part of me has always known that I love you."

"What part?"

"My heart."

In the glow of the streetlight, he could see her wet eyes. He bent to kiss both, tasting the salt of her tears. His lips touched hers, lightly, then firmly. Her breath was sweet. The sensation was strange and familiar at the same time. He held her body against his. She didn't resist. After a wordless minute, they drew apart and walked with their arms around each other. At every street corner, and sometimes in between, he pulled her close to kiss her, marveling at what was happening. They spoke little all the way home, although Obie knew there was much more to say.

After he put fresh sheets on the spare bed, they sat on the couch. He filled their wine glasses, and talk came, freely—at last.

"I'm not used to so much wine, but this is good," she said.

"I brought it back from my summer job up north."

"It reminds me of a conversation I had with your grandfather. I went to see him a few times after you left."

"I think I know what you're going to say. 'Making wine is looking to the future.' Is that it?"

"Yes," She said, "I've thought about that often. There was something special about Jacob, something spiritual. Didn't you feel it?"

"Often. He called my grandmother his 'excellent wine.' He said once that you reminded him of her and asked if you were my wine." He watched her face for a reaction to his words.

"And how did you answer?"

"I probably avoided answering. I was sixteen, Cassie."

"He asked me the same question about you when I was seventeen. I told him that you were already my wine . . . but in an unopened bottle."

He took her into his arms. "Are we each other's future?"

"Obie, I hope so. How I hope so."

"As do I!"

Without evidence of embarrassment, Cassie asked, "Why did you make up a separate bed for me?"

"I thought we might want to wait . . . for that."

"What would we be waiting for, Obie?"

"I want you to marry me, Cassie. Will you?"

There was no hesitation. "Yes, I'll marry you. I'll marry you tomorrow if you want me to."

"Tonight would be better. I'll settle for tomorrow, though." He pulled her close.

"No, wait. We have to be responsible. Do you really mean this, Obie?"

"With all my heart."

"I'm under contract to teach this year, and you have a year left here. As much as I'd like us to be together now, we should wait . . . and plan. We can be married next summer. I can teach anywhere. Wherever you go to seminary, I'll find work. What do you say?"

"It's a long time to wait, but yes, we *can* do that."

She smiled. "So, are we engaged?"

"We are. All we need to do is set a date."

"No, we need something more. Where's my engagement ring?"

"I'll get one . . . tomorrow."

She punched his arm. "I'm teasing, Obie." After they stopped laughing, she said, "How would you feel about returning to Stafford Rest someday, after seminary?"

"If it's what you want."

"I know I've said at times that I was going to leave, but in truth, the place tugs at my heart when I'm away. And it'd be different with you there. Don't you think about it . . . about Blackberry Hill?"

"Of course I do. It's a part of me that'll never let go. Let's keep that option open, however. And let's be open to going wherever God sends us."

"Yes, my darling. I'll be happy anywhere if I'm with you."

They sat on the couch for several minutes with their arms

around each other. Since Laura's betrayal, he'd not believed such happiness was possible, nor had he expected anything like this in his life. It was a new beginning, one he was sure God was offering him. "It'll be hard to wait, though." He looked toward the bedrooms.

"We don't have to wait, Obie." She stopped a moment, looked embarrassed, then continued. "We love each other. We're not children. Haven't we waited long enough?"

"Cassie, there's nothing I'd like more. But, do you know who I called last night after I talked to you? *Pastor Charles.* He was overjoyed that I'm applying to seminary. He gave me some advice. He said I should enter into a covenant with God to keep myself above worldly things for the coming year. And I did that. I promised God."

She scrunched up her face. "Well, I guess I can find someone else to fill my needs until next summer."

"Cassie . . ."

"I'm kidding. You'd better get used to it. You've forgotten what I'm like."

"No, I haven't. And, it's one reason I love you." He remembered something she had said. "You were to meet Judy tomorrow morning. There's so much here I want to show you and people I'd like you to meet. Do you think you could stay with me another day?"

"Yes, Obie. Judy will understand. You and I do have plans to make."

"Indeed we do."

"There's something I haven't told you. Yesterday morning, I had a visitor. Someone came many miles out of his way to see me."

"Who? Do I have a rival?"

"He's someone you know quite well. I can see why he's your friend. As of yesterday, he's mine too."

"Adam?"

"Yes, Adam. He made me promise to contact you. He said that you loved me. I can't say I wouldn't have called you anyway, at some point, but Adam is the reason I'm here at this particular moment."

"God bless Adam."

"He said to tell you something. He said he hoped his debt was paid in full. Said you'd know what he meant."

"Yes, I do. I know exactly what he meant." A warm tide swept through Obie, not unlike a summer breeze over Blackberry Hill. He and Adam were unlike in many ways, yet he was convinced that God's spirit moved through them both. Where the Spirit dwelled, love was there. Jacob was even wiser than Obie had imagined.

"Obie, you have tears in your eyes."

He blinked them away. Unexpectedly, an odd and ancient memory came. He was a five-year-old again, chasing two sisters around the Hunt lawn. He caught the one with yellow corkscrew hair. Cassie's child voice from the past was evident in his memory, "Obie loves me . . . don't you, Obie?"

"I do," he said aloud.

Cassie, sitting beside him, said, "You do what?"

"I love you, Cassie. With all my heart."

The End (for now)

Yes, there are unanswered questions, unresolved mysteries, and secrets yet uncovered. Look for the publication of *Blackberry Hill,* the sequel to *Wine for Tomorrow.*

A Last Word

All characters in this book are works of the imagination and not meant to resemble any person or persons, living or dead. A few prominent people mentioned have no interaction with the fictional characters.

It was a turbulent stage of our history, a time that I lived through as a child. My imaginary characters move through that time against the backdrop of real-world events. They deal with human fears, joys, and anxieties; they experience love, hate, betrayal, loss of faith, and in some cases, redemption.

Except for the imaginary villages of Stafford Rest and Evergreen, both set in the real Adirondack Park of New York State, the book is true to geography and topography. A few unnamed settings throughout are composites of real places.

The book's main character, Obadiah (Obie) Gainsworthy, becomes a member of the 34th Division (The Red Bulls.) This volume is generally accurate to that division's movement through the boot of Italy during the Second World War. However, some liberty was taken with the naming and activities of smaller units within that division, especially at the platoon level. You won't find Lieutenant Howard, Lieutenant Burnside, or Sergeant Silverman in the history books. And the members of Silverman's squad are purely fictional. Captain Forrester, a division chaplain, is also imaginary, but I followed the military chaplain guidelines of that time in depicting him.

This is my first novel, if you don't count the other unpublished ones in my wooden footlocker, or the half-dozen abandoned ones scattered around my apartment. After publishing two non-fiction books, each of which won a *Silver Medal for Biography* from the *Military Writers Society of America*, it's been quite a different experience writing this book. I intend to keep writing as long as possible, so I invite your criticism to help me improve.

Rupert Pratt
2022

ABOUT THE AUTHOR

Rupert Pratt grew up on a small farm in Salt Rock, West Virginia. He graduated from Barboursville High School in 1951, and after an enlistment in the United Air Force, he earned a BA degree from Marshall College (now Marshall University) in 1957 and a MA degree in 1959. He married Mildred Mereness from Schenectady, New York and taught in the Schenectady City School District for thirty-six years. Rupert and Millie have two sons, Gregory and Jonathan, and three grandchildren, Elizabeth, Nathan, and Andrew. Millie passed away in 2013.

In addition to *Touching the Ancient One: A True Story of Tragedy and Reunion* (2006, 2021), he is the author of *Tri-State Heroes of '45: Together With a Year in the Life of a West Virginia Farm Family* (2020). Information about Rupert Pratt's books and other related subjects is available on his website: https://www.touchingancientone.com.

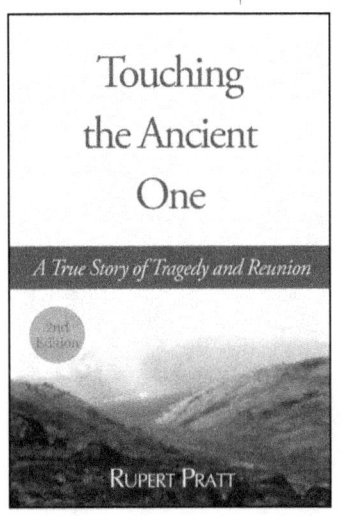

Touching the Ancient One–A True Story of Tragedy and Reunion is my story of a 1954 Air Force C-47 crash on Kesugi Ridge in South-Central Alaska that took the lives of ten military service members; I was one of six survivors. It's also the story of a reunion forty-two years later bringing together crash survivors, their families, families of the victims, and civilian and Air Force personnel from that time. There followed other reunions, the erection of plaques honoring the men who perished, a high military honor for rescuer Cliff Hudson, and a 1998 return to the mountain crash site.

Touching the Ancient One
was awarded a Silver Medal from
Military Writers Society of America.

https://www.amazon.com/Rupert-Pratt/e/B002BMD2DM

Independent Review:

Tri-State Heroes of '45: Together With a Year in the Life of a West Virginia Farm Family resurrects selected local, national, and world events of 1945, but hangs on a framework of diary entries of Pratt's mother, who was thirty-seven that year, while Pratt himself was only twelve. The daily life on their little farm in Salt Rock, West Virginia, presents a unique mosaic that tells an unforgettable tale of faith, family, and hope on the home front. Pratt honors military service members of the Tri-State area of West Virginia, Ohio, and Kentucky with 'mini-stories' from Huntington, West Virginia newspapers of that year [1945 Huntington Herald Dispatch and Huntington Herald Advertiser]."

There are over 8,000 personal names in the imdex.

Tri-State Heroes of '45 was awarded a 2021 *Military Writers Society of America* <u>Silver Medal</u> in Memoirs/Biography.

www.ingramcontent.com/pod-product-compliance
Lightning Source LLC
Chambersburg PA
CBHW072022020726
47501CB00006B/1902